ALEXIS ALBRIGHT—PRIVATE INVESTIGATOR

THE PLUM BLOSSOMS

ALEXIS ALBRIGHT—PRIVATE INVESTIGATOR

THE PLUM BLOSSOMS

JANICE MILLER

THOMAS NELSON PUBLISHERS
Nashville • Atlanta • London • Vancouver

Published in Nashville, Tennessee, by Jan Dennis Books, an imprint of Thomas Nelson, Inc., Publishers, and distributed in Canada by Word Communications, Ltd., Richmond, British Columbia.

Scripture quotations are from the NEW KING JAMES VERSION of the Bible, Copyright © 1979, 1980, 1982, Thomas Nelson, Inc., Publishers.

Library of Congress Cataloging-in-Publication Data

Miller, J. M. T. (Janice M. T.), 1944–
  The plum blossoms / Janice Miller.
    p. cm.
  "A Jan Dennis book."
  ISBN 0-7852-8208-4
  1. Private investigators—Hawaii—Fiction. 2. Women detectives—Hawaii—Fiction. I. Title.
PS3563.I4117P57   1994   94–21889
813'.54—dc20   CIP

Printed in the United States of America
1 2 3 4 5 6 7 — 00 99 98 97 96 95 94

My condo is bugged, *I said to myself.*
No kidding, *another part of me replied.*
*Aloud I said, "Same song, forty-sixth verse,
ain't no better and it's gonna get worse."*
*I stopped, slowly tapping my chin with my
forefinger as I considered my predicament. I felt indignant, furious,
and afraid. But after a moment, indignation swept the other feelings
aside. I squared my shoulders, jutted out my chin, and spoke directly
to my cream-colored walls. "Okay. I don't know who you are or
what you want with me. But if that's the way it has to be, then—let
the games begin!"*
They did.
Believe me, they did.

The whole rollicking mess started with tradition. Chopsticks to
chopsticks, chopsticks to chopsticks. Bad luck, *very* bad luck, my
dear friend Mrs. Osaka had informed me. Bad enough luck to bring
on an early death.

But then, I don't really believe in luck, good or bad. So perhaps I
should go back a bit and explain.

You see, traditionally pairs of chopsticks are allowed to touch
each other only at a special Buddhist death ritual. At all other times,
the good traditional Japanese is careful not to let sets of chopsticks
touch one another, even by accident. So firm is this traditional ban
that many older Japanese-Hawaiians of Buddhist persuasion never
so much as allow two sets of chopsticks to be *pointed* at one another,

lest even that act distill into death for whomever dares desecrate the ban.

These Old Country traditions and superstitions have, for the most part, been lost to the people of Japanese ancestry here in the Hawaiian Islands. But they often rest just beneath the surface. And every now and again, they heave up a gnarled, archaic head.

Such was the case on the day my story began. The cultural clash between the old and the new, between East and West, was in full evidence. The chopsticks were touching with full force, clattering all over each other like dry, rattling bones.

I was wearing my best basic black dress that day. Black Italian leather pumps and matching handbag, my good gray-pearl choker and earrings. Modern mourner's garb—the same clothing I had worn two years ago to my husband David's funeral. In fact, that had been the last time I'd worn the dress and the last funeral I had attended— and the last I had planned to *ever* attend.

But friendship is friendship, and Jess Seitaki had phoned me at one A.M. on Tuesday.

"Alex. I wanted to let you know that Victor died tonight." His voice was thick with grief.

"I'm sorry." It really was no surprise. All the members of our church had been praying with Jess and his wife, Yoko, during the five-day ordeal since his brother's massive heart attack, but we had all known there was very little chance Victor would survive.

"Apparently there was nothing more they could do," Jess explained.

"I see. I'm really sorry. Do you want me to come over?"

"No. No, thank you. Anne and the boys are here." Anne was Victor's wife—his widow, now. She had been born in Japan to a wealthy family—tradition all the way. Jess added, "Some of her family has flown in from Tokyo. We've already started the *otsuya.*"

Thanks to the wise tutelage of Mrs. Osaka, I knew that this was the traditional Buddhist wake, wherein the body would lie in state overnight while the family sat around it and burned candles and joss sticks, just in case the soul came back into the body—or the person wasn't dead to begin with. At the end of this time, the body would be washed in hot water, cleansed, the water poured carefully, backhanded, in preparation for the journey into death. Mrs. Osaka had caught me once, pouring lemonade backhanded from a pitcher when

I was in an awkward position. She had been disturbed by it, had explained to me that pouring this way was done only at the *otsuya*, that at all other times it was guaranteed to conjure up trouble, since it was a behavior associated with death. Even though Mrs. Osaka was a devout Christian, these cultural beliefs were still deeply ingrained in her, as they were in many others of her generation.

Chopsticks to chopsticks; chopsticks to chopsticks . . .

I said to Jess, "Let me know what I *can* do."

"Just come to the funeral ceremony. It would mean a lot."

Two years ago, Jess had seen me through David's funeral; now, I would help see him through his brother's. And so, on that star-crossed morning, I pulled my unruly blonde hair back severely and pinned it with a small black velvet bow, tugged on the basic black dress, applied a discreet amount of makeup, then reluctantly dragged myself across town and to the Buddhist temple.

The funeral was well attended. Victor had been a prominent man, friend to legislators, real estate developers, and other leaders of Honolulu's business community: people of every race, hue, and creed. The temple barely held them all. But immediately after the heavily ritualistic funeral ceremony, the body was taken to the crematorium and the crowd dispersed.

As we left the temple, Mrs. Osaka walked beside me. Barely five feet tall, she was tiny-boned and trim. Her silver hair was elegantly groomed, she wore a black-on-black dress, antique diamond jewelry, black cotton stockings, and sturdy, low-heeled shoes. As we made our way through the crowd and toward the parking lot, she said, "Drive me straight home, Alex. I'm tired."

So I chauffeured her to her stately old home in the upper Nuuanu Valley. She is, after all, eighty-five years old. Though she was not a member of the Seitaki family, she had earned her own place of respect in the community. The throngs of people at the funeral all seemed to know her, all stopped to pay respects to her. That much attention would certainly have exhausted me.

But as we neared her white house, with its wraparound veranda and two-story columns, she glanced at me and said, "To be honest, I'm going to spend the rest of the day cloistered in my flower garden. Avoiding crowds."

"Then you aren't going to the funeral dinner?"

"I've excused myself on the basis of old age." Mischief sparkled in her chocolate-black eyes.

"I envy you," I said. "I have to go back."

And I did. By late afternoon, the immediate family and several close friends, myself included, were back in the Buddhist temple to take part in an archaic post-funeral ceremony associated with this particular sect of Buddhism. The room was resplendent with life-sized gilt Buddhas, with brass ornaments, with black lacquered tables upon which sat numerous other artifacts of the Buddhist religion. It had rained earlier. The air was cloying and warm. I was using my handkerchief not to wipe away tears but to blot a thin veil of humidity from my forehead.

The black altar was covered with brass and gilt. Upon it, left there from the funeral service, was the *ibei,* the wooden tablet with Victor Seitaki's *kaimyo*—his spiritual name—inscribed upon it in the Japanese letters known as *kanji.* A photograph of him, gilt-framed and imposing, stood beside it. He'd been a slender, stern-faced man in his early forties, handsome in a way. There was a hint of arrogance in his facial expression that said he was used to wielding power.

Candles burned. Joss sticks wafted a pine-cinder scent throughout the temple. Two enormous bouquets of pure white chrysanthemums adorned the altar, and dozens more were displayed all throughout the room: white, symbolizing purity; round, symbolizing perfection—nothing with sharp corners can enter Buddhist heaven.

"Namu Amida Bitsu, Namu Amida Bitsu." Over and over, the incantation came. *Bless us, Lord Buddha, bless us, Lord Buddha.* The priest was clad in flowing blue robes; his head was stark-shaven. The few people who had been invited to this private ceremony chanted monotonously after him. I declined. Though I could honor my friend's brother by attending the ceremony, I wasn't about to chant to a statue. I saw that Jess and Yoko had their heads bowed in prayer but were also silent.

The chanting stopped.

The priest said a few ritualized words, then the closest blood family members lined up beside the altar. Anne Seitaki picked up a pair of simple wooden chopsticks. She dipped them into a brass container and withdrew a burnt shard of her late husband's bone.

Her facial expression was stoic, unreadable, as befitted a widow born in Japan. Her black dress was elegant but plain. Her jet black hair was pulled sleekly back from her carefully made-up face. Her almond eyes were wide, with just the finest gossamer of wrinkles around them. No jewelry except for the simple gold wedding band Victor had given her at their marriage some twenty-odd years ago. She'd never needed a diamond. She'd had everything else, everything that money could buy.

Chopsticks to chopsticks, chopsticks to chopsticks. The shard of bone passed from Anne to her eldest son, who was fourteen. He had a stricken look on his face, was just barely keeping it together. Chopsticks to chopsticks, he passed the object on to his twelve-year-old brother, whose bottom lip was trembling visibly but who managed to pass it along to Jess, the only other close blood relative still living. The in-laws from Japan and more distant family members sat with the rest of us, respectfully watching this New World adaptation of an ancient ritual designed to help grieving family members say good-bye as they escorted the soul into the spirit world.

A tremor in Anne's hand found its way into the chopsticks as she lifted, one by one, the shards of bone and brittle teeth from the brass receptacle where the larger remains of her husband's ashes had been placed after cremation. Anne's mother was long dead. She had lost her father only a year ago, and now her husband. I kept expecting her to break down, but except for the tremors and a dazed quality in her eyes, she remained surprisingly composed.

Jess was last in line, looking immaculately handsome with his gray-templed, short-cropped black hair, his blindingly white shirt, his gold tie tack and cuff links and expensively tailored black suit. He wore an intent expression, as if concentration could dull the pain. He scrupulously placed each remaining particle of his late brother's charred bones and teeth into the small urn called a *kotsutsubo*. When the ritual was completed, the priest would crush it all with a mallet and add the other ashes. Anne would then take the *kotsutsubo*, the photograph, the *ibei* and other objects home with her, to her home altar, the *butsudan*. There the urn would remain throughout the forty-nine-day period of mourning, with small rituals performed on various important days during that time. Then would come another ceremony; Victor's spirit would be fully released, and the urn of ashes would be permanently placed in the temple's *niche*.

Victor's remains would then rest alongside the ashes of many ancestors. Some had fled the Japanese famines of the last century to find indentured servitude on the plantations here in the Hawaiian Islands. The first generation of Japanese—the *issei*—had literally come to Hawaii by mail order, ordered in bulk by the plantation owners like the other supplies required to build their small empires. And for the most part they had been treated like supplies, commodities to be used up then replaced. Still, many Japanese laborers had chosen to stay when their contract time was up. Through tremendous effort, they had found acceptance, then relative affluence; finally, many had found even social position and immense political clout. The AJAs—Americans of Japanese Ancestry—now comprised about one-third of the population of the Hawaiian Islands, and their influence was felt everywhere.

Almost a hundred years of photographs graced a black lacquered sideboard in Jess and Yoko's house: men with gnarled backs from heavy plantation work, mail-order brides in wedding kimonos, their remains now resting in various Christian, Buddhist, and Shinto boneyards or in ash-filled urns in Buddhist temples throughout the Hawaiian Islands. The photographs showed generations with increasingly westernized airs, including Jess's father, a spare young man photographed while stationed in Italy. He wore an American World War II uniform with decorations for valor. He had been part of the famed 442nd Regimental Combat Team, a group of once-distrusted AJAs who had proved their loyalty to the U.S. by letting their blood be spilled all the way to Dachau, where they were among the first to open the gates and release the starving Jews. The 442nd had been the most highly decorated combat unit to fight in World War II.

The sideboard also featured photographs of Jess himself, a mere kid in uniform. He'd fought with honor in Vietnam, later graduating from college on the G.I. bill; and I remembered photos of Victor as well, who had made his own mark. There were photographs of him accepting service awards from diverse community associations, others showing him standing arm in arm with various business and political luminaries.

Chopsticks to chopsticks, chopsticks to chopsticks . . .

As I waited for the grim ritual to end, I cocked an eyebrow and scanned the room. I'd been in a Buddhist temple several other times, back when I'd first come to Hawaii and was curious about everything. There were around thirty temples to choose from and many different Buddhist sects and variations. But the Buddhist belief system was alien to my own now, an antithesis, and I hadn't been in a temple for many years. I looked around, recalling all the rich symbolism that my dear friend, Mrs. Osaka, had taught me during our long and rewarding friendship.

The huge gilt Buddhas on the platform behind the altar were enthroned on a dais of lotus blossoms. The bronzed lotus blossom was one of the perpetual offerings to the Buddha and held a deep, symbolic meaning for the Buddhist Japanese. It was not only the symbol of death; it was also a key symbol of overcoming the harshest difficulties of life.

Earlier that day, at Victor's funeral service, the mourners had carried silver and gold paper lotus blossoms. They had placed them reverently on the altar, and I had whispered to Mrs. Osaka, "What are they for?"

"It symbolizes purity," Mrs. Osaka had whispered back. Amidst the chanting, her cultural lesson was audible only to me. "It means if your heart is pure and you are strong," she said, "you will push your head up and blossom forth into beauty, like the lotus flower. The leaves will float on the water, but the blossom is always taller. Towering above."

Like other Japanese symbolism, this belief originated in the truth of nature. The blue-green lotus plants indeed drew their sustenance from the foul, still waters of swamps and fetid ponds. Yet, just as Mrs. Osaka said, from these plants grew strong white blossoms with a heavenly fragrance and purity.

Victor Seitaki had apparently done that: risen from the muck of social oppression and poverty. He and Jess, his brother and my friend, had both transcended hardship to become respected men. Victor had made his mark as a real estate developer, a profession that had made him profoundly rich. Jess, on the other hand, had found his fulfillment in police work. Now Jess was the head of the Hawaii State Police force's Homicide Division; and though he was far from rich, he and Yoko had enough. A beautiful home up in Nuuanu, not far from Mrs. Osaka's own, which they had inherited from Jess's parents; an occasional trip to the mainland; enough money to send their two children to very good mainland universities.

Chopsticks to chopsticks, the last shard of bone was passed to Jess. I saw the relief in his face as he placed it in the urn. These rituals had been a strain on him, a manifestation of the cultural schism between East and West, an abyss he had long ago crossed but was now being dragged back through.

It was over. I, too, felt a sudden vast rush of relief as the priest made the final blessings. At last, we could all step out into the fresh air and get back to appreciating life.

But as I walked out of the temple, I found myself remembering a verse from my own Bible—1 Peter 1:24:

> All flesh is as grass,
> And all the glory of man as the flower of the grass.
> The grass withers,
> And its flower falls away. . . .

The thought catapulted me back in time, for this verse had provided the grain of the sermon preached at David's funeral two years ago. Suddenly I was once again contemplating the brevity of life, and I felt the old seething anger and the same sense of injustice sear through me. Death wasn't fair. The very concept of death seemed to belie a loving, omniscient Creator who had the ability to create whatever kind of universe He chose.

And yet, I believed in God. My Christianity was deep, devout, as knit into me as my own bones. But how could a God who loved me as deeply as the Bible professed allow the vast evil of physical death to creep into His universe and mar His creation? How could an Eternal Being genuinely love *me* with a special, personal love yet force me to forfeit those *I* loved to this finality and separation called death?

That was what made me angry. Because I knew that God could have prevented my husband's death—could stop all death at any time He chose, for that matter. So why didn't He? If *I* ruled the universe, the funeral ritual I had just left would never have taken place. Anne would not be walking stiffly toward the black limo, leaning against Jess's arm, I would not be suddenly scalded with my own grief as I thought about my dead husband.

Because the first thing I would do, if I ruled the universe, would be to abolish this hideous pain called physical death. I would—

Ah, but I didn't rule the universe. God did. All that remained of Victor Seitaki were the ashes tucked away inside the *kotsutsubo*. David was dead, had been taken from me almost before I got to know him. Two years, only two short years of love and comfort and belonging and marriage. And then David had been caught in the crossfire between good and evil. He had been brutally gunned down, vanishing into that vast, all-encompassing loneliness we call death.

Seeing Anne brought my own pain back. I would never forget the hurt, the feeling of grief so strong that I'd barely been able to breathe for weeks after David's death. Nor would I ever forget the sense of cosmic betrayal that had quickly distilled into a steely, gnawing anger.

Still, after a lot of desperate effort, I had learned to cope. If I couldn't stop death from coming, I would at least stop it from destroying me with the pain of grief, even if that meant shutting down certain emotions, burying them along with David.

Death, ah death. It was the inevitable end of us all. Even if there was a heaven beyond, we would all have to go through that splintering agony of separation called physical death. But I was never again going to let myself love anyone so deeply as to be dragged through that unbearable, paralyzing agony of loss that I had felt when David was taken from me.

Never, never again.

ess Seitaki had been partner to my husband, David Albright, in State Vice and Narcotics for eight long years. He had been David's best man at our wedding, and Yoko had thrown the wedding party. But soon thereafter, needing college money for his two children, Jess had transferred to Homicide, where he was offered a promotion to Captain. David, on the other hand, stayed in V&N, at the cutting edge of the war on drugs.

Shortly after Jess's transfer, David had taken two 9-millimeter slugs in his head during a drug bust. And his death left a chasm in my life that now suddenly loomed large again, even after all this time.

I saw Jess and Yoko at church almost every week and spoke with Yoko occasionally on the phone, but being with them under these funereal conditions brought back a rush of memories. Many of my memories were good: David and I had shared a lot of special time with the Seitakis. But I had avoided serious social contact with them since David's death because being around them brought back the bad memories too, and believe me, these memories were *really* bad: being awakened in the middle of the night, rushing to the hospital, giving permission for the emergency surgery. Waiting, praying. Collapsing into Pastor Mike's arms when the doctor told me that even if David survived, he would never be able to move again, never talk, never walk, would never again communicate with me, would not even be able to feed himself.

The hardest day was when I made the inevitable decision to take him off life support. I spent the day on my knees, at David's hospital bedside. And that's where I was when he died.

Still, during those grim days Jess proved to be a friend of the first order. He and Yoko saw me through the long hospital vigil, through David's funeral arrangements, through the financial hassles of collecting the insurance. They helped me figure out the bills, enlisted Victor to help with the refinancing of the mortgage on the condo, helped handle all the other incidental details that seemed too difficult for me to deal with just then.

And because of all that, I was trying to help see them through this ordeal, paltry though my efforts might be. I had attended the funeral and the later ritual ceremony. Now, I would pay my final respects by attending the small traditional funeral dinner, even though being so close to death was getting to me more and more as the long and odious day progressed into evening.

I wheeled my dark blue Honda Accord through the iron gateway of Victor and Anne's immense Kahala estate—Anne's estate, now. I parked beside several other cars near the *porte cochere*, pulling in beside a Mercedes stretch limo with minimalist gold trim, a sleek black statement of wealth that I assumed must belong to one of Anne's Japanese relatives. Part of this assumption was based on the bald, bull-necked Japanese national who stood idly nearby, wearing pale-gray chauffeur's livery with black piping. As I stepped out of my car, the perfume of gardenias wafted in from the rich foliage that surrounded the house. The chauffeur took a long drag on the cigarette he was smoking and exhaled in my direction, killing the fragrance. He gave me an insolent stare, then looked away.

The notice of mourning, or *kichu*, was posted on a front door framed by jade vines and raucous fuchsia bougainvillea in full bloom. I rang the buzzer and waited until a crisply uniformed maid opened the door. She nodded a greeting, handed me a pair of cloth slippers, and waited while I stepped out of my shoes. I pulled on the slippers, then placed my shoes with the other pairs arranged symmetrically beside the door. She led me down a polished wooden hallway. I had my *koden*—incense money—wrapped neatly in the mandatory white envelope with white and silver strings, tied just the right way. I'd had it made up at a Japanese flower shop, where I'd also bought the huge bouquet for the funeral, honoring the rituals of both East and West.

I had never before been inside Anne and Victor's home, though I'd heard Jess and Yoko speak of it with pride. It was a three-million-dollar Japanese palace within a westernized framework.

Inside the hallway, the *tatami* mats beneath my feet were like finely crushed autumn hay, with the same sweetly natural smell. The sun was setting behind the *shoji* door to the veranda. The light tinted the wheat-colored panels into translucent crimson. The outside posts and railings showed through the paper as black geometric shadows upon which the shades of thick, wind-rippled foliage danced.

The maid ushered me into a traditional Japanese living area, complete with mats for sitting and tiny black lacquered tables although there were also chairs and settees. Anne stood and came to me. "Thank you for coming." She folded me into a quick, dignified embrace. I hadn't realized how small she was. Her arms felt like the frail wings of a trembling bird.

I put some warmth into my return hug. "Thank you for having me in your home."

The family members who had attended the funeral and post-funeral ceremony were there, about a dozen in all. A few were from Hawaii, cousins and other relatives by marriage: most were from Anne's extended family in Japan. There were also a dozen other close friends of Anne and Victor's. Jess introduced me all around as "Our dear friend Alexis," or "My late partner Detective David Albright's wife." A few local people took a harder look at me as Jess mentioned David's name. I knew they were remembering news headlines from two years ago, were perhaps recalling that the young drug dealer who shot David had in turn been shot dead by David's new partner, Derrick Green. There had been an investigation that lasted for a month, TV and newspaper headlines every day; but in the end Derrick Green had been fully exonerated for killing the drug dealer—even decorated—and David had been honored posthumously for bravery, a hollow reward indeed.

On a table at the front of the room, beside a wide window framing the dying light and the broad blue Pacific, sat the funeral urn and altar. Beside that, on each side, were two ten-foot-high potted plum trees, replete with black-barked trunks and delicate pale pink blossoms. Yoko had mentioned the trees when she'd phoned to tell me the time of the funeral dinner. They'd been flown here special from an exotic Tokyo hothouse that specialized in out-of-season plants and had cost several thousand dollars—but never mind, Yoko said. The plum blossoms were special to Victor, special also to Jess.

"Japanese tradition honors the lotus," Yoko had told me long ago. "But for the Seitaki family, the plum blossoms hold far more meaning. Oh, Alex, they are so beautiful at first bloom. One day you should go with me to Japan and I'll show you."

"Why are they so special?"

"The plum blossoms struggle out of the freezing cold to bloom early in February," she'd explained. "In Japan, that's the coldest month. The *haru ichiban*—an icy, violent wind—batters the countryside. But still the blossoms come out, long before the white freezing snow melts from the earth. True, the lotus blossom strives up from the muck to become pure and beautiful. But the plum blossoms? They must overcome the most impossible hardship, to become the purest, the sturdiest, to have the strongest heart."

Another time, we'd been sitting in her lovely back yard, in Hawaii's eternal summer, stringing satiny white plumeria leis for the church choir. She had told me about the black-barked plum trees shading us: "Jess's mother had plum trees on the family farm in Minoibu, Japan. She cherished these trees. To her, they symbolized everything honorable, everything good that she'd left behind in Japan."

I nodded. Like my own ancestors, who had immigrated into the eastern United States from Europe, the Japanese people had fled poverty and social systems that kept them bowed down beneath feudalistic power, even mass famines. Here in Hawaii, the Japanese laborers had been fed, at least. But they had also been brutalized and often worked to death during the earliest years. Still, our roots go deep. We all have nostalgia for those places in which we were born. And as bad as their circumstances might have been in Japan, the Japanese immigrants had been separated from family, culture, friends—

I had also seen the framed letter they kept beside Jess's mother's photograph in a place of honor in their living room. She had written it to Jess when he'd started college—the first one in their family to accomplish such a feat. In a barely literate English scrawl, the note said, "You honor us, my eldest son, for you and your brother have emerged like plum blossoms, out of our winter of poverty and hardship. Now, you are honorable and strong."

Years after those words were penned, Victor Seitaki had married his own Japanese bride, Anne, and brought her to Hawaii. Shortly thereafter, he made his first million through a major real estate development on the northernmost of Hawaii's five major islands, Kauai. He and Jess then built their aging parents the Japanese-style home in exclusive upper Nuuanu where Jess and Yoko now lived. The sons had imported half a dozen plum trees from Japan to plant in the wide, sweeping yard. These were the trees that had shaded Yoko and me as we strung the perfumed plumeria flowers into leis.

"But the plum trees have never blossomed," Yoko explained. She looked up into the dark filigree of branches, frowning. "Jess's parents watched them every spring and half of summer. Since we inherited this house, we've taken up their vigil. A couple of times there have been tiny buds on the limbs. But no matter what we do, we can't get the trees to bloom."

"Maybe they need a true challenge," I said. "A Hawaiian *haru ichiban* or a good heavy snowstorm."

Yoko had laughed. "Maybe. Maybe when the going gets difficult enough, they'll struggle through and show their stuff."

Now, Jess saw me studying the fragile, imported foliage of the plum trees that framed Victor's funeral urn and altar. He offered a faint smile that said he appreciated my understanding. He was still wearing his black dress slacks, though he'd taken off the jacket and tie and his shirt was opened at the throat. He looked a lot like Victor, though he was a few years older: a handsome, well-formed man who showed every bit of his Japanese heritage in his square jawline, his high cheekbones, his slender, almost willowy build, and his slightly less than medium height. But there were dark circles under his brown eyes, and he was showing his fifty years today.

Though he had made violent death his profession, the death of his own brother was hitting him hard. He came over and sat beside me. "We made it through," he said.

"Yes."

"Thank you, Alex. I know how difficult that was for you."

"Not so bad," I said.

"Nevertheless, I know how different all this is from our Christian beliefs. Thank you for being at the ceremony."

I shrugged. "The service just seemed so—I don't know, empty."

"I know what you mean."

Just then one of the relatives from Japan came up to speak with Jess. I nodded a greeting, then started to move away. Jess touched my arm and stopped me. "I believe you met Mr. Ko Shinda, Anne's uncle from Tokyo?"

I said yes, we had been introduced before the funeral. I offered Mr. Shinda the small series of stiff nods that serve as a modern day bow of respect. You nod, he nods, you nod again—I was never quite sure who was supposed to quit nodding first, though I knew I was supposed to bow deeper because he was my elder.

Mrs. Osaka had also taught me that bowing was very important in the traditional Japanese culture. You weren't supposed to bow from the neck, as many Americans tried to do. This was a way to keep eye contact, and the traditional Japanese did not like eye contact; it was a sign of rudeness and aggression. No, you were supposed to bow stiffly, from the waist, something like a small bob. Eyes politely lowered, please. Men kept their hands at the side of their trousers, women held their hands clasped in front, thumbs grasped in back of the hand.

And yes, the bowing was important. Politeness was everything to the traditional Japanese, prized above efficiency and accomplishment and nearly everything else—except, perhaps, social position. Though of course, one's social position was partly defined by one's awareness of etiquette. The patterns of tradition all link together, inexorably.

The Japanese were status conscious far beyond anything Americans could understand. In Japan, your status defined your being. People looked at your sex, age, background, economic position, friends, home—everything was summed up to define your status. And there was no such thing as an equal. You were always pegged as either inferior or superior, and it was hard to tell which was worse. If deemed superior, you found yourself the object of the deference and obeisance that Americans often saw as bowing and scraping—a most unpleasant situation. If deemed inferior, you were the object of haughty, though carefully masked, disdain, which wasn't all that much fun either.

To Mr. Ko Shinda, I was automatically inferior because I was younger, not Japanese, and—most of all—female. But I was so much inferior that he had no trouble at all treating me as an equal. The motivation behind that particular behavior was that when others saw with what graciousness he treated an inferior his esteem was elevated even further in their eyes—well, try to figure all *that* out.

I was nodding or bowing or bobbing back and forth with a slight, elflike man with razor-cut silver hair, a spiffy two-thousand-dollar black silk suit, and a sharp, intelligent face. His straight black eyebrows almost met over eyes that were deep-set and intense. Something that lay between merriment and malevolence escaped from their liquid depths; and though he only came to my breastbone, there was an impression of compact power about him, as if he could level me with a good, strong blink.

Jess said, "Mr. Shinda has been involved as a silent partner in the Golden Palms Resort project with Victor."

I let my eyebrows lift in appreciation. The Golden Palms was a major Hawaiian development, a hotel and condo complex complete with a world class golf course. I'd heard that the tab might run as high as five hundred million dollars before they were through. To Mr. Shinda, I said, "You visit our Islands often, then?"

Mr. Shinda's voice was deep, raspy. "Not so, no. I have only come this once for the occasion of this death." He scanned the room quickly, as if the death included everything within his range of vision, and then his piercing gaze fell back on me. His English was understandable, but his accent was thick.

"I'm sorry your visit couldn't have been under better circumstances," I said politely.

He agreed, in an even more polite fashion than I had managed. We shared a bit more small talk, then I finally excused myself and walked away. But Jess shot me a strange look as I left them, almost as if he was signaling an alarm, wanting me to come back. It puzzled me for a moment, but then I dismissed it as the stress of the occasion.

Jess and Yoko had not rested since Victor's heart attack. There had been the vigil at the hospital. Then the death and accompanying stresses and the traditional night-long wake. Then today had come the funeral service and post-funeral ceremony, not to mention the stress of the logistics of having so many visitors from Japan.

Yoko had taken over the duties of hostess, leaving Anne to chat gravely and daintily with the various guests. The traditional funeral meal was plentiful, yet simple: no meat, no fish, nothing bloody could be served. The meal was therefore made up of round rice balls, several meatless noodle dishes, *sake* (rice wine), tea, and round cookies. No corners to hurt anybody, no angles to keep the deceased soul from being able to enter heaven.

No one felt much like eating. The meal had been catered, so there was nothing for me to do from that angle. I mingled with the others and chatted vacuously about this and that. I stayed about an hour, making the right noises; then I excused myself to Anne and started out the door.

Jess caught up with me outside as I was stepping from the slippers back into my own black pumps.

"You look frazzled," I said. "So does Yoko. Can you get some rest now?"

"Before long." His face suddenly furrowed with worry. "Alex, I need to talk to you."

I glanced sharply at him. There was something deep in his eyes, something far beyond grief. "Why don't you come over later?" I said. "Bring Yoko, I'll make a late dinner with real food."

"I don't think Yoko needs to get involved yet."

That's when I caught the first scent of serious trouble.

He let his breath out between his teeth, his jaw clamped. Then he said, "I may need to hire you."

"*Hire* me? You're kidding. First, I'd do anything for you and you know it, and you'd never pay me a cent. Second, what on earth could a lowly private investigator do for you that the people at Hawaii State Police couldn't do better?"

Jess's gaze shifted to the distance. "That's just it. I may need some private work done, some things I can't do on my own. I—I don't want anyone to know what's going on—"

I lifted an eyebrow. "So what *is* going on?"

"Jess?" Yoko came through the door. She gave me a weak smile. I reached out and put my arm around her. She was taller than Jess, almost my height, five-nine, though smaller-boned and willowy. She had the haunting Japanese beauty that doesn't fade with age: the porcelain skin, heart-shaped face, raven hair and eyes so often portrayed in Japanese dolls. I reflected that this was probably the first time I had ever seen her look tired. She returned my brief hug, then said to Jess, "Anne is crying again. Can you go to her? She's just . . . I don't know . . ."

Jess nodded, then said to me. "I'll be in touch."

"Anything I can do to help," I said, careful to take in both him and Yoko, "just let me know."

Yoko said, "Thank you, Alex, but you know, there's really nothing. These things just need time, you just have to heal."

I nodded. "I do know about that," I said. "I'll keep you in my prayers."

And I did.

CHAPTER 3

And that's how the whole thing began. First with yet another death, then with a funeral, then with a plea from a friend. There was no clue, not so much as an inkling that I was being sucked headlong into a maelstrom; certainly no indication that I was about to be catapulted headlong into a major FBI investigation, or that the Japanese mafia—the *yakuza*—would soon deem it necessary to take a dangerous interest in my life.

But once again, I'm getting ahead of myself. And if you don't see how easily it happened—how it could also happen to *you*—you'll never understand.

I didn't hear from Jess for a while. I saw him on HGTV's six o'clock news the Friday after the funeral. He'd been filmed at a crime scene in Waipahu where a man had shot his wife to death. The reporter was asking questions, and Jess was answering them with his usual abrupt aplomb: Yes, the neighbors had heard shots; yes, they had found the man dead drunk, asleep in the pickup truck in back of the house; no trouble taking him into custody; yes, the perpetrator had a history of wife abuse; and so on.

I saw Yoko and the kids at church Sunday. We spoke in passing, and I asked how Jess was holding up. Not bad, she said. She'd never seen him so lost, but he was throwing himself into his work and that was helping. In fact, he'd had to work that very day. And with that, I figured that whatever personal crisis Jess had anticipated the day of the funeral must have resolved itself or been buried beneath the details of heading up the HSP's Homicide Division.

I didn't think much more about Jess after that. I had plenty of other things to worry about. I was in the middle of two investigations for attorneys who kept me on regular stipend, one a background check for a custody battle, the other a search for a missing witness to an industrial accident. Nothing really exciting going on, just nuts and bolts work that kept the bills paid. Then there was my nineteen-year-old nephew, Rick, aka "Troubles" Thompson, who had arrived on my doorstep, personal effects in hand, to take over my guest room while he was going through pre-med at the University of Hawaii. I enjoyed his companionship, but he managed to keep me on the move.

But about a week after the funeral, one fine day when my life was again spinning along full-speed, one of those peculiar events occurred that takes your tidy little reality, spins it like a top, and sets you off in a totally new direction. You never recognize these things for what they are until after the fact. Only then do you see the strong, steady hand of God at work.

On the afternoon that held this reality-spinning event, the Ala Wai Canal was a slate blue mirror reflecting the thickets of trees and shrubs that separate it, on the far side, from the wide green expanse of the Ala Wai Golf Course and the mountains beyond. Outrigger canoes were racing up and down the waterway, rowers practicing for the big waves of the vivid blue Pacific into which the canal flows. The sky was azure blue, the sun was shining . . .

I had already put in a full day's work by 3:30, and had decided to take the rest of the day off and relax for a change. I'd gone for a swim off Kuhio Beach, then came home and showered and changed into a striped white-and-yellow T-shirt and white denims. I had just started to dry my hair when the phone rang. I swept up the receiver.

"Albright Investigations."

"I must speak to the detective, please." There was a controlled terror in this voice that immediately shot me wide awake, and the man spoke in a flat, thick monotone with a heavy Japanese accent.

"This is Alex Albright."

"Your husband was a policeman?"

"That's me. Who are you?"

"I must see you immediately."

"About?"

"It is very urgent."

I thought for a moment. I don't like these cloak-and-dagger games where everything must be done immediately and secretively. The man hadn't even introduced himself. Still, I heard myself saying, "Where are you?"

"I am at a pay phone," he said. "A short distance from you. I must come to your office right away."

And before I had a chance to say another word, he hung up.

❖

The trades were up, so I decided to step out onto the corner balcony, the one with both mountain and ocean views, to dry my hair. I took my portable phone, and I could hear the intercom buzzer from there. But most important, I could see the street approaching the front entrance to my building, though there were several other entrances on the side streets. I stood there, contemplating the phone call—wondering what was going to land on my doorstep this time—as I ran my fingers through my short blonde locks and let the wind do its work and studied the street eight stories below.

Troubles had set up his telescope on the balcony beside my tangerine bougainvillea and other potted plants. As soon as my hair was somewhat dry, I stepped over and tilted it. The telescope had opened an entirely new world to me—a hobby I called recreational spying. To my eternal glee, I could now see the faces of the golfers across the canal, could read their lips as they cursed after missing a putt. I could see the muscles bulge on the rowers' arms as they sped down the waterway. I could see into hotel, condo, and shop windows for blocks and blocks around; I could turn the device, tilt it downward and watch every facial tic of every tourist who teemed along Kalakaua Avenue. I could scan then tilt once more, and I'd be gazing at the oiled, baking tourists strewn along the golden-sugar sands of Waikiki Beach. I could practically see through the windows of the Royal Hawaiian Hotel and learn what the luncheon buffet had to offer, or I could bring it back an inch or so and actually see through the wide plate glass window and into the inner workings of the Honolulu Police Department's tiny Waikiki substation.

Today I tilted it toward the perennial tourists and residents thronging the streets. I was pondering the mysterious phone call, hoping to get a glimpse of my mystery visitor in advance of his arrival, when something unusual caught my eye. I scanned backward, searched, then fixed on the movement.

A well-dressed Japanese national—white sports jacket, white shirt, navy slacks—had just emerged from the side doorway of the King's Palace Hotel. The differences between Japanese-Hawaiians and Japanese nationals were subtle to outsiders, sometimes imperceptible, but anyone who spent much time in Hawaii could distinguish one from the other. Hawaiians of Japanese ancestry were more relaxed in their mannerisms, more casual in their dress, their body language was less abrupt and kinetic. Almost a third of Hawaii's population were AJAs, and they were a fluid part of Hawaiian culture. But some five thousand distinctive Japanese nationals arrived at Honolulu International Airport every day, most of them to vacation in Waikiki. Which meant that there were so many Japanese nationals on Waikiki's streets that local residents often called the area Little Tokyo. So the fact that I had spotted a Japanese national meant nothing at all. There were hundreds of them on the street, and this man might or might not have been my mystery caller.

But whoever he was, he had paused and was looking furtively around him, his head jerking rapidly as he scanned the area. The furtive motion was what caught my attention. Now, he stepped to one side and bent down, as if looking under the thick hedges that decorate the building. People streamed past him on the sidewalk, but no one seemed to be paying attention to him. He leaned down again, and I thought maybe he'd lost something.

Just then a shiny brown UPS delivery truck turned the corner, blocking my view for a moment, and when I could see him again, he was standing erect. With a swift motion, he straightened his white linen jacket, then his tie. His head jerked right to left, back, then right to left again, as he did a rapid-scan of the terrain. The light turned green. He drew himself up, then strode toward the crosswalk.

I focused the telescope back on the place where he'd been stooping down. I looked carefully, trying to puzzle out what he'd been doing, but the shrubbery was thick, green, impenetrable. Suddenly the scream of brakes jerked me up, I heard a distant thud, and someone let out a hair-raising scream, followed by shouting. I forgot the telescope and leaned out over the balcony's edge, to see a white van careening to a stop near the crosswalk. I leaned out so far I almost took a nosedive, but the van completely blocked my view. I raced into my bedroom, grabbed my keys off the dresser, then hit the hallway at a sprint. I waited an eternity for the elevator to rise the eight floors, then jabbed the button that would take me down to the trouble.

By the time I hit the street, the police substation around the corner on Kalakaua Avenue was spilling out blue-black uniforms. Foot patrolmen came running, police radios barked scratchy, disembodied orders through the warm afternoon air, and cops were soon setting up bright orange cones and hot pink flares to divert traffic. One cop appeared with a roll of wide yellow tape, and began running it around the lamp posts to block off the area. Several more were bending over a form in the gutter: a form clad in a white linen jacket and sleek navy-blue slacks.

It was my Japanese national.

I maneuvered into a throng of tourists who had stopped to watch. I saw one kneeling cop look hopelessly at another, then the electric blue lights on the Cushman three-wheelers beamed in two blue-and-whites that screeched to a stop, blocking my view again. A wailing ambulance siren added to the din, the blazing orange strobes adding new color to the grim carnival of police lights. I angled around once again so I could see.

Two white-clad paramedics leaped from the back of the ambulance and began working on the man. The ambulance driver placed thick cotton pads around the man's head, trying to absorb some of the blood. They checked the man's vital signs, then looked at one another, again without hope. Even I could see it was useless. The man's head was at an impossible angle.

The crowd of onlookers was milling forward now, pulling me with them, but I edged to the left, to where I could now see the van that had hit him. Painted on the van's side were the words, "Big Bruddah's Plumbing." A thickset, dark-haired local man in a faded blue T-shirt and stained denims sat nearby on a swath of grass, his head in his hands, groaning, two cops with notepads interrogating him. Even from where I stood, I could smell alcohol. The left front fender was mashed in, evidence of where the vehicle had struck the victim. The driver's door hung open. As I watched, a cop reached in and switched off the engine.

Cops were measuring distances now, herding people away. A man with iron-gray hair and a mahogany face had taken over the operation. I knew who he was, though I didn't know him well: Sergeant Nathan Wong, who oversaw the Waikiki street patrolmen and rookies. A younger cop, a male Japanese-Hawaiian I didn't know, followed in his wake. They started asking the other cops questions.

The police had herded enough tourists away for me to be able to see the victim from a new vantage point. I watched as the paramedics cut away clothing, still looking for a way to save the the man's life. First the snow-white linen designer jacket fell apart into strips, then the tops of the slacks. But when they went to work cutting off the white shirt, one paramedic suddenly froze, then held up his hand for the other to stop. He motioned for Sergeant Wong, who stepped forward and looked down. His face collapsed into a worried scowl. I edged my way in and tried to see what was worrying them.

The paramedics were again peeling away the bloodied white shirt from the wounded man's torso. I made my way to a point just behind a tourist couple clad in matching neon green aloha shirt and muu-muu. I was close enough to hear what the paramedics were saying now, though I wasn't conspicuous to them. And as I watched the rest of the clothing being cut away, I heard—and saw—what was wrong.

". . . these tattoos," one paramedic said. He gave the other paramedic a meaningful look. He was down on his knees, hovering over the man, scissors in hand. Now, he moved back, wiped his forehead, and looked up at the cops.

"Probably flew to California or Portland then doubled back," said a plainclothes detective who had just joined the chaos and was now looking down at the artfully tattooed man. "That's the way they get past Immigration these days. Mainland doesn't care, they don't have to deal with them the way we do."

Wong nodded and said, "I'd like to have these tattoos photo-graphed on the spot."

The paramedic shrugged. "The medical examiner needs to pro-nounce him dead before we move him anyway."

"Did anyone get near him before we arrived?" The Sergeant had turned now and was talking to one of the first uniformed officers on the scene.

"Witnesses said no," the cop replied. "Some of us were around the corner, talking over in front of the substation, so close we heard the impact and the screech of brakes. We came at a run. Not much could have happened between the impact and the time we got here."

"Right. Well . . . any I.D.?" Wong was holding a clipboard, writing things down.

"There was a Japanese passport in his jacket pocket." He handed it over.

Wong looked, then handed it back, to be bagged as evidence. "What else?"

"Nothing in his other pockets but a bankroll, I'd guess close to six grand, all American hundreds. And some prescription sunglasses. Not even a hotel key, nothing."

"You see his Rolex and diamond ring?"

"Yeah, I'd guess those are worth another ten grand."

As Sergeant Wong and the police officers talked, they watched the paramedics cut away more cloth. I also watched.

The Japanese man was tattooed right up to his collar bone, down to his wrists, all the way to his waist, and below.

I stepped in closer, amazed. Every square inch was a filigree of exquisite needlepoint. There were necklaces of flowers and pyramids of beadwork; lacy, twisting trees and lattices of vines; sprinkles of rising suns and several ferocious varieties of coiling, writhing, spiraling dragons, some of them whiskered while others breathed fire.

The artwork was exquisite. The inks were brilliant: blue, green, red, orange, yellow, and, most dominant, black.

Most of the other police officers had stopped their work and were watching now. A sinister hush had fallen over the group, along with a growing sense of apprehension.

To the medical examiner, the sergeant said, "You sure he's dead?"

"No way he could be anything else."

He asked the police photographer, "You got your pictures?"

The answer was yes.

Only then did Wong say, "Roll him over. I want to see the back."

The paramedics complied.

The back was the same as the front, except that in the very center of the artistry, in the midst of the vivid orange, blue, black, and green inks, a Samurai warrior held a sword aloft, preparing to behead an unportrayed victim. Flowers and banners and dragons surrounded him. His eyes blazed orange hatred.

"*Yakuza.*" One of the cops had finally uttered the dreaded word.

"Just like in the police photos," said one of the fresh-faced rookies. A look of incredulity was stamped on his face. "It's the first time I ever saw a real one."

A young female cop jerked her thumb backward toward the driver of the white van, who still sat on the grass, apparently in shock. "Looks like our friendly neighborhood plumber just wacked out Japan's version of don Corleone," she said. "Much as I hate drunk drivers, I think I feel sorry for the guy."

I thought about that. I didn't feel sorry for the drunk driver. I hate drunk drivers. I guess I didn't feel sorry for the victim, either. Perhaps that's not very Christian, but the Japanese *yakuza* is one of the bloodiest crime syndicates in the world, certainly the worst in the Pacific basin. Furthermore, they're known to have a heavy hand in the recent flood of smokable crystal methamphetamine—Ice—that has people doing little things like plunging knives into their parents and spouses and killing cops, my husband among them. Things that go around have a way of coming around, and I save my sympathy for their victims.

I thought, too, about what I'd seen the man doing in the shrubbery beside the Hyatt Hotel. Had he been hiding something? And as I considered what I'd seen, I made a snap decision. I wasn't eager to admit to the Honolulu Police Department that I spied on Waikiki with a telescope from the eighth floor of a condo that could see square into the window of their substation. And how else could I explain seeing what I'd seen?

Besides, if there was anything interesting behind those shrubs, I knew I could always turn it in later.

CHAPTER 4

I went back up to my condo, back to the balcony to watch as they finished appraising and photographing the dead *yakuza* man's body, then loaded it onto a gurney, shoved it into the ambulance, and sped away.

I had already decided that my mystery caller wasn't going to keep his appointment. Either he had just been killed in the street—a probability that was beginning to give me a sickly, sinking feeling—or the crowd and the carnival of police lights had frightened him away. Still, I checked my answering machine, just in case he'd phoned again while I was down watching the action. No messages. I went back to the balcony and watched, my portable phone at my side, hoping to hear from him. I watched as the drunk van driver was cuffed and tucked into the back seat of a blue-and-white while the policemen measured the crime scene and finished taking photographs. Finally, the blood was hosed down the drain, and the plumber's van was towed away.

After about an hour, the coast was clear. I went back downstairs and turned casually toward the corner beside the hotel where I had seen the tattooed man bending toward the foliage, perhaps hiding something.

Someone was rummaging through one of the trash cans the city puts at intervals in order to try to keep Waikiki clean. He had picked the one closest to the place I wanted to search. In spite of his position, I could see that he was clad in brown twill clothing so soiled it was black in places, and his shoulders were bony, large for his reedy frame. He was bent so I couldn't see his face, but the back of his longish hair was oily black, obviously dirty. I stopped and watched him. After a moment, he came up out of the trash; as he turned around, I recognized him as a man called Snake, a longtime member of Waikiki's homeless community. He was an emaciated man with a mangled leg, demonic eyes, and turkey tracks all over his body—from pumping various white powders into various veins.

Snake had occasionally acted as an informant for my husband when David had been working the streets. Though I'd never met him face to face, David had pointed him out to me a few years back.

"Why do you call him Snake?" I'd said. "That seems a little demeaning to me."

"That's what he calls himself. The only name he'll answer to. Keep away from him," he'd said. "He's a twenty-year veteran of heroin and every other drug imaginable, most recently Ice. His brains are baked, and he's violent. I give him money once in a while, he gives me some low-level information about who's who in the streets. He may put it together that you're my wife and come to you for money. If he ever approaches you, let me know right away."

I'd seen Snake around for years, but he had never indicated he knew who I was, and he had certainly never approached me for money. Now, he glanced at me without recognition as I passed by. His eyes had the vacant, opaque quality of someone who had recently shot up heroin. I went across the street to a small deli, a place with windows all the way around. I grabbed a chilled bottle of lime sparkling water, then sat at a sheltered window table drinking it. I could see the shrubs where the Japanese national had been, and I could see Snake, though he couldn't see me. He scoured through the next garbage can, then did a casual search through the surrounding area, looking beneath a couple of news-vending machines, under a mailbox, peering under a few of the plants that bordered the sidewalk.

Even though I thought I had seen the dead man hide something nearby, I didn't think much about Snake's behavior. The homeless are always with us, even here in Waikiki. Some of them make a few odd dollars by recycling the aluminum soft drink cans the tourists pitch into the garbage, so its not unusual to see people sifting through trash cans and combing for discards, even in the middle of the day. The ones who consistently cause trouble are sooner or later locked up and invited to move along, or they're put into the state mental hospital, or jailed for the long term if there's a reason. There are good social services here, probably better than most cities. Shelters and ministries feed the homeless, provide places for them to go. The people who remain in the streets have usually established patterns of behavior that allow them to exist alongside the rest of us, in their odd little parallel universes. Most have either serious drug problems or mental problems, but not so serious that they can't function on the fringes of society. And so, you get used to seeing these people from time to time, maybe try to help out until you realize that many resent your help and just want to be left alone. I was more used to them than most because David had befriended a few of them, for both charitable and professional reasons.

Snake wandered off down the street, looked in another garbage can, then into a dumpster at the side of a hotel. I waited till he had vanished into the distance, then casually made my way into the bushes right up beside the hotel. Though people were coming and going on every side, nobody paid any attention to me.

I found it instantly: a small, fat, dun-colored ostrich leather briefcase, well hidden behind the thicket of leaves. I felt my heart lurch as I picked it up. This was *yakuza* property. So what had I discovered? Money? Diamonds? Secret documents worth millions?

I glanced around. Nobody seemed to notice my discovery. I tucked the briefcase under my arm, then casually carried it back up to my combination condo and office, strutting along like it belonged to me. Troubles and his friend Tess had a week's holiday from school. They were on the small island of Molokai, paddling our Zodiac inflatable boat around the rugged North Shore. They wouldn't be back till tomorrow, so I had the place to myself. I almost licked my lips in anticipation as I carefully settled the briefcase in the middle of the dining room table. I tried the latch. It was locked, of course. But I'd invested in a locksmithing class a couple of years ago and had bought a good set of picks. I retrieved them from my office closet, set to work, and in no time at all, the lock gave and I had the briefcase open.

The visions of precious gems, vials of methamphetamine, or bricks of heroin vanished as I saw the stacks of paper. A little disappointed, I picked some up and began to rummage through them. They appeared to be formally-issued legal contracts, written in Japanese *kanji*, with several columns of figures and some signature lines at the bottom, some of the signatures in *kanji*, some in scribbled English. I rifled through them. Not a thing I could understand. I put these documents to one side.

Several thick manila envelopes were next in the stack. I opened the first one and pulled out a sheaf of papers, written in English. I had brewed some peppermint tea by then, and I was just taking my first sip when I read the top words. My hand jerked, my heart lurched. The tea sloshed onto the table, I grabbed a cloth to dab it up before it could spread to the papers, and only then did I realize I was holding my breath. I let it out with a slow hiss. My hand was trembling as I picked up the document again and read it. I could not believe my eyes.

"Golden Palms Resort Corporation," read the legend printed across the top. I kept looking at the letters, but they didn't change. There was no mistake, no way. That's what it said. These papers pertained to the Golden Palms, Victor Seitaki's latest real estate development, the construction of which had been interrupted in mid-project by his sudden death. The papers were obviously financial documents. *Victor's* financial documents.

A dark feeling of dread began to creep into my formerly cheery dining room. What on earth had a dead *yakuza* man been doing with Victor's private papers? And why had he hidden them in the bushes? I remembered the undercurrent of terror in the man's voice. Had someone been following him? Had someone seen him stash the briefcase in the bush, and if so, had they seen me come to collect it? I thought about that one for a minute, then shook off what could have easily turned into some serious paranoia. Had the tattooed man deliberately stepped into the path of an oncoming vehicle, a bizarre form of suicide? Or had it indeed been an accident?

I retracked the man's every move in my memory, at least the ones I had been able to see. I couldn't recall anything unusual other than his dipping down to hide the briefcase, the act that had originally attracted my attention. But why had he ditched the papers? Apparently *something* had been going on that I'd missed. Suddenly, there were a lot of unanswered questions in my life.

Easy now, Alex, said the lucid part of my mind to the tangled part. *It can't be what it looks like. It's too much coincidence. There has to be a simple explanation for all this.*

But the more I thought about it, the less sense it made. What were the odds against a member of Japan's organized criminal faction toting around the late Victor Seitaki's private business papers? Then getting killed virtually in front of a friend of Victor Seitaki's brother, and that friend "accidentally" finding those papers, stashed, in front of her very nose? Add it all up, and the odds had to be in the billions. So—what did it all mean if it wasn't a coincidence?

The man who'd phoned me, who had needed to see me urgently, had been from Japan. No doubt about it, the accent was a dead giveaway. So—what if these papers were hidden in my neighborhood because it was my neighborhood? It was common knowledge that Victor was Jess's brother and that I was Jess's good friend as well as a private investigator. It was also no secret that my key connection to Jess was the fact that he'd been my husband's partner in police work for many years.

The man had asked if I was the one whose husband had been a cop. No doubt about it, the man who'd been on his way to see me had to be the same person who hid these papers in the bushes only moments before he was killed. Which meant he had been bringing these papers to me. But why?

And why had he hidden them beneath the shrubs? If they were that sensitive, why not leave them in the hotel safe—assuming he was staying in a hotel. Had someone been following him?

I was still playing with all the possibilities as I began to look through the papers. All of them, to a one, dealt with financing and building Victor Seitaki's new hotel project, and most of them bore what I now recognized as Victor's scribbled signature—even the ones written in *kanji*. And all the papers were highly confidential. There was Victor's personal financial statement, his construction corporation's year-end operating statement, and several financial papers that didn't make a lot of sense to me. There was a document titled "Property Description" that gave an overview of the hotel, the condos, the golf course, the grounds, and all the surrounds; there were several purchase notes and even a very complicated loan settlement schedule that talked about secured notes and unsecured notes and various financial institutions, here and on the mainland and in Japan, which had loaned money into the project. There were zoning variance papers, unsigned. And there were signed papers indicating that the Golden Palms had been following the state-required

practice of developing a share of the condos into low-income housing—which, here in Hawaii, meant units beginning at the quarter-
million-dollar range rather than the half-million-dollar or
million-dollar range. There were agreement papers that the Golden
Palms would donate money for new roads and even a small park
with a community swimming pool. I emitted a small, low whistle as
I read all this. The Golden Palms was an even larger project than I
had realized, and apparently the state had exacted a high price in
return for allowing Victor and his pals to make use of what had
formerly been prime agricultural land.

And at the very bottom of the papers, I found a personal letter,
written to Victor from the Bank of Oahu and dated almost a year
ago. It read:

Dear Mr. Seitaki:

*Please be advised that your loan with the Bank of Oahu
matures in two months and we continue to expect full repay-
ment of the loan on or before that date. Per our previous dis-
cussion, no extensions will be forthcoming. We trust that
your arrangement with the Wakizaka Bank Syndicate of Tokyo will be sufficient for you to meet these obligations.*

*Additionally, your interest reserve account has a balance of
only $803,444.03, an amount far insufficient to meet your
payments in arrears. Therefore, we are asking that on or before the due date, you remit the monies necessary to make up
that deficiency. Please have your staff call me for settlement
figures on or before the final date.*

Sincerely,

It was signed by Ed Grappner, the president of the bank's Commercial Loan Division.

I knew a bit about the Bank of Oahu because this was the bank
that had refinanced my mortgage after David's death. Refinancing
had provided a way to keep the inheritance taxes to a minimum and
lower my monthly payments. Jess had asked Victor to check into it
as a favor to me. I had wanted to use the insurance money to just
pay off the mortgage, but a loan officer had kindly crunched the

numbers that showed me if I did that, I'd end up spending a small fortune in taxes.

Still, before signing the papers I'd checked out the bank. And I had learned that like so many other corporations with conspicuously local names, the Bank of Oahu had been bought out some ten years back by one of the behemoth Japanese financial institutions which had, shortly thereafter, cut interest rates and flooded the Pacific basin with money. During that time, the Bank of Oahu opened numerous local branches, bought out several small, shaky savings and loans, blitzed the airwaves and TV waves with advertising that made the Bank of Oahu look as Hawaiian as a ukelele at a luau, and otherwise consolidated its position here in the Islands. And now, according to what I could figure out from the papers I'd just discovered, they had been threatening to pull the financial rug out from under one of the most successful real estate developers in Hawaii.

This was very bad *nichibei*: a *very* black mark on the Japanese-Hawaiian/American relationship. And it flat out made me mad.

But even as these thoughts formed in my mind, another thought stormed in and engulfed them. Victor? In financial trouble? *Victor?*

I thought about that for a moment. Maybe. Perhaps that was why he had a heart attack. After all, severe economic or personal pressure often precipitates illness, even fatal illness. And real estate development was always a precarious business. Most commercial developers hit an occasional snag. Especially these days.

Because of imbalances in the yen-to-dollar ratio a few years back, the Japanese had discovered that their yen bought as much in the United States as the dollar was buying in Mexico not all that long ago. Japanese investment had flooded into Hawaii, to the tune of 4.4 billion dollars in one year alone, and that's a lot of yen for a state with a year-round population of less than a million people. Hawaii's economy had welcomed the money, especially since the mainland was sinking into recession at that point and not so many mainlanders were showing up to spend vacation money. Tourism brings Hawaii some two million visitors a year and is our biggest legal industry, though some say marijuana growing is bigger business. But that's open to debate since the growers don't keep statistics; and since the feds and local police have been busy pulling up plants, that market tends to fluctuate widely anyway. At any rate, the Japanese visitors and investors were taking up the slack created by the slump in the mainland economy. Hawaii welcomed them, one and all, with open arms. As long as the visitors—from wherever—kept coming, all the hard-working people in what is called the visitor industry could keep their jobs, could keep their bills paid and their children fed—worthy goals, indeed.

But when Hawaii's heavy real estate speculation started, the old, stable Japanese companies that had been doing business in and with Hawaii for decades had taken their more conservative money and socked it away, folded their arms, and waited patiently as waves of speculators from the fast-track Japanese markets inundated the Islands with yen. These speculators had already rolled the economic dice that had made Japan's real estate prices skyrocket. Now they bought Hawaiian hotels by the dozens, and golf courses, restaurants, condos, hundreds of houses—anything that might allow them to catch the wave of the rising economic tide here and make a quick buck.

Then came the reckoning. Japan's go-go economy hit a serious snag and the bubble burst. Now, Tokyo's stock market had dropped by about 50 percent in the past few years—knocking the value of bank portfolios in half—and the Japanese economy was otherwise in decline. Unemployment was higher there than it had been at any time since the Second World War, and homelessness was an emerging problem. The Tokyo Evening News, a feature on Island television, showed people living in large cardboard boxes, just like the American homeless except that they had neatly placed their shoes beside the front entrance to their cardboard boxes and crates.

In addition, Japanese politics was in a turmoil as the citizens clamored for a cleanup of the deeply entrenched crime and corruption that was helping to drag down the economy. Any way you looked at it, the cheap Japanese capital was gone. Some American economic experts were actually predicting that Japan's banking system was on the verge of collapse. At the practical level, this meant that most of Japan's banks were calling in loans right and left, and things otherwise did not look good for Japanese investors. Especially investors who had taken a lot of risks in order to try to grab the fast bucks—which included a lot of investors who had put speculative money into Hawaii.

The Golden Palms Resort project had been planned and financed during the peak of Japan's go-go cycle, apparently with Japanese money. Adding it all up, I could see that Victor might indeed have been in a bit of financial trouble. Which meant that perhaps the *yakuza* man who had just been killed had somehow been trying to capitalize on Victor's troubles. But from the contents of Ed Grappner's letter, Victor had already been making a new loan with a bank in Tokyo. And Jess had told me that Anne's uncle, Ko Shinda, the wizened little man I'd met at the funeral, was also involved in the project. I knew for a fact that Mr. Shinda was fabulously wealthy, maybe even a billionaire. So—what did it all mean?

Trouble. That much was certain. Just the fact that a *yakuza* figure had access to Victor Seitaki's private documents made me so instantly furious that I didn't even stop to consider taking a moment to pray for guidance. I was certain that these documents had been illegally obtained in order to somehow give the Japanese investors an upper hand in the local building trade—and specifically in Victor Seitaki's forthcoming luxury resort project. That's the only way these papers made sense.

With my rage turning to a cold, steely affirmation, I looked through the rest of the briefcase's contents. The other manila folders and envelopes held more documents in both Japanese and English, more of Victor Seitaki's private papers. I stacked them all neatly to one side so that I could copy them later.

When I had finished scanning the rest of the papers, I felt down in the side pockets to see if I'd missed anything. I had. Stuck far into the corner was a pack of matches. There was also a single key with the numbers 656 etched into its hilt. Though hotels no longer put their names on their keys, lest one be lost and used for illegal entry, I recognized that this key had the distinctive square hilt of the nearby Royal Seashell Hotel, an exclusive resort built during the go-go cycle with Japanese money. Over the years, legitimate Japanese corporations had bought up about 80 percent of the hotels on Waikiki. This particular hotel was just past the Sheraton—also Japanese owned—and flush on the beach.

I let the anger seep into me as my hand snaked out, picked up the phone, and dialed Jess's home number. The machine answered with a polite recording of Yoko's voice. I waited, hoping a human voice would intervene, but the machine beeped, so I said to the recorder, "Jess, call me right away. There is something you *really* need to know." Next, I dialed Jess's office at HSP. They were sorry, but he had gone for the day. Would I like to leave a message? I didn't, they had me on recorder anyway, like all incoming calls.

I'd already thought about it. The police would still be there tomorrow, so would the contents of the briefcase. Getting this new information to Jess could even wait till tomorrow, if it had to. But whatever or whoever was in the newly deceased Japanese criminal's hotel room—656—just might not hang around that long.

CHAPTER 5

When I was a nine-year-old child in the Colorado Rockies, I'd read about a world-famous heiress who had taken a lover—a fortune hunter, no less—and they had been discovered commingling in Waikiki's Royal Hawaiian Hotel. He'd abandoned her soon thereafter, taking a nice chunk of her money with him. After that, my impression of the then very distant Waikiki was of opulence and lust, of despair and loneliness, of crisp white linen tablecloths and snobbish waiters doubling as gigolos. Enormous yachts waited just off shore. Cruel yet brilliant Asians with inscrutable eyes plotted intrigues. Large, drafty hotel lobbies with white-and-black tiled floors and potted palms and ocean waves lapping hungrily just outside a railing held 1930s intrigue, as redone in the 1960s by Hollywood.

Now, Waikiki was my home. I cut through the opulent pink lobby of the Royal Hawaiian Hotel every other day or so, on a shortcut to another hotel or to the beach, or on my way to their excellent brunch. Japanese investors had bought the building some years ago, had wanted to tear it down and put up a high rise. The powers that be in Hawaii had declared it an historic monument and forced them to keep it intact. More bad *nichibei*, bad blood between Hawaii and Japan.

If I saw any heiresses in the luscious pink lobby, I didn't recognize them. Though I did occasionally see today's version of a gigolo. And now I understood that Asians with inscrutable eyes were just socialized differently than I had been, what was inscrutability to me was good manners to them, what I saw as coldness was often behavior born of necessity from living elbow to elbow in an anthill society where today's citizens were all too often cogs in an industrial machine. I had learned that where physical distance from strangers was impossible, people created emotional distance.

But even with these myths blown apart, after midnight Waikiki could take on a slightly sinister air. There were still plenty of people out, but there was something harder in their features than in the daytime. Often, this was because they were simply up to no good— just as I was.

I'd waited till two A.M., using some of the time to dress in a simple sky-blue linen dress. I added dangling gold earrings, and dragged a comb through my short blonde locks. Then I draped an evening bag with a faux gold chain over my shoulder, after stuffing in my lock picks, a couple of bucks, and an I.D. in case some rookie decided I was one of the hookers who prowled Waikiki at this time of night and tried to roust me.

At just after two, I left my condo, crossed Kalakaua just *ewa* of the police substation, and walked with my shoes in hand along Kuhio Beach, down around the back of the Moana Hotel. I waded along the edge of the water, letting the breakers lap high enough to dampen the bottom of my dress, just another tourist out for a night stroll after the bars had closed. A couple of solitary men made motions as if they wanted to approach me, but I can give off signals when I want to, and I gave them off hard and cold. Both times, the men veered off and left me alone.

As usual, the city fathers had the seawall and the sidewalk torn up beside the Sheraton, so I cut through the hotel's green lobby, then their well-lighted parking garage, to get to the grounds in front of the Royal Seashell. Once there, I lingered outside and out of sight of the front desk until I spotted several other people walking in the direction of the lobby. I attached myself to their party by asking directions and walked in with them, one wife looking like she wanted to kill me for intruding into her domain at such a strange time of the morning, and her husband drunk and vulnerable, too.

I entered the elevator with them, then stood demurely at the back, waiting till they'd gotten off on three, then I touched the button that took me on up to the sixth floor. I knocked at the door of 656, waited, then knocked again. This time, when there was no response, I used the key.

A night-light showed me a suite that was rose and ivory luxury, one of those five-hundred-dollar-a-night jobs that included a full bedroom and a small sitting room complete with a wraparound balcony that overlooked the moonlit sea. I looked into the sitting room, then into the small kitchenette, then flipped on a dim lamp and took a quick look into the bathroom and the walk-in closet. Just as I'd hoped, the suite was empty. And, also as I'd hoped, there was a suitcase sitting beside the bed. A large, leather three-suiter with the Louis Vuitton logo on the clasp. *Yakuza* luggage. Filled with secrets.

I'd brought my lockpicks. No moral dilemma here. I wasn't going to steal anything, I was just going to look.

But the lock was a little sturdier than most, and I was still sitting on the ivory satin bedspread, my skirt dampening its skirt as I picked away, when the door suddenly opened and a man stood in the square of hallway light. I froze, and he actually didn't see me for a second, so dim was the lamplight. But as he flicked on the overhead fixture, there I was, warts and all and no place to hide. I quickly tucked the hand that held my picks in under my skirt.

"Hello," I said. And smiled my sweetest smile.

He narrowed his eyes and just looked at me. I pegged him for another Japanese national. About my age—thirty-three—and attractive, in a Japanese chairman of the board sort of way. His hair was dark brown and neatly cut, though a little short for my taste. He wore a crisp new aloha shirt in green and gray, and gray cotton slacks. He was poised, I didn't know if for flight or attack. But he was about six feet, tall for a Japanese. Lean and compact. And I knew the instant I looked at him that if he decided to nail me, the only thing I could do was jump off the balcony and die.

But my presence, rather than angering him, seemed to confuse him. He looked at the key in his hand, the one he'd just used to open the door, and then he looked at me. "Isn't this Room 656?"

His English was polished but a little too perfect, though there was no actual trace of a Japanese accent. But that didn't mean much. The Japanese kids start learning English while we Americans are still learning to crawl and watch the Flintstones.

"It is." I casually let go of the suitcase flap and adopted an air of indifference.

"Then this is *my* room," he said. "When I checked in, the bell captain said . . ."

Good. He hadn't actually been in here yet—the bell captain must have deposited his luggage for him. Still, I was waiting for him to realize what was going on, then roar into action. But there was no anger in his eyes. Yet. Maybe he'd been out sampling Waikiki's nightlife, in the form of a Mai Tai or two or four, something to numb his wits. In which case, maybe I could keep him confused just long enough to *shibai*—fast talk—my way out of there.

"I'm Elaine," I said. And that was true. My full name was Alexis Elaine Albright. "I also have a key to this room." And that was also true. I held it up so he could see it.

I try not to lie any more than I absolutely have to, though I do have a slightly different idea about what a lie is than what I learned in Sunday school. Still, just in case I'm wrong, I try to minimize untruths of every kind.

"But this is *my* room," he repeated. "I'm sure of it. I checked in then went to eat, and I'm sure this is the room they gave me." He looked at his key, looked back at me. "Look, we'd better phone the front desk and get this straightened out." And just then a sudden veil of anger contorted his face as he suddenly fixed on the suitcase on the bed. "That's a man's luggage," He said. He squinted, looking more closely. "That's *mine*."

I looked down at the suitcase, then flung my hands back as if I'd just noticed it. "I'm sorry," I said. I was mentally flogging myself—at least twenty lashes—as I thought about what he'd said about checking in. Apparently, the hotel hadn't wasted any time reletting the room after their former tenant was hit by a van and killed. I should have come earlier.

I stood up and said, "It looks like there's been some mistake." True, also. My mistake, and a big one.

The man had noticed my dampened skirt. He was staring indignantly at the dampened bedspread.

I stood up and walked toward him, my arms wide in an expression of confusion that I hoped equalled his own. I had already surreptitiously dropped my picks into my bag, then draped my bag over my shoulder, and I was ready to beat feet the instant I could get past him.

But he surprised me by stepping politely aside as I approached the door. "I really do believe they gave me this room," he said. "You'd better go down to the desk and find out what happened."

But as I tried to step daintily past him, his hand suddenly flew out and clamped like a steel vise onto my wrist—the hand that still held the room key—and he said, "I'll take that, too." He did. "I don't know where you got this key, but I'm beginning to suspect that you may not be a guest of this hotel at all."

I started to protest, but then realized that I'd be foolish to waste time arguing since he was apparently letting me go. And go I did, not bothering to wait for the elevator, not even waiting to see if he shut the door behind me. I was desperately relieved to be out of that room and out of that impossible situation. And it was only weeks later that I looked back and realized that I'd just met a professional to equal the best, and that in the very first move of the game I had been hopelessly outflanked.

learned later that they put in the bugs when I picked up my nephew, Troubles, at the Aloha Airlines terminal at nine the next morning. I was gone for several hours, so they certainly had enough time, and there was simply no reason why they should have been interested in me before my encounter with the man in the hotel. No doubt about it, that was the day.

Troubles and his best friend, Tess, had been rowing around the North Shore of the small island of Molokai for the past week or so, camping out on the beach at night. Now, they had just returned—sunburned, windblown, sandy, salted, and sated. I was bedraggled from staying up late exploring hotel rooms. I felt a hefty surge of envy as I thought about their week and compared it to my own.

"How was the trip?"

"Incredible," Tess said. She said that a lot about Hawaii's scenery, even though she'd been born and raised here. She was wearing battered Reeboks, a pair of cutoffs, a salt-stiffened T-shirt with a surf shop logo on it, and she still managed to look like she'd just stepped out of a TV commercial for soap or toothpaste or something else that featured blonde, leggy, suntanned, blue-eyed beauties. All this and straight A's in math, too.

"Water was a little rough," Troubles added, then slunk down and pulled the visor of his boater's cap over his eyes.

I was driving the clanky brown Chevy van I'd inherited from David—his fishing vehicle. I'd kept it for sentimental reasons and then, when I'd decided to finally get my P.I. license about six months after his death, I'd turned the van into a private-eye-mobile: an air mattress for comfort, tinted one-way glass in the back, even a cellular phone in case I needed to call out for a pizza or amuse myself by harassing the people with 1-900 numbers. It also worked fine for hauling things, and now the air mattress was neatly rolled up and the rubber Zodiac deflated and placed in the back, along with the rest of their gear. Troubles sat beside me in the front passenger seat, while Tess had climbed into the back seat. She stretched out and fell asleep the minute we started moving.

I thought Troubles was long gone too, but the minute we hit the H-1 headed home he sat up, shoved his cap back on his head, and said, "So how was the funeral?"

"Depressing."

"Jess and Yoko doing okay?" Though he'd only been here about eight months, he had adopted the Islands and its people as if he'd been born here. He was especially fond of most of the people in our church. He was a good kid and would have been at Victor's funeral if he hadn't already been on the isolated beaches of Molokai. I'd told him about the death only yesterday when he'd phoned and told me when to pick them up.

His mom and dad were divorced, and he'd had a hard time adjusting to the family breakup. I hadn't spent much time with him since he had been small, but now, to my delight, we were becoming good friends, and I was happier by the day that he was staying with me.

"Jess and Yoko are doing as well as can be expected," I said. "Matter of fact, I'm going to have lunch with Jess today."

I'd finally touched base with Jess at HSP Headquarters late the previous night. I phoned him right after returning from my adventure at the *yakuza* man's hotel room. Because HSP tapes and times all incoming phone calls (someone had once sued them for not responding fast enough), I hadn't told Jess about finding the briefcase yet. And there was certainly no point in mentioning the *yakuza* man's death, since all nonnatural deaths are initially investigated as homicides here and Jess would already know about the case.

I'd also decided not to tell Troubles about the peculiar series of events. He'd hear about the death of the *yakuza* man, of course. It had hit the front page of the morning paper and would be all over the TV evening news. But Troubles didn't need to know any more than that. In fact, I never told him much about any aspect of my work or my life away from him. He was immersed in his own life as a pre-med student. He didn't need the extra stress, and I didn't need the complications. Not that I thought Troubles would ever do anything intentional to clutter up a case. But things happen, David's death proved that. You couldn't really count on anyone but yourself, so why bring someone else in on your problems?

Troubles, unaware of my tangled thoughts, yawned. "After we drop off Tess, I have to study for a Nutritional Science exam. So I'll be busy most of the night. Must be nice not to have to work."

"Must be," I said, swerving to avoid hitting a rental car that had suddenly decided to take over my lane.

Troubles raised his eyebrows as I cleared the car then jutted out my jaw and held my position against the rest of the chaotic traffic. Then he grinned his cockeyed grin, tilted his head, pulled his cap back down over his hazel eyes, slouched down, and instantly fell asleep.

I was supposed to meet Jess at one o'clock at the Gourmet's Garden Restaurant on Palm Street, near the old HPD station on Beretania. The Honolulu Police Department had moved farther downtown into a bright and shiny new building; not too many members of the HPD still ate lunch in the old neighborhood. Not that many of them had ever eaten at the Gourmet's Garden before. Like cops all across the nation, most were far more likely to grab a burger and fries—or the local delicacy of spam and potato-macaroni salad—than to dine in a health food restaurant. Which was exactly why I chose the Garden. I didn't want to run into any cops except Jess.

I should take a moment here to explain that a lot of people confuse the Hawaii State Police (HSP) with the Honolulu Police Department (HPD). But the Honolulu State Police, where Jess is Chief of Homicide, is an altogether different entity from the HPD. Whereas the HPD is chartered to police the city and county of Honolulu (which county makes up the entire island of Oahu, even though the actual city covers only a small part of it), the state police had a charter to cover the entire state, which includes not only the island of Oahu, but also the islands of Kauai, Molokai, Maui, Lanai, and the Big Island, also known as Hawaii. If you aren't confused enough yet, there are also the smaller islands of Kahoolawe (unpopulated) and Niihau (populated only by Native Hawaiians who've lived there for centuries). Well. It used to confuse me a bit, too, when I first moved here. But you'll sort it out as we go along.

Anyway, the Hawaii State Police (HSP), for which Jess works, is usually considered to have more clout than the city police (HPD), though this is not always the case. But organizationally, HSP lies somewhere between the city cops and the feds.

Still, Hawaii is a small state, and the policing organizations often find themselves all working together on this, that, or the other case through practical necessity. This means that most of the longtime cops know each other, and they even manage to partially keep track of the undercover agents who come in from the mainland to do various jobs for the various federal agencies. Furthermore, not only is there an ongoing three-way rivalry between the state police, the city police, and the feds, but a rivalry also exists among the various federal agencies—DEA, FBI, BATF, Immigration, Customs, and so on. Law enforcement can be a cornucopia of confusion, here in Paradise.

One way or another, Jess knew a lot of people in police work, and I knew a few myself. Today we had to do some serious talking, and I didn't want to bump into anyone who might strike up a conversation that would interrupt us. So here I was at the Gourmet's Garden, bane to all but the most gastronomically discerning cops.

I arrived a few minutes early and did some shopping in an adjacent store. Some vanilla bubble bath, a pink beeswax lipstick, some green bath salts from the Dead Sea to soak the aches from my body on the rougher days. I also bought a new bottle of the vitamin B complex that I used to help ward off the effects of my high-stress lifestyle.

Then, in the adjacent dining room, I sat down at one of the small, glossily polished wooden tables next to the window. I liked the room. There were lush, green plants everywhere, and refurbished, mismatching wooden tables and chairs. Pictures in sepia of the early years of Waikiki adorned the walls—you know, the ancient-seeming photographs taken when the Royal Hawaiian and Moana hotels sat almost alone on the beach and the rest of the area was swamp, taro patch, and white clapboard houses. I liked to look at the pictures and identify the places, see what once had been. While I was waiting and looking, I ordered a glass of fresh carrot juice. The waiter, a Filipino kid named Paul, served it just as Jess walked through the door. It was frothy and cold and, as usual, just a trace too sweet for me.

Jess was wearing a crisply ironed yellow and white aloha shirt with dark blue background and dark blue slacks—more or less typical work attire for plainclothes detectives. I'd chosen a neatly pressed white cotton blouse with a heavy jade and gold necklace and matching calf-length skirt, flared. At the table next to us, two chunky middle-aged women bedecked in bright Indian gauze skirts and plenty of crystals discussed the merits of wheat grass juice as it pertained to weight loss and karma. A bright crowd today.

But Jess had come in frowning, his shoulders back and head high, like he was walking into the ring. He was so tense I could feel electricity zinging off him.

As he sat down, I said, "Sorry to bother you when I know you're so busy, but you have to eat anyway—don't you?"

He gave me a quick, distracted smile, then picked up a menu, frowned, and started speed-reading the print. "I've got about half an hour. What's good?"

I told him I'd already ordered. He accepted my choice with a shrug, folded the menu and pushed it aside, then glanced toward the kitchen and blinked at his watch.

Jess was always rushed. With good reason. The meth—Ice—traffic was way up. There was also more coke, heroin, and crack in the Islands these days. The inevitable correlation between the drug traffic and the number of homicides was proving itself once again; the murder rate was skyrocketing. The HSP Homicide squad was ultimately responsible for solving all the homicides statewide except for those that occurred on military bases and therefore fell to the FBI. The rest of the buck stopped with Jess. To make matters worse, an election was coming up, and that meant the police were under the gun to make Hawaii's politicians look good by making it seem like the Islands were running smoothly, murders or not. That took a lot of extra finessing, which meant extra time and energy.

I said, "Looks like you're hip deep in hammerheads again. I saw on TV that you made a bust out in Waipahu—"

"That one's already history. Two fresh cases today. Another domestic—a woman up in Manoa shot her husband—and a drug hit." He wrinkled his nose slightly. "Smells like lemons in here."

"My cologne," I said. I had spilled some while trying it on, and it was a little strong. "How's Yoko?"

"Busy. She's taken over the job of Choir Director. Pastor Mike bent her arm a bit."

"She'll be great."

"She's happy. She's been at loose ends since Romi and Peter went back to UCLA." Suddenly, he pierced me with a direct look and said, "How about you?"

He had caught me off guard, and I responded clumsily. "I'm okay. Staying busy, I guess."

"I know you're busy. I keep my ear to the ground, and hear nothing but good things about you and the business. David would be proud."

A sudden stab of loneliness left a near-physical wound at the mention of David's name. It came at me once in a while like that, his name out of the clear blue sky, and suddenly there I was, standing *beneath* a clear blue sky, dropping a blood red rose atop his coffin . . .

I made a quick recovery, though, and even managed a weak smile. "I'm getting some pretty good clients. By the way, you mentioned the other day that you might need some help—"

He made a dismissive gesture with his thick well-tended hand. "Just a temporary problem. Got it worked out."

"I suppose you'll be retiring soon anyway," I teased, "now that you're a rich man."

He shot me a probing, almost angry look, blinked, then looked away. "Victor's affairs are pretty complicated. Anne and the boys inherited a third of everything, there are some silent partners, and it's going to take my lawyer and my accountant months to figure out the rest of it. It may not be all that much by the time the taxes are paid. Victor was pretty heavily leveraged . . ."

I started to tell him about Victor's papers, but just then our waiter appeared with the sandwiches I'd ordered. They were made from a thick homemade ten-grain bread, mushrooms, fresh zucchini, avocado, crisp green lettuce, and a thin slice of melted cheese, no preservatives. Not bad, unless you counted the cheese. I'd spiced Jess's lunch up with a bowl of chili and a Pepsi.

Jess's attention turned to the food. I nibbled and watched him eat, chatting aimlessly while I thought about how to bring up the subject of the papers I'd purloined from the *yakuza* man's briefcase.

But suddenly he slugged back a jolt of Pepsi, washed down his bite of sandwich, and focused his full attention on me in a disconcerting way. "So why all the cloak and dagger, Alex? Why don't you just come right out and tell me what's up?"

I braced myself. "You're never going to believe this—"

Jess swallowed the last bite of his sandwich and wiped his mouth with his napkin. He glanced at his watch, and an intense frown transformed his face. "I've got an interrogation in fifteen minutes. Walk me to my car and we'll talk on the way."

"Okay," I said. "Okay, okay." I wrapped what was left of my sandwich in a large, thick napkin and stashed it in my purse and paid the bill over Jess's protestations, leaving too large a tip for the skinny young waiter because I didn't want to wait for change. Then I hustled Jess out the door and led him to my car.

"This will take just a minute," I said. "I found something you absolutely have to see. I didn't want to talk about it on your office phone. I know you'll want to keep this private."

He managed to look harassed and curious at the same time. I unlocked the Honda's passenger door, gestured him inside, then walked briskly around to the driver's side and slid in. I immediately leaned down and picked up the *yakuza*'s briefcase from the car floor, unlocked it, then set it, open, on his lap.

He looked at me, puzzled, then hesitated. But when I nodded, he picked up the first documents. I'd returned them to their original order, so he was looking at the ones written in *kanji*. As a third generation American of Japanese ancestry, he no more read Japanese than I did. He rifled through the papers, puzzled, glancing at me from time to time as if waiting for me to explain. I sat, silently watching him.

Suddenly he came to the first document with Golden Palms Resort written on it in English. His face crumpled up in surprise, then swiftly rolled right on into an angry glare. "What's this? Victor's papers? What are you doing with these?"

I told him. I started with the mysterious phone call from the Japanese national, then explained how I had been spying through the telescope—he knew I did it anyway; he and Yoko had tried it themselves a time or two. And then I told him about the tattooed man being killed on the street beneath my condo, how they'd cut away his clothing to reveal the fantastic artwork. And then I explained how I'd found the briefcase.

I had initially planned to tell Jess everything, even about my foray into the hotel that night, when I'd been surprised by the new Japanese tenant. But as I talked, I felt him drawing away from me, and I saw the look on his face transforming from one of hurried politeness to one of incredulity. Then suddenly he was staring at me in furious disbelief, his face stamped with such a dark, suffused rage that I stopped my story short at the point when I'd opened the briefcase and discovered Victor's papers, and said, "Jess! What's wrong?"

"You've had these papers since the man got killed yesterday?"

"Since shortly thereafter." I shrugged.

"I should arrest you." His voice was steely. His brown eyes had gone muddy with hostility and his square jaw was set in cement.

Taken aback, I said, "Why should I be arrested?"

"Why not?" The words were bitten off with such contempt that I felt like I'd been slapped.

"I don't understand you. *What* have I done?"

"You've concealed evidence in a possible homicide."

I felt my eyes narrow. "Jess, I don't understand—I mean—" I was beginning to feel the hot humiliation a child feels when being unfairly dressed down in public by an adult. I didn't like the feeling.

And though we'd been friends lo, these many years, I was suddenly having a hard time liking Homicide Captain Jess Seitaki. He'd transformed before my very eyes into someone arrogant beyond words. I'd never seen him like this, had never so much as suspected this side of his personality.

He fixed me with a rock hard stare. "I should cuff you right now and take you in. You, of all people, Alex, should know better. This thing—"

"Look Jess, I didn't find the briefcase till after the police had taken the man's body. I wasn't even sure he'd hidden anything in the bushes till I went and looked; it was just a suspicion. And when I found the briefcase and realized it contained Victor's papers, I tried to phone you immediately—I wanted you to know about it before I turned it over to HPD or whoever, so you could handle things in the best way. And you *are* knowing about it first. Here I am, telling you. So say, 'Thank you, Alex.' The police—you—have been informed, end of matter." I was angry, too, now. I drew myself up and looked pointedly at the passenger door, indicating I was ready for him to leave.

He said, "Why in heaven would this man phone *you?*"

The way he said it, it was insulting, like I should be a final choice in anyone's book—or like he didn't even believe me. I didn't reply.

But that didn't faze him. He said, "It's too late now to handle this in any decent way." His face had folded into a dark cloud.

His statement implied that I'd handled the situation indecently. Fuel for my anger. I said, "The papers are yours now. Handle it any way you want." I reached over and took the briefcase, angrily snapped it shut, then dropped it back into his lap, letting my fingers flare out in an indignant gesture as I let go.

He studied me, his own anger building until I thought for a moment he might actually explode. But he controlled himself and said through clenched teeth, "You don't have the slightest idea what you've done."

"Then why don't you try explaining?"

"Because I don't want you in it." He picked up the briefcase and opened the car door.

"In what?"

"In the middle of my business," he said, and I thought for a moment that I sensed a thaw.

I said, "So what are you planning to do with the papers?"

"That's my problem. As of right now, you're out of it. Got that? Just do us both a favor. Keep your mouth shut about this—"

A favor? With *his* attitude, he was asking me for a favor?

"—or I'll *have* to arrest you for concealing evidence in a possible homicide," he said. "The way things stand, I won't have any choice."

"Jess, I—" I was still hoping he would exhibit some vestige of sanity that would help me make sense of his reaction. Then I suddenly realized what he'd said. *Concealing evidence in a possible homicide.* I said, "You mean the man who got killed in front of my building was actually *murdered?*"

His eyes narrowed, and suddenly he was searching my eyes, searching, and I saw something different in him, something deep and disturbing that I didn't understand. His eyes thawed a bit, and I thought he was about to become himself again. Maybe he would even explain things.

I said, "Come on, Jess. What's going on?"

His brown eyes instantly iced over again. He said, "The van driver was a plumber's helper named Sonny Malinta—you probably heard the name on the news. He was drunk, period, but he claims that the Japanese national was pushed in front of his vehicle by someone who immediately vanished. Malinta didn't get a real look at him." His gaze suddenly became penetrating. "Did you see anything that might confirm that version of events?"

I thought very carefully before I answered, rescanning every part of the scene in my mind. "Nothing."

A cynical look crossed his face. "But of course if you were asked to testify to that in court, you'd have to tell them everything you *did* see and what you did in the aftermath. Which means I'd have to explain why I didn't arrest you the minute I realized you'd been concealing evidence."

But I was thinking about other things. I said, "So the *yakuza* man *was* murdered?"

Jess sighed. "Maybe. Maybe not. Sonny Malinta has a history of drinking and wife abuse, and his alcohol level was way beyond the legal limit. He could have cooked up the story to save himself from a manslaughter charge. But I still have to investigate it as a possible homicide."

"Having Victor's papers in the man's possession puts you in an awkward position, doesn't it?"

"Worse now than it might have been if you'd handed the papers over right away." His words were caustic again.

I started to make a heated reply, but he said, "Just keep your mouth shut, and I'll forget where I got these papers. I can claim I received them from a CI." A confidential informant.

"Fine," I said. "You just—"

But he'd shut—slammed—the car door in my face and was stomping toward his green Volvo with the briefcase clamped tightly under his arm.

Thanks for nothing, I thought. *Try to help out a friend, and this is what you get—*

I burned rubber leaving the parking lot. But it wasn't till I'd driven all the way home, parked my car, then inserted my key into the elevator door and started to ride up the eight floors to my condo/office that the anger suddenly welled up and dissolved into hot, salty tears.

Okay, God, I prayed. *Maybe I was a little irresponsible in the way I handled the situation. But You know that I wasn't being malicious, wasn't trying to cause trouble. I was just trying to understand what was going on, trying to help Jess, trying to protect him. So who's wrong here? Isn't Jess the one who's wrong? What about his obligations to our friendship? What about Christian love?* I felt more humiliated than ever before in my life, mostly because Jess had, until then, treated me with such pristine respect.

As I unlocked then opened the front door, Troubles looked up from the piles of school papers stacked on the coffee table. "Something wrong?"

I shook my head. "Just a little off the weather." I ducked straight into my office. I shut and locked the door behind me, then marched straight to the file cabinet where I'd stashed my photocopies of all the information I'd discovered in the tattooed man's briefcase. I yanked them out and started looking through them again.

I stayed in my office for the rest of a very long afternoon, studying the documents from every possible angle, trying to make sense of such financial horrors as corporate year-end financial statements, personal financial statements, partnership statements, current operating statements, and other dry and musty documents that I knew probably held some sizzling secrets amidst the numerous columns of figures. But they were as impossible for me to decipher as ancient cuneiform.

Nevertheless, if Jess Seitaki wanted me to stay out of this—whatever *this* was—I at least owed it to myself to figure out why. And if Jess didn't trust me enough to tell me what was happening, then I certainly wasn't going to trust him. And no way was I going to just step out of the picture and disappear. I hadn't asked for this situation. The man had phoned me, and he had been on his way to see me when he died.

Whether I liked it or not, I was in the middle of it now. I had best understand what was happening because, as usual, I had no one to depend upon but myself.

f you sit on the beach as daylight ends, you can watch a luminous Hawaiian sunset chased from the sky by translucent twilight. Far out on the horizon, the carnival-canvassed sailboats turn to-ward shore. As the light fades along the edges of the sky, the clouds become gold-rimmed, pale blue fleece, scudded along by the rising winds. The whitecaps grow brighter against the darkening sea, the palm trees turn black, the flaming tiki torches are lit in the hotel grounds along the beach, the primitive drumbeats herald the beginnings of hula shows and luaus. And the ghosts of the ancient *alii*—the ancient Hawaiian royalty who once ruled this land—are trapped in the shadows, shamed, waiting for the long night to end.

If you watch the sunset from the sand in front of the Royal Hawaiian Hotel, you can crook your head around toward the darkening jut of Diamond Head to see streetlights and stoplights blinking on along Kalakaua Avenue: gold, red, blue-green and am-ber, strung along the dark lushness of Kapiolani Park like tiny Christmas lights. Then, if you look seaward, you can watch the vanishing daylight weld sea and sky into an immense midnight-blue. Hawaiian midnight-blue: a special opalescent color, mixed in equal parts from decadence and deceit, from lushness, corruption, money, lust, survival—and violent death.

Night.

I'd put my copy of Victor's papers back in the file cabinet, then changed into my bathing suit and walked over to the beach that evening to think some more about Jess and his strange response to my gift of his brother's documents. From my position in front of the hotel, I watched the tourists vanishing from the beach as the light began to fade. When the sun began to slide behind the horizon, I swam for a half hour, savoring that last bit of half-light. The tide was in. The sea turtles were close to shore, feeding: huge, primitive creatures who surface, roll lightly to one side, then dive back down to their mysterious world. I also saw a school of tiny flying fish as they broke water, skidded along like silvery skipping stones, then dived back into the steel-gray depths.

But when it's totally dark, the bottom-feeders come in close to shore. And the sharks come out to feed, looking most of all for the sea turtles but prone to occasionally mistaking a person atop the water for a turtle's belly. There has never been a shark attack along the Waikiki shoreline—the reef is shallow enough to discourage most large predators. But it hadn't been all that long since a man netted a fifteen-foot tiger shark a short distance away, and shark attacks and sightings have been increasing for several years all throughout the Hawaiian Islands. I had given up my solitary late-night swims, so as the daylight fully died I let a wave wash me onto the sugar-fine sand, took a final look at the necklace of multicolored light along the shoreline, then took a quick, cold rinse under the public showers next to the police substation. I wrapped myself tightly in a huge beach towel then pressed into the tourist crowds; the people were back out, dressed for evening now, foraging for food and entertainment.

"Alex!"

As I headed for home, I heard my name and glanced around. But the traffic light was changing, and I had to sprint to make it across Kalakaua before the stream of traffic surged forward. When I got to the other side, I looked back but still didn't see anyone I knew. With so many people around, I figured it was probably someone calling another Alex, or perhaps I'd heard the name wrong.

The trade winds were rising. As I turned the corner, a gust blew in. I shivered, wrapped the beach towel tighter around my damp shoulders, and leaned into the wind. I live only a block from the beach, so I don't bother to carry a robe with me, especially since homeless people sometimes comb the beach in the evenings, looking for anything at all useful. I'd lost several beach robes that way before I'd learned my lesson.

I was beside my building, just ready to step into the side door, when I heard the voice again. "Alex! Wait up!"

I stopped, turned, and found myself staring square into the hard blue eyes of Derrick Green, the narcotics detective who had been with David when he'd been shot. His tan was golden and he wore a plum-colored shirt open at the throat to show a mat of black hair and a wealth of gold chains. Apparently my distaste for the costume showed, because he laughed and said, "I'm working a joint HSP-FBI investigation. Supposed to be a heroin dealer. Not exactly your type, I take it."

"Not at all. How are you, Derrick? It's been a long time."

"Too long."

I offered a tentative smile. I barely knew Derrick. He had joined the Hawaii State Police only a year or so before David's death, and they'd been partners for only a short time. David had kept his professional and private lives pretty much separate anyway, except for Jess and Yoko, who were friends from church and were otherwise special in every way. I'd met Derrick when he worked with David, of course, but only casually. And then he had been part of the swirl of events that followed David's death. We'd spent a modest amount of time together at that time, though everything had been on a very formal basis.

"I hear you're doing some private detective work these days," he said. "Good for you."

"Did you need to see me professionally?" I was a little puzzled by the sudden familiarity.

"No, no—I was just at the substation to pick up some paperwork and saw you walking down the street. Wanted to say hello." He looked a little embarrassed now.

"Well," I said, relaxing a bit, "it's nice to see you again."

"You—uh, have you had dinner yet?"

"No. But as you can see, I've just come from the beach. My hair is salty, and I'm not exactly dressed. Maybe we could talk another time?"

"You need to eat, I need to eat. I'll wait down here while you shower and change, then I'll buy you a steak."

"Really, I—"

"Please. I'm overdosing on sleaze. I need to spend an hour or so in some good honest company."

How could I say no to that? I thought it over, then said, "It will take me maybe half an hour to shower and dress."

"I'll wait down here in the lobby."

And of course, I could only do the polite thing, at that point, by inviting him up to wait for me.

Troubles was in his room with the door closed, sleeping or studying. I showed Derrick into the kitchen, gestured toward the table and chairs on the balcony, and said, "There's some fresh iced tea and some not-so-fresh limeade in the fridge, if you'd like a drink. Make yourself comfortable, I'll be a few minutes."

"Take your time," he said, grinning. "I'll just sit here on the balcony and keep an eye on the mean streets of Waikiki while I unwind."

I thought about Derrick as I showered and dressed. The first time I'd met him, he'd given me that look that said he was interested. I'd returned a look that said I definitely wasn't interested in anyone but my husband, and that had been the end of that. During the aftermath of David's death, Derrick had conducted himself in a sterling manner, showing just the right amount of concern, weathering the investigation the HSP conducted into his shooting of the man who'd killed David. Derrick had sailed through it all with a near heroic stoicness that I'd greatly admired.

I really didn't want to go out to dinner. I'd planned to resume studying Victor's private papers. There were answers there, if only I could find them. And there was also a good interview on Channel Twenty with one of my favorite ministers: a bit of TV wouldn't hurt me. I'd planned an early bedtime. But—it would have been impossibly rude of me to refuse Derrick's invitation, considering the way it was offered. Which meant I was more or less stuck.

Anyway, as I thought about it I started to get used to the idea. It would be nice to have some male companionship over dinner for a change.

I live within walking distance of some six hundred eateries, or so the tour ads tell me. Waikiki features the full range, everything from cheap and greasy fast food to five-star restaurants where you can easily spend a hundred dollars and more per plate. But frankly, most of my favorite restaurants lean toward good salads, fresh cuts of grilled fish, and similar simple fare. You don't need a white tie and tails to get into these places, so I pulled on an ivory silk-and-cotton sweater, matching knit slacks, then stepped into snow-white sneakers and socks. I brushed out my hair. I'd been wearing it extremely short since David's death, but I hadn't found time for a haircut lately, and to my surprise it had grown down to cover my ears—a rather flattering, softening look, I thought. Maybe I'd leave it that way for a while. I applied some light eye makeup, a dab of pink lipstick, and as an afterthought I added a tiny pair of gold earrings. I was almost overdressed, for me. Give me a choice, and I'd live in my fuzzy gray bathrobe or black one-piece swimsuit.

Derrick had left one lamp on and turned off the overhead light. He was sitting on the balcony, slouched down, studying the skyline that included the wedge-shaped Sheraton and other hotels, concrete oblongs cut through with light and framed against a backdrop of black water and sky. As I came into the room he sat up, and raised his eyebrows in appreciation. "You look great."

"Thank you." I checked my small leather bag to make sure I'd remembered my keys. "Any place special in mind?"

"Japanese sounds good."

"The Mirin is just down the street, and the prices aren't bad—though we'll go dutch, of course."

"Not on your life. I invited you. This is my treat."

"Let me check and see if Troubles wants us to bring him anything. Just a second."

He tensed up and frowned but quickly pasted it over with his friendly expression. "Who's Troubles?"

"Sorry, I forgot you haven't met him. His real name is Rick Thompson. 'Troubles' is a nickname he earned in childhood. He's my nephew, from the mainland. Studying pre-med at the university and living with me."

Derrick offered me a wolfish smile. "*That's* a relief. I thought for a minute you might be reattached to someone."

I felt faintly flattered by the implications in his tone of voice. I knocked on Troubles' door, heard a muffled "come in," then opened it a crack. I told him I was going to the Mirin with a friend and asked if he wanted anything. He said whatever I wanted to bring would be fine, he was cramming for a chemistry exam. I closed the door, and that was that.

The Mirin is in the bottom of a small shopping plaza on Kalakaua Avenue. The food is excellent, the decor is authentic Tokyo. It's dimly lit at night and decorated with colorful paper lanterns and tiny fairy lights. This night was busy, as usual. It's easy to find and therefore attracts a lot of the Japanese tourists, as well as locals.

The hostess seated Derrick and me at a small, square table near the back. There were wooden carvings on the wall, a few plants, some Japanese prints, and a sparkling glass sushi bar with wooden counter and rattan stools. The music was piped in: Japanese wooden flutes, intricate complexities of scales with occasional drums, zithers, and other unfamiliar instruments setting up chord structures and background that played out the sunlight and shadows of Japanese culture. I loved the woody, sylvan sound, and by the time the waitress—attired in a simple black and white flowered kimono—brought our hot tea, I was in a contented mood.

I knew from living with David that a narc obsesses when he's working a case. I figured the job would be all Derrick was interested in at the moment, so I asked about his investigation. He offered up some casual conversation about what was currently happening in the drug subculture and a few solemn comments about David's death and the aftermath we'd shared. Then he surprised me by saying, "I've thought about going private. What's it like?"

"Tedious, terrifying, and a poor way to make a living. No retirement, no job security, and people look at you like you've hit rock bottom and are about to start spending your time in a dingy office swigging from a bottle of gin."

"Your background is in intelligence, right? For the feds?"

"I worked in their Intelligence Analysis division for about six years after I got my degree."

"A degree in what?"

"A combination of sociology and statistics. The sociology because it was interesting, the statistics because it made me employable. I wrote my thesis on 'The Politics and Economics of the International Narcotics Traffic and the Covert Effect on U.S. Foreign Policy.'"

He offered up a low, appreciative whistle. "Pretty ambitious."

"I was, in those days."

"Did you like working in intelligence?"

"It wasn't what I expected. I ended up at the computer for days on end, trying to understand people and what they were doing by analyzing raw data, reality reduced to formulas and numbers and bureaucratic sludge. Impossible to do. I drew charts, graphs, maps of trafficking routes, tracked certain cartels. All in all, some pretty low-reward work."

"David mentioned once that you'd worked in Asia."

"I went to Thailand for a two-month stint once. Several of us went to the Golden Triangle to take a look at some of the opium interdiction programs. That was pretty interesting, but the rest of it wasn't much. Oh, the old-timers threw me a tidbit once in awhile, and some other interesting things occasionally happened. But it didn't take me long to figure out that I was too young and green to ever get the really interesting assignments, those went to people who'd been seasoned out in the field. So it was either apply for fieldwork or resign myself to bureaucratic boredom. Fortunately at about that same time a third alternative popped up. I met David."

"He was a good person."

"You have no idea. He was thorny, obsessive, yet the best-hearted person in the world. I've never known anyone like him."

"So you gave up drug busting?" He leveled an interested gaze at me. His eyes were a darker blue in the light from the paper lanterns. The Japanese flutes were playing something low and haunting, and the atmosphere was cordial yet exotic all at the same time.

"I had to either learn to live with the job I was doing or transfer," I said. "After I met David, a transfer was out of the question, so I just resigned. I went to work at the university as an assistant professor for a couple of years. That's what I was doing when David was shot."

"That was a tough break, Alex. For me, too. He was the finest partner I'd ever had, someone I could count on every step of the way. I mean, he was probably the first and only person I've ever worked with that I fully trusted."

I thought about that. "He was probably the only person I've ever trusted, too. There was something about him . . ."

"I know it's been hard for you without him." The statement was partly a question but mostly a way to draw me out.

Suddenly I didn't want to talk about David anymore. The evening had been progressing into a relaxed, pleasant occasion, and I was actually starting to enjoy myself. But now the old feelings of loss were surging back, washing in the old pain. I took a sip of hot tea, then said, "David was a special person. But we have to go forward, and now here I am, Alex Albright, Private Investigator, and wondering at least twice a day if I've done the right thing." I managed a smile.

"You do divorce investigations?"

"I try not to. Actually, I have a couple of pretty good accounts with lawyers. They pay on time and keep me busy with a variety of things."

The waitress brought us hot miso soup, served in little black lacquered bowls with lids, and tiny bowls of cabbage pickled in rice vinegar with daikon radish and grated lemon rind. She refilled our teacups. We drank the soup out of the bowls, used our thin plastic chopsticks to eat the cabbage. I chatted to Derrick about my work for a while—mostly about the case that was currently driving me nuts.

I said, "It's a custody battle. A nasty one. The father is a recovering alcoholic—at least, his lawyer is trying to convince the court that he's recovering. His wife says he's still a lush and has no business with the kid, at any time, and I'm afraid I'm going to find out it's the truth."

"She's probably right. I've seen alcoholic parents do some bad things to kids." He took a bite of cabbage.

"Problem is, I'm beginning to think our client—the mother—is a far worse bet than the father. I think she wants the kid just for the child support. She's a totally selfish person, and she treats the kid like an afterthought. The father, on the other hand, seems to really care, and all evidence so far indicates that his heavy drinking started when the kid was taken from him."

"I'm sure you'll figure out a way to make it work out."

"Hopefully. As a matter of fact, I have to fly to the Big Island soon—maybe tomorrow—to check out a few things."

"Troubles going with you?" He leaned forward and seemed keenly interested in my answer.

"No. He has classes."

"I see." He looked faintly disappointed for a moment, a reaction which puzzled me. But then he gave me a charming smile, picked up his soup bowl, and finished the last of his miso soup.

Derrick had ordered a tiny ceramic jug of hot sake, the Japanese rice wine that is potent as moonshine. He sipped the last of his second tiny cupful. He had mellowed out considerably, and was talking about himself now. "Marriage is never easy. My divorce was final in May."

I was surprised. "I didn't know you were married. I mean—sorry, I guess I didn't know you very well before David was—well . . ."

"That's okay. We narcs try to keep our private lives to ourselves."

"Still—you and I helped see each other through some tough times. At least, I know it was the hardest part of *my* life. And the subsequent investigation couldn't have been all that easy for you. So any way you look at it, we've been through a lot together. And yet, I suddenly realize I don't know a thing about you."

"We wouldn't have been strangers if you hadn't been my partner's wife." He gazed hard at me, measuring my reaction. I smiled what I hoped was a distant-though-polite smile and wondered why I'd never before noticed how handsome he was. Sort of a dark-haired Robert Redford type, complete with the crinkles around the eyes when he smiled, which he was doing plenty of tonight.

He said, "You and David weren't together very long, were you?"

"A couple of years."

"Tough on you, to lose him like that. Are you seeing anyone else yet?"

"I've been busy, starting up my business and—well, I guess I'm in no hurry."

"You should get back in the game."

I took a sip of hot tea. It suddenly had a bitter taste. "I guess that's the problem," I said. "It isn't a game to me." This conversation was leading down a slippery slope. I decided to change the subject, maybe even do a little probing, as long as I was here. After all, Derrick was a cop, he spent a lot of time out in the streets, maybe I could elicit some information from him, put things back on a level where I had a little control. It would sure beat talking all night about David, then going home and crying again.

"A man was killed in front of my condo a few days ago," I said. "Have you been following the case?"

His eyes narrowed, and he nodded. "A bit. I don't have much to do with Homicide, but I watch the news."

I started to tell him what I'd seen, just chatting, but something in his face made me feel suddenly evasive, so instead I said, "Strange, isn't it?"

The event had made the headlines, of course. It isn't every day that a *yakuza* soldier gets killed in Honolulu's streets, accidentally or otherwise. They had finally published his identity, after notifying the Japanese National Police. His name was Miro Ochinko, and he had a criminal record in Tokyo for gun running, gambling, and extortion. He'd been a top worker.

"Some Japanese gangster gets killed and they make a big deal of it," Derrick said, suddenly scowling. He set the sake cup down as if he'd lost interest in it and looked into an invisible distance. "There are people getting killed here every day, mostly over drugs, but you barely hear about *them*." He suddenly focused back on me. The scowl vanished and his face softened. "Look, I don't want to talk shop. I'm wrapping up this heroin investigation, high stress, and I'm burning out. I need a serious break from all that."

"Sorry. I didn't realize."

Fortunately, the waitress picked that moment to descend upon us with a red laquered tray laden with dishes of tempura, sashimi, and the grilled teriyaki steak that Derrick had ordered. The food was colorful, symmetrically arranged, a demonstration of the fact that the Japanese savor their food not only through smell and taste but also through sight. We both went to work on the food, making favorable comments on the quality and taste. I noticed, apropos of nothing, that Derrick used his chopsticks skillfully but not in the traditional manner. He frequently pointed them at me—holding them as he spoke, drawing little designs in the air with them to illustrate a point, or unconsciously pointing them in my direction as he picked up food. *Bad luck, very bad luck*, a tiny voice said in my mind. It sounded suspiciously like Mrs. Osaka. *Bad enough to bring on an early death,* it warned.

I almost mentioned the traditional Japanese ban against pointing chopsticks, then changed my mind. I didn't want to seem superstitious, and I certainly didn't want to seem nit-picking. Furthermore, I had learned long ago that these tiny cultural gems that I find so interesting often make other people's eyes glaze over with boredom or—worse yet—make me seem academic and intellectually pretentious.

So instead, I said, "I owe you a lot."

He looked surprised. "For what?"

"You put your life on the line for David. Even though it didn't save him, you were there and you did the right thing."

"You're providing a ray of light in an otherwise dark night." He smiled, almost shyly. "Consider your debt paid in full."

I thought it was a very nice compliment.

When we were finished eating, Derrick said, "Thanks for joining me, Alex. I enjoyed this more than anything I've done for a very long time."

"It was my pleasure," I said. I was a little embarrassed by his boyish sincerity and couldn't think of anything else to say.

Derrick paid the bill, refusing to even let me pay for the take-out order for Troubles. Then he walked me to my building, then into the lobby, then into the elevator. We were quiet by then, both full and relaxed and becoming comfortable with each other.

And when we reached my front door, Derrick said, "Maybe we could share an occasional dinner if you have any free time. I get to Waikiki a lot these days. And I learned tonight that it's highly therapeutic for me to spend time with normal people. You know— when you work the streets long enough, pretty soon you start thinking that everyone in the world is coked out or junked out or otherwise on the hustle."

"Most of them are, Derrick. Be careful out there. And yes, I would be happy to share dinner now and again. I'm listed under Albright Investigations. Just give me a call."

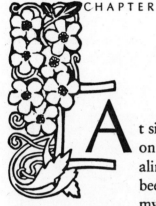

CHAPTER 8

At six A.M. the next morning, my alarm kicked on the radio, and I flew awake to some adrenaline-pumping rock music. Fine by me. It had been a short night, and I needed a jolt to get my system working again. On second thought, maybe this was *too much* of a jolt, all things considered.

I groaned, turned off the radio, then slid out of bed. Careful to avoid looking in the mirror, I dragged myself to the bathroom where I splashed cold water in my face. That jump-started my heart, then my brain kicked in, and at that point I remembered my short dinner with Derrick. I smiled at the memory, then forgot about him and started thinking again about Jess Seitaki. By the time I got around to squeezing toothpaste onto my brush, I had analyzed Jess's rude behavior, decided he had changed for the worse in the past couple of years, then dismissed him and moved on to think about my work. Heaven knew, there was a ton of it waiting for me.

Troubles was already up and in the kitchen, microwaving whole-grain waffles and frying up a couple of range-fed eggs. He was wearing blue denims and a green and white University of Hawaii Rainbows T-shirt. The colors showed off his sun-streaked blonde hair and deep tan.

I slid into the breakfast nook and said, "Make mine over easy, with a couple of slices of bacon." He was working at the waist-high counter that separates the kitchen from the adjacent dining area, and I could see past him and through the glass patio door. The sun's glint turned the sea beyond and beneath us to a shimmering blue mirror.

A couple of the brightly canvassed tourist catamarans were on their way in from their night's moorings.

"No bacon," Troubles said. "Clogs your arteries. Eggs are bad enough." He opened the fridge and took out my two eggs, cracked them into the sizzling skillet, and said, "You get your phone messages? I left them on your desk."

"Not yet."

"Fran Li called. She wants you to go to Hilo tomorrow, said to come by and pick up your tickets at her office, plus she needs to talk to you. Seemed sort of upset."

"So what else is new?" The sunlight was so bright that I had to squint to see the ocean. It was going to be a splendid day, in spite of the forever disgruntled lawyers who often dictated the terms of my life. Maybe I'd start it off right by going for another swim.

"And Yoko called and left a message last night. Said it wasn't urgent, she just wanted to see how you were doing."

"I'd be doing better if I hadn't tried to do a favor for her ungrateful husband. What a jerk."

"Jess?" Troubles shot me a surprised look.

"Jess," I said, nodding and pursing my lips in disapproval.

"I thought you were best friends. What happened?"

"Not much. I had some of Victor's papers I wanted to give him. He copped an attitude."

"That's pretty unlike Jess, isn't it?"

"That's what I thought, but I guess you never really know."

"He's going through a lot right now, don't you think? Maybe you should cut him some slack."

"Ha. That's easy for you to say. I was sticking my neck out for him, and he turned on me like a rabid pit bull."

Troubles actually looked disbelieving for a minute, then asked, "What were you doing with Victor's papers?"

I could see I had said too much. "It was just some real estate contracts I came across," I said, waving a hand to dismiss the topic.

Troubles, of course, knew that a member of the *yakuza* had been killed in front of our building. The people in the ground floor shops had been talking about it; the neighbors we knew occasionally mentioned it in passing, exclaiming how Waikiki was going downhill; and the news media had been exploring the possibility that Japan's largest crime syndicate might be trying to move into Hawaii to take over the local action, suggesting that this freak accident was a wake-up call for all of us.

But I hadn't told Troubles that I'd almost seen the accident, only that I'd seen the aftermath. Nor had I told Troubles about the phone call that had preceded the death or about the briefcase and papers I'd found hidden. And I certainly hadn't mentioned my escapade in the Royal Seashell Hotel the night of the death, how I'd used the purloined key to enter the dead man's room only to be caught there by yet another Japanese national. I always spared Troubles the heavier details of my life; he had enough on his mind trying to get through school.

Fortunately, he was already on to other things, namely breakfast. He blithely took two oranges from the fruit bowl on the counter and tossed them to me for peeling, one at a time. "Got to get your vitamin C," he said. "I left all your messages on your answering machine anyway, so you can hear them firsthand."

I set to work removing the rind from the oranges. "What's up for you today?" I asked.

"Class all day, then studying. Tomorrow, a few of us are going sailing with Donald Midori." Donald was the youth pastor at our church. "He's throwing a small party later at his place up on the North Shore. I'll probably spend the night."

"Good for you. I may end up having to spend a couple of days in Hilo anyway, depending on what's happening there. Think you'll have a chance to stop by the library today?"

"No problem. What do you need?" He had dished up the eggs and added two whole-grain waffles, then set my plateful in front of me. Now, he reached in the silverware drawer, retrieved a fork and knife and handed them to me, then settled down at the counter with his own breakfast.

"I need to scan some good books on Hawaiian banking laws," I said, pouring syrup on my waffles. "I need to know what it takes to put together a commercial real estate deal between local folks and the big money men in Tokyo. Just grab whatever you can find in that area, I mostly need a couple of general books on international banking and investment laws, state requirements, that sort of thing."

"You working a new case?"

"No, just checking into some problems that have to do with Jess's inheritance."

"Victor's papers?" He grinned. He hadn't lost interest after all.

"Sort of."

"Victor must have left him a bundle."

"There's some substantial money there, but Jess says everything is a mess. And I'm beginning to suspect that Victor may have been in a little deep with the Golden Palms project."

Troubles nodded. "I'll see what I can find for you. You doing the dishes this morning?"

"My pleasure," I said. All I had to do was rinse them and put them in the dishwasher. Troubles is an exceptionally neat cook, and he'd already taken care of the frying pan and spatula, right after using them.

An hour and a half later the dishes were done, Troubles had gone to class, I had indulged in a morning swim. After I returned, I sat at my desk wearing a pink and white striped terrycloth bathrobe, my hair still damp from my shower, sorting through reams of papers that had piled up, seemingly overnight.

The phone bill had come in—I'd have to talk to Troubles again about phoning his mother during prime time. The bills for my two credit cards were due, and so were utilities, that sort of thing. I had actually started generating enough business to be able to hire a bookkeeping service, and they did most of the major paperwork, entering my time sheets into the computer and returning them to me on disk so I could do my own billing, which was the way I wanted it. Other than that, I did the detecting and left the administrative stuff to them.

As I was balancing my checkbook, thinking about how little cash I had left, the phone rang. I still hadn't retrieved yesterday's messages, and I considered letting the caller pile yet another message on top of the ones the machine's indicator claimed it was saving for me. But when the caller's voice came on, I decided to answer. "Excuse me, let me just shut off my machine. There. Hello, Albright Investigations."

"Alex?" It was Derrick.

"Speaking." I wasn't really all that happy to hear from him this early.

He cleared his throat. "I wanted to tell you again how much I enjoyed dinner."

"Thanks, Derrick. So did I."

"Any chance we might do it again tonight?"

"Sorry, I'm a little tied up. I may have to fly to Hilo tomorrow, and there's a ton of work to do before I can leave. Why don't you call me later this week, we'll see what's up then?"

He reluctantly agreed and hung up, and I took one last, long, envious glance out my balcony door and to the ocean—even bluer now than this morning. I wanted to drop everything and spend the entire day at the beach, kicked back and soaking up the sun. But I made myself pull the drapes shut and returned to my backlog of work.

First, I hit the button that played back the answering machine's recordings. Seven messages. Three from someone who didn't leave a name or number, one from a charity I'd never heard of before, wanting a donation, two from girls calling for Troubles, and one from Fran Li.

Like I said, I was under contract to two attorneys who kept me on regular stipend and who therefore got priority on my time. I'd been with Fran Li longest. She was a tiny, formidable Chinese-Hawaiian woman in her mid-forties who practiced mostly family law, which is generally a grueling specialty. But she was good at what she did. She landed some interesting cases, and some of that work got passed along to me.

At the moment I was running a background check in the already mentioned custody battle. The father's name was Jimmy Villanueva. He lived on the Big Island and had shared custody of his eight-year-old son with his ex-wife until a few months ago, when he had been busted on a drunk driving charge. This had given his wife, Sally—a pretty but bitter woman—an opportunity to stop his visitation rights and reopen the custody battle.

Villanueva had then complicated the problem by quitting his job and missing some support payments. That had given Sally more ammunition, and she'd actually managed to get a judge to sign the order temporarily blocking the man from seeing his son. The forthcoming hearing would decide custody once and for all.

Fran Li was representing the mother, of course, and it was vital to the success of her case that I turn up as much evidence against the father as possible. Which, frankly, I didn't want to do. Because the more I learned about the father, the more certain I was that he was the better parent. On the other hand—there was his problem with booze. I didn't ever want to be responsible for sticking a kid with an alcoholic parent.

Because of all this, I took the investigation seriously. I'd known for a few days that I'd have to fly back over to the Big Island soon to see if anything new had come up and to update the evidence we already had. But now Fran Li was antsy for me to go immediately. Something had come up.

I dialed her number, waited while the secretary, Mindy, put me through, then heard her voice on the other end of the line.

"Alex?"

"Hello, Fran."

"Have you been out of town? I've been trying and trying to phone you." She wasn't chiding me, just getting right to the point as usual.

"Not really. Just tied up with a few things. Why, what's up?"

"Jimmy Villanueva came and took the child yesterday. Right out of the school yard."

"You're kidding me." I felt my face sag into disgusted disbelief. "What an utterly stupid thing to do."

"Not from our point of view. It's the best thing that could have happened." I knew she was right. By breaking the court order he'd put himself in a position to lose custody entirely, which meant our side won by default—I just wasn't sure that our side was really the right side.

"I guess this does prove he's rather irresponsible," I said. "Did he take the kid back to the Big Island?"

"Oh, immediately. The police have already picked up the boy, and they're holding him for his mother."

"Then you won't need for me to go over."

"On the contrary. Sally wants you to go with her. It will take the rest of today to get the paperwork in order, so she's flying over first thing tomorrow. Think you could go?"

I thought about it for a long moment. I really didn't like Sally Freedman and had thus far managed to avoid intimate contact. But I couldn't see a good way out, so I said, "I guess so. But why does she need me?"

"She's just feeling a little insecure. Not sure what to expect from her ex, I guess. I mentioned to her that you occasionally did some bodyguard work. She asked if you could go along."

"Just over and back?"

"That's the plan."

"What flight?" There were about a dozen flights a day to each of the outer islands to accommodate the tourists.

"I've booked you over on the eight A.M. You'll come back at 12:00, if all goes well. Sally just wants to pick up the boy, then come straight back home."

"That will work for me," I said.

"Another thing. We have some documents that have to be filed by four today, so Mindy can't get away to deliver your tickets. Think you could drive down here and pick them up?"

"Can't I just get them at the airport ticket counter in the morning?"

"I thought Mindy could deliver them, so we already have them here. Would it be too much trouble to come and get them?"

"I guess not. I'll be there in about an hour."

t was the end of June, the season when the torpid, tropical summer heat usually begins. But this year, the weather was more balmy than usual. The temperatures settled in at just about perfect. You could expect light showers in the morning and evening as a regular added refreshment, and even an occasional full-on tropical storm.

This morning had been a clear, translucent blue. But now, as I hit the McCully overpass and turned left toward the freeway, I could see gray-black masses of storm clouds piling up atop the emerald green Koolaus. The windward side of the island was getting drenched, and the Nuuanu Pali would certainly be under deluge. Within the hour, Honolulu and Waikiki were in for some rain.

I'm sensitive to the ionization of the air, and I felt a glowing sense of exhilaration as the bad weather approached. I navigated the traffic, took the Bishop Street exit, then hung a left on King Street and rolled into the entrance of the King Towers parking garage.

Fran's office was on the fifth floor of an old building which was a stoic remnant of the territorial days. Excellent ink drawings of Honolulu's many bluestone architectural treasures hung on the walls of her reception room. Several deep wine-leather chairs lined the walls, and a low matching sofa was placed so the clients could look out over the piers and the ten-story Aloha Tower while they were waiting.

Mindy was away from her desk, which was piled high with frantically churned papers and file folders. I stepped over to Fran's office door and opened it, to peek inside. She'd apparently stepped out.

I made my way down the corridor and into the copy room, where Mindy glanced up at me, then looked back at the copy machine, which was spitting out papers by the dozens. She was in her early thirties, a psychology grad whose education had prepared her perfectly for either unemployment or clerical work. She was pencil thin and had a mop of over-permed brown hair framing a sweet face, though her wire-rimmed glasses were so thick they enlarged her eyes and gave her the quizzical look of a harried, angelic owl. Her eyes seemed slightly out of focus at the moment, the way they always got when she and Fran were pushing a serious court deadline for filing papers and chances were good they weren't going to make it.

"Anything I can do to help?" I asked.

"Nothing, Alex. Sorry. I'd tell you where the tickets are, but everything is buried and you'd never find them. I'll just be a minute longer."

"I'll wait in front," I said.

I made my way back out to the reception area and dropped into an overstuffed chair. The *Pacific Business News* lay on the end table, along with some *Asian Wall Street Journals*, several *Pacific Architecture* magazines, and various other business publications.

I picked up a weekly news magazine and scanned through a couple of articles about the Hawaiian economy in general, more arguments about sewers and convention centers and hotel taxes and the general potpourri of Honolulu's political and economic problems. I checked out the local real estate sales. Then I thumbed through to the pages where they published the names and businesses of people undergoing tax liens, financial judgments, foreclosures, that sort of thing. I'd started reading the foreclosure pages when I was working a case that involved real estate, and I kept up with it. A little backdoor glimpse into the problems of Hawaii's business community. Who knew? Someday I may make a bundle on some exotic case and be able to swoop up a good deal.

Quite a few of the foreclosures were against Japanese nationals. You can usually recognize the names because they're longer and more unusual than the names of local Japanese. Of course, some of the foreclosures were bogus—the amount in arrears in the low thousands, which meant the foreclosure was being pursued only because common fees on condos hadn't been paid on time, or property taxes hadn't been paid, or other such trivia. Usually, these Japanese owners would have their asset managers send a check in the nick of time along with a hefty attorney's fee, and everyone would end up happy. Usually. But occasionally someone didn't come up with the money and a half-million-dollar condo was foreclosed on because some six or ten thousand dollars' worth of dues-in-common hadn't been paid to a condo association.

Still, this time a surprising number of the foreclosures were serious business, with amounts in arrears hitting hundreds of thousands of dollars. And a lot of these were properties valued at one million plus, and more than a few were mortgaged to the Bank of Oahu, the same Japanese-owned bank that held the mortgage on my condo and was coming down hard on the Golden Palms Resort project.

The truth was, the economic bubble had burst here, too. During the go-go years from 1985 to 1992, Hawaiian real estate had been a sure thing. In some areas, prices had doubled or tripled during that time and anyone smart enough to get in on the upswing and sell before the downswing had made a bundle. But a lot of people had bought high, thinking they'd sell higher. Now, many of the investors—especially the Japanese speculators who had plowed money into Hawaii in a big way—had been left holding properties that were worth half—or less—of what they paid for them. Contractors and developers were also taking some pretty good hits. To further complicate the problem, the sales market for the high-end residential properties was stagnant. The newspaper said there was a twenty-year surplus of million-dollar-plus properties. That's a sizeable real estate inventory for any state, even one where property is as expensive as Hawaii. A sure sign of a sluggish economy, a sure sign that a lot of heavy investors were losing money hand over fist.

The foreclosures included every kind of property, all the way across the board. Investors were getting stung with condos, houses, hotels, golf courses, commercial property, you name it. An article said that Japanese investors alone had lost more than twenty billion dollars in investments in California and Hawaii in recent years. Which was why the news weekly was publishing lists of tax liens or foreclosures on condos, homes, and commercial property in some of the cushiest parts of the islands and why a very large number of these very expensive foreclosures were listed under Japanese national names.

Reading all this yanked me back to the problem with Victor Seitaki's estate. I was becoming increasingly convinced that Victor had been in some real financial trouble before he died. Some of the hotels built less than five years ago with mortgages of up to six hundred million dollars were now worth less than half of that. Which meant that a lot of the local banks which had either financed or shared in the financing of some of these projects were taking a beating, and they were in turn putting pressure on anyone in arrears, anyone on down the line who might absorb some of their losses. Pressure was also coming from the Japanese banks that had come up with the bulk of the finance money, filtering it through local financial institutions. The whole thing was a mess.

Mindy came out of the copy room, her arms laden with documents. She stacked them neatly on her chair, then she went to work rummaging through her papers until she came across an envelope with the airline's logo on it. "Ah, here it is."

"Did you talk to Sally Freedman today?" I took the envelope from her then tucked it in my leather shoulder bag.

She made a face. "For a few minutes."

"How's she acting?"

"Miserable, as usual."

"I'm having a little trouble understanding why she wants me along, though I'm willing to go."

"Between you and me? She's thinking it will help her in court, you know, she has to take a bodyguard along because she's so afraid of him she has to have professional protection."

I rolled my eyes. "If it wasn't for Fran, I'd cut out."

"You and me both."

We chatted a minute longer about odds and ends, then I stepped out into the hallway and turned to look out the full-length window at the end of the hallway while I waited for the elevator.

A fine sprinkle of rain was falling over the city. The people in the streets far below were scurrying for cover. The sun was a dull brass disc, only partially obscured by cloud cover and the mist of rain. It always amazed me when it rained while the sun was still shining, even though it happened frequently. As I waited for the elevator, I continued to look out over the sleek white buildings, the historical bluestones, the waterfront straight out of a 1930s shipboard romance novel.

A tug was escorting one of the interisland cruise ships through the dark blue channel and toward the moorings at Pier Five. I halfway watched it, my mind on a dozen different things, my eyes scanning the sea horizon, then the skyline, then back to the sea, drinking in the beauty.

And then it suddenly hit me. I was right across the street from the central branch of the Bank of Oahu. The bank that held the mortgage on my condo, the offices that housed Ed Grappner, Vice President in charge of Commercial Real Estate, the man who'd written Victor Seitaki such a nasty letter about his overdue loans. I turned and took a long look at the glass and steel bank building, and then the elevator announced its belated arrival with a little "ding." Two men and one woman stepped out and I stepped in and hit the *L* for Lobby.

As I glided downward, I considered the possibilities.

Since I was in the neighborhood anyway, it would be foolish not to run across the street and see if Grappner had a spare moment.

After all, I had a right to know what was going on, didn't I? And Grappner was certain to be one of the keys to the puzzle. Because if Victor Seitaki had been in financial trouble—if the Golden Palms resort project was in trouble, to be more precise—then Grappner would certainly know what was going on and maybe, just maybe, I could learn something from him.

Besides, I hadn't asked the *yakuza* soldier to phone me—I was sure now it was him. And I certainly hadn't asked him to get killed right under my nose. And I hadn't exactly gone looking for the briefcase, it had come to me—more or less. Furthermore, I'd had to put up with Jess acting like an absolute jerk when he was supposed to be my dearest friend. So I at least deserved to know why all this was happening, didn't I?

I continued rationalizing as I rode down the elevator, stepped out into the heavy stream of pedestrian traffic, then crossed King Street and entered the eighteen-story office tower that housed the bank. A quick scan of the marble directory in the lobby told me that Grappner's office was on the sixteenth floor. By the time I was in the plush-lined elevator, riding up again, I had fully convinced myself that I was doing the only rational thing.

Grappner's secretary was Japanese-Hawaiian, probably in her early sixties though there wasn't a streak of gray in her raven hair and her body was trim as a teenager's. She wore a diamond the size of an almond on her wedding finger, and her freshly manicured nails were efficiently short. She wore several gold bracelets, one of them an inch wide with her name in Hawaiian inscribed in black lacquer. The bracelets were selling at Liberty House for right around nine hundred bucks apiece; I'd priced one recently and given up on it as too expensive. But the woman's clothing was surprisingly simple: a black cotton skirt and matching jacket that I suspected she'd made herself and a white blouse adorned with a red strawberry pattern. There was something elegant, maternal, and resolute about her all at once, as if she could simultaneously finesse you, nurture you, and nail you to the wall with a gimlet gaze, which she was giving me at the moment.

I said, "Would it be possible to speak with Mr. Grappner?"

She gave me the kind of smile made famous by disgruntled people everywhere—you know, the one that says, *My life is miserable and as of right now you're about to pay for it.* She said, "Mr. Grappner sees people only by appointment."

I tried on a superior smile, hoping it might make me seem rich. My own mortgage was with the noncommercial loan division on a different floor altogether, so I didn't have to worry about being unmasked. I said, "I understand that some of your commercial properties are undergoing foreclosure, and I'd like to know more about them. Since I was in the neighborhood I thought maybe . . ."

Just then the office door with the brass plate that read, "Ed Grappner, VP Commercial Loans" opened and a near-bald head popped out. "Glenda, do you have those letters—oh, hello." He looked at me quizzically, surprised to see me, and stepped forward so I could see the body beneath the head. He was *Haole*—Caucasian, perhaps of German ancestry. He stood about five feet, five inches, a good four inches shorter than me. His face was bland, flat-featured, stained to a golfer's tan. He was wearing navy slacks, a blue short-sleeved shirt and a tie—unusual for Hawaii, where even the downtown business community favors the informality of aloha shirts and slacks.

Grappner had a wadded handkerchief in his hand. He reached up to wipe his forehead, though I didn't see a drop of perspiration or other moisture on it. The muscles in his forearms were stringy, the skin fuzzed with honey-blonde hair. His watch looked like a Seiko— moderately expensive, tasteful. He wore a diamond-studded wedding band and a smile that he'd pasted on the moment he saw me. I noticed that his teeth were exceptionally even and slightly discolored by tobacco stains.

Not wanting to miss the moment, I stepped right up to him. "Hello. I was just asking to see you." I pressed forward so that he had to step back through the doorway, then I bore down on him, yielding no quarter. I talked fast as I moved. "I'd be so grateful if you could spare just a moment. I saw some of your properties listed in the foreclosure section of the business news, and I'd like to ask you some questions right away, it wouldn't do to wait, I always try not to let an opportunity pass, no point in letting the grass grow under one's feet . . ."

He frowned, backpedaling before my advance. "Wouldn't it be better for you to talk to your broker?" He stammered. He bumped into his desk and had to stop.

"I like to go right to the top," I said imperiously. "I can usually save some time and money that way." I resisted the impulse to give him a conspiratorial wink. I stepped swiftly back and closed the door behind me so that the secretary couldn't come to his aid.

He glanced around as if looking for an escape. When none appeared, his shoulders slumped in defeat. He went around his desk, dropped into his chair and motioned me into the chair across from him. I sat down.

He looked at me expectantly.

I said, "I need some expert advice from you. Mostly about the inflationary status of Hawaiian real property these days, and whether values are likely to continue to drop, or if you think it's bottomed out and we can look forward to some growth. I know the Japanese are still pulling out in droves. I believe that with a little private advice I might find an exceptionally good buy, and I'd certainly be willing to pay a generous consultant's fee to anyone who could steer me in the right direction."

He pasted on a fake smile. "I see you know the business. What type of property were you interested in?"

"Maybe a mini-mall. Or a medium-sized apartment complex. Maybe a cluster of condos I could use for vacation rentals or even some small part of a resort development." Might as well think big.

He hesitated, still wanting to throw me out. But apparently he decided it would be better to press forward and get my interruption over with because he began to recite his loan officer speech, the one no doubt tailored for clients who might have a few million to drop for a down payment on commercial property. He assured me that their bank was ethical, their properties rock solid. The only reason they were plagued with having to foreclose on so many properties was that people were so irresponsible and that too many speculators had invested in Hawaii in recent years. But because of that, several excellent properties were currently in foreclosure, and he expected several more to come back on the market soon.

I had checked this bank out before signing my mortgage papers, but it wouldn't hurt to do an update. I said, "I would like to know more about your financial institution. I recall reading in the paper some time ago that you're owned by a bank in Japan. How would I know that my investments were safe if the parent company is foreign?"

Grappner's eyes shot fire, then hooded over like a lizard's. "We're owned by one of the finest Japanese institutions, absolutely solvent and with a sterling international reputation."

"But didn't I read something in the *Asian Wall Street Journal* about this bank?" Might as well let him think I was really a sharp cookie. "Something about a major merger? Or was it some kind of scandal?" I didn't have the faintest idea what I was talking about, but when in doubt go fishing.

He sneered. "Our bank is one of the most respected in Hawaii, and all throughout the Pacific region."

I nodded solemnly. My glance had traveled to a stack of unopened letters on his desk. The top one was from A. Alton Realtors. Andrew Alton's company. Alton was a real estate broker, turning politician, who had just been appointed to head up the HSP's police commission. The name registered simply because it was familiar. It distracted me for a split second, then I looked up at Grappner and said, "One thing bothers me, though. I understand that the Japanese foreclosure process is altogether different from ours. Would you enlighten me as to what happens when you foreclose on a property? I don't want any international legal entanglements."

"That would depend on the project," he said, seemingly insulted. "Our branches here are chartered through the United States and subject to all U.S. regulations as well as to state regulations. Furthermore, the Japanese are far more solvent than U.S. press coverage would have you believe. A lot of this 'bubble bursting' nonsense is just wishful thinking." He folded his arms and adopted a facial expression that told me he had given this little speech before.

"Everyone seems to be under the impression that because the Nikkei Index is in a nosedive, Japan is on the brink of something resembling our Great Depression. This country certainly underestimates the Japanese. In truth, the Japanese government is deliberately manipulating the money supply in order to drive out the excess of foreign investment that swamped the market and artificially inflated many stocks. They're tired of foreign criticism, and they're tired of foreign interference and attempts at managed trade. They're also trying to create an environment that will lure some of the major investors' money back home."

The Honolulu newspapers had been full of items about Japan's economic problems for the past few years. Hawaii is firmly dependent on Japanese investment, and there's no way to miss what is going on. So I already knew that a lot of Japanese banks were in trouble because their stock portfolios were decimated in the wake of the three-year-long nosedive in the Nikkei Stock Index; I also knew that the banks made their loans against those portfolios and that this was part of what had frozen up the investment money. I'd also read that the Nikkei was being manipulated at the behest of the newly elected government, which was supposed to be struggling against the feudalistic Japanese system of the old government. Anyone who read the Honolulu papers knew that the old government was rooted in wholesale corruption, including massive *yakuza* infiltration and influence. And anyone who read the papers or watched the TV news also knew that the new government was a puppet government, put in just for show, and that the old guard still ruled supreme, *yakuza* buddies and all, and if anything gave, it was going to be the "reformist" politicians.

Well, Grappner had his own point of view, founded, no doubt, in his need to keep his job. I had been carefully studying him as he made his little speech. Now I decided it was time to get to the point. "I understand that several major Hawaiian resort projects have been in trouble and might present some good investment opportunities," I said. "I was thinking specifically about the Golden Palms Resort project, I understand one of the principles just died."

His eyes went flat, like a reptile's. His ears seemed to lay back like an enraged canine's, and he all but snarled, "Excuse me, but *what* did you say your name was?" His hands had balled into fists.

"I didn't."

"Well, whoever you are, you might do better to ask your realtor some of these questions." He stood up, then made it clear he wanted me to leave by stepping around his desk and opening the door. "If you'll excuse me, I have an appointment."

I tried to look hurt. "But I thought you might help me pick out some possibilities . . ."

"I'm afraid you've caught me at a bad time."

"When would be a better time?"

He snorted. "Actually, I don't handle the sorts of things you're interested in. We no longer hold the loan on the Golden Palms."

"Then who does?"

"I'm sorry, that's privileged information."

"Well, do you have anything else in your inventory that might present a good investment opportunity?" I still did not get up.

"I really think you need to look somewhere else." He nodded toward the door. There was a tic developing beside his right eye.

Well. No point in driving the poor man to a nervous breakdown. I wasn't going to get another thing out of him, anyway. So I finally drew myself up and offered him an imperious gaze; then, when the tic became more pronounced, I picked up my bag from where it had been sitting on the floor and left.

CHAPTER 10

The forty-five minute flight to Hilo was as unpleasant as I'd expected it to be. We sat beside each other, and Sally Freedman was obnoxious and demanding. She whined a lot about having to go to so much trouble to bring her child home. The kid's name was Mikey. He was eight years old, freckled, and small for his age, with red hair like Sally's and sad brown eyes like his father's. When we picked him up at Hilo Social Services, he made it clear that he wanted to stay with his father. Sally treated him like a piece of lost luggage that she had every right to reclaim. After she signed some papers, we grabbed a cab back to the airport and made the twelve o'clock return flight to Honolulu. On the way back, she either nagged at the boy or read a fashion magazine, and I sat in the row behind them, looking out the plane window into the clouds and wondering why I couldn't do anything to make the boy's life better. Which set me to wondering what I was actually accomplishing with my life.

I'd driven my Honda to Honolulu International. We retrieved it, and I dropped Sally and Mikey off at her Pearl City townhouse, then drove to Waikiki. After a quick stop at my office/condo to pick up Victor's papers, I drove to the copy center on Beretania and ran off yet another copy of the whole batch, stashing the first set in my car trunk. I then tooled toward the University of Hawaii and hung a left on Dole. That put me in a residential area. From there, I drove on over into the Nuuanu area, toward Mrs. Osaka's stately old house at the far upper end of the lush, green valley. By that time, it was almost three o'clock.

The thought of spending the rest of the afternoon with Mrs. Osaka had returned some brightness to my day. Mrs. Osaka was a plum blossom through and through, and we had developed the true, relaxed friendship that usually belongs only to close family members. And yet, there was a certain formal respect between us, a feeling of the difference in age and culture that caused me to continue calling her Mrs. Osaka, in spite of her countless invitations to address her by her first name.

She had been a professor of Cultural Sociology at the university during the few years I taught there; in fact, she hadn't fully retired till she was in her early eighties, after more than thirty-five years of what she called "service." For some reason, she had chosen me to be a part of her select inner circle: these were the old guard academicians who more or less ran things. Perhaps she had recognized the cultural schism I was trying to cross, had realized that I honestly wanted to understand the people in my adopted home. Or maybe she had merely recognized my cultural ignorance and had taken compassion on me, deciding to guide me along so I wouldn't be such a bumbling fool.

Whatever her reasons, she had decided, with no effort on my part, to mentor me. She had taken me into her heart, had invited David and me to her church—where his funeral had later been performed and which I still attended—and had otherwise become a guiding force in my life.

Silver-haired, tiny, still lithe as a cat, she'd been reared in Hawaii during the extremely racist Plantation era, which spanned the turn of the century and several decades thereafter. She was the daughter of a Japanese contract laborer and his picture bride. Both parents had died when she was a child, her father from an accident in the sugar cane fields, her mother from illness. Neither death was surprising—the life expectancy for contract laborers was short, at best.

Mrs. Osaka had grown up in a Christian orphanage. When she came of age at eighteen, she had adopted the Buddhist faith, more as an act of rebellion against a racist social system than from any intrinsic need to change faiths. Though the Japanese laborers had lived under the Buddhist/Shinto theocracy in Japan before the massive famines had forced them to immigrate elsewhere, the reigning *Haole* plantation owners here in the Islands had worshiped, for the most part, in conservative Christian churches, like their missionary ancestors. At first, the *Haole* didn't like the idea of their employees worshiping idols. But when they learned that the Buddhist faith stressed patience and acceptance of one's given status in life, as well as a strong reverence toward one's social superiors, they had decided the Buddhist faith wasn't so bad after all.

Certain Buddhist sects had finally come to the islands in spite of the protestations of other Christians, bringing along their vast brass and stone statues of Buddha, usually sitting on a dais of lotus blossoms. And at eighteen, Mrs. Osaka had stepped out of Christianity and into defiance.

The Buddhist monks had set up a Japanese language school. Needing teachers who could speak English as well as Japanese, they had sponsored Mrs. Osaka in a year-long study program in Japan, where she'd excelled at everything. She'd come back to Hawaii to teach until the Japanese bombed Pearl Harbor. Then suddenly the "Japanese Schools," which often taught strict Japanese patriotism and allegiance to the "sun-god" Emperor in addition to the language, were shut down as potential hotbeds of spy-craft and intrigue.

For most Japanese immigrants, World War II was an ordeal. Many found themselves in internment camps, selected for imprisonment on an arbitrary basis. But Mrs. Osaka had not been interned. Though authorities had questioned her because of her involvement with the Japanese School, they let her go. She had worked in a grocery store down on River Street during the rest of the war years. Though she was far past the proper age for marriage by Japanese standards, she had been very beautiful then; I had seen photographs. She had caught the eye of the owner, Curtis Osaka, and they had married. After the war, he swiftly built his grocery business into a chain of stores, and she could have lived, then, in relative opulence. But she chose to advance her education so she could continue to teach.

Curtis Osaka was, of course, a *nisei*—that is, a second generation Japanese-Hawaiian. He was also a firm Christian, and when they married, Mrs. Osaka returned to Christianity and became one of the most devout Christians I know. They had been married for forty-odd years until his death a decade ago—as she reminded me every so often. I could tell she missed him greatly.

At eighty-five, Mrs. Osaka was not only a unique repository of Japanese and Buddhist cultural lore, she was also a biblical scholar to match the best. In fact, she was still keenly intelligent and keenly interested in everything. She had become an icon to the community, a benefactor to our church, and though she didn't get out much anymore, there still wasn't much she didn't know about the Hawaiian Islands and the people who inhabited them.

So she lived in aging splendor, in the huge, two-story white clapboard house with a wraparound veranda. I could see the house now, up the driveway to my left. It had been built against the hillside amidst a rich green tangle of foliage that was the spillover of the subtropical forest, and she'd allowed the trees, foliage, and vines to creep in and around the pillars of the front porch so the house almost looked abandoned and you couldn't even approach the front door. As you drove up from the street, the stone foundation appeared to be crumbling. Rivulets from years of rain had cut deep into the asphalt of the steep, curving driveway, adding to the desolate look.

But the driveway ended at the back of the house, which was something else altogether. The ground here was level, and a wide glade had been sculpted out of the subtropical forest, the dark-green grass clipped to perfection by a gardener who came twice a week. The far left quadrant of the lawn was a classic Japanese garden, complete with symmetrical plants, swept sand, and stones reminiscent of Old Japan. A small stream spilled down the hillside and out of the wild forest, to run under the red laquered Japanese-style bridge. A small bamboo forest that had been planted long ago now towered above it all and merged into the wild plants and trees.

To the right was another type of garden—her late husband's creation, which she had lovingly kept up. He had loved flowers, and here was a rich riot of colored confusion: lavender and yellow hibiscus; bright red, black, and yellow lobster claw; anthuriums in red, pink, and pastel green; birds of paradise; and nearly every other luscious plant and flower known to Hawaii. The trees were also a rich proliferation of Hawaii's flora—plumeria, monkeypod, Norfolk Island pine, ironwood, eucalyptus, mango, avocado, strawberry-guava, even a chinaberry tree. The heavy foliage shaded the flower garden from the golden afternoon sun.

She had been sitting on her shaded back porch, reading. She saw me drive up and closed her book. As I joined her, she stood to embrace me, then rang for her Filipina housekeeper to bring us tea. Overhanging the back porch where we sat on her white wicker lawn furniture was a wonderful coral tree. Today, it was in full bloom, its lipstick-red flowers a brilliant shower of color, a blossom floating, now and again, to the green lawn. The smell of *piikoi* blossoms and freshly mown grass was heavenly.

I said, "All these wonderful plants, but no plum trees. Have you ever thought of planting some?"

She smiled. Like old-fashioned ladies everywhere, she wore a large hat when gardening, to protect her from excessive sunlight. Her soft, wrinkled face was the same patina as ivory kid leather. Her chocolate-black eyes were bright with mirth. "You've been spending time with Yoko Seitaki."

I laughed. "I see you know the story."

"Too well. When Jess's mother, Aiko, first got her plum trees from Japan, they were the talk of the island. Curtis went over and asked for clippings. Aiko refused. She told him he had to wait until after the first blooming, she didn't want to take a chance on damaging the trees."

"And they never blossomed," I said, smiling, "so he never got the cuttings."

"Yes, and I never heard the end of plum trees, either. Because Curtis decided he was going to have a cutting from Aiko's trees or nothing. And so we have no plum trees."

Mary, the housekeeper, served the tea, pouring it from a delicate blue and white china teapot into matching cups, then setting out a plate of almond cookies. She was a middle-aged woman, small and sturdy. She had recently immigrated from Manila to be with her daughter who had married an Army lieutenant. The daughter was now studying law at the university, a situation which made Mary eternally proud. Like most Filipinas, she'd had no opportunities of her own; to see her daughter succeed was the joy of her life. Mary could have lived with her daughter and son-in-law, but she wanted more autonomy; so she lived here with Mrs. Osaka, overseeing the household and tending to small needs. In return, Mrs. Osaka paid her a generous salary.

I said, "Hello, Mary."

She greeted me warmly. She wore faded denims, a starched and heavily embroidered white shirt, *zori* slippers on her feet. She was constantly busy yet completely comfortable.

There was no pretension in Mrs. Osaka's household—nor in her life. Each and every person was one of God's treasures to her, and she gave them as much freedom to be themselves as possible. It was a shame she had never had children because she would have been the world's best mother ever.

Actually, she had become motherly to me, for a time. But I hadn't wanted her as a mother. I wanted her as a friend, a role in which she could fully be herself, and so could I. She had gradually conformed to my definition of our relationship. And I had come to love, respect, and trust Mrs. Osaka implicitly. I fancy myself to be a collector of rare and unusual people, and Mrs. Osaka was an antique treasure beyond price.

But I was also aware of the fragility that came with her age and was therefore protective of her. So when I handed her Victor's papers, after some more conversation and a full pot of tea, I didn't tell her where or how I'd obtained them.

I merely said, "These have to do with Victor Seitaki's estate. A very confidential matter. I need a translation of the *kanji*."

She looked the English-language papers over, and a frown came to her face. And then, as she paged through the papers written in *kanji*, the frown deepened. "These papers belong to the developers and lenders of the Golden Palms Resort."

"Yes. But I desperately need to know what's in them."

She lowered her eyes and seemed to study the faded wooden floor. Then she spoke: "These papers say that Anne's uncle, Ko Shinda, was a silent partner in this project, that Victor was the full owner in name only."

"Yes, I believe that's true."

She set the papers to one side, removed her reading glasses, and fixed me with a penetrating look that I had never seen before. It was as if her liquid black eyes had invisibly honeycombed into a lens that probed deep into my thoughts. "I think you may have guessed something of what may be in these papers," she said quietly.

Her statement bewildered me. "I've studied them," I said. "But I'm drawing a total blank."

She kept giving me that odd look, and I could see now that she was taking my measure. "You may be stepping into something better left alone," she said. "Do you know that, Alex?"

"I don't know much of anything, at this point. I can't really explain the situation, but I'm not exactly stepping into it. It's more like I've been shoved."

The word made me think about the *yakuza* soldier identified as Miro Ochinko, lying dead in the street in front of my building as the paramedics stripped him to his waist and studied the tattoos he'd no doubt been very proud of. And that made me think about the plumber's story that the man had been shoved in front of his van, by someone who had mysteriously vanished. Which brought me full circle to the fact that the man may well have been murdered while on his way to see me.

Mrs. Osaka said, "I don't like to gossip. You know that, Alex."

I nodded. Her ability to keep secrets was one of the reasons so many people cherished her—and confided in her.

"But there are times," she said, "when it is better to tell the truth than to let a friend step, unwarned, into danger."

And suddenly I saw the depth of concern in her eyes and realized just how deeply she was troubled by whatever she had discerned from her casual look through Victor's papers.

I said, "What's wrong?"

"I am very old," she said. She rubbed her eyes with the heels of her hands, and when she finished, the pensive, distant look was gone, replaced with resignation. "I've watched many generations come and go on these islands," she said. "Sometimes I remember things that might best be left forgotten."

I was silent. A skylark chirruped deep in the forest, and then the world around me was silent too, except for a faraway siren, perhaps all the way down on the freeway, that whined into my range of hearing, then quickly faded out again. The wind gusted lightly through the yard, sending a full shower of coral petals floating brightly to earth.

And then Mrs. Osaka began to talk softly. She began to unfurl, like bolts of rich tapestry, decades and generations of lore, stories of the Japanese heritage in Hawaii, of the Seitaki family, of her own role in teaching Jess and Victor's father back in Japanese School, years even before the war. The words weren't gossip, they were treasured memories, and I listened with keen interest as she explained certain family connections, as she reminded me of the traditional role of Japanese women, how they had existed for centuries only to serve their households and husbands and were allowed little or no identity of their own.

"A woman in Japan may still be a possession," she said, "even to this day. But twenty-five years ago, when Victor and Anne were married, it was much worse. You know, I'm sure, that the higher a Japanese family's social position, the more strongly they honor tradition. Their fortunes are often protected by that tradition, for within the rigid Japanese hierarchical structure the lower classes are not even allowed to compete with their betters. Anne's family was very wealthy. Very respected. And so, Anne was bound by tradition to marry the husband who had been chosen for her."

I had heard stories of Anne's family's legendary wealth. Her father, Tuzumi Shinda, had been an industrialist. Before World War II, his family had owned a giant feudalistic industrial complex—a *zaibatsu*. These were vast family combines of interrelated businesses—imagine General Motors, U.S. Steel, Ma Bell, all the Baby Bells, American Express, several of the world's biggest banks, Sinclair Oil, Gulf Oil, IBM, and half a dozen other corporate giants combined. Then add in a tenth of all the agricultural and real estate concerns in the U.S., throw in some very serious munitions factories, an airline, and a couple of railroads, and you get the general idea of what a *zaibatsu* was all about. Add to this an iron-fisted grip on the throat of all key civil servants in government and the political clout to choose the highest ranking politicians, salt it all with an imperial family that is nothing more than a symbolic embodiment of the rigid hierarchical structure which keeps you up and running, and you get the full picture.

Before the war, several *zaibatsu*—the Shinda family's among them—had a stranglehold on Japanese commerce and politics. A lot of historians still blame these huge financial empires and their bulldozer greed for the Japanese role in World War II. In fact, after the U.S. dropped an atomic bomb on Hiroshima and conventional bombs on Tokyo, then rolled on in to occupy that country, one of the first things the occupational government did was dissolve the *zaibatsu*, grafting some of the U.S. antitrust laws into the Japanese law books in order to make the huge combines totally illegal.

But a select few of the old families had managed to recoup part of their fortunes, in spite of the new laws. And though the new financial combines were far smaller than the old *zaibatsu*—and though conventional wisdom had it that the old feudalistic, ultra-nationalist, fascistic mentality had been erased altogether by the efforts of the occupying Americans—it was pretty common knowl-edge that the bad *nichibei* between Japan and America came about largely because of the new conglomerates' unwillingness to give up their stranglehold on the Japanese economy and because of their protectionist economic policies. In other words, the old economic mind-set hadn't changed all that much.

These economic policies were the continuing focus of U.S. Con-gressional ire. There was constant talk of trade sanctions and other reprisals, for their economic policies gave the Japanese full range of most global markets, yet squeezed everyone out of their own sub-stantial market—you know, we can play in your yard with your toys, but stay out of ours. The trade surplus was some sixty billion dollars this year alone. That's sixty billion dollars going out of the U.S. and into the pockets of Japanese businessmen. Some of it—a very little—trickled back down to the rank and file Japanese people. But all in all, their lifestyles were getting worse, and most of them lived in dilapidated, rabbit-warren housing which was a direct result of land speculation, one of the key sources of postwar wealth for Japanese entrepreneurs. Single family homes in Japan often came with multigenerational mortgages—that is, mortgages that inden-tured the family all the way through the great-grandchildren, just so the family could have a roof over their heads.

In a nutshell, the economic policy of present-day Japanese corpo-rations not only hurt the United States, it also hurt all the Japanese who were not so fortunate as to own the marauding corporations or have top "salary-men" jobs within them. Furthermore, the mass accumulated wealth of the Japanese government went to pay farm and other subsidies in order to keep out foreign investment and goods, or it went to finance foreign marketing ventures for the corporations. Relatively little money was spent on parks or hospitals or roads or the environment or other social improvements that might directly benefit the Japanese people. Which meant Japan had become a very rich country with a few extremely rich entrepreneurs, while the rank and file worked longer hours and lived in far poorer conditions than the average American yet continued to pay exorbi-tant prices for their housing, food, and other goods because the economic system was tightly sewn up.

Well, Anne's family was one of the few which had managed to hold on to some of their prewar wealth and expand it into another fortune after the war. Her father and his brother, Ko Shinda, had managed this feat together. They had made a fortune through real estate speculation, then some more by retooling various factories, financed with U.S. guilt-money. But however it had been made, the really big money had been made at the expense of the common people—in Japan, in the United States, and anywhere else the corporation did business. At least, that's the way it looked to me.

People with such opinions are often accused of Japan-bashing. But it seemed to me that the ones bashing the Japanese people were the feudalistic Japanese corporations and the politicians they owned. The combination had the Japanese people locked into a neo-fascist system with ultranationalist underpinnings, not all that far removed from the old prewar days.

None of which was Anne's fault. Anyway, her father had died, and his share of the Shinda fortune had gone to Anne's younger brother in Tokyo; according to Japanese tradition, the first son is always the full heir. Still, I had heard that the family was instrumental in obtaining the financing for Victor's first major real estate development here in Hawaii, and now apparently Ko Shinda had a part of Victor's enormous Golden Palms Resort project. The family ties were apparently still binding. Linked up by solid gold chains, in fact. Still, it seemed that for Anne the chains, gold or not, were merely a way to enslave.

Tradition, always tradition. Chopsticks to chopsticks . . .

I said, "Anne certainly never seemed like a possession to me."

"Perhaps not in recent years. She and Victor went their own ways. But when she and Victor were first married, she certainly was chattel. The family arranged it to be so. The custom is known as *miai* marriage," she said, "what we would call an arranged marriage. In Japan, in the upper classes, it is unusual to have a *ren'ai*, or love marriage, even today. Social position and wealth must be protected at all costs, and frequently the daughters of wealthy families find themselves more or less auctioned off for the greater interests of the family."

"Sounds terrible." Actually, it sounded worse than that. It was almost suffocating for me to think about a society in which every move had to be precalculated, every action prescribed, in which your self-image was predefined by the status of your birth, in which you could be auctioned off through marriage like family property.

"Marrying Victor deeply shamed Anne," Mrs. Osaka said, nodding sagely.

That threw me for a minute, and I looked at her, puzzled. *Victor?* I thought Victor had been remarkably attractive, and most other women seemed to share my sentiments. He was surrounded by women the few times I'd seen him at parties or other social functions. I had heard rumors, of course, of his infidelity—which was nothing new. The Old Country double standard of female fidelity and male infidelity had carried over to many of the traditional non-Christian marriages here in the Islands. Not that this was a flaw in male-female relations peculiar to the Japanese. But even though I deplored the deception and betrayal that was part and parcel of such an arrangement, I could easily see why women found Victor attractive. I supposed that for most of them, his financial success merely added to his appeal.

Mrs. Osaka said, "You see, the father met Victor when Victor was a young man in the Navy, on leave in Tokyo. It was most unusual that Victor was soon chosen as Anne's husband. It was a great insult for a girl from such a prestigious family to be betrothed to a foreigner, even one of Japanese descent. Just a cut above betrothal to a *Burakamin.*"

This was a word I was familiar with from other conversations with Mrs. Osaka. The *Burakamin* were Japan's outcasts, people who were like other Japanese in appearance, but who, for various reasons, were considered inferior and were therefore forced to separate themselves, to the extent of living in ghettos called *buraka*. At one time these people—some two million strong—had been called *eta*, or filth. These people were strongly shunned, and though most modern Japanese claimed to be socially enlightened with regard to racial disparity, part of the marriage selection process of any person still included a careful background check to make sure the intended had no *Burakamin* heritage or blood. All this meant that if Anne considered marrying Victor just a step above marrying a *Burakamin*, she thought he was inferior indeed.

"Anne was the youngest daughter," Mrs. Osaka said. "I remember it all well. Aiko Seitaki was furious when she learned of Anne's attitude. She forbade Victor to marry her. This was quite a scandal for the Seitaki family, though only a handful of us closest friends knew about it. First, there was the matter of religion. Aiko and Masao

Seitaki were strong Christians, some of the first members of our church. They didn't want Victor to enter the Buddhist faith, which was required of him if he was to marry Anne. The elder Seitakis had a strong pride in their family. Though they had little money, Victor had just finished college, Jess would soon go, thanks to the G.I. bill, and the future looked more promising."

"Was Anne *hapai*?" Pregnant.

Mrs. Osaka shot me a quizzical look. Then she shook her head, smiled, and said, "Oh no, no, you do not understand. She wasn't even allowed to be alone with Victor until after the marriage ceremony. This was a true arranged marriage. Anne had gone to bridal school, she had learned flower arrangement, the tea ceremony, music, and classical dance. She had been very sheltered and was preparing to marry a man worthy of her own social class."

"What caused her family to marry her off to someone they thought was inferior? Was she getting old enough to be an embarrassment? Or did she do something to shame the family?" I had learned of these Japanese customs during my long friendship with Mrs. Osaka.

"I don't believe it was anything Anne did at all," she said. "I think it was a business arrangement. I believe that the Shinda Corporation wanted a way to invest in Hawaii without alarming the local people as to the true scope of their interest. Foreign investment was not so welcome at that time as it is now. This was not all that long after World War II, and Japan was not yet forgiven for bombing Pearl Harbor. Even the local Japanese didn't look fondly on the idea of the Japanese nationals buying the land from beneath them, not at that time. So what better way to silently invest in Hawaii than to marry off one's daughter to a local boy who was all too eager to go around acting like a big shot?"

"So that's how Victor got started in business?"

"Of course. These papers tell me that Victor has for years been fronting for the Shinda Corporation. He owns most of the properties in theory, the Shindas own them in fact. Though it appears that the uncle, Ko Shinda, became involved in the Golden Palms project only after Anne's father died last year. I'll need to look further into that. It seems to be a very complicated arrangement."

"You gathered all that just from scanning those papers?"

She chuckled. "And from my memory. Aiko Seitaki and I were good friends, Alex. She confided in me, more so than in even her own husband. And Victor was the youngest son, her baby. He told her many things that may well have best been left unsaid, for they troubled her greatly. The house where Yoko and Jess now live, for instance. It was more or less a bribe from the Shinda Corporation for the elder Seitakis to look the other way. Aiko did not want to live in the house at first. It was a great shame to her, that she should take charity from people who thought her inferior. She would never have done so, except that interfering would have hurt Victor more than anybody."

"And now Jess is in the middle of it all," I said, suddenly beginning to understand the situation.

"He will find himself in an awkward position. Because he has inherited not only Victor's paper interests. According to the Japanese tradition of reciprocity—*giri*—he has also inherited his brother's *on*—the obligations to the Shinda Corporation."

I thought about Jess saying the day of the funeral that he might want to hire me for something. He'd been in a jam, all right. Furthermore, for the first time I realized why he might be aggravated by my interest in Victor's private papers. There was nothing strictly illegal about what Victor had been doing, of course. But it was certainly dishonest and not the way Jess would have done business, given a choice. Still—I was guessing that Jess would quickly extricate himself from the arrangement, even if it cost him a bundle.

"Victor saw a way to rise quickly above poverty, and he compromised," Mrs. Osaka said. "And now, as usual, his older brother will have to clean up after him."

The daylight was dying. The streetlights down the hill were blinking on, the insects were singing their evening song. Inside the house, the kitchen light came on. I could smell something with sesame oil, *shoyu*, and onions cooking.

I said, "I'd still like to leave these papers with you and have you translate the *kanji*, if you would, please."

"I think, Alex, that you would be wise to leave this matter alone."

"I can't. I'm beginning to wish I could, frankly, but—I just have to know."

"Have you prayed about this?"

"Yes. Off and on for days."

She was silent for a moment. She set her jaw stubbornly, and I thought she was going to refuse. But instead, she said, "Very well. If you feel it is in the Lord's will, I'll try to help. Do you need them soon?"

I didn't even try to hide my gratitude. "A day or two would be fine."

I hesitated, then drained the bit of liquid left in my teacup and picked up my purse, preparing to leave. I felt uneasy and didn't quite know why. I said, "I want to remind you again that this is all highly confidential."

"Of course." She gave me that penetrating look. "Alex, is something else bothering you? You're really not yourself today."

I gazed past her into the darkening tropical foliage, then started as the wind riffled a tree branch. I felt foolish for being so jumpy. I looked back at Mrs. Osaka. She was watching me intently. Finally, I braced myself and said the words that had been trying to erupt out of my mouth for the past hour.

"When I first saw these papers, I thought someone was trying to capitalize on Victor's death," I said quietly. "But now I'm concerned that Victor Seitaki might have somehow been involved with the *yakuza*."

She froze in place, gazing full at me. And for the first time in my life, I saw a deep and abiding fear creep into her widening eyes, a fear so strong that it chilled me.

She touched the gold cross she wore on a chain around her throat, as if for reassurance. Then she said, "That is possible, Alex. There is much about Victor's arrangement with the Shinda Corporation that has always been cloaked in secrecy." She gazed past the dark foliage and into the dying light. She was looking back through time.

After a moment, she said, "You should know more about the *kuroi kiri*. The black mist that has for centuries choked the freedom from the Japanese people."

"Black mist?"

"This is what my people call it. It is a pall, like an evil incense wafting up from the poisonous grip of the *yakuza* and the corrupted forces that empower them, a symptom of the moral corrosion that enslaves Japan. When we Japanese first came to these Islands, a hundred years or more ago, my people tried to leave that terror behind. But because of the conditions on the plantations, we often found ourselves in even deeper slavery than we had escaped. Over time, we fought to be accepted. We have struggled hard. We have earned our freedom . . ."

"This frightens you," I said.

"It poisons me with fear. It is a slavery we have fought for centuries to be freed from. It is something to dread at night, like a child dreads demons, like being buried alive. It is an evil so invisible, so deeply rooted that it seems impossible to change."

"But the *yakuza* has never really gotten a stranglehold in Hawaii," I said. "Not at the operational level. Maybe these so-called 'black mists' blow in from time to time, but the authorities have always managed to send up a good stiff breeze and blow them right back out again."

"I wonder," Mrs. Osaka said. "So much investment and tourist money has come in from Japan, especially over these past few years."

I thought about that. In truth, the experts estimated that between five and fifty major Hawaiian businesses had been bought by *yakuza* money over the past few years. It was equally true that the feds had no way of knowing what money came from the *yakuza* and what was legitimately gained. Organized criminals of all nationalities had long ago learned how to bury their ownership of legitimate enterprises beneath layers and layers of camouflage, hush money, and deceit.

Still, the covert nature of these investments meant that the overt presence of Japanese organized crime was kept to a minimum, so as not to attract attention. Therefore, there hadn't been much indication of a strong *yakuza* presence in Hawaii. Oh, there had been an occasional incident over the years. A state senator had been murdered in the early seventies, and a known *yakuza* enforcer had driven the getaway car; a prostitution ring in a major Waikiki condo project had proved to be owned by the *yakuza*, another had been uncovered in a major hotel. A *yakuza*-affiliated heroin dealer had been shot to death in a university area apartment, along with his hostess-bar mistress. Japanese tourists could find porno shops, escort services, and hostess bars that catered exclusively to them; police said there was bound to be *yakuza* money involved, but there was no way they could trace it. And veiled rumors occasionally circulated about the *yakuza* affiliations of several prominent Hawaiian people who had been "blessed" with phenomenal good luck in their business dealings.

The truth was, law enforcement officials believed that the *yakuza* did indeed operate certain prostitution, pornography, gambling, and gun smuggling operations that at least had branches here. Furthermore, this was a perfect place for them to rub shoulders with mainland mob bosses—the Italian Cosa Nostra—who had long ago declared Hawaii an "open territory" and whose operations had long since gone global, linking up with organized crime from every segment of the world. Though La Cosa Nostra (LCN to the FBI) had decreed that no single crime family could have jurisdiction over the Hawaiian Islands, any crime family could invest here, members could retire here, money—much money—could be laundered here. Apparently that same principle had been passed on to the *yakuza*.

Furthermore, the *yakuza* were smart enough to send men in thousand-dollar suits with no tattoos and all fingertips intact to serve as their front men in the major enterprises. The Immigration and Naturalization Service (INS) keeps an eye out for people who fit the *yakuza* profile and detains them at the airport. Most of them are guilty of visa fraud, for the visas that allow them entry ask about police records, and some 90 percent of all *yakuza* have police records in Japan. If they don't lie, they don't get the visa; therefore, possession of the visa alone is enough to bust most *yakuza* who are caught entering Hawaii. Several now reside in Mainland prisons, where they serve one- or two-year federal sentences. All are fined heavily and at the very least deported. While they're here, the INS photographs their tattoos for identification purposes.

Unfortunately, the *yakuza* profiles fit only the lower echelon criminals, equivalent to our street thugs and pimps and gun-runners and porno traffickers and so on. The INS looks for men in silk suits with short permed hair (called "punch perms") or ponytails, missing fingertips and wraparound sunglasses, who might be stripped down to reveal elaborate tattoos. These men are like the lowest-level Mafia soldiers, and they're generally ill-bred, rude, and swaggering smallfry. The *yakuza* man who had been killed in front of my building partially fit that profile, but he came the long way around, via Los Angeles, and therefore didn't go through Immigration at the Honolulu airport. Anyway, the INS agents don't look for polished, prosperous Japanese businessmen carrying laptop computers and expensive briefcases. No indeed. These are the people that we *want* to lure to the islands, for they bring millions—even billions—of dollars in investment capital, and that means prosperity for all. And if an occasional *yakuza* money-man slides in among them—well, perhaps that's the price you have to pay . . .

"There is so much we do not understand about the way these things are done," Mrs. Osaka said, reflecting my own thoughts exactly. "And now you tell me that Victor Seitaki, a man I have known since his childhood, may have been serving a *kuromaku*."

"I'm sorry?"

"A 'black curtain,' Alex. A *kuromaku*. The curtain they pull across the stage in *kabuki* theater. It's also someone who controls people from behind the scenes: a *yakuza* crime lord, perhaps a godfather."

As I thought about that, the black mist she had spoken of seeped into my awareness like a freezing wind, and the world around me turned ever so slightly alien. I felt a threatening, suffocating sensation as I entertained this new concept of some dark, evil, unknown force behind the scenes, pulling the strings that had gotten Miro Ochinko killed.

I had apparently stumbled into a deep and evil labyrinth. And in that moment I suddenly realized that no matter what I did, no matter where I ran, if this thing was as big as it seemed, I was certainly going to find out exactly who this *kuromaku* was and why one of his soldiers had died while trying to deliver Victor's private papers—*to me.*

CHAPTER 11

W hen you drive back toward Waikiki from Nuuanu, the fastest route is to catch the freeway at the Pali Highway, drive toward Diamond Head and the Kaimuki area till you reach the Sixth Avenue exit, then turn right till you hit the first stoplight. There, you turn right again, hit Kapahulu Avenue for the few blocks of mostly fast-food restaurants—Troubles calls it "Grease Row"—then you turn right once more and cruise on down the palm-lined length of Ala Wai Boulevard, alongside the canal.

Which is what I did that evening, letting my instincts guide me home. My mind was totally tangled up with thoughts of Mrs. Osaka's reaction to my suggestion that Victor Seitaki might have somehow been involved with the *yakuza*, and that led me to think about the *yakuza* itself.

I was familiar with the organization. I had, after all, spent a few years as an intelligence analyst for the feds, and the *yakuza* had just been emerging as a high priority on the agency's agenda at that time.

Yakuza was actually a slang term. Most experts believed this name was derived from the words for the lowest score in Japan's favorite card game, *hanafuda*, and that the name had originated as a way of saying the criminals who gambled at this game were no-good outlaws, born to lose.

Perhaps that had been the people's general opinion of the gangsters a couple of centuries ago when the first criminal gangs began to organize. Perhaps some people in Japan still felt that way, in spite of the formidable power the *yakuza* now wielded over both Japanese society and Japanese government. But myths had grown up around the organization, much as they had grown up around the Italian Mafia. And these myths had wrapped the organization in a feudal camouflage that portrayed them as noble descendants of *samurai* warriors, modern-day Robin Hoods with swords and guns, who championed the Japanese people, defending them against evil aggressors of various kinds—though most Japanese secretly knew who the true aggressors were.

These legends were honed through a barrage of *yakuza* movies and pulp novels which were of course financed by *yakuza* money. The *yakuza* controlled Japan's entertainment industry, all the way from the brothels to the porno movies to the legitimate, prestigious theater. They also controlled vast blocs of Japan's most expensive real estate, certain sporting events, various industries, trucking, waste disposal, gun smuggling from the United States into Japan, illegal gambling, and loan-sharking—in fact, anything that might make them a few yen. Sort of like a criminal *zaibatsu*.

Whether the explanation for the origination of the name *yakuza* was true or merely another fanciful legend, the police on both sides of the Pacific formally referred to the organization as the *Boryokudan*: "the violent ones." Believe me, from all I had learned, this name fit. Still, in private, most cops, federal or local, called the gangsters by the more common name of *yakuza*.

The *yakuza* had started in Japan some two hundred fifty years ago as loose groups of thugs, thieves, waterfront gamblers, and other hooligans who, for whatever reason, had dared to step outside the rigidly structured and unforgiving conformity of Japanese society. Now, they had become one of the world's largest crime cartels, made up from nearly a hundred thousand members and comprising over two thousand different subgroups. The Japanese National Police Agency had recently published statistics stating that in one year alone, the Gross National Product of this shadow nation within a nation was nearly ten billion U.S. dollars. U.S. law enforcement put that number at between fifty billion and a hundred billion. And contrary to my reassurances to Mrs. Osaka, there was a great deal of evidence that the *yakuza* had been trying for some time to expand into Hawaii, California, and even New York, in part because there was rising pressure in Japan itself to stem the political and economic corruption that was threatening to swallow the country whole.

One form of *yakuza* expansion came in the guise of an expanded interest in marketing drugs—crystal methamphetamine, in particular, once known as speed. This drug especially lent itself to Japan's frenetic lifestyle and had therefore been their drug of choice for many decades. Now, according to FBI data, one full third of the *yakuza*'s revenue came from the smokeable form of crystal methamphetamine that is known on Hawaii's streets as Ice. Although the local drug dealers handled it at the street level, although international gangsters as diverse as Taiwanese tongs and Korean syndicates did the actual trafficking, much Hawaiian Ice was financed by *yakuza* money-men, brokered through *yakuza* channels, even processed at *yakuza* labs in various places throughout the Pacific basin.

I knew a lot about Ice. David had been shot dead by a mid-level dealer who had been selling large wholesale quantities of Ice.

Ice is probably the ugliest drug yet invented. It mixes the dangerous paranoia associated with the 1960s "speed freaks" with the affordability and convenience of crack cocaine. Worse yet, drug experts say it's more addictive than crack or heroin. It's also far more likely to turn a user violently psychotic—in fact, the only drug abusers I've ever been afraid of are Ice-heads. Hawaii's court system recently found a murderer not guilty by reason of insanity, on the basis that he had used Ice for a short period of time before committing the murder and the drug had literally driven him insane. A bad legal precedent, yet one that was grounded in the truths of the drug. I knew from firsthand experience with various addicts that Ice bakes the user's brains in nothing flat while at the same time setting them up for irrational, out-of-control, flash-point violence. It rips away every shred of humanity.

What kind of people could originate and supply a market for such a drug? Any drug, for that matter? And if Victor Seitaki had indeed been involved with the people who did this, what did it mean?

It certainly didn't mean that Victor had been dealing Ice. That thought was absurd. No, whatever was going on at the upper levels had been related to real estate, maybe even to the Golden Palms Resort project. Maybe Victor had been running a laundry for Ice money by rinsing it through his various developments. Or maybe it was Ice money that had literally built those developments. The thought stopped me cold. Because if that were true, then some of

Victor's real estate developments had been mortared with my husband's blood.

It was fully dark by the time I parked my Honda, retrieved my copy of Victor's papers from the trunk, then rode the elevator to my floor. I unlocked the door with the large brass placard that said ALBRIGHT INVESTIGATIONS, then stepped into my office.

When I had my mind on work, I often came in through this entrance. It was a few feet down from the main front door, the one that opened into a small foyer and then on into the large living room. I'd had this separate entrance put in while remodeling the master bedroom into my combination office and small waiting room. At the far side of my desk, one door opened into my bedroom and bathroom and another door opened into the living room, beyond which was the kitchen, a small dining area, and the wide balcony that wrapped around the front of the condo, overlooking the beach, and all the way around the side that held my bedroom and this office, with its beach and mountain views. Troubles' bedroom and bathroom were on the far side of the living room, down a short hallway and also fronting on the balcony overlooking the beach and Waikiki's beachfront hotels.

My office was pitch dark. I usually leave on a small night-light, but apparently it had burned out, or maybe Troubles had turned it off before leaving for his North Shore camping trip. I switched on a lamp, put Victor's papers into my small safe and locked it securely, then opened the door to the living room—odd that it was closed—and stepped through.

I stopped short, a few steps shy of the light switch, and felt an involuntary shiver.

Someone was in the room with me.

I turned my head soundlessly from left to right then back again. The beige drapes had been pulled tight across the wide glass balcony door. They were well-lined, and the lights from the hotels and street offered only faint illumination. The lamplight that shined from my office made an oblong slant that left the rest of the room pitched in darkness.

But someone was here. I was certain of it. The hairs stood up on the back of my neck; I felt the fear-pumped adrenaline surge through my body, readying me for fight or flight. The sensation of an unwelcome presence was overwhelming, like too much heavy incense wafted by a black, suffocating mist.

I hoped for an instant that it was Troubles after all. Maybe his camping expedition had fallen through and he had stayed home, fallen asleep while it was still daylight. I actually started to say his name, but stopped myself.

For even as these split-second hopes bolstered me up, I knew better. I heard a sudden small scraping then, maybe the motion of a rodent, or the brush of a limb from my ficus tree against the wall. I braced myself and started to turn toward the noise.

He came at me from behind.

I jerked backward, slammed into the wall. I smelled his foul breath, felt his thick, scaly hand on my shoulder grabbing for me, and then I was away from him, running back through the office door and slamming it shut behind me and shooting home the bolt.

I dived to the desk and yanked out my .38 Chief Special, then checked to make sure it was loaded and ready. Something crashed into the door. I turned, ready to fire. I heard someone curse, then heard something slam, something slammed again—the front door. I opened the door that separated the living room from the office, moved carefully back through the semidarkness, my gun out now, ready to fire. I moved swiftly to the light switch, ducking so I would be a less certain target. And in that instant, just as the light came on, I heard a crash, saw the front door give and swing open; the light from the hallway illuminated a black-clad figure wearing a low black watchcap and a turtleneck, pulled up over the lower half of his face.

He was out in a blur, but I was in the hallway in four long paces, and then I was running after him, panting down the hallway. But he had found the exit to the fire stairs, was through and gone. I stood there, trying to focus on what had happened, trying to get my breath back and stop the shaking in my legs. And I knew in that instant that the stupidest thing I could possibly do was step through the fire door and try to follow him. Because if he was playing for keeps—and most people did these days—then I'd be walking square into his sights.

I stood with my back to the wall, my arm still out, gun aimed, and watched the fire door for a long moment. And then a thought hit me. What if he wasn't the only one?

Cautiously, I went back inside, my gun still ready. Fully aware of the front door gaping open behind me, I switched on the lights, one by one, until I had combed every possible hiding place in every single room.

Only then did my ragged breathing begin to normalize. I let my gun drop to aim toward the floor now and went back into the hallway, looking once again at the door to the fire stairs, the one through which the intruder had disappeared. I remembered then that the door had an automatic lock, the kind that allows you to enter it from the hallway, but you can't open it from inside the stairwell. A security precaution for which I was suddenly very grateful.

I went back into my living room, phoned the night security supervisor, Tommy Blake, and told him I'd had an intruder. There had been no point in phoning him before; actually, I didn't want to put him in a position to have to confront the man, since Tommy was pushing seventy and wasn't even allowed to carry a gun. I described the intruder, asked him to keep an eye out for anyone matching the description, warned that he might be coming out of the stairwell, might be dangerous. Then I asked if they could please send someone up to fix the broken lock on my front door. Tommy was concerned, and he assured me that someone would be up right away.

I sat down, then, and thought the event through. There was no point in phoning the police. The intruder was certainly long gone now, and besides, I didn't want to get them involved. Because there was something disturbing me, something I couldn't quite pin down, and the more complicated this whole thing became, the smaller the chance that I'd get it sorted out.

As I was putting a pot of coffee on to brew, I suddenly realized what was bothering me most. There was something vaguely familiar about the figure. Though I had seen the person only in flight, I knew it for certain. I had seen that form, the wide, bony shoulders, that odd gait, before, and not so very long ago.

But try though I might, I was too keyed up to be able to fully remember where I'd seen the man.

The handyman came to replace my lock. He wanted to phone the police too, but I finally convinced him it was a waste of time to report the incident, that too much time had passed. But when the lock was repaired and I was once again safely ensconced in my comfortable abode, I wasn't comfortable at all.

I checked everything in the place. Nothing had been stolen. The intruder had apparently picked the front door lock from the outside, then closed the door behind him as he came in, unaware that it would relock automatically, unaware that he'd be needing to make such a speedy exit.

I spent the rest of the night on the living room sofa, the balcony door tightly locked, the other locks likewise, deadbolts on, night chains intact. I watched TV till dawn, catching an old movie and a couple of good talk shows, even one unusual church service from Tokyo, complete with Japanese evangelists, subtitles, and a rousing rendition in Japanese of the old gospel song "Power in the Blood." This was a rare find, considering that less than 1 percent of all Japanese are Christians. Frankly, it set me to thinking. And praying for guidance. There was so much in this world that transcended stereotypes, so much that I didn't begin to understand.

For the better part of two hours, I prayed and puzzled over everything that had happened, trying to add it all up to make sense of my terrifying night visitor. Only when the sky turned fully light did I finally pull an afghan up around my chin, burrow in, and fall soundlessly and dreamlessly asleep.

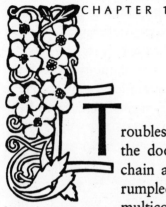roubles awakened me at nine A.M. by leaning on the door buzzer. When I dislodged the safety chain and opened the door, he glanced at my rumpled clothes, then at the wrinkled sheet and multicolored afghan atop the sofa. He raised his eyebrows questioningly, then tossed the morning paper onto the kitchen counter and said, "What's with the night chain?"

"Paranoia." I felt grouchy and had a headache. I sat down and massaged my temples with the heels of my hands. "Why are you home so early? I thought you'd be hiking and swimming all day."

"Got rained out."

I went into my bathroom, took a hot shower, then a cold one. I dressed in bleached denims and a navy T-shirt, brushed my teeth, and felt a little better. When I got back to the living room, Troubles was in the kitchen, whipping up whole-grain pancakes. One of the many nice things about him was that he loved to cook.

I pulled open the drapes that covered the sliding glass balcony door. The weather had indeed gone bad. The sky was overcast, the ocean was a choppy gray. The catamarans and outriggers were all tied up at the beach, and the beach vendors had draped plastic tarps across their stalls to protect their inventories from rain. I climbed aboard one of the high wooden stools at the kitchen counter and said, "Someone broke in last night."

Troubles had been holding the hand blender, stirring up the batter, and now he turned it off and stared at me. "In here?" He sounded skeptical, like he expected me to deliver a punchline.

I told him everything that had happened. When I had finished, he was frowning hard. "So who do you think it was?"

"I don't know." I had already puzzled over every single client, acquaintance, and friend who might have a reason to secretly enter my residence. I couldn't come up with a thing. "My best guess is a burglar," I said. "Probably just a coincidence that he targeted our place." I didn't want Troubles to worry. On the other hand, I wanted him aware of the situation. After all, he lived here, too.

After a few moments of questioning me about the break-in, Troubles returned to whipping up pancakes. I relaxed a bit, then idly reached over and picked up the morning paper from where he'd tossed it onto the counter.

I unfolded it and heard myself let out a long, low whistle.

Jess Seitaki had made the headlines. His photograph stared up at me from the front page, just beneath the masthead. He was wearing a shell-shocked expression. The contours of his face were fuzzy, like he'd been walking fast and someone had shouted at him, then popped the photo just as he turned to look full at them. Right beside Jess's photograph, in another frame, was a smaller photograph of a local man with a jowled face and unruly dark hair. He had the worn appearance that comes with heavy boozing and hard living, and he looked vaguely familiar. Suddenly my memory kicked in. It was the man who'd been driving the plumber's van that had hit and killed the *yakuza* soldier last week.

The caption covered two columns, beneath both pictures. It said:

CAPTAIN JESS SEITAKI, HEAD OF THE HAWAII STATE POLICE'S HOMICIDE DIVISION, HAS BEEN SUSPENDED, PENDING AN INVESTIGATION INTO HIS HANDLING OF A HIGHLY CONTROVERSIAL CASE WITH INTERNA-TIONAL IMPLICATIONS.

My whistle had caused Troubles to turn and stare down at the newspaper too. He was looking at it upside down, so the caption was hard to read. He said, "That's Jess. What's wrong?"

I read him the caption, then skimmed the rest of the short accompanying article, reading out loud:

Homicide Captain Jess Seitaki has come under fire for mishandling evidence in the accidental death of Miro Ochinko, a visitor from Tokyo who the HSP identifies as a member of Japan's criminal organization known as the *yakuza*. This mishandling of evidence resulted in Honolulu resident Sonny Malinta being prematurely released from the county holding cells yesterday afternoon, where he was being held pending bail for driving under the influence and was awaiting a possible charge of negligent homicide. Mr. Malinta was the driver of the van that hit and killed the Japanese national. Andrew Alton, Head of the Hawaii State Police Commission, informed *The Honolulu Examiner* last night that Seitaki's judgment has been questioned. "Jess and I have been friends for a long time, and he's always been a first-rate cop," Alton said. "However, this is a serious matter and I'm required by the police rules to suspend him, pending an investigation. Still, I feel certain that Captain Seitaki will be vindicated on all counts and will soon return to work." *The Honolulu Examiner* was reminded that it is illegal for the Hawaii State Police Commission to comment on the specifics of any accusation until after the internal investigation has been completed. When our reporter tried to interview Captain Jess Seitaki, he said, "No comment."

I slammed down the paper. "I don't believe it."

Jess had won more awards than any cop who'd ever worked for HSP. He was meticulous and methodical in his work, and the idea that he could screw up a case was incredible. But another thought had invaded my mind, even as I automatically defended him. The news article said he'd been accused of mishandling evidence. What if Jess had turned in the papers I'd given him? What if that was the evidence he'd "mishandled"? What if he was taking the rap for something I had done? A sinking sensation filled me with lead.

"It sounds bogus," Troubles said. "Not like Jess at all." He had stopped stirring the pancake mix. Now he straddled a stool on the opposite side of the counter and was reading the paper himself.

I picked up the wall phone and dialed Jess's house. The number was busy.

"I'm going over there," I said, hanging up the receiver.

"You'd better eat first. You'll get one of your stress headaches if you don't eat something."

"No thanks, I—"

The phone rang. I swept it up. "Alex here."

"Glad I caught you home." It was Derrick Green. "Everything okay?"

I frowned. "Yes. I—"

"How was the trip to Hilo?"

"Short. Look, Derrick, something urgent has just come up. Can we talk later?"

"You mean the front page of the morning paper?"

"That's it."

"I know you and Jess are friends. Frankly, I think the whole thing is a crock. Alton has had it in for Jess for a long time."

That got my attention. There was information to be gleaned here. I made my voice more friendly, and said, "What on earth are these so-called complaints against Jess?"

"The state prosecutor insists they have a slam-dunk negligent homicide charge against Sonny Malinta. They claim they'll get a plea bargain or a conviction in nothing flat. Jess, on the other hand, thinks it's a full-on homicide. He believes Malinta's story that Ochinko was pushed in front of the van. Anyway, that's the talk in the cop-shop."

"So why is Jess in trouble?"

"Everybody wants to push this one under the rug, and Jess won't let go. This thing about *yakuza*—it isn't good for tourism, you know, Mom and Pop from Duluth don't want to vacation in the middle of a bunch of foreign thugs, especially violent ones, and the economy stinks as it is. All the hotel big shots are apparently putting pressure on Alton to downplay the whole deal, and he'd be happy to do it, but Jess won't play ball."

"Now *that* sounds like Jess," I said. I felt slightly relieved. No mention at all of Victor's papers.

"Anyway, Jess will land on his feet," Derrick said. "There's just so much that Alton can do to him. So—what are you doing for lunch?"

Lunch? I looked at Troubles' bowl of pancake batter, abandoned as he listened to my side of the conversation, his eyebrows raised in curious concern. And now Derrick was trying to feed me lunch at ten in the morning. What was it with men that made them always want to feed me?

I said, "Maybe dinner. Call me later."

"Good enough." He said good-bye and hung up.

I decided to try to reach Jess and Yoko one more time before driving up to their house. This time Yoko picked up the phone on the second ring. "Seitaki residence."

"Yoko? It's me, Alex. I just read the papers. What can I do to help?"

"Oh, Alex." Her voice was suddenly filled with dejection. "I can't tell you what a mess this is. Look, Jess is in his study. He's asked me not to bother him. He knew a lot of people would be calling to offer support, but I think he's just going to stay in there for a while and pray."

I thought about that. "I'll send up a few prayers myself," I said.

"That's the best thing you could do. I don't understand how all this happened. I'm not even sure I understand yet *what* happened. But I'm sure it will work out somehow, it's just a matter of riding through it."

"Let me know if I can do anything at all."

"We certainly will, and thank you."

I placed the receiver gently back in the cradle, then told Troubles what Yoko had said.

And then I made my second major mistake, right up there at the top of the list, just under my brief sojourn into Miro Ochinko's hotel room the night he died. You see, Troubles can be a very good listener at times. Also a very good source of common sense. And so, *against* all common sense, I found myself confiding in him. I didn't realize yet that *they* would also be listening.

As he flipped pancakes, I pulled out the plates and cutlery and filled Troubles in on what Derrick had said concerning Jess's theory that the *yakuza* soldier had been murdered. And one thing led to another, so before I realized it I was telling him about the strange phone call on the day of the accident, about seeing the man place something in the bushes, about my view of the accident. Then I explained how I had found the briefcase in the bushes beside the hotel, how I had discovered the hotel key and had used it to check out the dead man's hotel room.

"Actually," I said, "going to the hotel was pretty stupid. It didn't accomplish anything, and I could have gotten into a lot of trouble."

"Could this have something to do with the break-in last night?"

He's sharp, I'll give him that. Puts things together almost too fast.

"I don't know," I said innocently. "I guess it's possible."

He said, "Maybe the intruder was after Victor's papers?"

"I doubt it very much. Nobody even knew I had them." I started to add *except Jess, and he already had a copy*, but something stopped me before the words could roll off my tongue.

"So where are the papers now?"

I started to tell him they were at Mrs. Osaka's, that she was translating the *kanji*. But again, something stopped my tongue from divulging the information. I decided, too, that there was no need to tell him that I'd made yet another copy, which was locked securely in my safe. All these copies would only confuse him. So I simply said, "They're safe."

Troubles' hazel eyes were flooded with concern. "Don't you think this situation is a little dangerous? I mean, I don't know much about the *yakuza*, but if you're involved in their business, you could get hurt."

"No doubt," I said dryly. "But then, what isn't dangerous? Have you checked the traffic statistics lately?"

"Okay, point made. By the way, I got the books you asked for," he said. "A couple of volumes on international banking, with a long section on Japan–U.S. law, and a couple of other things that might help you figure things out. I put them on your desk."

"Thanks. I'll get to them later."

"Are you going to be all right?"

The question surprised me. "Of course. Why?"

"I mean it, Alex. This sounds like heavy stuff. I think you should just turn it all over to the police and let them handle it."

I told him then what Derrick had said about the Hawaii State Police Commission wanting to sweep it all under the rug. "That's the way it is sometimes," I said. "And frankly, I'm getting a little weary of the whole thing. But Miro Ochinko was apparently on his way to see me when the so-called accident happened. And I believe he was bringing those papers to me. That's the only way this makes sense. I don't know what it means, or why he chose me out of all the people on this earth, but he did. And now he's dead, and I feel morally obligated to find out why."

"Are you praying about it?"

I had to smile. First Mrs. Osaka, now him. "I pray about almost everything," I said. "Especially when I don't have a clue as to what I'm doing."

"Then I guess it will be okay."

I agreed. But believe me, if I'd known then that they had my condo hard-wired and were listening to every word I said, I would have packed a quick bag and hightailed it for the mainland that very hour. And I certainly would have taken Troubles with me.

But isn't that the way it always goes? You can never see the true pattern of events until after the fact, and by then it's always way too late.

CHAPTER 13

They picked me up that evening, just after sunset. I was walking down Kalakaua Avenue, on my way to the automatic teller machine beside Woolworth's. A sleek black limo slid up beside me, a dark-tinted window slid down, and a haughty Japanese face turned regally toward me. A well-manicured hand went up to remove opaque designer sunglasses—obviously an affectation at night. I was looking into a pair of brown-black eyes containing just a hint of scorn. The eyes were set above high, square-cut cheekbones, a blunt nose, and a sullen mouth. The man, who appeared to be about forty years old, appraised me for a moment, then his mouth slid into a thin, formal smile.

"Mrs. Albright?"

I ignored him while I took a mental snapshot of the limo. It was the brand new Mercedes stretch that had been parked in front of Anne's house the day of Victor's funeral dinner. I even recognized the bull-necked chauffeur, though now, instead of formal livery he wore a white polo shirt that emphasized his thick muscles.

But I didn't recognize the man who'd said my name. I took a quick snapshot of him, too. His face rose up out of a starched white-on-white collar, an Italian silk tie in wine-red and white, a black suit that would have paid off the rest of my mortgage, solid gold cufflinks and tie tack. Except for the faint scorn, the man's facial expression was stoic, unreadable.

I analyzed all this, then made a split-second evaluation that painted him in a very unpleasant light. I said, "Yes, I'm Alex Albright." I stood well away from the car, like a wise child giving directions to a stranger. I knew they must have followed me from my building, must have been cruising along after me.

"I am Kuzio Takio, special consultant to Mr. Ko Shinda," he said formally. "Mr. Shinda wishes to speak with you."

That surprised me. "I hadn't realized he was still here."

"He has stayed on to attend to business matters."

"Well, of course, he's welcome to phone me any time—"

"He would like to see you in person right away."

This man seemed to think that when Mr. Shinda called, people jumped. For an instant, my dislike of authoritarianism got in the way of my professionalism, and I started to say something rude. But my curiosity quickly brushed aside the impulse. "What time?"

"I would be happy to escort you there now."

I gestured down at my clothes. I had pulled on my bleached, frayed denim slacks, a blue and white shirt, and scuffed white tennis shoes without socks. "I'll need to change clothes."

"That won't be necessary. It will be a private meeting, and he would prefer to see you immediately."

So there I was. Picked up on the street and taken for a ride, just like the old mob days in Chicago. Except that these people operated with a certain style, I had to give them that. Of course, this was the Japanese way. Flawless manners, the gracious deference that was in truth a carefully calculated act designed to placate one's inferiors. The thick-necked chauffeur climbed from the front seat and opened the rear door for me, without looking me in the eye. I climbed into the new-smelling plush interior beside the man who'd just introduced himself as Kuzio Takio, and settled myself into the banquette seat as if I tooled around in hundred-thousand-dollar limos every day.

After the initial, uncomfortable greeting, I felt obligated to make some small talk.

"I met Mr. Shinda at Victor Seitaki's funeral," I said, trying to show manners as perfectly polished as his own. "I don't believe you were there."

I had folded my hands properly in my lap. He glanced down at them, then quickly away. I looked, and noticed that my light pink nail polish was chipped. I curled my fingers under, in spite of myself.

"I have only just arrived this afternoon," he said. He was staring straight ahead, as if it was difficult to look at me. The sliding partition between us and the chauffeur was partly open, and I could see out the front window too, as we pulled away from the curb and into the flow of traffic.

Takio fell silent. I didn't feel much like chatting either, so I tried to relax and forced myself to think hard as I tried to figure out this strange turn of events. I watched the dark ocean, the glittering, white-pillared Moana Hotel, the tiny police substation sliding past. There was a thick undercurrent of tension in the car, and the black side windows made the enclosed compartment unpleasantly murky in spite of the small lights on the ashtrays and the folding bar. I was getting claustrophobic.

After a long moment, Takio said, "I have come to help Shinda-san settle certain business affairs caused by Victor Seitaki's death." He glanced sharply at me then, as if hoping to catch some expression in my face. I sensed a rush of hostility from him.

I kept my face blank. "Yes, I imagine there is a lot to do."

He continued his small attempts at courtesy. We chatted stiffly about his flight, about the cold weather he had left behind in Japan, about the excellent surf rolling in to the right of us on the black velvet sea. He tried to seem interested in my answers and comments, but I could tell I was insignificant to him, a minor inconvenience in an otherwise important life.

We cruised through Kapiolani Park and past the old Natatorium, past the large, lighted fountain. Then the lights of Waikiki fell away behind us and we swung inward to the residential areas where the streetlights were at more distant intervals and the night seemed darker. Then we were again skirting the water, driving up the slight hill to Diamond Head lighthouse, the beam rotating to illuminate the sable-black sea in wide rotating swaths of light. I caught a brief glimpse of triangular ships' lights—perhaps one of the many dinner cruises that go out at night. Then we were past the lighthouse, rolling on into the exclusive Kahala region, named for the mythical Hawaiian goddess of rainbows. We were moving in the general direction of Anne's estate, and I decided that's where they must be taking me.

But instead, about three blocks shy of the turn, we hung a sudden left, then another, and pulled into a private garage at the Conch Shell, one of the expensive condominiums where retired movie stars and multimillionaires hole up in order to get away from the unwashed masses. The Conch Shell had been one of Victor Seitaki's first major developments.

The building featured two main towers separated from the street by tall trees and a long private driveway. We cruised past beds of flame-red torch ginger, past brilliant birds of paradise and orange lobster's claw, all illuminated by small all-weather lights set back in the lush green-black foliage. I knew the wide new golf course was to our left, the ocean to our right, so close that if I rolled down the window I'd hear the hiss of the sea rolling in to froth the moon-silvered beach.

I didn't know what the units in the Conch Shell were going for these days, but I was betting that my whole three-bedroom corner-unit condo wouldn't make a good down payment on even one of the private parking garages. We pulled into one of these, a small condo in itself with concrete walls, storage cabinets, and a private elevator. Two other vehicles were in the stalls: a white Land Rover and a green Jag.

The chauffeur opened the door for both of us, Mr. Takio graciously gestured for me to precede him, and we entered the elevator—studded leather walls, a mirrored ceiling—then floated upward. The elevator stopped, the door slid silently open, and we stepped into a foyer decorated with blue-tinted mirrors and towering ferns and full-sized trees. There was a small stone fountain in one corner, trickling water; a pedestal holding a three-foot gold statue of Buddha in another, with joss sticks in front in case someone wanted to say a prayer or blessing. The *makai* side of the room was all glass, overlooking the golf course and the dark ocean beyond.

A middle-aged Japanese housemaid in old-fashioned brown kimono admitted us into a penthouse that swallowed up the top floor. You almost never see Japanese women in Hawaii wearing kimonos, except during ceremonial occasions or when they're working as door hostesses or waitresses in Japanese restaurants. Seeing this diminutive, authentic woman with her deferential manner was like stepping into the past.

The semidark interior of the penthouse showed that elegant simplicity of design so characteristic of good taste everywhere, a simplicity the Japanese have turned into a literal art form. There was a lot of polished wood and small brass sculptures, but the place seemed unlived in, like a designer's showroom. About a third of the rooftop was open to the sky and had been landscaped into an elegant garden, a perfect blend of Japanese simplicity and lush Hawaiian foliage. It was dramatically illuminated by occasional pole lamps and colored paper lanterns. I was quickly ushered through the living quarters and out to the open air.

There, the diminutive Mr. Shinda sat on a wooden high-backed bench beneath a hanging lantern that glowed green. He was shaded by ten-foot koa trees, surrounded by ti plants and tree fern. Beside him was a small stone table, and upon it was a stone brazier, filled with dying embers. Beside that was a round stone table which held a pewter tea service and pot. This section of the roof had been planted in rolling, perfectly manicured moss-grass, and Takio and I stepped onto a wooden boardwalk—artificially weathered—that connected us to the place where Shinda sat, clad in a short wheat-colored kimono and trousers, snow-white socks on his feet beneath the thonged slippers they call *zoris*.

When he saw us, he stood up and waited till we'd reached him. And suddenly there I was again, offering Mr. Shinda that familiar series of nods. I still wasn't sure who was supposed to quit nodding first. I really needed to ask someone about that sometime.

Tonight, in his own setting, Shinda seemed far more massive, in spite of his slight size—rather like the teaspoons of matter from collapsed stars that are said to be so heavy their weight could knock a hole all the way through the earth. The razor-cut silver hair was still perfect, though a breeze agitated the tree ferns beside him and caused me to lightly shiver. It crossed my mind that the hair was sprayed in place, but that assumption did nothing to diminish the impression of compact, ruthless power. And though Shinda was smiling graciously, the hint of merriment that I'd seen in his deep-set eyes the first time I met him had now been swallowed whole by a deep, hypnotic malevolence.

Mr. Shinda motioned for me to sit on the bench beside him, then turned to face me, though the bench was long and he was still more than an arm's length away. Takio took a seat on a polished wooden chair opposite. Mr. Shinda beamed at me, but his eyes were chilling.

He said, "Thank you for coming." His accent was thick, but his words were understandable.

"Thank you for inviting me," I said, leaning forward in my seat. The atmosphere was sodden with hostility, yet these two men pretended to welcome me. These signals were so mixed they were bound to be explosive. And yet my curiosity was piqued. I wanted to know why I was here.

Mr. Shinda spoke slowly now, carefully, as if I were a little hard of hearing or slow of wit. "Takio-san will be taking Victor's place as *kumi-cho* of my business interests here in Hawaii."

He added the "san" as a term of respect, much as we use the word "Mister." I knew the other word, too. *Kumi-cho* meant boss. What I didn't know was why he was bothering to tell me this.

"I hope to see Takio-san start fresh," Mr. Shinda said. "That is why I have stayed here for a time, to settle outstanding problems with Victor's affairs."

"Yes," I said, thoroughly puzzled now. "That would seem wise."

"Those affairs are suddenly made more complicated by the fact that Victor's brother, Jess, has inherited part of his brother's property, which is interlinked with my own. And at the moment, Jess seems to have many problems that prevent him from attending to his inheritance." His thick, black eyebrows knit themselves into a concerned frown.

I nodded. So this was going to be about Jess and his obligations to the Shinda Corporation. I said, "Yes. Things aren't going very well for Jess at the moment."

"I have asked you here because our cultures are different. I do not always understand the way things are done in Hawaii. Yet I feel I can be of some assistance to Jess Seitaki in the very serious matter of the charges against him," Shinda said, "if only he would allow me. But I have been unable to talk to him."

"I don't know what can be done right now," I said. I started to add that I hadn't been able to talk to him either. But again, something stopped my tongue from moving.

"I am of course acting as a friend. Nevertheless, my first obligation is to my business colleagues, with regard to the pressing matter of our development at the Golden Palms Resort. There are permits, other problems that require immediate attention. If these matters are not addressed, vast amounts of money may be lost—money which is not only ours, but Jess's. But even more important, this money is a large part of the inheritance for Anne and her children. Our obligation dictates that we make certain everything is properly taken care of. But we have been unable to get Jess's full attention since these foolish problems with his job have erupted." He spread his arms in a studied gesture of helplessness.

"I see," I said.

"Yes. But I know that he is your friend. I saw at the funeral that he deeply respects you. Therefore, we have decided to ask you to speak with him on our behalf. You must make him understand the urgency of these matters."

"He's hard to reach these days, but I'll certainly do what I can."

They were both exquisitely polite now. The view was beautiful, the night air was perfumed by piikake flowers and the musty, ancient scent of the sea. But I suddenly felt as if a heavy weight was descending on me, trying to press me into the damp, gravelike earth.

As if he had sensed my withdrawal, Mr. Shinda leaned quickly forward, his eyes a malevolent glare until he blinked, and a kindly expression returned to his face. "We would of course express our appreciation for your help in this matter," he said.

He nodded to Takio-san, who nodded back, then Shinda opened a briefcase that had been sitting beneath his chair. He withdrew a thick slab of American money. I felt my eyes go wide.

He handed it to me, and I automatically took it, feeling its heavy weight in my hand. And as I thumbed through it, I saw hundred dollar bills—at least ten, maybe twenty thousand dollars' worth.

The money felt strange. Even my hand holding it, the arm attached, seemed suddenly numb and alien to me, as if all the nerves had died.

But before I could assimilate the feeling, Shinda said, "There are also missing papers."

Bam! It came at me so suddenly that there was no way I could hide my astonishment. I tried to say something witty that would quickly mask my involuntary reaction, but instead I felt my mouth moving in little o's, like a fish gasping for water. I let my mouth flap shut and sat there, busted, my hand holding a fortune in hush money, my integrity on the auction block.

"We require the missing papers in order to settle the financial affairs of the Golden Palms project," Shinda said, as if he were discussing the most common problem in the world. "I am sure you understand."

He leaned back then, a satisfied look on his face, and exchanged a meaningful glance with Takio-san. Then he turned back to me, keen-eyed, and said, "Certain sources inform us that the papers were stolen from Victor's safe. We believe the thief planned, for some reason, to give them to you."

That startled me back into some vestige of self control. I leaned forward and placed the money on the brazier beside Mr. Shinda—dangerously close to the still-glowing embers. I said, "I'm sorry, but I don't know what you're talking about."

"Whoever possesses my papers does so illegally," he said, frowning deeply. "We require their immediate return."

"I'm afraid I can't help you there."

"Perhaps not," he said, very polite again. "But you are after all an investigator. The Shinda Corporation would like to hire you to help us find these missing papers. We will of course pay you handsomely for your troubles, in addition to the gift we wish to give you for acting as our intercessor with Jess Seitaki." He nodded toward the money I'd put down beside the brazier.

Well. I was talking with a master of covert communication, I could certainly see that. After all, if he had lived every detail of my life right beside me for the past week, he couldn't have gotten much closer to the bone. But—the real question was, what did he really know about Victor's papers, and how much was just a lucky guess? He knew something, that was for sure. Was it possible an informant had really told him the thief would bring the papers to me? Highly unlikely. After all, what did I have to do with all this? I had to be a peripheral player, at best. No, Shinda was most likely fishing for information, trying to make me think he knew what was happening so I'd talk to him.

"We would of course require that the papers be returned to us as soon as possible," he continued. "Otherwise, certain building permits for the resort project will expire, and the papers will have no further value."

I said, "I'm sorry. There seems to be a misunderstanding here . . ."

His jaw set stubbornly, and the same scorn I'd seen in Takio's eyes flooded his own. "There is no misunderstanding on our part. We wish to make certain there is no misunderstanding on yours. I do not wish to make you uncomfortable or rush you in any way, so please consider this matter. We will contact you tomorrow morning to learn of your decision. Thank you for coming."

And with that, his eyes shut down as if a light switch had been turned off. He nodded abruptly to Takio-san, who in turn nodded to the chauffeur, who had stepped beside the doorway into the penthouse and now held it open for me.

There was nothing I could do but walk over and go through it, through the penthouse and back out into the elevator. The chauffeur walked beside me, seemingly oblivious to my existence. But when we reached the limo, he opened the door and waited till I'd climbed in the back seat, then slid in behind the steering wheel, used the automatic device to open the garage door, and rolled the limo back out into the real world. When we reached the street and were only a few blocks from Kahala Mall, the claustrophobia of the enclosed compartment suddenly washed through me as a wave of panic. I rapped on the closed partition—I didn't have a clue as to where the speaker-phone was—and he slid it open and looked back at me as if he were inspecting an insect.

"You can stop here," I said. "I'd really rather walk."

He blinked, then pulled to the side of the road, in front of someone's low-slung Spanish-tiled house. It was only eight o'clock, and the buses didn't stop running in this area until midnight. I climbed out and started walking toward the closest bus stop, back near the mall. But I glanced back over my shoulder and watched the limo till it was well over the hill and far away.

Only then did I let myself relax. I walked two blocks, to the unlit bus stop, then settled onto the bench and waited. Occasional cars whisked past through the quiet residential area, their headlights crossing angularly as they turned a corner or pulled into a driveway. Chopsticks to chopsticks, chopsticks to chopsticks . . .

The stars hung pure in the sky above me, as pure as I wished I could be. The night winds still carried the sweet, clean scent of piikake. I sat there, trying to untangle my thoughts, sorting through everything that had just happened to me. And I finally began to realize, in that moment, that there were things going on beneath the surface here that I hadn't yet begun to fathom.

CHAPTER 14

The bus service in Honolulu is excellent, and the ride from the Kahala area to Waikiki was short. I got off at the stop nearest the bank machine, my original destination. I used my bank card to take out cash for the weekend, then grabbed a couple of submarine sandwiches, stopped at the Food Pantry for some fresh fruit, and was back home by a little after 9:30.

Troubles was stretched out on the living room sofa, Tess was curled up on a rose-flowered floor cushion. They were plowing through a huge bowl of popcorn, watching sumo wrestling on TV.

I tossed one paper-wrapped sub to Troubles and said, "Sorry I didn't know Tess was here, or I'd have brought another one."

"No big deal," he said. "We can split one." He promptly tore the sandwich in half, paper and all, and tossed a ragged half to Tess.

She caught it, fully intact, and laughed. Everything Troubles did seemed to delight her. She was wearing Levi's, a splashy flowered T-shirt, and she looked terrific, as usual. Ah, youth . . .

Troubles shot me a curious look. "You sound a little edgy. You okay?"

"Just a bad day," I said. "I'll recover." I settled onto David's old black leather recliner, used the lever to raise the foot rest, then leaned back and unwrapped my own submarine. I checked to make sure they'd put extra olives on it, then started to "grind out," as the local kids say.

"Derrick phoned," Troubles said, between bites. "Three times, actually." He shot me a sideways look, and grinned. "Getting to be a serious item, huh?"

"Getting to be a serious pest," I said and hunched down, to finish my sandwich and watch TV.

Sumo was big in Honolulu, and getting bigger, though most of the action came from Japan. For the first time ever, three Local boys—HAJAs, or Hawaiian Americans of Japanese Ancestry—had gained maximum rank there. One had made *yokozuna* (Grand Champion, considered to be a "walking god" in Japan). Two others had made *ozei* (champion). Having a foreigner achieve that status was almost a miracle, considering the still-closed society in Japan and the enormous status of the sumo wrestlers there. This was heady stuff for three local boys who had grown up eating shave ice and plate lunch and body surfing off Makapuu. The *yokozuna* was now pulling down better than 1.5 million dollars a year and had an entire stable of people to wait on him and cater to him.

I had once belonged to the ranks of unenlightened Americans who made fun of a sport that pitted two painfully obese men in fancy diapers against one another in order to force each other out of a tiny ring. But as I learned more about the sport and the immense skill required to participate, about the thousands of years of tradition involved and the obscure Shinto symbolism incorporated into every move, I'd gained a bit more respect for it. You know me, I'm a sucker for ritual and symbolism, as long as it helps me figure something out.

Now I chewed and watched intently as the tiny ringmaster paced back and forth, back and forth, scowling. He wore an elaborate long-skirted costume, and every part of it had a complicated symbolic meaning.

The *dohyo*—the ring itself—was built up from over fifty tons of dirt that had been specially selected, sanctified, then turned into an actual sculpture. The graceful, fluted roof above it was modeled after the roof of a Shinto shrine. The ring was surrounded with rice straw blessed by a Shinto priest through a dousing of sake. In Japan, there was no contradiction between the high percentages of Buddhists and the state-sanctioned religion of Shinto. Neither religion was exclusive, and more often than not, people practiced both simultaneously.

The referee waved a huge paddle and shouted, "*Nokota!*" which I had been told meant "keep fighting." And then the competing *sumotori*—the wrestlers—paused and flung something into the air above the ring.

Tess said, "Why do they do that?"

I started to answer, but Troubles beat me to it. "It's salt. They do it to drive out any evil spirits that might be lurking inside the ring."

"Weird," said Tess.

The *sumotori* stepped into the ring, and the battle of bulk began as they squared off—350 pounds on one side, over 400 on the other. They were immense, their muscle and mass almost mythical, their agility incredible. They were both naked except for loincloth-aprons, and their haunches were enormous. And both wore the distinctive top-knotted hairstyle known as *chonmage*.

They leaned into each other, straining and struggling for leverage, one of them grabbing hold of the other's belt in an attempt to torque him off balance. The four judges, sitting at the four poles of the universe—north, south, east, and west—and clad in the colors associated with each direction, remained stoic while the referee ran to and fro, watching every move. The applause and shouting from the crowd ebbed and flowed. The match would be over when a contestant was shoved over the outer boundary of the ring or when any part of his body except the soles of his feet touched the floor of the ring.

"They're supposed to be mountains," Troubles said. "Something to do with the power of nature."

I thought about that. This was news to me, but then I sure didn't know everything.

"Look, whoa, there he goes!"

And indeed, the larger of the two mountainous men had been shoved over the side to collapse down into the fringes of the crowd, which was going wild. The entire match had lasted all of twenty seconds.

The event was coming live from Tokyo. Now, two frenetic Japanese commentators in spiffy business suits came on the screen, speaking furious Japanese and making elaborate hand gestures. A score was posted, along with certain names and words in *kanji*. English subtitles translated at the bottom of the screen as the commentators excitedly rehashed the action and discussed future matches and championships and replayed segments of the contest.

I had watched the brief match intently, thinking about the immense respect with which the Japanese approached this sport—more a ritual than a sport, actually. I was also thinking about Mr. Shinda, about Takio-san, about all the intrigue of my unusual afternoon, the

Japanese mind-set, their often befuddling culture. But as the *kanji* names came on the screen, I was suddenly reminded of Mrs. Osaka. I had meant to phone her as soon as I got home. Before I decided whether or not I was going to give Victor's papers to Shinda, I was going to know what was in them—*all* of them—and hopefully she had the answer to that puzzle.

I went into my office and dialed her number, and she answered on the third ring. I greeted her, then said, "I was wondering about the translating job on Victor's papers. How's it coming?"

"Oh, Alex. I had company all day, and then the water heater broke this evening and I had to phone a plumber. It almost ruined the kitchen cabinets. I promise you, I'll get to it first thing in the morning without fail. I'll try to have it done by noon."

"That would be great," I said. "You know I appreciate you doing it at all."

We talked a moment longer, then I signed off.

I suddenly realized I was tired. My Bible lay on my bedside table. I glanced at my watch. Only ten o'clock. Still—

I brushed my teeth and washed my face and hands, then undressed and put on my yellow cotton pajamas. Yelling through the door to say good night to Troubles and Tess, I lay down on top of the bed, leaned on one elbow, and opened my Bible to 2 Peter. It's one of the most uplifting books in the Bible, and I hadn't spent enough time lately being uplifted. After my visit with Ko Shinda, Incorporated, I felt even more tangled and confused. But I couldn't blame it all on him. I always got like this if I didn't spent enough time praying and reading my Bible. I needed a spiritual fix.

But before I could finish the first chapter, I fell sound asleep, and my mind transported me back to Mr. Shinda's penthouse.

I still held my Bible tightly in my hands, trying to anchor to it. Shinda and Takio-san were both there, as were a dozen or more other men, all of them Japanese nationals, some as large as sumo wrestlers, some painfully thin and wiry. To a man, they all wore white sumo loincloths, they all had short permed hair or mid-length ponytails, and they all sported tattoos with elaborate and brilliant designs from stem to stern. They sat in various places on the roof garden, engaged in various endeavors and watching me intently. One of them pointed at my Bible and looked puzzled.

"*Konichi-wa, Alexis-san,*" said Mr. Shinda.

"*Konichi-wa, sochi*," I replied. Good afternoon, boss.

But even in my dream, I knew I was not addressing him as just any old kind of boss. No, this was the word reserved for the *oyabun no oyabun*, the top dog of all the *yakuza* gangs in Japan.

"You have been brave," he said. "You have earned your tattoos."

I shuddered. "No, thank you."

He looked genuinely puzzled. "Why do you disobey?"

I shrugged. "I don't like for people to tell me what to do."

His scowl was fearsome then. "You are a selfish person to put yourself above the common good. You must atone." He turned to Takio-san. "Bring the dagger."

I gripped my Bible harder, clutching this anchor to my own beliefs, my own culture. I didn't belong here, this wasn't supposed to be happening to me. I looked down with embarrassment as I realized I was still dressed in my tatty yellow pajamas.

Takio-san quickly returned from the kitchen holding a sharp, serrated carving knife and smiling with wicked anticipation. He handed it to me as Mr. Shinda reached out and firmly took the Bible from my left hand—I seemed powerless to stop him—and guided that hand until it was laying face up on the stone table beside him. I knew there was no point in struggling.

He handed me the knife. I took it in my right hand, inhaled and held my breath, and prepared to perform the ritual of *yubitsume*, wherein I would sever my little finger at the first knuckle, then place it in the piece of fine linen that Takio-san had thoughtfully provided along with the knife. I would then present the tip of my little finger to Shinda as atonement for refusing to obey his orders.

He smiled coldly and waited. I was bewildered by what I was doing, yet I was strangely paralyzed and unable to stop myself. I wanted to pray, but my spirit was paralyzed, too. I raised the knife, started to bring it down . . .

Chop! I awoke with a start.

I looked around and was pleased beyond measure to find myself lying on my own bed, the Bible beside me, the bedside lamp still on. I spread out my hands and looked hard. All of my fingers were intact.

I got up then. With the hypnotic sensation of sleepwalking, I was drawn out the sliding door and onto my balcony. I looked down at the street, to the place where the *yakuza* man had been killed.

It was late, and there was no traffic. The street was wet with rain. The colorful neon lights from the surrounding shops melted on the pavement into rain-shined filigrees and flowers, into dragons and giant carp and other elaborate patterns. As I watched my world reshape itself, I tried to scream, but no sound would come out of my mouth. Then a sudden furious rain began to pelt the earth. The pavement was suddenly awash, and the painted tattoos melted into a blood-red fluid that raged down the rain gutters, poured into the drain pipes. The street was scoured clean again, and a voice was calling from far away, "Alex . . . Alex . . ."

I really woke up then. I sat up straight, realizing that my Bible was indeed still beside me, though it had fallen shut. I touched my damp forehead, surprised to find that I had been sweating, and then I looked up with a start.

Troubles was standing in my bedroom doorway. His eyes were narrowed with concern. "Alex! Come on, wake up! Are you okay?"

I was groggy beyond belief, but I was honestly awake now. I sat up and shook my head, hard, trying to clear it. I mumbled, "Yeah. I guess I'm okay. I was having the strangest dream, layers of dreams, actually. A nightmare."

"You sure you're all right?"

"I'm fine." I slid my legs over the side of the bed, then realized that Troubles was trying to hand me the portable phone.

"It's Mrs. Osaka," he said. "She says she needs to talk to you."

"Whoa, boy. I hope this isn't going to be another dream."

"Wake up, Alex. She really sounds upset."

I slapped my cheeks a few times, then said into the receiver, "Alex here."

It was indeed Mrs. Osaka, and it wasn't a dream. "Alex, you'd better come right away." Her voice sounded too controlled, as if she were fighting back hysteria.

That brought me fully awake. I stood and reached for the clothing I'd peeled off and tossed over the back of an armchair. Troubles, realizing I wanted to get dressed, left the room as I said into the phone, "What's wrong?"

"Just come," she said. "Right now."

"*Who's there?*"

"No one. They've already gone."

"Are you okay?"

"Of course. But you need to come here."

I stepped into the denims, pulled them up and buttoned them while holding the portable phone under my chin. I moved the phone from one hand to the other while I quickly pulled a shirt over my head. Then I said, "*Who* was there? Shinda's thugs?"

She was silent for a moment, and when she spoke, her voice was cautious yet bright and curious, more like her old self. "Mr. Shinda has thugs?"

"He either has them, or they have him. But I guess you'd know that if they'd been to see you. So—if not them, then who? Are you in danger?"

"Of course not. But I'm worried about *you*." A tremor had found its way into her voice. She was indeed deeply upset, even though she was doing her level best to sound normal.

"What happened?"

"The authorities came. The FBI." Her voice caught. "They knew I had your papers—Victor's papers. They took them."

"*Wha-aat?*"

"Please come, Alex. Please explain this to me."

"The *FBI?*"

"Yes."

"They had a *warrant* for Victor's papers?"

"Yes."

"You sure you're okay?"

"Yes. Just come. Please."

"You sure it was the FBI?"

"Alex." She was losing her patience now. "Of course it was the FBI. I'm not a fool. I made them show me badges and then they had the warrant to search my house and take the papers."

"*You have got to be kidding me.*" Even as I said it, I realized that now *I* was the one slipping a bit.

"No, this is no joke. And I'd appreciate it very much if you could come up here and explain."

I was already at my front door, hair disheveled, portable phone in hand, car keys ready. "It'll take me about fifteen minutes to get there. Shall I phone the police and have someone check on you in the meantime?"

"There is no need for police. Mary is here. She's made tea. I really will be fine, but please come."

nd so I found myself speeding down the freeway at one A.M., rocketing past the soiled night-glitter of downtown Honolulu, taking the Pali cutoff toward the lush dark mountains, burning rubber up through the Nuuanu Valley, up to Mrs. Osaka's house.

It was a harbor of lighted windows within a thick cover of black feathery foliage, nested up against the dark, jagged background of the silent Koolaus. I screeched around to the back, parked, then sprinted up the steps and onto the lighted veranda. Mary opened the door before I could knock and stepped aside so I could go through. She was clad in a long blue robe and fuzzy slippers. She'd been watching for me, and her eyes were wide with worry.

I don't know what I'd expected: the house trashed, blood and mayhem, maybe someone with a *ninja* mask and a *samurai* sword waiting for me behind one of the immense black koa trees or just inside the door. But I made it through and into the living room without incident, and Mrs. Osaka sat on her wide rattan sofa with the peach and gray cushions, seemingly intact. She had the television tuned to the Cable News Network, which was showing a feature story about dog shows. Beside her was a basket overflowing with brightly colored yarn, and she was holding knitting needles and the beginnings of an afghan featuring pink, yellow, white, and blue squares. As I walked into the living room, she set her work down, clicked the remote to turn off the TV, then motioned for me to sit in the wide armchair across the coffee table from her.

I sat and peered at her. She was shaken but feigned composure so well that I suspected no one else would have realized the extent of her agitation. A flash of anger shot from her eyes, but she instantly masked it. "You must have driven fast."

"I did."

Her silver hair was as unruly as my own, and she had either been preparing for bed or been in bed, for she was wearing a long white cotton nightdress and a frayed pink silk robe. I looked for broken bones or blood, heaved up a prayer of thanks that she was okay, then saw the anger in her eyes melt a bit as her face skewed into a schoolteacher's stern frown. I was about to be dressed down.

"Okay," I said, "what happened?"

"If you had trusted me enough to explain the circumstances, I could at least have been prepared for them," she said, and her small jaw jutted out.

"I think you'll have to start at the beginning," I said. "I'm not following this so far."

Her frown deepened, and she studied me intently for a moment. Then she nodded, satisfied that I was truly bewildered. Only then did she relax and say, "They came at 11:15."

I squinted, puzzled at that. But I let it pass. "What did they look like?"

"There were two of them. A tall local Japanese man and a midsized *Haole* woman with light brown hair."

"And you're absolutely sure they were FBI?"

"I'm certain."

"What did they do?"

"They knocked on the door. Mary had stayed up late to read, and I had already gone to bed." Her jaw set hard as she remembered and grew angry again. For a second I had the impression that tears were about to well up in those brown-black eyes.

"It was the way they did it," she said. "Even though the young man was Japanese, it was almost like the other time. I thought I had forgotten, Alex, had gotten over it. But these things all come back so easily, I guess you never really forget."

Her voice broke then, and suddenly I realized what was really bothering her.

On December 7, 1941, at 7:57 on a sleepy Sunday morning, the Japanese had bombed Pearl Harbor Naval Base. Under the influence of the *zaibatsu* and their ultranationalist military lackeys who were trying to swallow up the Pacific Basin, 360 warplanes painted with the bright yellow-red emblem of the Rising Sun, wave after wave of them, had dropped enough explosives to level the better part of the United States Navy's entire Pacific Fleet within the brief, cataclysmic space of half an hour. The explosions had thundered and reverberated across the Hawaiian Islands, in various ways. When the planes had turned and vanished, some 3,500 people lay dead or injured, enormous aircraft carriers and other ships were sinking, their crews drowned. Everyone was in a state of shock, and by three o'clock that afternoon the Hawaiian Islands had been placed under strict martial law.

Twelve hours later, at 3:00 A.M., the FBI came to Mrs. Osaka's door—though she wasn't Mrs. Osaka yet. Four men in dark suits took her into custody. She had been astonished, then humiliated, then terrified.

"Because I was *kibei*," she had told me. We'd had the conversation about a year ago, in her backyard, after a small church barbecue. A friend of hers from the war years had recently died, and the conversation had turned to the past and the losses of the past and the things that still haunt Japanese-Hawaiians of her era.

"*Kibei* means those who went to school in Japan, then came back to Hawaii to teach or act as Buddhist priests or otherwise continue the Japanese culture," she'd explained. "The FBI agents were suspicious of all Japanese-Hawaiians, but especially of those who taught the Japanese culture and language. They thought we were sympathizers or spies for the Emperor. They had already compiled a list of us, about a thousand in all: the Buddhist priests, leaders of the local Japanese community, and of course those of us who taught at the Japanese language schools. Because yes, we taught the old customs along with the language. And some of the older people still even worshiped the Emperor as the sun god, and we all honored him, of course. But we mostly honored our U.S. president. We wanted to keep our identities, our heritage. But we wanted to be Americans too, we thought we *were* Americans. Those of us in the *nisei* generation had been born here, we had automatic citizenship, we could vote. We knew there were still hurdles to cross, but we really thought we were Americans. I remember, when I heard what the Emperor's warplanes had done, that I cried and cursed them. We had worked for so many years to be accepted here. And there it was, gone, all at once. When I think about it, I can still get angry at those dirty Japs."

It shocked me to hear that word escape from Mrs. Osaka's gentle lips.

She saw the shock and disapproval in my eyes, for she smiled sadly and said, "Such an ugly word, isn't it? But many of us felt the same way as the *Haoles* or Chinese or Filipinos or Koreans or Native Hawaiians. Oh, we honored our Japanese culture and wanted to keep the good elements of it. But Hawaii was our home, too, by then. These Japanese foreigners had bombed our home. We were angry with them too, and we called them the same ugly names that everyone else did." She smiled bitterly.

I could full well understand her feelings. I was mostly of Scottish descent, but also partly German. Americans of German descent had also been suspect during the war years, and many had been arrested back east under suspicion of spying for the Nazis. It usually bothered me to hear German people referred to as Krauts, but when that racial slur was used to describe the Nazis of the war years, the defamation bothered me not at all.

Mrs. Osaka paused for a moment, then said, "But then others started calling *us* those names. People said some of the Pearl Harbor warplanes were piloted by Japanese-Hawaiians who had defected to serve the Emperor. People said we were all spying, especially those of us who had gone back to study in Japan. They said that the bombing couldn't have happened if we hadn't helped lead the warplanes in. They searched my house for radios . . ."

That first night had been the worst for her. No one had known what to expect. Rumors were flying—that the Japanese planes were coming back to level everything on the island, that the U.S. military was going to line up all Japanese-Hawaiians before firing squads. The fires were still burning at Pearl Harbor, and people could see the smoke. Everyone was frightened of something that day, and when the night came, it was worse.

After the FBI arrested her, they took Mrs. Osaka to the immigration center, where scores of other Japanese—mostly men—were being detained. They interrogated her for hours, trying to make her confess that she had helped guide the Japanese pilots to the island. But there was no proof, of course, and in the end they let her go. They couldn't inter everybody in work camps. After all, the Japanese made up more than a third of Hawaii's population back then. They were needed to work the cane fields and otherwise continue the menial labor. The head of the FBI had also proved to be more humane than he originally seemed, for he basically trusted the Japanese-Hawaiians and had intervened on their behalf, insisting to the people in Washington, D.C. that most of them could be trusted.

Mrs. Osaka had spent the rest of the war living in fear of both the Japanese warplanes and the FBI, as had all the others rounded up in that first sweep. Under martial law, the FBI's power was absolute. They acted as an enforcement arm for the military, and their logic was sometimes irrational, for they were also caught up in the fury of the war. Mrs. Osaka and the many like her trod on eggshells during the war years, worrying each night that they might be arrested again, accused of treason, forced into the camps. Nearly 1,500 local Japanese were eventually interred, their property confiscated. Families sometimes lost track of those who were taken and thought they had been executed. The Japanese-Hawaiians—no matter their loyalties—were generally tarred with the same brush as the Japanese nationals, and deep and abiding wounds had been inflicted, wounds that still remained unhealed.

Mrs. Osaka had said occasional disparaging things about the FBI from time to time. She was an educated professional, an intelligent woman. And yet, the old feelings still remained, buried deep in the memories of the past. An unexpected visit in the middle of the night from the FBI could disturb almost anybody. But though the Japanese now controlled the better part of Island politics, though AJAs now worked for the FBI and other law enforcement agencies in a variety of capacities, though Japanese-Hawaiians sat in the U.S. House and Senate, this visit had nevertheless stirred up tiny poisonous memories that had exaggerated her feelings and fears.

"I'm really sorry," I said to her. "If I'd had the slightest idea this might happen, I'd never have given you those papers."

"I feel foolish for letting it upset me so much. But some feelings and memories just run so deep."

"I know. I have a few ghosts like that." I thought about David's death, how any mention of it made the pain suddenly new and raw again. Some feelings just didn't vanish with time. Some didn't even dim.

"Ah, Alex." I could see she was feeling better. Talking had helped. "What can we do to get your papers back?" she said.

Mary had been sitting on the far side of the sofa, listening to the conversation with a concerned look on her face. Now, she said, "We made them sign a receipt for the papers. Would you like to see it?"

"Please," I said.

She stepped to an old rolltop desk in the corner—an antique with brass fittings—and took a slip of paper from one of the tiny cubbyholes. She handed it to me.

I read it. And then I felt my face tighten.

Mrs. Osaka said, "Well?"

"This certainly complicates things."

"What do you think it means?"

"Just what it says, I guess."

I knew they'd both read it already, so I didn't bother to elucidate. The receipt was for one set of documents, written in both *kanji* and English, consisting of vital evidence in an ongoing investigation, which papers were henceforth being confiscated by the Federal Bureau of Investigation. It was signed by FBI Special Agent Frank Yoshida.

I folded the receipt and stuck it in my pocket, after getting a nod from Mrs. Osaka. Then I said, "You never got a chance to work on the *kanji* at all?"

"I'm sorry, Alex, I didn't. As you know, everything went wrong today. I had the papers on the desk there, was going to work on it first thing tomorrow." She looked at the floor, ashamed for having let me down.

"Don't worry about it," I said. "I have another copy."

Suddenly she smiled, and I saw all the tension and worry roll off her. "You'd better bring your copy back first thing in the morning," she said. "I'm beginning to agree that we need to see what's going on."

"Maybe," I said. I had already decided not to get her further involved. "You told them where you got the papers, of course?"

"I didn't have to. They didn't ask, didn't even seem interested. They just knew I had the papers. They came in with the warrant, I gave them the papers, then they left."

This was not good. Not good at all.

I quizzed her some more, but that was all she could tell me. I stayed for another hour. We had tea and talked about the FBI's visit to her home, then about other times and problems. But I was only halfheartedly engaged in the conversation. Frankly, I stayed only because I felt obligated to help put her back at ease with her world, which had been disturbed because of me.

And as we talked, in the background of everything else, one question kept rolling over and over again in my mind, shaping and reshaping itself in a thousand different ways. *How had the FBI agents known where Victor's papers were? Who could possibly have told them that Mrs. Osaka, of all people, was in possession of them?*

Finally, about three A.M., I began to burn out. I hugged Mrs. Osaka and Mary good night, then drove home—playing a jazz tape full blast to keep from dropping asleep at the wheel—and then I fell swiftly into bed.

But just as I started to slip into a troubled sleep, a sudden realization bolted me upright.

I sat and stared, wide-eyed, at the walls around me.

The room was suddenly unfamiliar, belonging to someone else. Oh, the burnished mahogany furniture was mine, the mirrors and plants, the charcoal gray carpet and gray and white drapes. The wine-striped Queen Anne armchair in the corner was mine, the creamy, pink-flocked wallpaper. The closet was mine, the clothes, the wine and white bathroom I could see through the opened door. But I realized at that moment that the world I inhabited was no longer mine. It had been invaded.

My condo is bugged, I said to myself.

No kidding, another part of me replied.

A wash of cynicism hit me. Aloud, I said, "Same song, forty-sixth verse, ain't no better and it's gonna get worse."

I stopped, slowly tapping my chin with my forefinger as I considered my predicament. I was swept through with a combination of indignation, fury, and fear. But after a long moment, the sense of indignation shoved the other feelings aside.

I squared my shoulders, jutted out my chin, and spoke directly to my walls. "Okay. I don't know who you are or what you want with me. But if that's the way it has to be, then—let the games begin!"

I sat there for a long time, thinking, watching, and listening, almost as if I expected the walls to talk back to me.

But when they didn't, I finally said, "And by the way, just for the Congressional Record, you seem to have a hole in your operation as big as the city of Tokyo. You really need to get that fixed."

ntense anger can be exhausting. After about an hour of sitting on my bed, legs crossed like chopsticks as I glared at my walls and silently fumed over what was happening, I finally adopted a fatalistic attitude, climbed beneath the covers, stretched out, then fell into a troubled, dreamless sleep.

At 7:30, after a couple of hours' tossing and turning, I rolled over and shot wide awake, suddenly certain of what I had to do.

I got up, took a quick hot shower, and dressed, and on my way out the door I grabbed a banana muffin for breakfast. A scant half hour later I was back up in Nuuanu, at the base of the jagged, volcanic Koolaus. But this time I hung a left a half mile before I reached Mrs. Osaka's street. I cruised up a roadway and steered my Honda into Jess and Yoko's wide, curving driveway, then parked right behind Jess's black Jeep Cherokee. Yoko's new white Pontiac was parked beside the garage and I didn't want to block her in, but Jess wasn't going anywhere until I had some answers.

I ascended the steps and rang the front doorbell once, twice, then leaned in on it and didn't let up. After a moment, the curtain over the tiny leaded window in the top of the door moved and an eye peered out at me, then the door quickly flew open and Yoko stood there, already immaculately groomed yet wearing a wine-red bathrobe. "Good heavens, Alex. What's wrong?"

"Plenty," I said, "is Jess home?"

"We were just finishing breakfast. Come in."

"No, thank you. I don't want to seem rude, but this is really private. I'd like to talk to Jess out here."

Yoko looked perplexed. "Of course." She turned back down the hallway, toward the kitchen.

Standing there, I could see through the open doorway and past the hall into their comfortable living room. I wondered if the techies had Jess bugged too—and if so, where the listening devices were. Surveillance agents were ingenious, the possibilities were many. I looked with a jaundiced eye at the television, the VCR, the light sockets, the electric outlets, the telephone, the track lighting, the stereo. In fact, the tiny microphones could be attached almost anywhere there was a lead-in to the electricity. That, of course, assuming the techies had the house hard-wired with tiny listening devices linked to near-invisible filaments then spliced into the wiring, so the electric current could directly power the mike and transmitter. This allowed the surveillance to continue indefinitely. As an added advantage, the bugs could be switched off and on by the surveillance agents at the point of origin, thereby complicating the possibility of detection.

The bugs were always voice activated. The transmitters emitted radio beams of a special frequency, which were normally picked up at headquarters. There, in a special, highly secured room, a large bank of reel-to-reel tapes recorded information around the clock, when an electronic surveillance was underway—which meant most if not all of the time. But the transmissions were picked up there only if the bugs were legal—that is, if a court order had been obtained before the techies—technical experts—placed them. Which wasn't always the case.

There was another way to do it, though. My mind was whirling with possibilities. If the Technies had Jess soft-wired, the bugs could be anywhere—even in the yard. But soft-wiring was used only for very short-term surveillance, since it meant finding a place to set up and conceal the recorder as well as the microphone. I was betting they had the place hard-wired—assuming they had it wired at all. Which meant the microphones would be restricted to places where there was access to electricity.

Which was why we were going to talk outside.

Just in case.

It had been a long time since I'd done a debugging job. It wasn't my specialty. But believe me, as an ex-Intelligence Analyst for a federal agency, I knew plenty about electronic surveillance and the possibilities therein. Enough to be absolutely certain that my condo was bugged, even though I hadn't yet seen the concrete evidence. But I'd hashed and rehashed everything that had happened, and there was absolutely no other way that anyone could have known that I'd taken Victor's papers to Mrs. Osaka for translation. She was the only person I'd discussed it with, first of all at her own house, then later from my condo, on the telephone—and that a scant few hours before the so-called FBI's invasion of her life and conscription of the papers. Far, far too much for coincidence. Whoever they were—FBI or not—they'd somehow heard Mrs. Osaka tell me she'd have the papers translated by noon the next day. They had apparently decided they'd better grab the papers before then. Which told me that at the very least, my phone was tapped.

It isn't all that easy to do a legal wiretap on a telephone. You have to work through the telephone company, which means you have to first of all convince a judge that the surveillance is warranted, then get the judge's signature, then present the warrant to the phone company, and so on. In a legal wiretap, everything has to be more than aboveboard because there's a paper trail all the way through it; the tapes have to be locked down and transcriptions are made of everything heard—and the only words you're supposed to listen to are those parts of the conversation relevant to what you're trying to investigate. If you get involved with anything other than that, your whole case can be tossed out of court. Tricky stuff.

On the other hand, anybody can put in an illegal phone bug these days. You hook your hidden mike up to the telephone's electricity, then leave it open so it's voice activated, phone conversations included. That way you don't have to worry about judges or warrants or the phone company or anyone except the person who's monitoring the wire—usually you or your accomplice in crime. And believe me, an illegal electronic surveillance is definitely a crime. Last time I checked, it was a Class C felony—a major offense that could land you some heavy prison time.

I had my detector and debugging equipment locked in a private storage area in the basement of my building, along with a number of other things I seldom used. My first instinct after realizing what was going on had been to storm down there and retrieve it, then sweep every square foot of my condo/office until I found the bug or bugs.

I wanted the satisfaction of stomping into my bathroom, dropping the devices into the toilet, and flushing emphatically.

But Tess had stayed late, watching TV, and had decided to spend the night. So she'd been sleeping serenely on the sofa in my darkened living room. The last thing I wanted to do was have her awaken in the middle of the night to find me, wild-eyed, wandering around with a weird electronic device, probing into all the nooks and crannies of my condo. I didn't want her to think I was losing my mind, of course. But even more importantly, I didn't want to explain to her that the whole place was probably bugged. I would have to tell Troubles sooner or later, of course. To keep the surveillance secret would make me an accomplice in the violation of his privacy. But that would have to wait until later. In the meantime, since I already knew beyond doubt that my condo/office was bugged, my best bet was to find out who wanted to listen to me—and *why*.

After a brief moment, Jess came down the hallway, dressed in a white T-shirt and worn gray cotton cords. His dark eyebrows were fixed in a puzzled frown, but before he had a chance to say anything to me—I hadn't forgotten our last meeting—I held up the palm of my hand to stop him. "Look, Jess," I said, "maybe you're still angry with me, maybe not. But we have to talk."

His face was unreadable for a moment, then he seemed to resign himself to the fact of my presence, and his muscular shoulders slumped. "You don't give up, do you Alex?"

I leveled a steely look at him and squared my jaw.

He spread his hands wide, in a simulated gesture of truce, and almost smiled. "Okay, okay. What's up?"

I jerked my thumb toward the backyard.

"Look, come on in, have some coffee . . ."

"Outside," I said. "In the back."

He looked puzzled and annoyed. But he came outside and shut the door behind him.

The minute the door was shut, I said, "Someone has me bugged."

His eyes narrowed; his body wrapped up tight.

"Yeah, I know," I said, watching him. "It has something to do with Victor's papers, doesn't it?"

He didn't say anything, just stared hard at me with depthless eyes.

"Do you have anything to do with it, Jess?"

He looked like I'd hit him. "No. Why would you think. . . ?"

"Then is there any indication they also have you bugged?"

He really frowned then, but his eyes radiated a keen intelligence, and I could see him mentally scanning his circumstances. After a moment, he said, "I don't think so. No. Why would anyone want to bug me?"

"I've been asking myself the same question," I said. "Anyway, I'm in the middle of it, and I don't even know what 'it' is. I think it's time you talked to me."

He nodded to himself, thinking, then finally said, "I guess I don't have much choice, do I? Come on."

We went around the side of the house, along a flagstoned path that took us into the beautiful backyard that Jess's parents had begun and now he and Yoko continued to improve. There was the Japanese garden, of course. Smaller than Mrs. Osaka's, but far more regal. The garden was a sign of status for all Japanese-Hawaiians of a certain age, for only the aristocracy in Japan had been able to afford such treasures. The wide lawn was well manicured, and it sloped up to meet the tangle of ferns and shrubs and trees that blanketed the lower slopes of the Koolaus. I knew that Jess found comfort—and a place to do his deep thinking—by coming out here and sitting cross-legged on the grass and manicuring the yard with long garden shears into its perfect, even length. There was a small stream—those who lived on the lower slopes of the lush Koolaus were blessed with such luxuries—and a small *koi* pond that David and I had helped to build during weekend gatherings several years ago. Jess had stocked the pond with prize carp—flashes, now, of orange, gold, and black brilliance darting beneath the placid green water. Lotus leaves emerged from the water in clusters, displaying an occasional snowy blossom. As I watched, a brilliant petal spiraled down from the flowering golden-shower trees to be caught in a tiny eddy as the fish churned the water. There was a fresh-mown, minty scent to the scene—perhaps wafting from Yoko's small herb garden beneath the kitchen window. And near the edge of the yard were the regal, black-barked plum trees.

It was cool this morning. The cloud cover snagged on the upper Koolaus manifested itself here as a misty fog that laced the treetops and hung in shreds off the lower shrubs. The grass was damp with dew. I was glad I'd worn my hooded gray sweatshirt. We sat on the white wooden lawn furniture beneath the sheltering plum trees. The stream rushed past with the runoff from last night's rain.

Jess looked at me, shook his head hopelessly, and said, "I tried to stop you, Alex. But you just don't stop, once you lock your jaws onto something. You remind me of a moray eel."

I didn't know if that was a compliment or an insult. The morays are famous for locking their teeth into people, then the person's flesh has to be cut away, or the eel's head has to be cut off, because the moray's jaws just don't open up again.

"Jess," I said. "I need to know what you did with Victor's papers—the ones I gave you."

He bowed his head, then rubbed his forehead hard with the heel of his well-tended hand. "This really isn't your business, Alex. Go home and stay out of it, and it will blow over for you. If you keep going the way you are, you're going to get hurt."

That surprised me. I said, "By you?"

His head shot up, and he looked astonished. "Of course not!"

"Well—you can't blame me for wondering. I feel like I don't even know you anymore. The way you acted that day after lunch, when I gave you Victor's papers—"

"I was trying to keep you out of it. I figured that maybe if I was unpleasant enough, you'd go away and leave me alone." He actually smiled then. It was nice to see the crinkle of his eyes, the even, white teeth—the old Jess. "I should have known better," he said.

"I didn't go looking for this, Jess. I told you, Miro Ochinko phoned me—I'm sure it was him. He was on his way to see me about something—probably the papers—when he was killed."

"When he was *murdered*," Jess corrected me.

I studied him closely. "I hear you're catching a little flack for sticking to that line of reasoning."

"Who told you that?"

"Derrick Green."

Disapproval swept across his face. "Are you seeing Green?"

"Not really. I run into him once in a while, and I naturally asked about you after I read in the paper you'd been suspended. He says Alton didn't like you investigating the *yakuza* man's death as a murder. Is that true?"

"That's about the size of it. But Alex, has it crossed your stubborn mind that *if* Ochinko was murdered—and I'm convinced he was—then it was almost certainly because of what was in those papers?"

"That had occurred to me," I said dryly.

"I put the papers in my safe," he said.

"Aha. Withholding evidence in a possible homicide."

He shot me an amused look, remembering the words he'd hurled at me the day I'd given him the papers. "I figured if you could get away with it, so could I."

"Did you have the *kanji* translated?"

"No. No one's seen any of the papers but me. No one *will* till the timing is right."

"And you don't read *kanji*," I said, "so we don't really know what's in that part of the papers."

"I can make an educated guess."

"Jess—" I hated to admit the truth since we were just beginning to get along again. But I had no other choice. Slowly, I said, "I made a copy of the papers before I gave them to you. I figured I had a right to know what was in them."

He shot me a long-suffering look, then shook his head in resignation. "Just how bad does this get?"

I told him, then, about taking the papers to Mrs. Osaka for translation.

"Get them back, Alex. Bring them to me and leave this alone."

"I can't. A couple of people claiming to be from the FBI confiscated the papers from Mrs. Osaka last night. That's how I figured out that my condo was bugged."

The starch melted right out of him at that, leaving him deflated. He thought for a moment, shaking his head hopelessly, then he looked up. "What do you mean, *claimed* to be from the FBI?"

"Just what I said. There are some other things going on here that make me wonder. Mrs. Osaka is certain they were FBI, but I didn't see them and I trust nothing until I've seen the evidence with my own eyes. Besides, the receipt they left was handwritten on a sheet of Mrs. Osaka's paper. No letterhead."

"If it wasn't the FBI, then who?"

"There are several possibilities. For one thing, they could have been from the Hawaii State Police," I said. "I thought it might tie into your suspension, somehow. I saw on the news that the van driver—Sonny Malinta—is still missing."

"He is."

"What do you think happened to him?"

Jess looked sick. "He may be dead."

"In other words, he did see somebody shove Ochinko in front of his van. He was apparently the only witness, and when he got out of jail, that same somebody shut him up for good?"

"I'm praying that isn't true. I'm hoping he had the good sense to go into hiding."

"I'm sorry, Jess."

"I wasn't responsible for getting him out."

"I wondered when I read the newspaper. It didn't sound like something you'd do. Was that a setup?" I asked.

"It was. Alton is a political appointee, I'm sure you know that. He's a high-powered commercial real estate broker who lobbied for the office of Police Commissioner to add a little status to his resume. Unfortunately, he got the job. He sent down the papers that won the release, then blamed it on me."

"But—why?"

"Good question, one I've spent the past few days trying to answer."

"Any luck?"

"Not yet."

"Nail him, Jess."

He gave me a grim, determined stare. "I will, if he doesn't nail me first."

"Well," I said, mulling over all this new information, "you're full of surprises today. I thought that even though the papers belonged to Victor and dealt with his project, you had probably turned them over to HSP as part of the investigation into Miro Ochinko's death. That's what you indicated you were going to do when I gave you the papers, remember?"

"I guess I did at that. Anyway, whatever happened, it all boils down to the fact that the whole thing is going to explode in my face, and there's not a thing I can do about it. Except, of course, make sure you don't get caught in the blast."

I had never seen Jess like this before. He was a fighter, a leader, everyone else looked up to him for common sense and strength. Now, he seemed dejected, even fatalistic.

I said, "Jess, let me help. That's all I really want to do."

"I can't, Alex. It's too dangerous. Besides, I'm a long way from understanding this one myself."

"Why don't you start by telling me what you *have* figured out. I can throw in my two cents' worth, and maybe it will actually add up to something."

He smiled, though it was a thin smile. "It's cold out here this morning. Let me grab a jacket and some hot coffee. Want some?"

I shook my head no.

He stood up. "Wait right here."

He went through the back door of the house. I sat there, arms wrapped around myself against the chilled air, and thought about all that was happening. Jess came back, carrying two steaming white mugs, despite my declining his offer of coffee. I asked, "What if it really was the FBI who took the papers? Would that mean they were also investigating Miro Ochinko's death?"

He looked puzzled for a moment. "I can't really answer that. You know the feds. There are probably a lot of agencies looking into this one. The FBI's Organized Crime Task Force would have an interest, just because the man was *yakuza*. And since Ochinko had a record with the Japanese National Police, U.S. Immigration is trying to figure out why Los Angeles Customs didn't double check his visa—he came to Hawaii via L.A., you know, and sailed right through Customs. That's pretty suspect. But so far as I know, HSP still has the case, and it's still being called an accident." He handed me one of the mugs. "Here. Hot chocolate."

"Thanks," I said, using the mug to warm my hands. I took a sip, then said, "If the FBI *is* getting into it, maybe they'll dig up some evidence that will help you."

"If the FBI gets into it, I'm history," Jess said. His eyes turned to flint.

"Why? If they step in, Alton won't be able to shove things under the rug, you can prove Ochinko was murdered—if he was—and the truth will come out."

"I'm not so sure I want the truth to come out anymore," he said.

I was silent for a moment. Then I said, "It's Shinda, isn't it?"

He looked at me sharply. "You really *have* been busy."

I told him then about Shinda sending his chauffeur to pick me up. I told him about the cold eyed, immaculately groomed Japanese national named Takio.

As I said Takio's name, Jess let out a long, low whistle then started peering at me as if I was under a magnifying glass.

"You know him?" I said.

"I know who he is. Tell me everything, every word."

I tried to remember every detail. I studied Jess's reactions as I told him about Shinda's attempted bribe, about his request that I intervene to convince Jess that he needed to serve the Shinda Corporation's interests. As I talked, Jess's face went through the full range of emotion, from indignation to rage to disgust.

When I finished talking, he fell into a morose silence. The tension in his body was palpable, harboring an impending fire-storm.

I waited, silently, for a respectable time. Then I said, "There's no easy way to ask this, Jess. But I have to know. What about Victor? This whole thing started to spin out of control when he died. Do you think his death might have been something other than it seemed?"

I almost winced at the sudden flood of sorrow that poured into Jess's face.

But he braced himself and said, "I wondered too. Victor had been in some serious financial trouble. When the economy bottomed out in Japan, Victor and other Hawaiian developers got left holding the bag."

"I know," I said. "A lot of commercial property in the Islands plummeted in value, and everyone was scrambling to cover their losses."

"Right. Anyway, Victor's problems really started when Anne's father died a year ago. The banks in Tokyo were already freezing up their money and calling in loans. The more speculative the project, the more precarious the loan, the faster it was called in. Victor was a gambler through and through. Anne's father cushioned him a lot. But when Anne's father died and Anne's uncle, Ko Shinda, stepped in to handle the Tokyo side of the Shinda Corporation's affairs, the banks in Tokyo started putting serious pressure on the Hawaii side of the operations. Which meant the pressure landed squarely on Victor."

"But I thought Ko Shinda was rich-on-rich."

"He is. But from his point of view, he's not rich enough. Anyway, it's not really the money with people like him. It's the power. Money matters only because it buys him power."

"It gets to be an addiction, doesn't it?"

"One that can destroy you just as fast as any other addiction. But it gets even worse. Appearances are always deceiving when it comes to high finance. The money in the Shinda Corporation doesn't all belong to the family. You don't get that far that fast without making some connections. Certain stockholders hold a sword over the corporation. When the corporation started losing money, Ko Shinda started feeling some serious heat from them. He passed the heat on to Victor by forcing him to take a smaller share of the Golden Palms project."

"How?"

"He pulled the backstage strings that translated into the Bank of Oahu pulling out of their loan obligations to Golden Palms. That all but stopped the project, and it put Victor in pretty bad shape. Ko Shinda then offered Victor alternative financing—in return for about three-quarters of Victor's share of the project."

"In other words, Shinda was legally ripping Victor off," I said.

"That's about it."

"But—do you think Ko Shinda had anything to do with Victor's death?"

"In a nutshell, yes. But was it murder? No. Not technically. You know Victor—at least, you're bound to know the rumors. He drank, fooled around on Anne—all the things a prosperous Japanese businessman is supposed to do."

I felt a disapproving frown furl my face. "That's not fair, Jess. I know a lot of Japanese men who are faithful unto death to their wives and families and who never touch a drop."

"I'm talking about Japanese nationals. Victor was impressed by them. Anne's family never thought he was quite good enough, and he wanted to be accepted by them. So he tried to outshine them at everything they did. I don't have to tell you that Japanese culture condones—even encourages—heavy drinking and infidelity. The wife stays home and tends the children, the mistresses or bar hostesses or whatever exist for the purpose of tending to the husband. It's one of the things about my native culture I'm not very proud of, but that's the way it is. I talked to Victor, tried to help him get straightened out—" He shook his head, and I could see an irrational guilt welling up.

I cut it off. "Okay. So Victor fooled around."

"Constantly. He was out every night, drinking, dining, wheeling and dealing, and otherwise wrecking his health. No, the heart attack was for real. I checked it out in every possible way, from the doctors who took care of him to the coroner's reports. But the stress of the Golden Palms situation definitely accelerated Victor's heart attack, and Shinda definitely played a part in causing that stress."

"How much money did Victor actually lose?"

"The dust hasn't settled yet. But some of his private investments seem pretty solid, if they're not wrapped up in the Golden Palms. Hard to tell so far. If they aren't, on the books I've inherited about a million, Anne stands to gain a little over a million, and there's half a million each in trust funds for the two boys—that's all before taxes, of course. But the investments that involve the Shinda Corporation run into the tens—maybe hundreds—of millions, and a good chunk of that is wrapped up in the Golden Palms. Unfortunately, the speculative developments were begun near the end of the boom-bust cycle instead of catching the wave. The Shinda Corporation really took a bath. From what I can figure out, the properties are currently worth less than fifty cents on the dollar, and that's a lot of yen down the drain."

It was. I remembered what I had read in Fran Li's office—that in the past few years, Japanese investors had lost more than twenty billion dollars in California and Hawaii. Several massive developments on Oahu were sitting half built. Prime real estate had been cleared all over the island—lots that had formerly held quaint ramshackle houses and older apartment hotels, places where the lower-income Hawaiian residents of all ethnic makeups had lived. The intention had been to replace these older, locally-owned buildings with brand new Japanese-backed hotels and condos and office towers that catered to the high-end tourists and wealthier Islanders. Now the lots stood empty because the development money had dried up, and a whole new segment of Hawaii's lower-income people had been dispossessed.

The developments that had actually been built weren't faring much better. Hotels that had been developed at a cost of six hundred million dollars were on the auction block for two to three hundred million dollars and weren't finding any takers at that. Some of the really big projects were currently losing up to forty million a year, and no matter how mammoth a corporation is, not many can take a hit of that size.

"What's the deal with the Golden Palms?" I said.

"It was Victor's pet project. He went to his father-in-law for backing. By the time Japan's economic bubble burst, Anne's father and Victor had already dropped a bundle into the project. But they were getting things put together when Anne's father suddenly died."

"How did he die?" I asked.

"An accident, outside Tokyo."

I rolled my eyes.

"No," Jess said, "nothing suspicious there. It was a train derailment. A car hit his limo, such a freak accident that no one could possibly have staged it."

"And so Victor ended up in trouble?"

"During the chaos of settling the estate and separating his affairs from his father-in-law's interests, Victor ended up getting a few payments behind at the Bank of Oahu. Apparently, from what I saw in the papers you gave me, that—along with the pressure coming from Tokyo—gave the Bank of Oahu the excuse they needed to bow out. Still, new backing immediately came through, from the Wakizaka Bank Syndicate in Tokyo."

"The Wakizaka Bank Syndicate?" I said.

"Right. That was all clearly spelled out in Victor's papers too, wasn't it? In the process of saving his *okole*"—his tail end—"Victor made some serious compromises. I'm not sure whether or not he realized just how serious at the time. But Ko Shinda certainly knew what he was doing because he'd been personally involved with these people for years . . ."

Jess abruptly stopped talking. He turned to appraise me, as if he was taking my full measure, wondering just how much more he should say.

I said it for him. "*Yakuza*."

He gave me a heavy-lidded look. "So you've figured it out."

"It didn't take a genius. After all, it was the death of a *yakuza* soldier that got me involved."

"Well, Victor became very distant from me right after his father-in-law died. And he really started drinking, harder than ever. And carousing. Looking back, I think he was eaten alive with shame when he had to really take a look at what he'd been doing. In spite of everything, Victor was basically a decent person. He just saw a chance to get ahead, and he wanted it so desperately that he started to compromise."

"It's always so easy for these things to snowball out of control."

"Exactly. Anne's father shielded Victor from the truth of what was happening with the Shinda Corporation's shareholders for years. I didn't have a clue. But Ko Shinda doesn't shield anyone. From what I understand, he was always the one who worked the dirtiest of the deals. He wants his full pound of flesh everywhere he can get it. So when Ko Shinda took over, Victor had to look at the truth. Apparently, he couldn't live with it."

I was thinking hard. The Wakizaka Bank Syndicate no doubt featured some of the same shareholders as the Shinda Corporation— people who were straw men for Japan's crime syndicate. I thought about my theory that drug money had built parts of Victor's empire. I had been right on target.

I said, "And Takio. The man who picked me up yesterday. Who is he?"

Jess's eyes went flat and dead. He grew very still. "He's someone you really don't want to mess with, Alex. Believe me. Even Ko Shinda jumps when he calls. And if he's here in Hawaii, you can bet your bottom dollar that something heavy is going on. Something heavy enough that if any part of it rolls over on you, you're going to end up a statistic."

Jess settled back with his still-hot coffee. His face was stiff with worry. He took a sip, then carefully set the mug on the white wooden table beside him and put his head in his hands.

The cold sun was climbing high up in the sky. The mists were shredding apart and wafting away. But behind them, high atop the jagged Koolaus, new storm clouds were massing. I stood, bracing myself against the chill, and set my mug down. I then leaned forward and gently touched Jess's arm. "I'll be in touch, Jess. We'll pray about this . . . It will all work out."

But as I climbed back in my car, I wasn't so sure. I shivered, then turned my heater on against the cold, damp day. As we'd talked, I had felt a growing sense of dread. And the feeling wasn't going away.

CHAPTER 17

When I got home, Troubles and Tess were both at class. I used the opportunity to go down to the storage area in the basement and rummage around until I found my dusty black bug sniffer. I carried it back up the elevator—wrapped in its scuffed black leather case, of course, and buried inside a paper shopping bag.

But the truth of the matter was, if my eavesdroppers were willing to shoot the moon, they could bug me with impunity anyway. Today, listening devices came in such sophisticated high tech wrappings that many were virtually undetectable.

Take, for instance, the methods that true spies use. I had recently read that Chinese spies had bugged the highly secured Soviet embassy in Beijing for decades, hearing all the whispered words inside the most secretive rooms, and this without a single trace of electricity, no mikes, nothing. When the Chinese built the embassy, they erected specially formed chimneys made from highly acoustic clay in the main buildings. These had transmitted all sound outward. The Chinese had then dug tunnels to channel the sound to a point near the edge of the embassy compound, where they set up listening posts under the guise of posting courtesy guards. The building itself was the bugging device: a huge acoustical microphone. The chimneys and tunnels were the transmitters! Ingenious—and a technology far and away beyond the scope of my expertise.

The Russians in turn did quite a job on the U.S. embassy in Moscow, though they used more conventional techniques. The U.S. State Department had foolishly allowed the Soviets to precast all the concrete and girders for the new edifice and to participate in other phases of construction. Just as the new three-hundred-million-dollar brick embassy was finished, tests revealed that the building was literally riddled with electronic surveillance devices: bugs in the steel girders, bugs in the concrete walls, bugs in the very rafters and floors. And even though the KGB had thawed out and had given the CIA detailed diagrams showing where the thousands of bugs had been planted, the CIA still hadn't managed to clean up the new embassy enough to be able to move in, even after all these years.

As long ago as 1952, the Soviets had bugged the U.S. Ambassador's Moscow office by putting a cavity resonator inside the Great Seal of the United States that hung on his wall. It worked by bouncing back microwave beams sent out from the building across the street. The Soviets knew every word that was said in the office until one brilliant debugger figured it all out and hacked the seal to pieces.

Modern surveillance technology is even more complicated. One technique utilizes the electromagnetic waves emitted by ordinary light bulbs to transport sound waves; so common is this technique that the CIA stations and U.S. embassies around the world have long since changed to fluorescent lighting. And then there is the method of picking up the acoustical waves that are reverberated by window-panes and whatever, so that you don't need a mike at all, just a listening point and the proper resonance and receiving equipment.

Well, that level of spy-craft was way out of my league. But I did know my way around the rank and file bugging devices used by most law enforcement agencies in order to catch the bad guys. That's Surveillance 101 these days, since about half the world seems to be spying on one another at any given time. Husbands want to know what their wives are up to, wives spy on their husbands. Kids spy on parents, parents spy on kids, employers check up on employees, salespeople target customers, and so on. Believe me, these days the smallest part of electronic surveillance is done by law enforcement agencies.

Consider industrial espionage. That's the *really* big game. International wars are increasingly fought in the boardroom rather than on the battle field. Plant a bug at any corporate headquarters so it will transmit the incoming faxes or computer data on to you, and you've most likely tapped into a gold mine, if you want to peddle what you learn. Statisticians say that some 37 percent of all U.S. firms have at one time or another been the target of industrial spies. Most of the companies don't even want to admit it, lest they incur the wrath of their stockholders. But a good investigator who wants to work the world of industrial espionage will get all the work she wants, no matter which side of the fence she wants to sit on, and a large part of her work will be planting and detecting bugs.

Furthermore, in the world of covert listening, any amateur can apply. All you have to do is order your gadgets from one of the many catalogues or stores that offer up spy technology to anyone who has the price of the game. There are infrared cameras for less than five hundred dollars, with lenses that fit inside a pinhole. You can film your friend or spouse in their most intimate moments, even in the dark. There are voice-activated wireless gadgets as cheap as $39.95, that will turn a telephone into a room-monitoring device. The accompanying pickup system will run you around two hundred dollars, not much more than your average tape recorder. If you really want to get serious about the game, you can buy voice curtains to mask your conversations behind white noise or scramblers that will turn the words to static. If you're sitting on the other end of the wiretap, you can buy descramblers and penetrators that will make all your opponent's efforts futile, or you can purchase an electronic voice changer that will let you call up your prey and worry them a bit. If you want a little protection on your end of the line, you can set up a system that will give you a digital read-out of your caller's phone number while simultaneously patching his voice into a computer that will measure the stress-level of the caller's voice, thereby indicating whether the caller is lying to you or is otherwise under stress. The technology of surveillance is amazing.

My own little bug sniffer was an RTB3-900, designed to find hidden transmitters in rooms, walls, or on the telephone line. It was a small black box with a sensitivity dial on it, a silent red-light alert, and an antenna similar to that of a Geiger counter. It had a twenty-step solid-state meter that indicated signal strength, so you could hone in on the bug. I had paid 1,800 dollars for it through a law enforcement supply service, and it was a good deal at twice the price.

I pulled it out of the bag I'd used to transport it upstairs, then checked the batteries, which were worn out, of course. I replaced them and went to work probing and scanning and sniffing. Two hours later, I'd discovered a raisin-sized mike hard-wired into my

VCR; another, smaller one in the antique phone on my teakwood office desk; one hard-wired into an electric outlet in my bedroom; and yet another one hard-wired into the electric socket beside the cherry-red wall phone in my white, red-accented kitchen. Between the four of them, they just about covered the condo.

I went out onto my balcony then. I scanned the small fig trees, the peach and tangerine bougainvillea that sheltered my balcony wall; I looked for filaments that might run from the electric outlets to my potted torch ginger, my jade vines, and the flowering, potted poinciana beside my umbrella table. I checked the lounge chair and even the telescope. The balcony came up clean.

Back inside, I plopped down onto the living room sofa, folded my arms, and glared at my cream-colored walls. I was silently furious. I wanted to rip the bugs out, toss them over the balcony railing to the street eight stories below, then find the people who'd invaded my privacy and rip off their faces.

But if I tore out the bugs, I was never going to know who those people were. And the more I thought about it, the more I realized that I really did need to know who wanted to listen to my every word. At very *least*, I needed to know that.

The bugs had something to do with the *yakuza* soldier's death and with Victor's papers; I knew that much. Nothing else made sense. But the more I thought about the rest of it, the more confusing everything became.

In retrospect, Ko Shinda had seemed to know way too much about what was going on in my life. He hadn't come right out and said enough to make me certain, but he'd coiled around me like smoke, mentioning Victor's affairs, talking about Jess's reluctance to "honor" his obligations to the Shinda Corporation. I recalled the sensation I felt as I was talking to him, a sudden heavy weight descending on me. Had my unconscious mind—or more likely my guardian angel—been trying to tell me that there was more to the conversation than mere coincidence?

And then there had been that sudden thrust, when Shinda mentioned the missing papers. The timing had been impeccable, almost rehearsed. Far too much for mere coincidence, as if he knew I had them. How could he have known that? I shut my eyes, and again saw that knowing look Shinda had shot to Takio-san while he'd been putting me together. And in that moment I realized that I had been sitting in this very room, discussing my possession of Victor's papers with Troubles for the first time—only hours before the limo had pulled up beside me.

Maybe my listeners were Japanese nationals instead of American cops or feds. But if that was true, how long had they been listening to me, and why? Had my phone already been tapped when Miro Ochinko called and told me he was on his way? Had they overheard him and intercepted him before he could get here?

That didn't make sense. There would have been no reason for anyone to be interested in me back then. Before the day of Victor's funeral, Mr. Shinda and his thugs hadn't even known I existed. Even after that, there was certainly no reason for them to have bugged my quarters.

But there was also no reason for the FBI to have been interested in me before Miro Ochinko was killed. No reason since then, either—at least, no reason that they should have been aware of. But the bugs were the same type the techies had used when I was an Intelligence Analyst for drug enforcement. And the installation was A-1; no doubt about it, the operation had the fingerprints of the FBI all over it.

Suddenly I felt suffocated. I needed to get out of there, to be able to think. I went into my bedroom, changed into my black, old-fashioned bathing suit, grabbed my beachmat and the latest copy of my weekly news magazine—I hadn't had a chance to read it yet—dropped that and my sunscreen into my beachbag, then went into the kitchen. It was after two P.M., and Troubles would be home from class soon. I left him a note, in monster lettering, that said: GONE TO BEACH: COME IMMEDIATELY. URGENT!, then stuck it to the fridge with the dolphin-shaped magnet.

He'd go straight to the fridge the minute he walked in the door. And he'd know exactly where to find me.

Half an hour later, I felt a cube of ice hit my sun-baked back. I rolled over, scowling, and looked up at Troubles, who was standing there in his baggy orange and purple swim trunks, his blonde hair tousled, a paper cup in his hand and a grin on his face.

"I forget," I said. "Did the name Troubles stick because you had so many troubles, or because you caused so many?"

"Both," he said proudly. He dropped onto the sand beside me. "Okay. What's so urgent?"

"I felt an urgent need to get out of the house," I said.

"Let's rent kayaks and catch some waves." He was gazing wistfully out beyond the shallows to where the surfers were catching four-foot sets.

"No." I sat up and adjusted my sunglasses. "I want to tell you something."

"Okay. Tell me something, and *then* we'll rent kayaks."

"Rick," I said, using his given name. "It looks like we're going to have some unwanted visitors for a while."

He frowned, surprised at my sudden seriousness. "Who?"

I told him then, though I toned it down a bit. I explained that the FBI was probably interested in me because of some evidence I'd stumbled across during an investigation and that they'd placed bugs in our living quarters. I told him I wasn't sure exactly who was listening to us or exactly what they wanted, but I assured him the situation should last only a few days, till I had it all straightened out.

He looked at me with a growing expression of concern, and when I had finished explaining, he said, "You know, Alex, we've been studying paranoia in my abnormal psychology class . . ."

"Don't bother," I said. "I know the symptoms."

And I did. I'd thought about the possibility that I was losing it ever since I'd first decided I was bugged. After all, thinking that someone is listening to you or watching you is the first step into that distorted delusional system, and most serious paranoids believe that they have transmitters or receivers in their teeth, or that they're being monitored by aliens, or that the CIA or FBI is living in the walls of their house and beaming voices to them, or something equally weird.

According to the text books, the basic characteristics of the paranoid were free-floating hostility, unwarranted suspiciousness, projective thinking—that is, projecting your thoughts onto someone else, assuming that because you were angry, they were; because you were afraid, they were; because you were interested in something, they were. Paranoids also became obsessively self-involved and felt generally threatened. And most of all, they felt that they were the center of the world's attention; therefore, their every thought and act became the object of nefarious interest for those invisible beings who watched them.

"Believe me," I said, "I considered the possibility that I was getting paranoid. But I can assure you, the fillings in my teeth aren't exactly picking up messages from UFOs. I found the bugs. Real miniature mikes. I'll show you when we get home."

"Let's go," he said eagerly.

I began to gather up my things. "You can't let them know I've told you," I said. "Everything goes on just as normal. But—if you'd like to move into a hotel for a while, or stay with a friend, I'd understand. It's a lot of pressure having to think about what you're doing or saying every moment of the day."

He looked hurt. "I wouldn't leave you there by yourself."

"I'd be okay. I'd rather have you stay home, of course. It's just that we'll have to be really careful."

He thought about that, then his face crumpled into an expression of defiance. "Ah, nuts to them. If they want to live with us, they have to take what they get. Come on, I've never seen a real bugging device before."

I laughed. "That's the spirit."

But as we passed the pay phone in our lobby, I said, "Just a sec. I want to touch base with Jess, and I don't want to use our phones."

Troubles nodded, understanding. "I'll grab the afternoon paper," he said, turning toward the machine on the corner.

I dialed Jess; he was home. He said, "Alex. I was just getting ready to call you. Can you talk?"

"I'm at a pay phone. What's up?"

"I need to fly over to the Big Island tonight. I've been going back through Victor's papers again, and there's a lot in here about the Golden Sands project, Victor's smaller hotel in Kona. I want to ask the General Manager there a couple of questions, things I can't get answered by phone, and I just learned that he's leaving tomorrow for a two-week vacation on Guam."

"Jess, excuse me for a minute, but I forgot to mention something last time we talked. I stopped by Ed Grappner's office on an impulse the other day and annoyed him a bit. And while I was there, I saw a letter from Alton's real estate agency on his desk. Do you suppose there's a link there that might help you make sense of some of this?"

He was silent for a long moment, then he said, "It's worth a thought."

"Okay, I just wanted to make sure I didn't forget to tell you again. Now, you're going to the Big Island? What can I do?"

"I was wondering if you'd mind bringing your bug detector up here to check out my house. I don't think anything is wrong, but in light of what's happening to you, I'd rather be sure. And—would you like to stay here tonight, with Yoko?"

"You think someone might try to hurt her?"

"Not really. It's just that she's feeling the ripple effects of my stress, and she's pretty edgy. She's used to having me here, and with the kids on the mainland she really feels alone when I'm gone. Plus, I thought that you might like a break from the pressure, you know."

"I found the bugs, Jess." I told him where they were and the type.

"Sound like federal issue," he said.

I agreed. "Okay if I bring Troubles along?" I asked.

"Of course."

"Tell Yoko I'll be by about six, that I'll bring some take-out Chinese for dinner."

"I'll let her know. And Alex?"

"Yes?"

"Thank you. A lot. I'm sorry about my misguided rudeness to you that day. You really are a true friend."

❖

Tess's father was a chiropractor of long standing in the Islands. He'd recently treated himself to a brand new Hobiecat, and while I was throwing a few things into an overnight bag, he phoned to invite Troubles for a weekend sail. Troubles decided he'd rather spend the weekend with Tess than with me—surprise—and so I ended up visiting Yoko by myself.

When I got to her house, I didn't want to alarm her, so I left my bug sniffer in my overnight bag while we sat at the kitchen table and used simple wooden chopsticks to eat the Chinese food, and talked.

Yoko told me that Anne was still crying most of the time. She was still sitting the wake. Yoko was deeply concerned about her. "The family isn't close, you know. A lot of very wealthy families are that way. I believe the uncle is still here, handling Victor's business affairs, but the rest of them immediately flew back to Japan."

I didn't say a word.

She talked next about Jess's suspension, and I gently pried, trying to get a fresh perspective on the situation. But I didn't learn much. She'd been aware for some time that there were unpleasant politics going on with regard to the HSP, but she had every confidence in Jess. She didn't really understand everything that was happening; Jess was overprotective of her when it came to his work. But she knew he would tell her what she needed to know, in his own time.

At half past midnight, when Yoko had gone to bed and I was sure she was sound asleep, I rolled out of my bed in the guest room, took my bug sniffer out of my bag, and went to work scouring the house, missing—believe me—absolutely nothing. I worked my way past the family photographs on the mantle, through Yoko's collection of antique laquered fans and glass-cased Japanese dolls, through the silver in the teakwood hutch, through the overflowing bookshelves and past the upright piano, around the wide verandas and through the utility room. I probed every nook and cranny of the old-fashioned kitchen, the bookcases and desk in Jess's study, the dining room and sewing room and all the other rooms. I especially checked the areas where there were telephones.

I found nothing. Their house was absolutely clean.

I returned to the guest room, just off the back patio, and climbed back between the soft pink sheets. To unwind, I read several chapters from the book of Psalms—Yoko kept a Bible on the bedside table—then I finally turned off the light and fell into a restless sleep.

About three A.M., the rains came. They sliced into the mountains with a fury, and—suddenly wide awake—I heard a muffled crash. I pulled back the curtain. A rain-veiled yard light faintly illuminated the plum trees, which shivered and cowered against the deluge. I could see that a wind-shaved frond had fallen from a palm tree in the backyard and crashed against the house. The stream that ran down the mountain had become a small, rushing torrent.

I thought at first that the rain had awakened me. I lay in bed and listened as it pounded like a waterfall onto the roof. I found the sound rather pleasant. But suddenly, I thought about the prize carp in the backyard pool that David and I had helped to build. What if the dam wasn't holding?

I got up. In spite of the storm, enough light came through the window for me to be able to feel my way around. Yoko's bedroom was in an alcove at an angle from this guest bedroom. If her drapes were open, she might be awakened if I turned on the light, so I left it off. But I didn't want Jess's beautiful carp to wash downstream.

It was only when I opened the back door and the cold rain hit me in the face, bringing me fully awake, that I realized something more than the storm had awakened me. I was almost felled by the heavy, unfocused feeling that something was dreadfully wrong. As I looked out into the rain-soaked night, I was washed through by a vast, suffocating sensation of evil. Yet I wasn't concerned that an intruder had awakened me. No, this was a cosmic evil, something far more dangerous than mere mortal flesh and blood and bones.

I didn't switch on the big yard light. Instead, relying on the smaller yard light and distant street lamps, I edged my way past the baby's breath that Yoko had planted beside the stream—getting drenched in the process—and found the edge of the rock wall that formed the dam. Anxiously, I felt the edge. For some reason, I needed to actually touch it, feel its solidity, in the same way I use to awaken in the night and reach out to touch David's shoulder, just to make sure he was there. The dam was holding just fine. I wasn't sure I could say the same about me.

Aware of the threatening, rain-misted shapes around me, I made my way back to the house, closed and locked the back door, then tiptoed back to my room. Only then did I finally turn on a small, bedside light. I used a fluffy bathtowel from the adjacent bathroom to dry my hair, then stepped out of my damp pajamas, dried my shivering body, and pulled on my thick terry cloth bathrobe. I climbed between the still-warm sheets, then reached over and switched off the lamp, pitching the room into darkness. But as I nestled down, listening to the rain and trying to fall back asleep, I slowly realized why I'd awakened with such a sense of dread.

I had been dreaming about David.

About death.

Now, as I approached that state that welds consciousness to sleeping, the dream came drifting back.

Chopsticks to chopsticks, chopsticks to chopsticks, Anne stood passing charred bones and teeth along the gauntlet. Except it wasn't Anne now, it was me. The sallow-faced addict-dealer who had shot David dead was passing David's charred bones to me, chopsticks to chopsticks, and I was passing the fragments of David's bones on to Jess, who was inspecting them carefully before passing them on to Mrs. Osaka, who was passing them on to Mr. Shinda, who placed them with impatient distaste, into a brass urn. Takio-san stood in the background, arms folded, smiling a grim, knowing smile.

The dream shot me up straight, trembling. I turned on the bedside light. And I knew in that instant that the imagery had been more than an ordinary dream, that in that semi-waking moment my world had been flooded with an evil that was beyond my comprehension and reckoning, beyond my ability to transcend.

This evil was called death. It was omnipresent, inevitable, waiting like a sinister, gleeful essence to swallow us all. It was the nightmares of childhood, the stuff of horror movies and horror books, the blood on the vampire's teeth, the shroud of the ghoul, the hand sticking out of the grave at midnight, the decay and suffering and the separation that made you bleed with sorrow for the rest of your life.

Even the very knowledge of death was a prison—an oppression, a mental coffin from which you never escaped.

I prayed, silently, desperately, trying to shake the oppressive feeling. I picked up the Bible and read several more chapters of the Psalms. Still, in spite of King David's beautiful words, in spite of the paeans of praise, the grim, gnawing impression of impending death stayed with me for a very long time, till the sky began to show the faint silken gray of a damp false dawn.

But finally, at the end of an intense prayer, a vestige of peace descended and I fell asleep again. This time, I didn't dream. In fact, I didn't even awaken until Yoko knocked on my door, black hair already brushed to a sheen and make-up carefully applied. She was clad in a snow-white satin bathrobe with pink silk piping.

"Sorry to bother you, Alex. But I thought you might want some breakfast before church."

I rubbed my eyes. "It's Sunday?"

"Yes." She smiled. "We have to rush, I'm directing the choir."

"I had forgotten what day it was," I mumbled.

"Well, I'm here to remind you."

Though I was exhausted from my night's misadventures, I climbed out of bed, showered, then borrowed a trim gray blouse and mid-calf skirt from Yoko. We shared some microwaved waffles and sausage, then we drove her white Pontiac down the hillside and into the overflowing parking lot of our church.

hurch was just what I needed. Yoko had taught music before her children were born, and under her skilled direction the choir's performance was contemporary and uplifting, the styles ranging from resounding black gospel to Bach. The small church orchestra was getting better every week, and Pastor Mike preached a joy-filled sermon on Christ's love that dissolved every vestige of the night rains and nightmares.

Troubles and Tess were still at her father's beach house on the North Shore, sailing. They'd most likely attend the small grass-roots church up in Haliewa. But Mrs. Osaka sat in the pew in front of Yoko and me. She was in the company of her ninety-year-old gentleman friend, Yoshi Tanaka, a spry and keenly intelligent kindred spirit. Mary sat to one side, with her daughter and son-in-law. Other friends were there as well, and it was nice to see smiling, normal faces. After the service, I chatted with Mrs. Osaka for a moment, careful to steer clear of the subject of the FBI's recent invasion into her life.

Yoko and I had lunch at the Ti-Leaf, a family-style restaurant up in Kaimuki. I had planned to go home after that, but over our grilled opakapaka and Maui onion salad we started talking some more, catching up, and after dinner I continued to enjoy her sparkling humor.

So when we arrived back at her house, I phoned home and punched in my code number to retrieve my messages, just in case anything was happening that required my attention. Derrick had phoned four times, sounding petulant because I wasn't returning his calls. His attitude made me decide not to return these calls either. One of Troubles' friends had also phoned to ask for class notes, and that was it, home free.

Yoko and I spent the rest of the afternoon and evening noshing on almond cookies, drinking tea, talking like teenagers, and working on an elaborate and colorful Hawaiian quilt Yoko had started over a year ago. Our church was featuring a three-week-long seminar on rearing children—a subject that neither Yoko nor I felt relevant to our own lives—so we weren't going back to the evening service. Instead, we enjoyed the serene day, the peaceful setting: a rare vacation for me.

But as the sky turned dusky and began to envelop the hillside, as the city lights beneath us began to slowly twinkle on, I suddenly realized I'd had enough serenity. I was ready for some serious chaos.

Just as I was preparing to leave, Jess phoned from the airport and asked Yoko to come pick him up. Though I wanted to find out what he'd learned on the Big Island, it could wait until tomorrow. I embraced Yoko and thanked her for her hospitality; then I climbed into my Honda and sped back down into the coldly glittering city.

It's amazing how quickly the bugs take over your life. The instant I unlocked the door and stepped into my office, I was aware of their presence. Remembering my recent intruder, I switched on lights as I went, carefully examining all the rooms to make sure I was alone. Then I went in and changed into a baggy pair of khaki slacks and a matching multipocketed safari shirt. Finally, just to reassure myself that I really hadn't slipped into a state of paranoia, I checked to make sure that all three mikes were still in place, still active.

They were. And I don't know what possessed me at that moment. Perhaps the sermon I'd heard that morning had spun me into a particularly heady and carefree mood, or perhaps the long, comfortable visit with Yoko had revived my good humor. At any rate, for some reason I sat down on my living room sofa, put my feet up on the coffee table, and addressed the mike inside the VCR.

"Hi, bug-people. Looks like you've decided to spend some time with me. I can't exactly say you're welcome, but I'm not all that sure you're unwelcome, either. The truth of the matter is, I won't be sure *how* I feel about you until I know who you are and what you want from me. So—why don't we do this the easy way? You phone me and introduce yourselves, then tell me what you want and I'll see what I can do to comply." I told them my phone number then—as if they wouldn't already have it—and added, "Call anytime. If I'm not here you can leave a message."

My spontaneous speech gave me the illusion of being at least somewhat in control of things again. At any rate, it took the vast, ephemeral evil I'd been associating with the bugs and reduced it down to something I could actually deal with. That alone made me feel a whole lot better.

But not good enough. I still wasn't comfortable in my own home.

Still, I knew that the feds rarely considered a surveillance important enough to actually put live, round-the-clock listeners on the wire. That was an expensive operation, reserved for top-level investigations into mob bosses and other major criminal enterprise. It was expensive, tied up a lot of manpower, and therefore required clearance all the way to the top. I knew my federal bureaucracies well enough to know that no one was going to stick their neck out far enough to authorize an investigation of that scope in order to eavesdrop on poor little me.

Therefore, I knew the bugs would almost certainly relay my words to the reel-to-reels downtown, where they would sit as electronic imprints until the word processors pulled the tapes Monday morning and transcribed them; or—if something really hot was going on—until the surveillance agents pulled the tapes and played them. But even though I understood the time delays, I still felt as if someone was watching me.

It was an irritable, restless feeling that stayed with me while I tidied up the kitchen, while I searched the near empty refrigerator for something to eat. Finally, just to scratch the itch, I grabbed my handbag, turned off all but a couple of lights, locked up the condo, and went for a walk.

Waikiki is a mile-and-a-half long, quarter-mile wide swath of hotels, restaurants, boutiques, condos, apartments, churches, cinemas, parks, shopping bazaars, T-shirt stands, street peddlers, office towers, videogame rooms, cocktail bars, *karaoke* bars, gun clubs (where Japanese tourists can fire handguns at targets, handguns being illegal in Japan); and an occasional cubbyhole porno shop, where soul-suckers stand in curtained doorways and beckon and the outside come-ons are written almost exclusively in *kanji*.

Waikiki makes up a world within the larger world of the city and county of Honolulu. Waikiki itself harbors only some twenty thousand full-time residents, yet a million or more tourists roll through here every year. Certain promotional literature would have you believe that it is the number one tourist destination in all the world, and perhaps it is. The seaward, or *makai* side of Waikiki is bordered by Waikiki Beach—which, in turn, is broken into various sub-beaches: Kuhio, San Souci, and so on. The *mauka*, or mountainward boundary is the long, man-made sweep of the Ala Wai canal, beyond which lies a wide golf course, a wide residential area, and then the serrated, lush-green Koolau mountains. Lengthwise, Waikiki is bounded on one end by the extinct volcanic tuff cone known as Diamond Head, on the other by the region where the land narrows and the canal pours into the sea.

Kalakaua and Kuhio Avenues are the main streets, running the length of Waikiki. The hundreds of stores that line these avenues are open till ten or eleven P.M., even on Sunday night. They glitter with various beguiling kinds of light and offer elaborate window displays filled with a bewildering variety of goods: eelskin handbags, Asian cloisonné, gold jewelry, sequined baseball caps, windup hula dolls, shell plant hangers, wind chimes, plastic leis, wooden tikis, conch shells, and every other variety of tourist schlock. There are also the better stores, where you can pick up platinum wristwatches, rare pink diamonds at a hundred thousand dollars a carat, fifteen-hundred-dollar Italian leather handbags, clothing and accessories from all the major designers, rare perfumes, expensive golf bags and clubs, and other exotic and special purchases. In these better stores, the clerks almost always speak Japanese—some *only* Japanese—and the advertisements are often written in *kanji*, with English subtitles, rather than the other way around.

That Sunday night, all the stores and the wide tree-lined sidewalks in front of them teemed with tourists of every nationality. There were Swedes with finespun hair and sunburned skin, California girls in cut-offs and tank tops, couples from America's Heartland in muu-muus and matching shirts. There were Filipinos, Koreans, Chinese, Guamanians, Australians, New Zealanders, Europeans—the list is a long one. But a goodly number of the tourists, as usual, were Japanese nationals.

The Japanese nationals came in couples, in clusters, and in large tour groups. They came as pairs of youngsters wearing grungy clothes with backpacks; as elegant women attired in sleek black Pierre Cardin knits, Ferragamo pumps, tasteful gold and diamond jewelry; they arrived as businessmen clad in elegantly understated sports coats or golfing shirts or brand new aloha shirts and razor-creased slacks. There was the occasional young couple pushing a baby stroller; the preteens wearing the Japanese version of rapster and gang-banger attire, oversized baseball caps with the bill turned to the back, sloppy shirts and baggy pants and affected street-ghetto mannerisms that amused rather than offended, in their naïveté. I was brushing past simple Japanese shop girls; past teachers, businessmen, housewives, and others who were here as part of their well-earned corporate benefits, or because they'd saved up for years, or even because they'd gotten filthy rich by capitalizing on the trade imbalance.

But whatever else I was doing, I was most likely *not* brushing shoulders with any members of the Japanese *yakuza*. In fact, the rank-and-file Japanese national had about as much in common with Japan's *yakuza* as I did with La Cosa Nostra or the Chinese Tongs.

On any given day, some 5,000 Japanese nationals were likely to arrive through the gates at Honolulu National Airport. Only a very small fraction of these even resembled the *yakuza* profile, and the Immigration service nailed only a few actual *yakuza* every year for trying to enter on visas that hid their criminal history.

Unfortunately, those few created some bad *nichibei* indeed in Hawaii-Japanese relations. In short, it caused the fear of the old "yellow peril" to rear up its ugly, racist head as Hawaii's citizens became aware that Asian criminals with nefarious intent were seriously trying to infiltrate Hawaii and subvert our lives, our hopes and dreams. The fact that the *zaibatsu* mentality of many massive Japanese corporations was fascist in and of itself, that the *yakuza* gangs often served as enforcers for these corporations, further complicated the issue. Hawaii desperately needed Japanese investment and Japanese visitors. But the bad *nichibei* caused by the few predators too often tarred the perception of others who arrived from Japan—normal people doing normal things, wanting to enjoy the trade winds and swaying palms and roaring surf in an atmosphere that allowed them their human dignity—which they well deserved.

Well, for the most part, Hawaii *was* grateful for the Japanese yen. Most of the Japanese investors were honest businessmen who followed the rules and helped fuel Hawaii's economy. Japanese tourists spent almost twice as much money per day as did the other tourists, and their money fueled the tax base, created and sustained jobs, and otherwise benefitted Hawaii's economy. Furthermore, the Japanese tourists were for the most part courteous, exceptionally well-groomed, and easily entertained.

Oh, sometimes they irritated me. I realized this was because their patterns of behavior were marginally different from my own. They would cluster in the aisles of the supermarket and fail to let you pass, or they'd cluster together when boarding the bus, then stop for what seemed like no reason, clogging the doorway. They tended to look right through you, as if you didn't exist—a disconcerting mannerism that was in truth a coping strategy for living in a society so overpopulated that people were forced to live nearly on top of one another. And more often than not, when I was walking down the street, one of the men would light up and blindly blow gusts of cigarette smoke into my personal breathing space—but that obnoxious behavior certainly wasn't restricted to the Japanese.

But the real source of my occasional discomfort around Japanese nationals was far more easily explained. They were a people who emphasized the good of the group over the needs of the individual, and that ran contrary to my lone-wolf nature. Not that I'm indifferent to the needs of others, but I'm just not the sort of person who is ever going to travel with a group, and I frankly don't fully understand those who can. There is a weight of conformity there, an absence of spontaneity that automatically makes me want to start fighting my way out of jail. And yes, it is a cultural rather than racial bias. Because my Japanese-Hawaiian friends are, by contrast, spontaneous and every bit as independent as I am. For good or bad, they're Americanized, and I'm as comfortable with them as with my own family. So my small beef is not with the people—the race, if you will. It's with certain aspects of the Japanese culture. Especially that subculture known as the *yakuza*—Japanese organized crime. And even there, my dislike is focused on certain behaviors that transcend race: drug dealing, murder, and extortion among them.

With that exception and in spite of my small discomforts, I enjoyed the Japanese presence: the children with their wide, dark eyes and snowflake skin, the occasional Old Country grannies clad in kimonos and shuffling along, the elegant, modern youngsters in their Calvin Klein or Pierre Cardin clothing, the constant light of curiosity in their eyes, the chopping buzz and lilt of Japanese conversation. I liked the ebb and flow of being around a people different from myself, and it pleased me that an occasional small courtesy was enough to grease the social wheel and keep us all flowing smoothly past one another.

And so I strolled along Kalakaua Avenue, brushing shoulders with the various peoples of the world, mulling over the intricacies of the Japanese presence and my relationship to it. As the night grew deeper, the lights became garish and the street traffic thickened: the usual montage of taxis, pickup trucks, tour buses, city buses, mopeds, bicycles, and occasional limousines jockeyed for positions in turn lanes and at turnouts. I kept a close eye on the limos, especially the black ones. I wasn't about to let Ko Shinda's cronies slip up on me again.

I was wondering, too, why Shinda hadn't phoned or otherwise shown up. After all, it had been two days now since I'd had my command performance with him. He'd said then that he'd contact me the following morning, to see whether or not I'd decided to sell my soul. Yet since then, not a peep from him.

Well, that was fine by me. My soul was spoken for anyway, thanks be to God. And I didn't have anything more to say to Ko Shinda and Corporation.

I was passing a store that sold silk and cotton T-shirts and coordinated slacks. Expensive, but the fabric and fit were beautiful, and I'd had my eye on a mint green outfit in the window for a while now. On an impulse, I went inside and tried it on. It fit perfectly, and I put it on my credit card, waited while they wrapped it, then tucked the package inside my oversized handbag.

That put me in a shopping mood. Not that I usually buy much in Waikiki. Even though I live here, I live on a budget like everyone else, and other parts of the Island offer far more in the way of shopping— at least, as far as prices go. Troubles and I made an occasional trip to the big discount stores on the outskirts of the city to buy household and cleaning supplies, and I did a fair amount of my grocery shopping in the health food markets up by the university. But on a rare occasion, I found myself in the mood to go out and look at "stuff," and this was one of those nights.

I wasn't really interested in the objects I examined and appraised and invariably put back on the shelf, though. I was practicing the ritual known as shopping as something to do with myself while I thought and mulled over all that was happening in my life. And as I was trying on a dazzling blue topaz ring, complete with diamond accents and a thousand percent markup over the wholesale, I came to the conclusion that I needed to peel myself away from the swirl of trouble that seemed to surround Victor's papers at least enough to get back to work on the other investigations that I was supposed to be conducting. No matter what else was happening, my life had been knocked out of orbit ever since Miro Ochinko's death. I needed to regain control of my life.

I handed the ring back to the shop clerk, wandered out of the store, and thought, now, about work. Fran Li's client—Sally Freedman—had apparently won her child custody case by default. That went without saying, since Fran hadn't phoned to ask me to gather any more evidence against the husband. But even though I didn't like the way that case was turning out, I should have at least phoned Fran as a courtesy, to make sure she didn't need my services. Furthermore, she owed me a check, and in order to get it I was going to have to sit down and do my time sheets. Boring. I also had another case I needed to take care of. I'd been looking for a missing witness to an industrial accident and hadn't been able to turn up anything at all. Now, I needed to at least tie off the case and write up my report for Matt Goldstein, the lawyer who had requisitioned the work, so he could take the next step, whatever that might be.

These thoughts led me into and through a bookstore, where I bought a news magazine and the Sunday paper. That put me next door to the International Marketplace, with its profusion of trinkets and T-shirts and tropical glitz. I walked past the $100,000 per stall carts heaped with tourist treasure, and to the Food Court, with its many windows opening onto the various foods of the world. I stopped off at the kiosk operated by Chan, my newfound friend from Hong Kong. He squeezed me a glass of fresh, frothy grapefruit-apple juice and asked after my health. Before I could answer him, he fell into a frenzy trying to fill the orders of a dozen customers who had suddenly swirled up.

I sat down at one of the white tables beneath the wide, green awning. I was in the no-smoking section, beside the trees and the narrow alleyway. On the other side of the alley was the double row of slope-roofed vending kiosks they call Duke's Lane. Fairy lights dangled from the trees above the carts, in the shapes of sailboats, stars, a half moon, and other fantasies. Even though the economy was suffering and tourism was down, the carnival-like bazaar was overflowing with shoulder-to-shoulder shoppers looking for bargains.

I watched the crowd for a while, as I sipped my juice. Then I opened my Sunday paper. I had just locked onto an interesting article about the possibility, once again, of trade wars with Japan when I heard the short, low growl of a siren. I looked up to see a blue-and-white crawling along the alley. The cop had hit his siren briefly, to warn a tour bus to move out of his way so he could pass through the narrow lane. I glanced in the direction he was headed. There was a small commotion near the street. I finished off my juice, refolded my paper, then stood up and walked down to see what was going on.

As you already know, there are street people in Waikiki, as in every other city in the world. There are people who eat out of dumpsters, people who beg at the back doors of restaurants and grocery stores for their food. You see some of them in the daytime, of course. But they all seem to come out of the shadows as soon as the sun goes down. Then, in an enterprising variety of ways, they begin to work the fringes of the constant hustle that is the nighttime carnival of Waikiki. Though shelter and food is available to most of them through social agencies and churches, a scattered few are missed by every safety net because they either don't or won't fit in. Some you get to know by sight or reputation, the way I knew the man named Snake, the one I'd seen rummaging in trash cans the day I'd discovered Victor's papers inside a briefcase. Others, you see around for years and years, and you get to know them a bit better.

Such a person was Kenny Dexter, another street person who had been a snitch for my husband, David. After David's death, Kenny had approached me and offered his sincere sympathy. Then one day he'd pigeonholed me as I was leaving my building and had asked if I'd like to buy some interesting information. It was obvious that he was broke and hungry, so I'd paid him twenty bucks and he'd told me about a pair of paint-sniffers who had taken up temporary residence beneath a downtown bridge and who were stealing cameras from tourists' cars. I'd pretended the information was useful.

I still bought information from him now and again. Most of it was equally useless to me, just an excuse to help him out. And I'd taken him to church with me a few times, hoping that it might make a difference in his life. He'd gone, reluctantly, but he had never responded, and he soon learned to avoid me on weekends.

Now, to my immense surprise, I realized that the commotion at the end of the alley centered around him. Although he was almost hidden in a cluster of uniformed cops, there was no mistaking that shock of gray hair or that abrasive voice.

As I approached, the police uniforms divided like the Red Sea waters and suddenly there he was, his dirty gray hair disheveled as if he'd been fighting, his sinewy arms sticking out of a sleeveless red-striped tank top above a pair of cut-off denims that showed his short, bowed, gray-haired legs. Unlike most of the homeless, he kept himself up, and his clothing was passable. But even from my distance I could see a look of vile hatred on his nut-brown face. With good reason. Two cops towered over him, and a young blonde cop wearing an expression of steely determination was locking a pair of handcuffs on his bony, extended wrists.

Kenny is a man of extremes. I've heard him called *lolo*, which is the Hawaiian word for nuts. I knew that he had indeed been in and out of the State Hospital at Kaneohe, mostly because of recurring problems with various types of drugs. But the people who perceived Kenny as mental were making a big mistake. Because Kenny was a brilliant man during his lucid hours. Too brilliant. He was easily bored, and like a lot of small-time criminals, he thrived on intrigue and longed for bigger things.

Unfortunately, he's not above creating intrigues just to stir up some action and make himself seem important, so you can't always trust what he tells you. Once he'd tried to convince me that an elderly Italian man was a Mafia thug from the mainland, here to do a hit. I checked it out and quickly learned beyond any doubt that the man was a doctor from Duluth, a devout Catholic who was here on a short vacation with his wife and two grandkids. Well, like I said, you can't always trust Kenny. His tall tales could add up to tall trouble. But at that moment I could at least trust my eyes, which told me that Kenny was on his way to the slammer. The small swirling storm of trouble that seemed to constantly surround and energize him had tripped him up once again.

I was standing at the stoplight across the street. He spotted me at the same time I spotted him. He leaned forward, squinting to make sure it was me, then shouted, "Hey!"

The blonde cop had him cuffed now and was carefully steering him toward the open back door of a blue and white transport car. I didn't know whether or not I should respond to the shout.

But Kenny wasn't going to let me get away. "Hey!" He shouted again. "Come down and bail me out!"

The cops all turned to look at me.

I struck a nonchalant pose for their benefit. The light changed to green just then, so I crossed the street and joined the fun. The cops were all young, probably on the force no more than a year or two. Which was good because that meant they had no reason to know or remember me. The blonde one had just helped Kenny into the squad car and was standing erect again, rolling his eyes to heaven for the benefit of his scowling comrades.

I stepped up to him. "What did he do?"

"Shoplifting. Tried to take a bottle of Cutty Sark." He nodded toward the small convenience store beside us. I could see the shelves of liquor through the window and was now aware that a pudgy Vietnamese man in his fifties, probably the store's owner, was standing beside the wall, watching with judicious glee.

I said, "How long to get the paperwork processed?"

"It's been a busy night," the cop said. His shoulders sagged to emphasize the point. "Probably be at least midnight before we get him processed through."

"Bail?"

"Depends on his priors. You can call Booking in an hour or so, they'll be able to tell you more."

And then he looked at me, really seemed to see me for the first time, and surprise smoothed out his face and caused his white eyebrows to shoot up above his bleached blue eyes. "You know this guy?"

"He's an old friend," I said.

The young cop looked even more surprised, and for some reason it irritated me.

"He's been having some hard times lately," I explained.

"I guess so. This is the third time this week we've hauled him in. You ought to let him stew for a while, might teach him something."

"It might," I said.

Throughout this conversation, Kenny had been sitting in the back of the transport car, window down, listening. Now, the cop behind the steering wheel turned the key and the ignition caught. I stepped to the back window, which was still rolled down and covered with wide mesh. Up close, I could see that Kenny's eyes were blank from exhaustion and drink, and there was also a tiny trace of shame there. I told him not to worry, that I'd do what I could to make bail. He managed a skeptical smile, muttered a thanks, and then the car rolled away.

On my way home, I stopped at the bank machine and took out a couple of hundred dollars. Bail would have to be paid in cash.

CHAPTER 19

When I got home, Troubles was sitting in the living room, kicked back and gnawing on pretzels as he watched a movie about giant ants crashing through the jungle and attacking some people in a canoe.

I watched for a few minutes, and asked him how his weekend had gone; he said splendidly. I went into my office and phoned HPD Booking. They told me Kenny wasn't processed yet, to phone back in an hour. I went back and watched some more of the movie, interested in a analytical sort of way. Troubles and I discussed the 1950s monster movies, the techniques by which they made the miniatures, how they made the ants move, and so on. We were both aware of the electronic bugs in our walls. Our conversation seemed stilted, as we carefully skirted the subject of electronic surveillance in all its many aspects.

Finally, I phoned Booking again to learn that Kenny couldn't be bailed out until after four A.M., for some bureaucratic reason. I went to bed then and read till well past midnight. And then I fell asleep.

My alarm went off at four on the dot. I groaned, stretched, then rolled over and hit the redial on my portable phone. Apparently the rush had died down because the HPD's booking room answered on the first ring. Yes, Kenny Dexter had been processed through. His bail was set at three hundred dollars. I got up, stepped into my new green shirt and slacks, knocked on Troubles' door to tell him where I was going, and took off.

Though Waikiki has a small HPD substation—the one I occasionally spy on from my balcony—the booking room, jail, and main offices are at the central station downtown, on Beretania.

The booking room was large. The holding cells were just off the receiving area, the taffy-colored bars separating those who offend from the rest of us. In an adjacent open office area, a dozen or so men and women of all ages, shapes, cultural backgrounds, and sizes were pecking away at computer keyboards, or filing reports, or staring worriedly at papers, processing the paperwork that plagues bureaucracy. Vice cops and narcs were coming and going through the corridors, some wearing disguises that looked incongruous in these hallowed halls, though I knew they'd look right at home on the street. Some were even cracking jokes. No rats here—this was a brand new building. No one screaming as someone worked him over with a rubber hose. I've seen uglier police stations—uglier cops, for that matter.

"You want this in your name or the subject's?" I had peeled off the three hundred cash, and now the clerk was shoving some papers at me for my signature.

I thought for a moment. If Kenny showed up in court, he'd get the money back. That might be an incentive for him to do the right thing. If I got the receipt in my name, I'd have to accompany him to court in order to get the money back anyway—a nuisance I didn't want to commit myself to. Either way, if he didn't show up in court, I wasn't going to see this money again. Might as well try to encourage him to do the right thing. I had them put the receipt in his name.

Finally, after we'd signed all the papers, Kenny was sitting in the passenger seat of my car, and we were riding home from downtown. It was that tarnished, gauzy predawn hour when the sky is melting from black to gray and all the revelers and skilled predators have slipped back into their holes, for the most part. The only people in the streets during these hours are the ever-present cops, the die-hard party animals, and the transvestites and other hookers, rejection permanently etched into their various faces. Most of the hookers are doing hard time here in the streets. They carry their drug habits and sexual enslavement around like weighty bundles that eternally bow them down.

We were passing through the area of Waikiki where several bars, restaurants, and shops make up a nexus for the gay community. They were shut up tight now, but the neon lights still burned. I said, "Where do you want to go?"

Kenny held up his hand like a traffic cop. "Stop!"

I hit the brakes and rolled to the curb. "What?"

"There."

He pointed to the closed, darkened doorway of a bar. A person slept there, hidden by shadow, no blanket, not even his own hands beneath his head, just stretched out cold on the concrete. I felt a wave of despair.

I climbed out of the car with Kenny and checked the man. He was still breathing, at least, and the instant I'd stepped out of the car, the sickly sweet smell of vomited wine made me nauseous. I stepped back, suddenly angered by the waste. Here was that most amazing of all miracles, the human brain, lying besotted by alcohol—and who knew what else—against the cold concrete.

"I could phone the HPD," I said. "They could put him in jail to sleep it off."

Kenny shot me a disapproving frown. "Yeah, and he may not know anyone to bail him out." He hunkered down then. He took one of the man's hands in his own—the nails were black with filth—and astonished me speechless by bowing his head in prayer. I prayed too then, silently. Something about the situation seemed staged and surreal.

Kenny crouched beside the man, then lifted his head up and cradled it. The stench grew more pronounced, but Kenny didn't seem to notice it. Suddenly the man's eyes opened, and he smiled and slowly shook himself awake.

Kenny seemed to know the man. I asked what we could do for him, but the man shook his head again and staggered to his feet. He told us he was going to walk the two blocks to the nearby homeless shelter and refused my offer of a ride. It was almost daylight by then, and I was beginning to get a serious headache, so I didn't argue.

When Kenny and I climbed back into the car, I said, "You surprised me. I wasn't aware that you had such a kind heart."

He looked at me and started to say something, but he stopped himself short. His eyes suddenly grew dark and evil, like those of a cornered wild animal, and the hard street hustler was back in his bony face. I'd seen the paradox in him before, when he felt threatened, but the transformation was so swift this time, so intense, that it fully startled me and I felt myself shrink back from him.

He turned to look full at me then, and a craftiness came into his eyes. "I could make money off of you."

"Perhaps. Or I could just help you out. How much do you need?"

He thought, then smiled wolfishly. I didn't like the smile a bit. He said, "A lot."

"I don't have a lot."

He appraised me, and I saw the street hustler melt right off him as he softened. "Then twenty. You already bailed me out, just twenty so I can get some food."

I negotiated a traffic light while I rummaged in my handbag and pulled out a twenty-dollar bill. I handed it to him and said, "Kenny, please don't spend it on booze. I can't stand to see my money used to destroy people. Feed yourself with it, something healthy. Please."

He pocketed it, furtively. When you live in the streets, you learn to be furtive with money. Then he said, "I wouldn't really make money off of you. Not if I had to hurt you to do it. But I got something to tell you that might be worth the three hundred."

"The three hundred is so you'll show up in court and get some of your stuff straightened out," I said. "Why don't you let me get you into Habilitat?" This was the local rehab center, run by an ex-junkie who knew every hustle in the books. It was, in fact, one of the few rehabilitation programs in the nation that worked, and their doors were always open.

"They'd just put me in the state hospital. I ain't going back there. You want to let me work off the three hundred?"

"I don't know, Kenny. That's a lot of money. I'm willing to invest it in you, but I'd like to see you get straightened out."

"This information is worth three hundred." He nodded his head to encourage me.

"Okay, tell me, then I'll decide."

He swung his head around to look at me, and there was an awful, dark knowledge in his eyes. His voice dropped to almost a whisper, and it was tight with fear as he said, "They're going to kill you."

The words shocked me. I laughed in disbelief. "*Who's* going to kill me?"

My laughter seemed to insult him. "Dunno, exactly. But there's an open contract out on you."

"*Who would want me dead?*" The situation seemed to get more surreal by the moment.

"The *yakuza*, maybe."

I felt myself grow cold. How on earth would Kenny know I had any involvement with the *yakuza*? Or did he know? Probably not. He was probably just making a lucky guess. He'd probably heard about Miro Ochinko being run down in the street in front of my building. But why mention the *yakuza*? If he was just guessing, why go halfway around the world to find a villain, why not pick on some homegrown criminal? There were plenty of them . . .

But my mind was suddenly racing. Who had I told about finding the briefcase? Mrs. Osaka, Jess, and Troubles. None of them would have talked to anyone about it, not even Jess—especially not Jess. Would he?

What if Jess had inadvertently mentioned something to someone and it had gotten back to Kenny? That bit of information would have found fertile soil in Kenny's darkly creative brain. He could easily transform that scrap of information into a mad scenario in which some *yakuza* capo put out a contract on me and *yakuza* hit men stalked me. This was the way the world looked to Kenny, during his darker moods: half television drama, half street paranoia, and all life-or-death threat. But would Jess have talked to anyone who might—even accidentally—leak this kind of information back to the street level? Not on your life.

So how did Kenny know I had any involvement with the *yakuza*? What if he really had heard something? The coconut wireless—that constantly busy word-of-mouth communications network—was especially active at the street level. It constantly amazed me what the street people knew and heard. What if the *yakuza* really had put a contract out on me? What if Shinda and Takio had decided I was in the way of something they were doing?

I felt a chill wind blow in off the ocean, carrying with it the scent of ancient ghosts, the wailing of ancient and alien intrigues. I actually shivered.

Kenny was watching me through slitted eyes. He had shrunk back to lean against the car door. "What about the three hundred?"

"You'll have to do better than that. Where did you hear this?"

He snorted derisively.

"Then at least be more specific. *Who* wants to kill me?"

I had just stopped at a red light, and in that instant, he jerked open the car door and stepped out.

"Wait," I said. "I'll take you—"

"If God really was in charge like you say, things would be a whole lot different," Kenny said. He slammed the car door, hard.

And then a perversity seemed to overtake him. He stomped off, cursing, loudly threatening to kill anyone who had ever gotten him busted or otherwise rolled over him. He reached a row of garbage cans and kicked one, toppling it over with a renewed curse and a clang, sending the lid rolling off down the street, then he kicked another.

I sat in my car long after the light had turned green and watched him, thinking that the forces of darkness and light seem to do stronger battle within him than they do within most of us. He was in worse shape by far than the last time I'd talked to him. The drugs and booze were taking their toll. I wanted to drive after him, ask him more questions. But though I'd never seen him quite this bad before, I'd seen him in similar moods. I knew better than to interfere. These rages of his were what caused people to call him *lolo*, and confronting him at this moment would be a sure recipe for a barrage of curses or maybe even a physical attack. I shouldn't have gotten him out of jail. He'd never hurt anyone yet, so far as I knew, but there were reasons that he got busted so often. He really needed help.

As he walked off into the distance, shoulders hunched in anger, an early morning traveler pulled up behind me and honked, reminding me that the light was still green. I pulled away, turned down Kuhio, and headed toward home. And as I passed through the silent, tarnished streets, I reminded myself that Kenny was a professional liar who said whatever was necessary to get what he wanted. He'd wanted my three hundred dollars. He hadn't realized that he already had it, if only he'd go to court and get his problems straightened out.

Well—I wasn't going to worry about what he'd said. He'd pulled the *yakuza* up out of the hat of villains he used to threaten people; next time it would be the Mafia or the CIA. I shook my head, chiding myself. He'd just been working me, and it *had* worked. He had me nervous. His street sense was intact, even if his common sense was not.

When I got home, I brewed a cup of carob tea, carried it into my bedroom, changed into pajamas, and crawled into bed. But I lay awake for a long time. I was still thinking hard about what Kenny had said.

ess and I had arranged a signal that allowed us to communicate without tipping off the bugs. At seven the next evening, the phone rang four times, stopped ringing, rang twice, then again stopped. The first four rings told me that Jess needed to talk to me, the double ring at the end meant he was at home.

I grabbed my keys, then rode down to the lobby and stuck a quarter in a pay phone. When I had Jess on the line, he said, "I just got a call from a friend at HSP. There's been a homicide at an apartment over on Mango Lane. A man was shot once in the back of the head with a .22, looks like a professional hit. From the description, I'm guessing the victim is Sonny Malinta."

I got a sick, sinking feeling. "What can I do?"

"I can't show my face right now. Maybe you could just go down there, see what you can pick up by watching and listening?"

I agreed, and he gave me the address. I hung up and went back upstairs. I had finally slept off the feeling of dread caused by Kenny's "information," waking up about noon. I spent the afternoon at my desk, getting time sheets ready so I could collect some money, typing up the report for Fran Li, doing other paperwork. About two o'clock, it had started raining again, drizzling off and on ever since. Now, I pulled on my trenchcoat—yes, I really have one, a genuine gray Burberry I use when it rains. Then I was on my way.

The streetlights illuminated the apartment building on Mango Lane. It was a two-story faded pink stucco with perhaps a dozen small apartments in it on the *ewa*—northwest—side of Waikiki, a couple of blocks from where the Ala Wai canal spills into the ocean.

It was set amidst a dozen other apartment buildings, all equally run down. The building's front yard was paved over, soaked black with rain. Three blue-and-whites were parked at odd angles, where they had come to a sudden stop. Their electric blue flashers reflected in the rain puddles on the pavement, cutting across the black wedge of foliage and trees that sheltered the building on both sides and in the back. Where the blue lights washed across the pink stucco facade, it turned a sickly lavender.

On the second floor, past the black iron balcony railing, a square of light shined through an open doorway. Two windows, one on each side of the door, also blazed with yellow light. Outside the open doorway stood two uniformed officers, absorbed in conversation. They wore yellow rain slickers over their uniforms, yellow plastic covers over their hats. I could see a third cop moving around inside the apartment.

A small group of neighbors had come outside. I stood among them and watched as HSP's mobile evidence lab and the medical examiner's car pulled up. As usual, they were in tandem. Their offices were side by side, they got their calls at the same time.

People climbed from both vehicles, carrying black bags. They rushed into the apartment, and the uniformed cops stayed outside, roping off the area and talking among themselves. An ambulance pulled up.

A faint, fine rain was falling now. Two plainclothes cops came out of the lighted apartment. Ambulance attendants were carrying in a gurney. I edged closer to the detectives and heard one of them say, ". . . wife's name is Rosie Malinta. Someone will have to tell her."

The wife! Of course. I wasn't going to get into the building to see what was going on, but if I could get to the wife before the police did, I was bound to learn something useful. I turned away from the crime scene, hurried to the hotel across the street, and called Jess from a pay phone. He had the wife's address, of course; he had tried to interview her several times during his investigation, with no luck. But her husband had still been alive then. Perhaps now, things would be different.

"I learned a bit about her," Jess said. "She was a bar girl in Manila, one of those pits where the women take the abuse in return for the money. She married an American soldier named Martinez and came to the States with him about five years ago. He turned out to be a loser. Beat her bad enough that she finally left him. Would have lost her green card if she hadn't had a couple of his kids. She's been working at the Black Cat as a bar hostess, earning the family bread. She met Malinta there and hooked up with him. They've only been married a month or so."

"Thanks, Jess, that will help."

"You sure the deceased is Malinta?"

"That's what I overheard them saying."

There was a long silence as Jess absorbed the information. Then he gave me the address. As soon as I'd committed it to memory, I spun around and raced back to my car.

Rosie Malinta lived in an area just *ewa* of downtown. It was a district where aging public housing leaned into low-rent apartment houses. There lived the newly dispossessed: recent arrivals from the Philippines, from Southeast Asia, from China. Depending on the geopolitical picture in the Pacific Basin, someone is always fleeing from something. Most of the current immigrants were fleeing poverty or war. Most of them arrived with little or nothing, and a good percentage of them were illegal aliens.

Half an hour later I arrived in Rosie's neighborhood. I slid out of my blue Honda Accord and double-checked the doorlocks. Two tough-looking teenagers lounged beside the stoop of a dilapidated three-story apartment building with grimy windows, their listless forms hovering at the edge of the arc of light provided by a streetlight. I'd seen the glow as they passed a joint back and forth, but as I approached they dropped it, ground it to a pulp, then stared at me with resentment. Beside them, two green garbage dumpsters overflowed and reeked of rotting fish.

I moved up to them, and said, "Can you tell me which apartment Rosie Malinta lives in?"

The boys scrutinized me with silent hostility, and suddenly I saw myself through their eyes. *Haole.* Blonde. Slim, wearing a gray raincoat, snow-white shirt, gray slacks with a sharp crease, a gold cross around my neck. To them, I was one of the privileged class, one of the enemy. One boy spat on the pavement to show his defiance, the other smiled contemptuously. They weren't going to tell me anything.

I turned away from them and climbed three wooden steps, then entered a small foyer. The mailboxes were set into the back wall and a single barren light bulb dangled from the ceiling, barely illuminating the area. Most of the locks had been broken and graffiti had been scrawled and spray painted all over the walls, the strange hieroglyphic symbols of the various local gangs. I carefully read all the insertable placards in the mailboxes, but none read "Malinta." I was about to start pounding on doors when the closest one opened and a wizened old Chinese man stuck his neck out and glared at me. "Excuse me," I said quickly. "I'm looking for Rosie Malinta. Can you tell me where she lives?"

He rattled something in Mandarin, saying the word "Martinez" several times, and then he pointed toward the stairwell. Well, at least I had someplace to start. I went back to the mailboxes, found the name Martinez on number 208. The old man watched me through his cracked door.

I climbed the stairs. The walls were thin—strident voices argued, children cried, TV sets blared. The strangely blended cooking smells of hot chili, curries, garlic, soy sauce, onions, roast pork and chicken reminded me that I'd skipped breakfast. But my appetite vanished as a large black cockroach crept out from beneath a doorway, paused, then skittered off down the hall.

At apartment 208, I rapped on the door. The predictable noises came from within. I knocked again, louder.

The door swung inward. A man with the posture of an upright cricket stood there scowling. He was ancient, with broken, black-rimmed fingernails and a shock of dirty white hair. His teeth were long gone, and his face was a solid mass of wrinkles. I shouted over the television, "Are you Mr. Martinez?"

His scowl deepened. He said something in Tagalog, and then he turned his head and stepped backward, craning his neck to see as a sudden burst of gunfire came from the TV.

I looked around him into the dirty cubicle. This first room held two narrow beds, both unmade. The floor was strewn with clothing and toys, with potato chip and candy bar wrappers and other debris. Two small children sat on an unmade bed. Their wide, brown eyes were riveted to the TV, which was tuned to a western. I hesitated, then stepped past the old man and stood between him and the TV. "Where's Rosie?"

He muttered something at me that sounded like a curse, and then he shouted into the kitchen. A woman's shrill voice shouted back.

I took a step toward the kitchen just as a woman came through the door. She held a spatula in one hand. Her face might have been pretty if it hadn't been marred by a sullen scowl. She stopped short, surprised, then glowered at me.

"You cop," she said flatly.

I shrugged. "Something like that."

"What you want?"

"Are you Mrs. Martinez?"

Her shoulders slumped. "No more Martinez. Rosie Malinta. Me and Martinez, we're divorced, I stay with Malinta now. What you want?"

I turned to look at the old man. "And he is—?"

"My father, from Manila." She pointed at him with one long fingernail. "He no speak English, you talk to me." It was an order.

She was in her late thirties, maybe early forties, very thin. She was wearing a soiled green robe, and her makeup was smeared, as if she'd slept in it and only recently awakened. Deep lines pulled her mouth downward. Her eyes had narrowed suspiciously. "What you want?"

"Did Sonny Malinta live here?"

"He gone. I get him out of jail, he come home one night, he no come back." She stared at me defiantly.

Apparently the police hadn't yet notified her of Sonny Malinta's death. And now that I was standing face to face with her—now that she was a real person—I was having reservations about manipulating such a grievous situation. Should I tell her Sonny was dead? Certainly not. But under the circumstances, was it even ethical for me to try to question her? I decided to play it by ear as I went along.

"Bail was pretty steep for him," I said. I didn't have a clue, but it seemed like some place to start. "I guess it took you a while to put the money together."

"Why you talk to me about bail? What Sonny do? He no run over Japanese man. Why you come to put him back in jail?" Her jaw jutted out defiantly.

"He's not going back to jail. But I would like to know where he is."

Irritation washed her face, but her eyes were unreadable. "I no care where he go. He take my money. He want money, all the time. Money, money, money. I no give, he leave me."

I thought about that. From what Jess had told me, Sonny Malinta had worked for Big Bruddah's Plumbing only part time. He was a boozer and a gambler, both expensive habits. Rosie's job in a hostess bar supported the family.

I said, "Did Sonny tell you who pushed the Japanese man in front of the van?" I watched her closely.

A crafty look darkened her eyes, then she made them go round and innocent. "You ask question, you give money."

"How much?"

"Other man, give me money. You give—twice as much."

"Which man?"

"Man who give me money for bail." She shrugged, feigning indifference. "I don't know name."

My eyes involuntarily widened, and I ventured a guess: "A Japanese man?"

"No. *Haole*."

Okay. So much for that theory. None of this was adding up the way I'd expected.

"Mrs. Malinta, could you tell me something—anything—about this man?"

"He come one day, tell me Sonny is in jail, he give me money to get Sonny out."

"And you did?"

She nodded her head sullenly.

"Can you describe this man?"

She gave me a certain look. I opened my purse, checked my cash, pulled out a fifty and handed it to her. "Sorry, but I'm almost broke."

Her hand swallowed the money. She said, "He *Haole*," again, as if this explained it all.

"What color was his hair?"

"Brown."

"His eyes?"

"I no see. He wear dark glasses."

"Height?"

"I no can tell."

After another five or so minutes of this piece by piece interrogation, I had learned absolutely nothing. Finally, I said, "Does Sonny have any other friends I might contact?"

She froze up. "No friends."

"Sonny didn't have *any* friends?"

"Sonny no good, always trouble. He drink, always money, money, money."

I took another good hard look at her, wondering how she'd react when she learned Sonny was dead. Maybe she wouldn't react. Maybe she couldn't any more. I had a sudden impulse to reach out and take her hand, to tell her about Jesus and how He changes lives. But somehow I knew she'd just jerk away, that she wouldn't listen to me. To every thing, there is a season, and she wasn't going to trust or believe anything I said to her just now.

I said, "What about the man Sonny saw? The one who pushed the Japanese gangster in front of Sonny's van?"

"Not Sonny's van."

"Yes, I know. I mean the van Sonny was driving. Did Sonny describe the man to you?"

"Said man who pushed was ugly. A devil. Pushed Japanese man, Sonny no could stop, now everyone blame Sonny."

"What do you mean, 'ugly'?"

"Sonny no say. He tell me shut up. He act scared."

"Did Sonny say anything else at all about the man?"

She started to shake her head no, but instead a cunning look came into her eyes. She looked at my purse.

I thought about giving her more money. But somehow I knew I wasn't going to learn anything else, no matter how much I paid her. I stood up, said, "Thank you," and turned to go.

I hesitated for a minute, wishing I could do something more. But I knew this was it. Neither the time nor the place. Reluctantly, I left. On the way home, I stopped at a pay phone and filled Jess in on the futility of my visit.

"So we at least have one new lead," I said after I'd told him about the conversation. "The man who paid Sonny's bail. Doesn't it stand to reason that whoever wanted him dead would first of all have to get him out of jail?"

"But the man gave the money to the wife," Jess pointed out. "Do you think you can get anything else out of her?"

I had to admit it. "No. She sees everyone in simple terms: money or no money. She probably never looked past his wallet."

"Think it would do any good to show her some photographs?"

"Of who?"

"Good point."

"It could have been one of Sonny's friends, it could have been someone he worked with, it could have been anybody."

"But it probably wasn't."

"Right. So, let's say it really was the man who killed Sonny, or at least someone working with him. Where do we start looking for this guy? Rosie's a dead end."

"That's about what I figured," Jess said with resignation. "It looks like whoever killed Sonny Malinta has stopped this side of the investigation dead in its tracks."

"So now what?"

"I guess we check out some different angles. By the way, your tip about Alton may pay off. I found out a couple of things you'd be interested in knowning."

"Tell me."

"Frankly, Alex, I'm busy at the moment. Tell you what. Give me a call first thing tomorrow, and we'll meet and talk. Is that okay?"

"Not really, but it sounds like that's as good as I'm going to get."

"It's just that it suddenly crosses my mind that we say way too much on the phone."

"I'm at a pay phone, Jess."

"Yes," he said, "but I'm not."

"Good point," I said. "I guess they could move in at any moment."

"Enough said. Call me tomorrow?"

"Consider it done."

had decided not to see Derrick again. Yet there I was, sitting across the table from him while he slid into the booth. He picked up the worn brown leather menu, flipped it open, and said, "Hello, Alex. Sorry to be late."

"That's okay. I just got here."

He wore denims and a lightweight leather bomber's jacket over a gray turtleneck. He was more attractive than I remembered him being, perhaps because he'd discarded the drug dealer's clothes. I was suddenly aware of my own baggy stonewashed pants, the oversized shirt. I wished I'd changed into something more attractive.

Our young waiter wore a thin Mexican serape over his own shirt and slacks. He had the muscular, sun-bronzed look of a surfer working part-time. He stopped beside Derrick and said, "Cocktail?"

Derrick looked at me. "What are you having?"

"I don't drink alcohol. Maybe a cola."

Derrick nodded judiciously. "Make mine the same."

After the waiter had moved away, I said, "I'm going to have the smothered bean burritos and a side of guacamole. Their guacamole is the best in the world."

"I'm a meat and chili peppers man, myself. I think I'll have the beef fajitas." He closed the menu, then shot me an electric look that said he was more than glad to see me.

I wondered what I was getting myself into. Last night, after visiting Rosie Malinta, I'd gone home and rechecked the bugs—still there—then had sat on my balcony and stared out at the city, brooding over my situation and wondering who the bugs belonged to. Troubles had been out with friends and hadn't returned until almost one A.M. He'd gotten up early this morning to go to class, so I hadn't seen much of him. All in all, I'd spent another restless, solitary night.

First thing this morning I'd tried to phone Jess, only to learn that he had already left the house and wouldn't be back until after noon. I'd then driven downtown and presented Fran Li with my time sheet and picked up my check from her. I'd tooled by the market and bought a few groceries, gassed up the car, and had the oil changed. I was still feeling restless when I returned home. I'd paced the floor for a while, then shuffled some papers, unable to stay interested in my work. Around 11:30, I had just decided to step out for a bite of lunch when the phone rang.

It was Derrick. The timing was right, and my resolution dissolved. I met him here at Amigos, a restaurant on lower Kalakaua. The white stucco walls were decorated with huge sombreros studded with colorful glass shards. There were only a dozen small booths. The place was cozy, colorful, and featured the best Mexican food in the Islands.

"I thought you were going to avoid me forever," Derrick said. He smiled. His teeth were white and even, he had a golden tan, his dark hair had been recently cut, and his eyes were even bluer than I remembered.

"I got busy with a few things," I said.

"Working a case?"

"More or less."

"Helping Jess out?"

"Not really, though I would if I could."

"How's Jess doing?"

"Good. But he'll be doing better once his problems with Commissioner Alton are straightened out and he's reinstated."

Derrick nodded. "You've heard that Sonny Malinta is dead?"

"Yes." I made my eyes go opaque. "I caught it on the morning news." That was true. It just wasn't *all* of the truth.

"Malinta was murdered, Alex. This isn't going to help Jess's situation."

Suddenly uncomfortable, I said, "But Jess isn't responsible for the paperwork that allowed Malinta to be bailed out of jail."

He shot me a surprised look. "Who says Jess isn't responsible?"

I caught myself before I blurted out the whole truth and shrugged. "I just know he isn't. And anyway, doesn't Sonny Malinta's murder bolster up Jess's theory?"

"That Malinta saw the man who shoved Ochinko in front of the van?"

"Yes. Doesn't it look like someone bailed Malinta out, then murdered him to shut him up?"

He shook his head. "Doesn't make sense, Alex. Malinta's wife put up the bail money. Why would *she* set him up to be killed?"

I started to argue that an unidentified man had given the bail money to Malinta's wife. But that wonderful little something that often clamps my mouth shut did its job, and instead of blurting out that bit of privileged information, I just said, "I guess Malinta's murder could be unrelated to Ochinko's death. Stranger things have happened."

Derrick nodded sagely. "Very perceptive. The cops in Homicide say Malinta was into some of the local gamblers for quite a bit of money, that they shut him up as a warning to others."

"I guess that's possible."

Derrick studied me for a moment. "Alex, I think you should know. Other rumors are starting to surface about Jess."

"Such as?"

"Confidential cop talk, I'd rather not repeat it. But I'm beginning to wonder if Alton didn't have a legitimate reason to suspend him."

I skewered him with an angry stare. "How long have you known Jess?"

"A few years. David introduced us, we all three had coffee together now and then."

"How *well* do you know Jess?"

He made a dismissive gesture with his hands. "Not very well."

"Then let me assure you, Jess is one of the best people you'll ever meet. He's innocent of anything they say about him. Trust me."

"I only brought it up because I'm concerned about your involvement. I hope you're doing the right thing, sticking by him."

"Of course I am. Jess hasn't done anything. He'll work this out."

"Jess is lucky to have a friend like you."

"Thank you."

A look of annoyance crossed Derrick's face. "Too bad he isn't equally loyal to the people who depend on him."

Surprised, I said, "What is *that* supposed to mean?"

He suddenly looked uneasy, as if he may have said too much. "Nothing. People just talk," he said offhandedly.

"*What* people talk?"

His eyes darted back and forth; I thought he might be looking for an exit. Then he seemed to regain his mental footing and said, "Just rumors."

My voice went steely. "*What* rumors, Derrick?"

He held his hands wide in mock surrender. "Nothing that matters, Alex. There are just a few people in HSP who feel that Jess let them down."

"It's exactly the other way around," I snapped.

"I agree. Don't be so touchy. I meant what I said, Jess *is* lucky to have you for a friend. Look at you, ready to go to the mat to defend his honor." He chuckled.

"Sorry," I said. "I'm a little on edge."

He looked at me with fond amusement. "Let's change the subject. I hear you bailed one of my street snitches out of the slammer a couple of nights ago."

I looked at him, surprised. "Kenny?"

He nodded, then explained. "David used to buy information from him. I inherited him."

"No kidding," I said cynically. I had also inherited him, but I wasn't about to divulge that to Derrick. My street informants had the utmost confidence in my silence, and they deserved that silence. Even Kenny, whose information was often crafted out of cunning or madness, deserved my discretion. Selling information to people in law enforcement—even to a private cop—is serious business for those who live in the same dangerous environs as those they inform upon. Sometimes snitches get killed, even over little things. The fact that Derrick so easily labeled Kenny a street snitch—even to me— made my estimation of Derrick's integrity plummet.

The waiter returned with our colas. They were garnished with wedges of lime. He set a bowl of guacamole and corn chips on the table between us, and I immediately scooped up a chipful, delivered it to my mouth, and chewed heartily.

"I was thinking about you last night," Derrick said. "I've thought about you a lot lately."

I swallowed. "Depending on what you've been thinking, I may or may not be flattered."

He made that dismissive gesture with his hands again. "I was just thinking about your commitment to your work. Wishing I could be that way again, you know, spontaneous and interested, wide-eyed and eager. These streets eat you alive."

"Literally," I said, suddenly thinking of David.

"But you remind me of a kid, in a way. Everything seems sparkling new and fascinating to you."

"Not really." I blinked away the memory of David and forced myself back to the present.

Derrick said, "Speaking of kids, how'd your child custody case work out?"

I made a wry face. "Not good. The guy blew it, the wife gets the kid. Too bad. If he'd done it the right way, he could have at least gotten shared custody."

"I always wanted to have kids," Derrick said. He held the cola glass in his hand, staring down into it. "Bonnie—that's my ex-wife—didn't want any. Guess it's just as well, since our marriage didn't last."

"What happened?" I had to ask the question or seem rude. But I really didn't want to have this conversation, I really wasn't interested. When you start talking about marriage, the conversation invariably expands to include the past, the present—and the future. You end up sharing confidences, and then you invariably regret it . . .

But he surprised me by saying simply, "It just didn't work. Look, I'm boring you." He lifted his glass to clink against mine. "Here's to better days."

"Amen," I said, repeating his gesture and slugging back a sip of cola.

Then I said, "How's the undercover work going?"

He smiled again, but this time it had a smug, predatory quality. "I had a good week. The prosecutor's office has everything they need to put several local dealers away for a few decades, courtesy of me." He made a little mocking bow.

"Good work," I said. And suddenly I appreciated his integrity again and was glad to be with him, a kindred soul and fellow champion of justice, someone who saw how dark and evil the underbelly of society really was, someone who wasn't afraid to lay his life on the line in order to lock up the bad guys.

The waiter brought our food, and we ate and talked about incidentals: Honolulu's new mayor, the cutback in federal funding for drug enforcement, the increase in international drug trafficking, how it was worse now than at any time since the war in Vietnam and most people were so oversaturated with the problem that they no longer cared. And that led us back to our friendly neighborhood *yakuza* soldier, who'd been run down in front of my building. And that took us back full circle to Jess's investigation of the death and his subsequent suspension for believing the man had been murdered.

Derrick had loosened up now, so I said, "What are these rumors about Jess, anyway?"

"I didn't mean to worry you, Alex. It's just a few disgruntled people in administration grinding an axe. But Jess has a lot of friends, too. They're putting on some pressure, but Commissioner Alton is still playing hardball. The suspension stands."

"I don't understand this Alton," I said. "Jess is one of the best cops on the force. Why is Alton picking on him?"

"That's not so tough to figure out. Alton's a power freak. He's made a few bucks in real estate, now he has major political aspirations. That's why he worked so hard to be appointed as Hawaii State Police Commissioner. Most people consider that job to be sort of a glorified public relations appointment. But it's a highly visible position, and he's using it as a first step into the political arena. He interfaces a lot with the suits who run public relations for the hotels. They want to keep this *yakuza* death under wraps. Think about it. So far, it's gotten a couple of days in the headlines of the local papers, a spot on national news, and then it died off. Somebody ran over a tourist who just happened to be linked to Japanese organized crime, no big deal. The problem is, Jess's theory that the man was murdered could stir up the media again and keep it stirred up for a while. *Mucho* negative publicity for Paradise, and at a time when tourism is down anyway and the Hawaii Visitors' Bureau is spending millions on TV ads to try to lure people *to* Hawaii. So—that's the immediate beef he has against Jess. Jess is in the way."

"What else?"

"Glad you asked. The deeper problem is that Alton has to control everyone around him. He can't control Jess, so he hates him. I get a little flak from Alton myself, for the same reason."

I grinned. "David told me once you had a mind of your own."

"Yeah, but I'm learning to work the system," he said, taking a long sip of his fresh coffee. A new, dark look had come into his eyes, and an expression of distaste drifted over his features, then vanished.

"Were you born here in Hawaii?" I said.

"I was. My dad ran a tour boat operation here for a few years. But he wasn't much of a businessman, so he went belly up. We moved back to California when I was about six. Later, I was stationed here in the Marines, at Kaneohe. When I got out, I decided to stay and seek my fortune. And here I am, ten years later, with no fortune to speak of." He laughed darkly. "And not much future, either."

"There are different kinds of wealth," I said. "You have your health, your integrity, a job that makes a real difference . . ."

He shot me a sudden, angry look that puzzled me, but the look vanished, and he smiled sadly. "I think my biggest problem is loneliness. You know. Working the streets, you spend all your time with people—women, mostly—who deal drugs, who are hooked on drugs. Maybe they're not bad people, but their lives are so wrecked that they've gone emotionally dead, they're out for what they can get. There's no way you'd dare get close to any one of them. I don't mean to sound holier-than-thou, but, well, sometimes I just want to spend time with someone decent. Like you."

I decided the direct approach was best. "I'm happy to be your friend, Derrick. I admire what you do. And if you think I'm decent, I'm pleased. But don't put me on a pedestal, I'm a long way from perfect."

"Who needs perfection? It's the imperfections in a woman that make her beautiful. Take, for instance, the way your hair always looks a little windblown. Or the fact that your face is ever-so-slightly asymmetrical—"

Whoa. This conversation was going off in the wrong direction, and fast. At least, that was my first reaction. But on the other hand, what was the harm in hearing someone say something nice about me for a change? My vanity began to overcome my common sense, but I caught myself in the nick of time and said, "I'm sorry—would you mind if we talked about something else?"

"Why, Alex? I'm only telling you the truth."

"Derrick, I'm just not ready for this kind of relationship yet."

He leaned back in his chair and shot me a charming, mischievous grin. "Why not? Neither one of us is getting any younger."

And I heard a little voice in the back of my mind say, *Why not, indeed?*

But something else shot into my mind at that same moment. For a Christian to get romantically involved with a non-Christian was emotional suicide. And though Derrick was handsome and considerate, he wasn't a Christian. In fact, I'd even heard that he was something of a womanizer. I thought about what he had just told me regarding the kind of women he spent most of his time with. Maybe he was being honest about his feelings toward them, maybe not. And I suddenly remembered a little definition I'd heard or read somewhere long ago: "A womanizer is a rock upon which women dash themselves to pieces."

I quickly said, "I really believe serious male-female relationships should be sacred. Sanctioned by God."

He grinned and shrugged. "I'm not exactly asking you to marry me—at least, not right now."

"Derrick, I'm an ironclad Christian. I don't know if you really understand what kind of commitment that takes . . ."

"So are you saying you're chaste?" His grin turned derisive.

That seemed like such a cheap shot that it angered me. "That's exactly what I'm saying."

"So why not get unchaste?" He said it as if he was kidding, but the question in his eyes was serious.

"You don't understand," I said. "My faith forbids me to have sex outside of marriage. I also think it's asking for trouble for me to develop a serious relationship with anyone who doesn't share my faith."

"You've got to be kidding me."

"No. I'm very serious." I took my napkin from my lap and placed it beside my plate. Though my food was only partly gone, I'd lost my appetite.

"I thought you and David both belonged to the same faith," he said casually. He speared a slice of beef with his fork, then poised it in midair.

"We do—that is, we did."

"But David didn't—oh, never mind."

"David didn't what?"

"It's nothing, just a passing thought." He pilloried me with a serious yet somehow boyish look, and said, "Sorry. That comment about your chastity was in poor taste. I was trying to tell you that I really like you. I didn't mean to come off like a jerk."

I felt myself thaw a bit. "Don't worry about it."

"Anyway, I'm out of line. I'm supposed to be acting like a big brother here."

I frowned. "A big brother? Why?"

"A promise to a friend."

"Excuse me, but you've lost me."

"Look, I've been trying to reach you because I know that something is wrong, Alex. Something heavy is bothering you."

I felt myself draw back, felt my muscles tense up. Was I so troubled by this situation that even someone almost a stranger to me could tell I wasn't myself? I said, "What makes you think that?"

He grinned again. "Maybe I've never spent much time around you, but David used to talk about you so much, I feel like I know you. He thought you were a pretty special woman, and he was right."

"He talked about you, too."

There was a sudden, quick glint of concern in his eyes, but he masked it immediately. "I'll tell you what he said about you if you'll tell me what he said about me."

"Deal. You first," I said.

"No, you."

I smiled, put my napkin back in my lap, and scooped up the last of the guacamole on a chip. "No, you go first."

"Okay. He said you ate a lot when you were worried, but you never gained weight."

I laughed. "Is that why you say something is wrong, because I'm hungry?"

"No wait, there's more. David said you were the most loyal person he'd ever known. That you would literally lay down your life for a friend."

I looked at my plate. I wished I'd been there to lay down my life for David.

"He said he loved you, but that most of the time you were impossible to live with."

I looked up at him sharply. "David really said that?"

Derrick grinned and held up the palm of his hand toward me. "Scout's honor."

"Why?"

"He said you were so intense that you wore him down. That everything you did, you gave your all, even if it was washing the windows."

I had to laugh at that. "I guess that's why my windows haven't been washed lately. I've been overwhelmed with other challenges."

"And he made me promise that if anything ever happened to him, I'd keep an eye on you."

That surprised me. I looked at Derrick, studied him. "Is that what you're doing? Keeping an eye on me?"

"I know something is wrong, Alex." He leaned forward, and his blue eyes were suddenly flooded with concern. "You're into something heavy, maybe the same thing that your friend Jess is into. There are rumors in the streets. Bad rumors."

"Tell me."

"I've heard that certain Japanese nationals have decided you know too much, that you're better off dead." He skewered me with a dark, questioning gaze. "Don't lay your life down for Jess. You don't even know what he's really involved in."

I swallowed the sudden rush of fear that swept through me like an icy wind. "You said Kenny is your snitch. Did he tell you the *yakuza* wanted me dead?"

He studied me. "I heard it from someone much more reliable."

"*Who?*"

"That's a confidential source, Alex, one I don't talk about."

I leaned forward, my face furrowed with concern. "And you believe it?"

"I do."

"But—why would they want me dead? I mean—"

"That's what I was hoping you'd tell me, Alex."

I saw the eagerness in his eyes then, and my mouth clamped shut. When it opened, I said, "I don't have a clue."

"Something to do with Ochinko's death, I think."

I shook my head. "Your guess is as good as mine."

"You really should reconsider your loyalty to Jess. He may be using you, jeopardizing you."

"Impossible." But even as I said it, I was feeling the first small seeds of doubt.

"I'll keep my eye on you."

"Don't, Derrick. Please. I don't really believe I'm into anything that could get me killed. I'm not afraid."

"All the same, I'll continue to keep my eye on you. I want to keep my word to my partner. If you're in trouble, I want to help you."

"Please don't."

He smiled then. "That's another thing David said about you. That your biggest problem was your inability to trust anyone."

I had to think about that, and after I'd thought about it, I didn't answer.

"Trust me, Alex. Even if you don't trust anyone else, trust me. Can't you see I want to help you?"

I suddenly felt an overwhelming urge to lean forward, place my head in my arms, and weep. I wanted so badly to trust him—to trust anyone who might be able to extricate me from the chaos and confusion that was swirling up around me. But I stifled the impulse. Because people really couldn't be trusted. Even if they didn't deliberately betray you, they invariably let you down. David had let me down. He had left me when I needed him the most. It was true that David had remarked on my lack of trust from time to time. But he had trusted people, and look what happened to him. They killed him.

Slowly, almost hypnotically, I took the napkin from my lap again. I placed it carefully on the table, arranging it just so. And then I fished two tens out of my wallet, stood up, and placed them on the table. "Lunch is on me, Derrick. Gotta go." My voice sounded thick to me.

"Alex, what's wrong?"

"I'm leaving. If I stick around much longer, I'm probably going to tell you *exactly* what's wrong, and there's no way in the world that telling you is going to make anything better."

"Alex, let me help."

He was standing up too now, putting his own napkin down beside his plate. I held up my hand, and what he saw in my face apparently stopped him short because he stared at me hard for a moment, then sat slowly back down.

As I walked toward the door, he said, "I'll be in touch, Alex. And remember, I owe it to David. If there's anything I can ever do for you, please let me know."

"I'm sorry, Derrick, but I'm going to have to work this one out for myself."

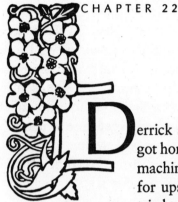

errick started phoning within minutes after I got home. I screened his calls on the answering machine—he left two messages, apologizing for upsetting me, wondering if I was okay. I tried to call Jess again. He still wasn't home.

I felt exhausted, depressed. I didn't really believe that the *yakuza* was out to kill me. The concept seemed fanciful, even egotistical. After all, who was I to warrant such fearsome attention? But my life had turned into chaos. Too many things were unexplained. Why, for instance, had Shinda invited me to his quarters, all but threatened me regarding the return of Victor's papers, then failed to make contact with me again? And why had Miro Ochinko phoned me and stashed Victor's papers on his way to see me? And why had he been killed?

Whatever was going on, it cut close enough to the bone to cause me some real concern. Because *something* evil was swirling around me. Something that indeed felt dangerous. And no matter how hard I tried, I couldn't put all the pieces together in a way that made any sense.

I had been pacing my office floor. I stopped, looked at my watch. It was still early—only one o'clock. I sat down at my desk and dialed Jess's number again. This time, the machine answered. I tried to work for a while, but the tension wouldn't go away, and I felt a serious headache coming on. Finally, I shut off my phone and lay down on my bed, wanting to read my Bible for a while and relax. Instead, I quickly fell asleep.

About an hour later I awakened, feeling a bit better, and headed downstairs to check my mail. As I entered the small mailroom and inserted my key into the mailbox, I was thinking about all Derrick had said. *Could* he be trusted as a friend? Maybe. He'd killed the man who shot my husband, after all. Not in time to save David, but he'd tried. Not many people would do that.

But could he be trusted as a potential mate? Never. There were countless opportunities in the streets for action if a person—male or female—was interested in destructive and superficial relationships. I saw it all the time, tourists flirting with the beat cops, handsome young men and women in uniform. It was even harder for narcotics detectives, most of whom were men. They had to get close to people in order to do their jobs, very close, and there were women galore in the drug subculture; many of them were prostitutes or other man-manipulators who considered sleeping with a cop a status-builder. They used the cops, of course, to get information, favors, status, immunity from arrest, whatever. And unfortunately, some cops took advantage of the situation and used them in return—for information, for mindless sex. This was one of the many reasons why the divorce rate among vice and narcotics cops was exceedingly high. And it was yet another reason why I wasn't about to get involved with Derrick. David had been different, our shared faith had made him more or less bulletproof when it came to womanizing . . .

Bulletproof. I shook my head. What a disgustingly ironic way to put it.

I opened the mailbox. There was the electric bill, a couple of credit card bills, a letter to Troubles from his mother, a letter from the university for him. I removed them, sifted through them, and had started to close the box when in the very back, stuck up against the corner, I saw a small pink envelope, the kind used for wedding invitations. Thinking that was exactly what it was, I pulled it out. My address was scrawled on it in elegant handwriting, no return address. I absentmindedly tore it open.

The small stiff card inside was pale-pink, an expensive linen paper. There was no design, nothing upon it except the elegant handwritten script:

Dear Alex:

We have to talk. I'll be at the Ocean Bar at the Royal
Seashell Hotel every day this week, from 2:30 to 3:30 P.M.
Please come quickly. I'll be watching for you.

It was signed, "The Bug."

I felt a chill scamper down my spine. I glanced around behind me, as if someone might be peering over my shoulder. No one there. I read it again. The sense of unreality stayed with me, an almost paranoid feeling, but it was quickly joined by an equal sense of glee. I had done it, almost without trying. I had smoked them out!

I checked my watch. Two-fifteen. Perfect. If anything could yank me out of my depression, it was some serious intrigue. I took my mail upstairs, dabbed on a bit of makeup, decided not to change my clothes, and thirty minutes later I was stepping through the looking glass and into the Ocean Bar on the tiled terrace of the Royal Seashell Hotel.

I slid onto one of the empty rattan barstools and ordered a glass of pineapple juice, garnished with the inevitable little purple vanda orchid. The ten or so tourist-patrons were sitting beneath the giant banyan tree around which the terrace had been built, at round metal tables, consuming tropical drinks or beer or sodas and presumably sharing war stories collected during their travels. I watched them all surreptitiously as I sipped my juice.

One slender woman in her early sixties was regaling a pudgy couple in their thirties with a loud critique of the food on the dinner cruise she'd been on last night. Actually, I'd heard every word of the conversation a million times before. When you live here, the two million plus tourists who move through every year tend to fade into a buzzing background; the rest of life emerges into foreground. It's not that the tourists are unpleasant. And they certainly aren't insignificant since they drive Hawaii's economy. But they're just not part of my essential daily reality most of the time, so I tend to overlook them.

Usually. Which is why I thought at first glance that this woman was just another tourist. I mean, she had her act down pat, I'll give her that. She had been sitting at a table by herself, glancing at her watch now and again as if she was waiting for someone. Now, she moved up and sat down on the barstool to my right, sporting a pink flush of sunburn across the bridge of her nose and on her bare shoulders. A really nice touristy touch. She was wearing a rose-colored halter top and matching skirt, and she was fresh-faced and pretty in a high school cheerleader sort of way. Straight brown hair that hung just past her shoulders, nice brown eyes, high, almost Indian, cheekbones. She was wearing White Gardenia cologne—I could smell it.

She placed a white canvas handbag on the bar and said to the bartender, "Looks like my date stood me up. I'll have another Mai Tai." Then she turned to look at me, and I saw the bruised and worried look in her eyes. I knew it was her.

"It's too early to drink, isn't it?" she said. "But—I seem to need a little lift."

I waited, saying nothing.

The bartender set the drink in front of her, and she pulled a five-spot out of her bag and handed it to him, indicating with a little flip of her fingers that he should keep the change. When he'd moved down the bar to the cash register, she turned, checked to make sure no one else was within hearing distance, and said quietly, "So you're Alex."

"That's me. And you are—what. My worst nightmare?"

"I don't expect you to be intimidated. But you could at least be a *little* impressed after all the trouble we've gone to." She gave me a self-deprecating smile. In spite of myself, I decided I liked her.

Behind us, on the lawn, white-jacketed porters were busily unfurling snow-white cloths to cover the long metal tables being set up for the hotel's featured luau. Others were setting up high partitions, to block nonpaying passersby from the action. The sun was cruising toward the horizon, and I felt the adrenaline singing through my veins.

"I never sleep anymore, so I get salted really easy these days," she said, "so I'm only going to have this one more drink." She reached in her bag and pulled out a clump of fresh but wrinkled tissues, then placed them on the bar and pulled a piece of paper from beneath them. She used her hand to secretly slide it to a place between her glass and mine.

Her next words were so soft I almost didn't hear her. "Here are your directions. Read them, then swallow the paper."

I shot her a sideways, incredulous look. She was glancing at me, and she grinned. "Seriously. Just read them and follow instructions like the good girl I know you are, then dispose of the paper safely. I promise, you won't be sorry."

"Cloak and dagger," I said. "I hate cloak and dagger."

"Well, that's what we do, you know. I hear you aren't so bad at it yourself."

"People talk too much. By the way, did you get a court order before you put your little insect infestation into my condo?"

She lifted her eyebrows innocently, then lifted her Mai Tai glass, drained it, and set it back down with a flourish. "Ah. Good."

"Did you?"

"That's one of the things we'd like to talk to you about," she said. She looked long at the paper on the bar between us, indicating that I should pick it up. I did, unfolded it casually, carefully. One never knew who was watching these days. I read the directions—just a few words—then said, "Okay."

"Thank you, Alex. We knew we could count on you." She stood to go, picking up her handbag. "You know, we apologize for having to do things this way. But, well—we do what we must."

"Yes," I said, "I guess that's more or less what we all do."

he instructions advised me to drive to the Aloha Tower parking lot at five o'clock. Rush hour traffic was hitting the downtown area with terminal gridlock, thereby making it difficult for anyone to tail me. I sat in that parking lot until 5:30 then drove into the lower level of the parking garage directly across the street. I parked and locked my car, walked to the elevator, making sure I hadn't been followed, then took the elevator up to the eighth floor. My mystery date would be in a beige Chevy sedan parked right beside the elevator door, waiting expectantly for me.

I followed the directions perfectly, though I added a few tricks of my own. Just before I got off the elevator, I checked to make sure I had my small handgun firmly in place in the waist holster. It was freshly cleaned, fully loaded, and camouflaged by the folds of my oversized lemon-yellow jacket.

I stepped out of the elevator carefully, not sure what to expect. But only one car sat there, a beige sedan with lightly tinted windows. This was the only possibility; the rest of the garage gaped emptily around it. I was still carefully scanning the area to make sure that no goblins lurked in the shadows when the driver's door suddenly swung open and a tall man unfolded up and out of the driver's seat.

I stopped short—stopped breathing. I knew that face, and it wasn't a face I'd expected to see.

The man narrowed his eyes, just like the last time, and stared hard at me. And in that moment I belatedly remembered Derrick's warning that the *yakuza* wanted me dead.

I wasn't sure whether to go for my gun or not. If I did and the man didn't intend to shoot me, perhaps my motion would activate his own instinct and we'd be drawing down on each other, playing out Honolulu's version of the O.K. Corral.

On the other hand, if he *was* going to hurt me—and why else had I been lured here?—then I'd be better off to take the first shot, maybe wing him and stop him.

This was the man who had surprised me the night I'd invaded the dead *yakuza* soldier's hotel room. The man I had pegged for a Japanese national, the man who was attractive, in a Japanese Chairman of the Board sort of way. His hair was still dark brown and still neatly cut, though today he wore a white shirt open at the throat and a light tweed sports coat. His body was still lean, unusually tall, compact yet somehow explosive. But today there was a suffused anger in his fine-boned face.

His hand dived inside his jacket.

I whipped out my .38 and aimed dead at him. "Stop! I don't want to shoot you!" I shouted.

He stopped in mid-motion and stared at me in sheer astonishment. Then, in a voice dripping with sarcasm, he said, "Well, *thank you* for that." He held his hands wide, not bothering to hide his disgust, and said, "I *was* going to show you my I.D., but under the circumstances I guess you'll just have to take my word for it. I'm Special Agent Frank Yoshida. FBI."

In that sinking instant, I knew he was telling the truth. I quickly replayed my memory-tape of the events in Ochinko's hotel room, the night I'd first seen this man. With a wilting sense of embarrassment, I realized that from the very beginning of this irritating and perplexing game I had been outwitted, and I'd been misreading everything about the whole tangled mess ever since.

Sheepishly, I tucked my gun back into its holster and said, "You're the same agent who confiscated my papers from Mrs. Osaka's home, aren't you?"

"*Your* papers?"

"Okay, Victor Seitaki's papers."

"That's better." His English was still polished and perfect, but now there was a trace of the local lilt in it rather than that extreme precision with which the well-educated Japanese national speaks.

I said, "What were you doing in Miro Ochinko's hotel room that night?"

He stepped around and opened the passenger door of the sedan. "Climb in," he said. "We need to talk, and we might as well be comfortable."

"No thanks," I said. "I'm tired of being recorded."

He sighed, with the kind of exasperation a parent feels when dealing with an unruly child. "No bugs here, Alex. And I'm too tired to deal with any *shibai*. So climb in."

I wanted to argue some more, but my humiliation had deflated my arrogance. So I walked around and meekly climbed into the passenger seat.

He slid back behind the wheel and locked his door—causing me to follow suit. He said, "Let's get right to the point."

"I get the first question," I said, trying to regain my composure, to take some control. "Why the bugs?"

"Because you stuck your nose in the wrong place at the wrong time. We've had you under surveillance from the moment you left Miro Ochinko's hotel room."

Frustration welled up in me. "But *why*?"

"My partner had been waiting in the lobby. I phoned down, she tailed you home. We wanted to know how and why you beat us to Ochinko's hotel room, why you were carrying his key, what your interest was in him, whether you had anything to do with his death. We kept a watch on your place all night while we simultaneously ran a check on you. The next morning when you went to pick up your nephew and his girlfriend, we had someone follow you to the airport; at the same time we sent in a technician to plant the listening devices."

"You got a warrant for the bugs?"

"We did."

"Based on what?"

"Based on your direct involvement in the murder of a Class-I Confidential Informant."

I felt my eyes grow wide. "Miro Ochinko?"

Yoshida nodded, then said, "My turn for a question. Why *did* you go to Ochinko's room the night he was killed? We've heard it all before, of course, when you explained it to Troubles. Every word is on tape. But tell me again, in case you left something out."

I said, "Ochinko phoned me. He asked if I was the one whose husband had been a cop, then said he had to see me immediately. I was watching for him, through my telescope. You know about my telescope?"

He nodded, and I thought I saw a momentary twinkle of mirth in his eyes, but he immediately went stony again.

I hid my annoyance and repeated the rest of Ochinko's phone call word for word. I explained how I had seen Ochinko hiding the briefcase, everything.

When I had finished talking, Yoshida nodded solemnly. His eyes were opaque, hiding his thoughts.

I said, "My turn for a question. What's in Victor's papers that warrants all this interest?"

He looked mildly surprised. "You've seen the papers."

"Yes, but I never had the *kanji* interpreted. What does it say?"

I hadn't really expected a forthcoming answer, but without missing a beat, he said, "More of same, actually. Financial documents, contracts. Not what we'd hoped for. Look, Alex—" he frowned, and suddenly I saw how deeply troubled he was. "We'd like to ask you and your nephew to take a little vacation at FBI expense." He offered up a friendly smile. An all-American Japanese boy—all that was missing was the Huck Finn haircut and a few freckles.

"Why?"

"It seems we have a real mess here. And you've landed square in the middle of it."

I rolled my eyes toward heaven. "Tell me."

"It's extremely sensitive. In fact, top secret. But I've checked your old files. You used to have top security clearance with drug enforcement."

"I did. And I can still keep my mouth shut."

"When you want to," he said pointedly.

"If you don't like what I have to say, you don't have to listen." I stared him down.

He sighed.

Then he squared his shoulders and said, "Well—you're right in the middle of this now, and I'm not sure how to get you back out without getting you hurt."

"Just how bad does it get?"

"It's complicated. Let me tell you what's happening, then we'll go from there."

He started talking then. I listened hard, adding some of my own background information about Japanese organized crime into what he was telling me. And finally, the whole thing began to make sense.

Like I said before, the *yakuza* had enjoyed more than two hundred feudalistic years of tyrannical power over Japan's politicians and civil servants. The ninety thousand or so organized criminals who made up the various gangs had racked up cumulative incomes estimated to be from fifty to a hundred billion dollars yearly, and their power tainted everything in the country. But finally, in March of 1992, a few courageous Japanese citizens had enacted the first serious anti-*yakuza* laws, patterned after our own RICO act. For the first time, the Japanese National Police found themselves with legal clout against organized crime.

The anti-*yakuza* factions had started using those laws to put on the pressure. But the *yakuza* hadn't exactly rolled over and died. They had long received protection by funding powerful right-wing, ultranationalist politicians, and they began calling in favors. They pulled strings in the country's financial markets, in the diet, in the stock market, in every ministry and governmental office. Some very powerful people helped the *yakuza* move vast amounts of money into overseas investment, where it could be laundered and kept safe from the prying eyes of the reformist government and policing agencies.

"We fought for years to penetrate the money pipelines that were bringing *yakuza* money into the United States," Yoshida said. "Because the criminals follow their money, it's as simple as that."

He had my full attention.

"You probably already know that they were buying up golf courses and hotels, office towers and restaurants, and any other businesses where they could rinse their cash. We started various investigations designed to penetrate their pipelines and bring them down. There was a very real danger that they'd get locked in so tight they'd begin to control politicians and street action here, as well as in Japan."

I nodded. "It only takes a few rotten politicians to destroy the whole barrel."

"Right. We set up major sting operations in the cities they'd made their major targets: Palm Springs, Las Vegas, Los Angeles, and

Honolulu. Japanese money was flowing like water into all these areas at that time. We knew that a substantial stream of *yakuza* money was hidden inside the flood of yen. But we finally focused our primary investigation here."

"Into Victor Seitaki's developments and investments," I said.

"Right."

"I should have figured more of this out," I said. "But I thought you were a member of the *yakuza* when I first saw you. I started from the wrong premise, and it's kept me off base."

He nodded and smiled grimly. "I was posing as a *yakuza* then. I'm good at what I do. Anyway, so much money was flooding into Honolulu back then that it was almost impossible to parcel out what came from where. Japan doesn't even have money laundering laws, so we weren't getting any help from that end. But finally, when the money slowed down to a trickle and things started getting tight, we got a lucky break. We busted Miro Ochinko for trafficking about sixteen kilos of Ice into Honolulu International. To our amazement, he turned out to be our primary target's second in command!"

I was skeptical. "Isn't it unusual for someone that high up to actually handle drugs?"

Yoshida nodded. "Right. But Ochinko had gotten into some trouble gambling in Tokyo. He didn't want his boss—Takio—to know about it, so he did the Ice deal on his own to grab some fast cash. An abysmally stupid move for a man in his position, and one that indicates how desperate some of Japan's criminals are getting for fast cash."

The picture of a sullen-faced, haughty man sitting in the back of a death-black limo flashed across my mind. "Did you say Takio?"

Yoshida nodded. "The same Kuzio Takio you recently met. He's the *oyabun*—top gun—of the *yakuza*'s biggest family—the one we're after. Anyway, his sidekick, Miro Ochinko, was looking at about thirty years in a U.S. prison. So after some effort, we managed to turn him."

I was paralyzed by the immensity of what I was hearing. But a few things were finally beginning to make sense.

Yoshida said, "Ochinko was right up there at the top of Takio's dealings. He was helping us penetrate the financial quagmire surrounding Victor Seitaki's dealings with the Shinda Corporation, which was in part a front for Kuzio Takio's crime syndicate. We almost had an airtight case that not only locked down the *yakuza* money hidden in the Shinda Corporation's U.S. investments—an airtight RICO case we could try here in Hawaii—but we also had Kuzio Takio and his boys linked into a good share of the Ice that's being trafficked into this state by all his little mules and spiders and ants from half a dozen different Asian-Pacific countries."

I bit my lip and stared at him.

He looked back at me, levelly. "We initially got a court order to plant the bugs in your place for only a week, just to check out your relationship to our deceased informant. But after we realized who you were, we got curious and got it extended. Your husband was gunned down during an Ice bust—"

"Yes."

"You ever wonder about that?"

I frowned. "Not really."

"Well, think about it now. Your late husband was linked up with Jess Seitaki. Jess's brother, Victor, was indirectly linked to the people who wholesale most of the Ice that finds its way into this state."

I felt sick. "I didn't have a clue about that part of it. David never said anything—"

"Well, he wouldn't have talked about it if he was dirty. If he wasn't dirty, maybe he really didn't know ..." Yoshida looked unconvinced.

"Did you say 'dirty'?"

"I don't mean to tarnish your late husband's image, but there is evidence that someone inside the HSP was working with Takio's people to facilitate the Ice traffic."

I felt my fist flex, felt my arm draw back, ready to slug him.

He stared at me. "Alex, I'm not saying it was David. But there are a lot of things going on that we still don't understand."

I forced my fist to open, forced my hand to fall to my lap. "I'll explain one thing real fast. Nobody hated drugs more than David. He was the cleanest cop who ever worked the streets."

"What about Jess Seitaki?"

I gave him a scathing look. "Get serious."

"Then what about Derrick Green?"

I thought about that, then shrugged. "I don't know him very well, but he did shoot the man who killed David. It seems to me like he's on the right side."

Yoshida leaned back. His shoulders had been tight and now they slumped a bit. "Okay," he said, "that leads me to the next question. Can we trust *you*?"

"Nobody asked you to."

He turned to look full at me and skewered me with an impenetrable look. "Ah, but we have to, Alex. Because there's a wrinkle in our investigation that has ricocheted back to you in a big way."

I felt my eyes slit up suspiciously.

"You recently visited Ko Shinda's penthouse," he said.

I kept my look level, as impenetrable as his own.

"This thing has gotten so big that Takio himself flew in to straighten things out. The top gun. He personally drove down to pick you up. Not many people warrant that kind of attention. Which tells us they're not taking your involvement lightly."

"Keep talking."

"They tried to frighten you, but you didn't respond to their demand that you deliver Victor's papers to them, along with Jess's loyalty."

I was still puzzled by that, myself. "Shinda said he'd contact me the next day to get my response. I never heard from him again."

"That's because they knew it was too late. We'd confiscated Victor's papers by then. Think about it. You came home from Shinda's penthouse, watched sumo wrestling for a while with Troubles and Tess."

I felt the sense of violation well up in me again as I realized just how familiar he was with me and my private life. He was talking as if he was a member of my family.

He smiled thinly, amused by my reaction. "You sit on the wires long enough, you get to know people better than they know themselves," he said.

"I might not mind so much if the relationship wasn't so lopsided," I said, in what I hoped was a scathing tone of voice.

"Come on, Alex. It isn't like you to be ungracious. Anyway, you phoned Mrs. Osaka that same night, asked her if she'd finished transcribing the *kanji* portion of the papers. That's when we first learned where those papers had ended up. Man, you should have seen us scrambling."

"You had someone sitting on the wire, directly? Not taping me?"

"This is a serious investigation, Alex. We needed immediate action on any information the tap provided. Anyway, before we learned you had the papers, we were interested in you only because we'd seen you in Ochinko's room the same night he'd died, and we wondered about the connection. Once we learned you had the papers Ochinko had been delivering to us—well, then we really got interested."

"Why are those papers so dreadfully important?"

"Ochinko was supposed to be handing us the final nails in Shinda and Takio's coffins. But after we'd confiscated the papers from Mrs. Osaka, we saw that some of the papers Ochinko had promised us were missing. We thought at first you still had them, so we intensified our surveillance."

"Did you break into my condo and search it?" I was thinking about the intruder, who had surprised me right after I'd first taken the papers to Mrs. Osaka—in fact, the night I'd first taken them up there I'd returned home to find the man in my living room. Had I mentioned anything aloud about the papers before that happened? By phone, or to Troubles? No, so far as I could remember, I'd been totally silent about them, no reason to breathe a word until the night I'd asked Mrs. Osaka about translating the *kanji*.

Still, the break-in didn't necessarily have to relate to the then-missing papers. Maybe I'd stumbled across one of the techies. Maybe they'd gone in to check the bugs, replace a battery or something.

But Yoshida frowned, confirming my worst fears. "No. That wasn't us. But we had you bugged then, and it got us concerned enough to redouble our surveillance."

"I see," I said, though I really didn't. "So what's the bottom line here?"

"Let me sum it up real fast. Your appearance at Ochinko's hotel room the night he died got us interested. The fact that you had ended up with the papers kept us interested. Especially after we confiscated those papers from Mrs. Osaka and learned that the critical documents were still missing."

"So you figured I'd kept the missing papers?"

"That was our first thought. But after we listened to you a bit more, we realized that Ochinko had been holding back. Maybe he was going to play us for more money. Unless—maybe you did keep something back and were smart enough not to mention it aloud?" He peered hopefully at me.

"Sorry. You got everything I had, including most of my sanity."

His hope vanished. "I was afraid of that. Anyway, let's move back to the fact that Ochinko phoned you. He had stolen those papers from Takio's offices in Tokyo. He flew into Honolulu International via Los Angeles the next morning. Didn't contact us before he left, or we'd have had someone at the airport to take receipt of them. Apparently he knew that someone was on to him, even then. So far as we can tell, he was alone when he arrived at Honolulu International. He came by cab straight from the airport—we interviewed the cab driver. He checked into the Royal Seashell, then phoned us, saying he was here and wanted to deliver the papers immediately. I was supposed to meet him in a coffee shop a couple of blocks from the Royal Seashell. But when he was late, we started to worry. Finally he phoned again, from a pay phone, and told us someone was following him. Headquarters relayed the message to me. He wouldn't tell us exactly where he was, but he said he could lose them and was still going to make the meet. That's the last we heard of him."

"But that's the time period in which he phoned me?"

"Apparently. We figure he contacted you within five minutes after he last phoned us."

"The Honolulu Police Department's substation is only a block or so from where he was killed. If he knew he was in danger, why didn't he go there?"

"Good question, something we've wondered about, too. Our best guess is, he didn't trust cops at that point."

"Why would he come to me?"

"That part is still a puzzle," Yoshida admitted. "The best we can figure, he must have been involved with your husband at one time or another."

I felt a sudden cold chill.

"He apparently realized you were nearby. Whoever was after him wasn't giving up, so we think he decided to hide out with you, where he'd be safe till we could get there. Unfortunately, he was too slow getting to you."

"So he *was* pushed."

"Without doubt."

"By who?"

"By the same person who also killed Sonny Malinta, to shut him up."

"You don't have any idea who the killer is?"

"It all went down fast. They must not have realized Ochinko had the papers till after he'd left Japan, or they would have killed him there. And they didn't have time to bring in a hit man from Japan. But they have local contacts, they must have used a local contract killer."

"But Ochinko hid the papers, and instead of the killer recovering them, I got there first?"

"Apparently." His eyes narrowed and his concentration intensified. "Are you sure you didn't see anything else, Alex? Tell me one more time. Who was around, probe your memory. Did you see anything at all suspicious?"

I didn't have to stop and think. I'd been over it all in my mind so many times that I could honestly say, "Nothing. Not a thing. When I went down to recover the briefcase, there was a homeless man rummaging through the garbage, but that's certainly not unusual. I've seen him around for years."

"Anybody see you pick up the briefcase?"

"I'm sure they didn't. I was careful."

"That fits. If anyone had seen you take those papers, you'd already be dead."

I felt that cold chill again.

He sat back, and his face relaxed a bit. "Well, now you know a bit about where you are."

"My turn to ask a question," I said.

He nodded.

"How do you know what Shinda wanted from me that night I went to his penthouse? You knew I didn't respond to their demand that I hand over Victor's papers and manipulate Jess's loyalty. Do you have Shinda bugged, too?"

He threw back his head and laughed out loud. "Bingo," he said. "They told me you were sharp."

"Then explain something, please. I've been told twice recently that Shinda and his thugs are planning to do me in. Any truth to that?"

The smile plummeted from Yoshida's face. "Who told you that?"

"A fairly credible source."

"They might have killed you in the beginning, if they'd known you had the papers. But there's no reason now." He thought. "No, I can't think of anything I heard about them hitting you. But you know, they think you know a great deal more about their business than you apparently do . . ."

"Like what?"

"They seem to think you and Jess Seitaki are deliberately trying to sabotage their Golden Palms project. Something about revenge."

"Do you think they killed Victor?"

"No. Victor's heart attack was the real thing. That has nothing to do with it anyway. They seem to think Jess is deliberately sabotaging their project by not signing the papers that would allow them to get the variance they need to continue building, and they think you're helping him."

"Well—if Ice money is the foundation of their developments, I'll be happy to exercise some revenge if I get a chance. But I didn't even suspect that Shinda was connected to the Ice traffic until this whole thing started. Jess and Yoko were my friends, but I never traveled in the same circles as Victor. I knew nothing about his business—apparently Victor was far removed from the dirtiest side of all this, anyway."

"I know that, Alex. But apparently Shinda and Takio don't. They make little references to something that apparently goes back a few years, something that indicates an involvement with your late husband. Frankly, that's another reason we think Ochinko may have known David."

I felt a sick, sinking sensation that momentarily disoriented me, as if a small earthquake had rolled through my world, leaving it distorted. I forced the fear to recede, then said in a voice that sounded small and faraway, "Did you know David?"

He shook his head. "I was at Quantico when all that happened, just going through the academy. Listen, about this possible threat on your life—in light of what's happened to Ochinko, I don't want to take that lightly. But there's no reason to believe it's true—yet. Let me look at the transcripts we have from the Shinda tapes again, see if I've missed anything. In the meantime, that offer of a vacation still stands."

"I don't think so."

"We'd really like to get you and Troubles out of the line of fire. This thing just escalated so fast, we—"

"No. I'm not leaving."

"Well, we'll assign someone to guard you, then," Yoshida persisted.

"Thanks, but I can take care of myself."

He was studying me again with a peculiar, systematic evaluation that made me feel like I was under a microscope. Then he said, "That brings me to the final and most serious part of our problem."

"How much worse can it get?"

"Nothing you can't handle, if you want to."

I rolled my eyes again. "Okay, tell me."

"Well, if you do decide to stay in the middle of this, we'd like to leave our bugs in your house for a while. Our warrant expired yesterday, and we don't have sufficient reason to convince a judge to sign another one."

I felt my facial expression collapse into incredulity. "Why would I agree to that?"

"Because we'd like to put you on the payroll as a confidential informant."

That set me to thinking hard.

Being a CI brings with it a whole new set of problems and responsibilities, and if you don't know exactly what you're getting into, you're stepping dead into the barrel—you know, the one in which they shoot the fish.

There are several ways to become a CI. The cops might bust you for something, then "turn" you; that is, cut a deal if you'll play ball, like they did with Miro Ochinko. Or, for one reason or another, you might volunteer. This usually happens when people need money or when they want to get even for something.

Once you're on the books as a CI, you're assigned a CI number. Thereafter you usually feed in your information by dialing a certain phone number—to the FBI, DEA, local police, Military Intelligence— whoever owns you. You give the operator your CI number, where-upon your information is confidentially recorded and passed on to the right person. Or, if you're a good CI with access to good information and the cops or feds have learned to trust you, you're patched through to your contact (spies would call this person the control agent), and you can talk directly to the big people. Or, if you're *really* a good CI and they've *really* learned to trust you (or if they're using you for some very specific purpose that's very important to them), you can actually set up a clandestine meeting and talk face to face just like a real spy.

The trouble with all this is, in spite of what they always promise you, you have no control over your anonymity. Which means that if you draw a contact who doesn't take his or her work seriously, or who likes to brag, or who is otherwise a little short on brains or integrity or both, it usually isn't all that long before your cover is blown and you're branded as an informant by all the wrong people.

Which is not always the end of your world. Because if you really want to, you can still accomplish a great deal, even with that label. I learned that lesson well, back when I was writing my doctoral thesis on the politics and economics of the international drug traffic. I was honest with everyone who seemed interested in what I was doing, and I got along just fine, in spite of the wealth of information that was literally poured into my lap by people as diverse as top-level Mafia bosses to gutter junkies to all the people in between—including a bent politician or two. In the "peripheral world" there's always infighting. Malice, envy—someone always trying to knock someone else out of the box. These guys always try to use the police to rid themselves of rivals or enemies, but they don't want to stick their own necks out far enough to actually go to the police (even a recording of their voice leaked to the right people and saying the right things might get them killed). So what can they do? They come to the people who are known informants. They drop interesting tidbits into conversations, then cross their fingers and hope that the informants, whom they see as bottom-feeders, will pass those tidbits on to the police, who will do their dirty work for them.

Most good people in drug enforcement know all this. Most good people in law enforcement would never consider getting themselves into a situation where someone else controls their action to the point of being able to turn them into a confidential informant. That's the sucker's game.

I said, "Your plan is neatly thought out. If I agree, you can bug me legally. No possibility of repercussions, since I'm a party to the bugging, and all I have to do to keep you up to date is talk to my walls. The problem is, I don't have anything to talk about."

"We don't need you to dig up information. We just want the situation intact."

I said, "Since you already know more than I do, and I'm not going out digging for you, why do you want to leave the bugs in my condo?"

He surprised me by slumping against the car door and looking hollowly into the distance. "Ochinko held out on us. We can't build a case without the rest of those papers. But it gets worse. The HSP's narcotics division is working with us on this investigation, handling the link into the local Ice traffic. Somebody from either their end or ours ratted out Ochinko to Takio, and got him killed. You were right when you said we have a leak the size of Tokyo."

I said, "I'm sorry. Seriously. But I still don't understand what this has to do with me."

"You're our long shot. When Ochinko died, we watched about five years' worth of hard work go down the drain. The chance that we'll ever recover the missing evidence is almost zero. We figure now that Ochinko never took it out of Takio's office. He'd been hitting us up for more money and a better deal in the Witness Protection Program. We figure that he was going to use that last bit of evidence as leverage. On the other hand, whoever killed Ochinko and Malinta is a new link into Takio's operation. If we could nail the killer, we could almost certainly turn him, get him to inform on the next person up the ladder, and that would put us back in the game from a different angle."

I asked, "Did your people give Rosie Malinta the money to bail her husband out of jail?"

Yoshida sighed. "That's pretty cynical, even for you. No, Alex, we're not in the business of setting people up to get them killed, even to win a case of this size. That wasn't us. But we did interview Rosie—right after you left, by the way; she described you for us. And we'd also like to know who gave her the money."

"Okay. Sorry. But, well—now what? You know why I was in Ochinko's hotel room that night—sheer stupidity. Furthermore, I can understand now why you put the bugs in my condo, and no hard feelings, I got what I deserved. But I still can't understand why you want to leave the bugs in."

He turned back to look at me, and there was exhaustion and defeat in his eyes. "Like I said, we want the situation intact. The genie's out of the bottle, Alex. The Japanese have some high-powered surveillance technology these days; Shinda and his people have intercepted our wire."

"You mean—"

"Right. They have a device that intercepts the radio signals out of your condo. It works a bit like the intercepts that people use to pirate cellular phone frequencies and bill their calls to that number. Which means—they listen to every word you say, right along with us."

I was incredulous, speechless for a moment. Then I managed to sputter, "Why on earth would anyone want to do that?"

"I told you. They think you know a lot more about their operations than you say you do. Something to do with the dirty money behind their overt investments here in the Islands. They're worried that our surveillance of you might give us some kind of edge on them. And we're hoping—praying, actually—that we may be able to somehow manipulate that situation to our advantage."

"How?" I was furious. My fists had balled up again, I was just barely holding back my temper.

He shrugged his shoulders. "Forget it. It's a bad idea, anyway, such a long shot it would never work. If I were you, I'd take a vacation and just get out of the whole mess. Our expense, like I told you."

"To where. Tokyo? *That* would get me out of your hair, wouldn't it?"

"You could fly back to the mainland for a few weeks, wherever you want to go. We don't really want to force you into anything here."

"I'm not leaving my home."

"Then what do you want us to do?"

"Go away and leave me alone," I said.

"I wish it were that simple."

I looked at him, measured him. He seemed dedicated; he'd been decent enough to care about what happened to me. *Some* people I'd worked with in federal law enforcement would have just offered me up in the interests of winning the game. I decided that all in all, he was a first-rate professional who had been trapped into this ridiculous situation by a cruel turn of circumstance. Or, more likely, by someone in his own organization who had been bought off. Still, I wasn't going any further in this direction.

"Pull the bugs out," I said. "I'll take my chances with the bad guys."

He stared hard at me.

"Okay," I said, "don't remove the bugs. That means I'm working for you, doesn't it? Because at this point I know about the bugs, and if you leave them in, that's implied consent. Which technically makes the bugs legal and therefore makes me your CI, whether I officially sign on or not."

He was trying to read my mind through my eyes now. "That would be the simplest solution."

"But a dangerous one," I said. "Sort of like chaining one of my legs to the post in the center of a snakepit, then watching me try to charm the snakes."

"We need help, Alex. You of all people should know that we aren't superheroes. If we're going to win this war on drugs, sometimes we need some help—"

"No. I don't trust you. Two people are dead, your operation is a mess, you've got the *yakuza* eavesdropping on everything I say . . ."

"We didn't do it, Alex. Someone did it to us."

"Perhaps. But they're not going to do it to me."

He looked at the floor. "They're already doing it to you. If we pull out the bugs, we can't guarantee your safety—"

"No."

His shoulders slumped another quarter inch. "Then I guess that's it. Maybe I can come up with some other way to smoke them out."

I thought, long and hard. "Is this why Shinda and Takio have a contract on me? Because they think I'm informing for you?"

He looked up at me, surprised. "I really don't think they have a contract on you. There's nothing at all to indicate that. But I'll recheck our surveillance transcripts and see what we can learn. We certainly owe you at least that much. And if you change your mind, we can offer you full-time protection, of course, until this thing blows over."

Suddenly I saw Ochinko, lying in the street, the paramedics cutting away his expensive clothing to reveal the brilliant, ancient symbols of oppression that had been etched into his flesh like a brand. And then I remembered Sonny Malinta, bailed out of prison, then shot in the head, dead long before his time because of someone else's mindless greed. The sensation of death boiled up around me like a black incense, and there was the grinning, toothsome skull again, the all-devouring blackness.

"Look," I said, making a sudden decision. "Tell you what. Leave the bugs in. You have my permission. But I'm not signing on with you. Not with anybody. Just leave things as they are for a few days, let me think it over. Then we'll talk again, and I'll let you know what I've decided to do."

A bit of spirit came back into him then. "Thank you, Alex. There's more, of course. This thing links all the way into the Japanese National Police, all the way up to the highest levels of Japanese politics. I wish I could tell you everything that's going on here, maybe you'd have a bit more confidence in what we're trying to do and how hard it actually is. I don't want to leave you thinking we're a bunch of bumbling oafs. But you know how it goes. I've already said a lot more than I was authorized to. But I do want to emphasize that there's an awful lot riding on your decision. An *awful* lot, and we appreciate you . . ."

"Don't mention it. I mean, really don't mention it. Just tell me how to reach you on a regular basis, then let me get out of here and into some fresh air so I can start thinking again."

ollowing my conversation with FBI Special Agent Frank Yoshida, I walked around in a state of bewildered agitation, unsure of my next move. Troubles was home that night, studying chemistry, but he caught my mood. I noticed him glaring, from time to time, at the walls, the VCR, the kitchen phone. He was unconsciously mimicking my own behavior with regard to the bugs, and like me he grew tight-lipped and silent.

Troubles slept with a night-light on that night, for the first time since I had known him. The following day, he communicated through body language and facial expressions more than with words. Finally, at about two o'clock that afternoon, he scribbled a note telling me the place was beginning to feel creepy to him, like it was haunted. He couldn't concentrate, so he was going to the library to study; he'd be back when it closed at eleven P.M. I was relieved to have him out of the line of fire.

Alone, I set about tidying up the place, keeping my hands busy as I offered up fragmented prayers and tried to think things through. I couldn't even imagine how I'd stumbled into such a mess. I'd simply wanted to satiate my curiosity about a simple odd act—a well-dressed Japanese national stashing something in the bushes. Now here I was, skewered on the horns of an international dilemma, sitting on a barbed wire fence smack in the middle of a major FBI investigation.

As I threw a load of towels into the washer, I thought about Agent Frank Yoshida and all he'd said. According to him, both the good guys and the bad guys were interested in me. Yet I realized that neither of them was really interested in *me*, per se, they were interested in each other. I had merely fallen through the looking glass to become a part of the lens through which they were trying to see each other. Now, I was trapped. Yet though the situation was disturbing, it was interesting in a peculiar sort of way.

But it was also embarrassing. I had badly mishandled the entire situation, digging myself in deeper with every move I made. Now, I wanted to redeem my professional self-respect. But even more than that, I wanted to know if there was indeed a death threat hanging over me, and if so, why.

The situation was turning into a call to action. I wanted this thing straightened out. I was tired of having to think about every word I said, every move I made. It had been hard enough when I'd thought my listeners were in law enforcement. Now that I knew the *yakuza* was also listening in, the situation became impossible. But Agent Frank Yoshida wasn't going to solve my problems for me, no matter what he'd said. I had learned by long and hard experience that if anyone solved my problems, it would be me.

About an hour after Troubles left, while I was stripping the sheets from my bed, I made a decision. I tossed the sheets into the washer, walked back into my bedroom, and spoke directly to the bug in the electric outlet.

"Okay. Now I know who you are, all of you. And this isn't a game anymore, is it? But I still don't know what you want with me. I've been told you want to kill me. But if that's true, *why* is it true? And if it's not true, why is someone spreading lies and trying to make me afraid?"

I was speaking, of course, to Shinda and Takio, on the chance that Yoshida's information was accurate and they might actually be wasting their valuable time sitting a wire someplace, listening to me. Or—more likely—recording the message to be played later, which was just as good—or bad. But assuming Yoshida had told me the truth (and there was no reason to suspect otherwise), then he or other FBI agents would also hear the words—and they'd immediately know what I was doing. They'd be furious with me for taking the reins into my own hands. They would read it as a usurpation of their authority and a betrayal of their trust.

But if I was going to straighten this situation out, some lines of communication were going to have to be established, one way or another. I was going to have to work with the tools at hand. And so long as I didn't jeopardize the FBI's investigation in any way, maybe—just maybe—I could do something constructive with the peculiar situation in which I found myself.

But I was going to have to be very, very careful. There was a vast cultural schism between me and most Japanese nationals, but there were galaxies between my value position and that of the *yakuza*. Any word I said might be misconstrued, anything I did might be misread as menacing. Even if they weren't already planning to kill me, their minds might be easily changed. They were bound to be hair-trigger tense. Their investments were threatened, their freedoms were threatened—and if they perceived me as in any way causing that threat, I was going to become that statistic Jess had told me about.

So I certainly didn't want to strike up a direct enmity with them. On the other hand, I wanted the FBI to nail every last one of the death merchants, from both sides of the ocean and of whatever nationality, and if that included Shinda and Takio—so be it.

But strangely enough, the more I thought about the situation, the more the *yakuza* seemed to become the lesser of two evils.

Not that Shinda and Takio weren't evil men. They trafficked guns and drugs into their own country, they corrupted their own society, they and other fascists like them had caused Japan's moral and economic and political decay for centuries. The *yakuza* was indeed the essence of the violent, terrifying black mist that Mrs. Osaka had spoken of; their nefarious deeds were indeed veiled by the black curtain. They were the paramilitary force that continued the ultra-nationalist mind-set that oppressed both Japanese nationals and foreigners; they were the Japanese tentacle of the growing global octopus of totalitarian fascism.

But for some reason, Shinda and Takio's alienation from my own society was a mitigating factor to me. It didn't excuse the destruction they were causing, and they needed to be stopped, of course.

But those people who were facilitating the *yakuza*'s activities here in the Hawaiian Islands were quite another matter. There was no cultural divide for them to hide behind—they knew exactly what they were doing. Like me, they saw firsthand the results of the Ice traffic, every day. Their own families and children were being poisoned and murdered, their own society was being undermined and destroyed. These facilitators were busily shaping the razor-sharp cutting edge of the end of the world. Stop them, and you stopped the rest of it.

While I was thinking through all this, the phone rang and I swept it up without thinking. It was Fran Li. She had a new assignment for me. I was brusque with her, told her I'd phone her back tomorrow. A few moments later, about half past three, Derrick phoned. I let my answering machine record the call, didn't even pick up the receiver. I was thinking, thinking, driving myself crazy by hashing over the same tired hypotheses—over and over again.

As I took the towels out of the dryer and folded them, I remembered that I still needed to phone Jess. But I didn't want to go out, didn't want to see anybody—and most of all, I didn't want anybody to see me. I wanted this situation solved; I wanted out. And I didn't want to walk away from it by taking a vacation to the Mainland. Every negative experience in my life had taught me that when you walk away from something, you either return to a worse situation or you can never return at all.

On the other hand, I wasn't going to become a confidential informant for an organization that was, by its own admission, penetrated by the bad guys. No way. I'd liked Yoshida, even trusted him. But he was only one of many, and the rest of them were faceless, nameless phantoms, perfect strangers, trapped all too often in bureaucratic sludge. There were heroes there, to be sure. But no superheroes, Yoshida had been right about that. Not one of them was bulletproof, not one made a good enough shield to make me feel safe hiding behind them.

As I mulled all this over, the events of the past few weeks began to distill down to one single event. Miro Ochinko's death.

I put the towels away, then walked outside and stood on the balcony, looking down at the street where Ochinko had been killed. The ever-present tourists scurried to and fro. The foliage beneath which Ochinko had hidden the briefcase was to my left, the place where his tattooed body had lain was just beneath me. Why had he tried to find refuge with me? How had he even known about me? What had he been thinking when he phoned me, when he'd died? Had he indeed known my beloved David? If so, why? If only I could get to the bottom of these small mysteries, the rest of the pieces of the puzzle would surely fall into place.

I walked back into the bedroom, sliding the balcony doors shut behind me but leaving the drapes open, so the sunlight flooded through. I stepped through the wide doorway into my office and took out my copy of Victor Seitaki's papers, then pushed them aside and began to doodle on a notepad while I tried to understand. There was indeed a leak in the FBI's operation. The *yakuza* had known that Ochinko was informing on them. They'd also learned that the FBI was bugging my condo, they'd even learned the frequency that was routing the transmissions. Who had that kind of access? It had to be either someone in the FBI or someone involved in HSP's end of the investigation.

Yoshida had mentioned three people: David, Jess, and Derrick Green. I didn't want to think about it, but I had to evaluate the possibilities. I forced myself to look at the worst-case scenario.

Even assuming that David had been corrupted—a thought that was almost impossible for me to even fathom—he certainly had no influence on the present events. No, if he'd been involved in something illegal, he'd been working with either Jess or Derrick, and one or another of them was carrying on the dark legacy. *If* David had been corrupted . . .

I felt sick, even allowing myself to think the thought. *I'm sorry, David. If you can hear me, I'm sorry, but I have to figure this out.*

Jess had investigated Miro Ochinko's death. By the time I'd handed him Victor's papers at the restaurant that day, he must have known that Ochinko was a major informant. So why hadn't Jess mentioned any of that to me? What was he hiding?

Perhaps he had just wanted to keep me out of it, like he said. It was indeed a dirty business. Even here in Hawaii, the traditional Japanese community placed an extreme significance on social position and respect. If it came out that Victor had been acting as a facilitator for *yakuza* money, the Seitaki family was going to suffer immensely. Victor's actions would bring dishonor to the family beyond anything a Westerner could imagine. But would that threat be enough to compromise Jess's integrity? And if he hadn't done it for himself, might he have done it to save Anne and the boys, Yoko and his own children, from the disgrace? And what had Derrick meant when he'd said that Commissioner Alton might actually have a good basis for Jess's suspension?

The possibilities were staggering.

Worse yet, it was beginning to look more and more as if this macabre roller coaster ride actually had something to do with David's death. One way or another, everything kept coming back to David.

I tried to step back emotionally and force myself to objectively analyze the possibility that David had been involved in corrupted activities. The implication was that he'd somehow helped facilitate the Ice traffic. But I couldn't make it fit. Everything I knew about David belied the thought. He had been killed trying to *stop* the drug traffic. There was no way he could have been involved in anything dirty. My loyalty to David remained absolute, my confidence in his integrity was equally certain.

That left Jess and Derrick Green, one or the other or both of them working without David's knowledge. But Jess was a friend. Even though he'd been Victor's brother, even though Victor had sold his soul, I couldn't roll that over onto Jess. No, that, too, was impossible. Jess was out of it. And Derrick? I didn't know him all that well, but he had, after all, shot dead the Ice dealer who had killed David. And he'd seemed sincere in his wish to help me. No, Derrick too was out of the picture.

That meant Yoshida was wrong. Perhaps the leak originated inside the FBI itself, and Yoshida was trying to pin the blame on someone in the HSP because of his own loyalties. Now *that* made a bit more sense.

Maybe.

The more I thought about the situation, the more I felt as if I was trying to measure the dimensions of an expanding fog that was slowly but surely swallowing me up even as I tried to find its boundaries. And in the middle of this thinking, the sense of the bugs in the condo was beginning to create a near-hallucinatory atmosphere, heightening the sense of danger that had lingered with me ever since my conversation with Agent Yoshida. All this intrigue had elevated my adrenaline levels. I needed to step back from it, to catch my breath and see if I could look at it all from a different vantage point.

With that in mind, I changed into my black velour warm-up suit, stepped into my jogging shoes, stashed my keys and a five-spot in the pocket of my jacket, then headed out the door. I had a couple of hours before night fully swallowed the island. I planned to run down Kuhio beach, through Kapiolani Park, then, if I had time, to Diamond Head lighthouse and back, just to work out the physical kinks and the growing mental fog.

But I had only made it about half a block when I spotted Kenny and Snake, sitting together on a covered concrete bench at the closest bus stop, their heads together, talking. Two of David's street snitches. It had never crossed my mind that they might be friends—I guess I'd never really thought about either of them that much. But seeing them together I realized that they'd both been part of Waikiki's fringes for as long as I could remember. Of course they would know each other.

It was the first time I'd seen Kenny since bailing him out of jail. I hesitated, wondering if I wanted to approach him. I certainly wanted to ask him—again—who had told him the *yakuza* was after me. But in my present frame of mind, perhaps it would be better to avoid both of them altogether until I'd worked out some of the tangles.

I decided to do just that and was in the process of turning around when Kenny looked up. He started when he saw me, as if I'd caught him at something. He was too far away for me to see his face or hands clearly, but I assumed he might have been scoring drugs from Snake or was otherwise engaged in something illegal. I hesitated, still ready to take an alternate route, but he'd leaned close to Snake, probably saying something, then he locked onto me like radar and was now striding toward me, wrapped tight, with that fast-frame motion that tells you when a person is super-wired.

I waited.

He stopped short in front of me, buzzing with negative energy, and said, "Hey, howzit? Gotta sec?"

"Of course." His pupils were pinpoints, and he was practically scratching at himself. He was on meth. Probably Ice. Unusual. He was usually drunk or stoned on pot; I'd never seen him wired like this before.

"I got something for ya."

"About what?"

He darted a paranoid look both ways as if he expected something or someone to pop out at him, then mumbled, "Japanese."

I hid the zing of fear that raced through me. "How much money do you need, Kenny?"

He looked furtively around again, glanced back toward Snake, then back at me. "A hundred."

The price surprised me. He usually asked for ten or twenty bucks. For him, this was high finance, and I was betting he needed the hundred to give to Snake for more drugs. Experts said Ice could string you out after just one or two highs. I said, "I just paid your bail money a few days ago. I'm running a little short."

"I gotta have a hundred," he said, almost pleading.

I knew I was beginning to look like a pure sucker in Kenny's eyes. In the streets, kindness is all too often mistaken for weakness. On the other hand, I can't stand to see someone beg, so I said, "Okay. Tell you what. I'll make it a hundred on one condition. Tell me where you're getting your information." I didn't bother to add that I was going to parcel the money out ten bucks at a time for the next ten days.

The blood drained from his pruny face. "I—I can't do that."

"Why?"

"They—he'd kill me."

"Who would kill you?"

"I—I can't say."

I waited for a minute, measuring him. He was really afraid. I said, "Okay, Kenny, forget it. Back to the original deal. You give me the information. If it's worth anything, then I pay."

I knew the arrangement wouldn't ordinarily have been fair. But considering the fact that most of Kenny's information was made up or otherwise worthless, it was the only possible way to do business with him.

He darted another look at Snake—sitting, head down, at the bus stop—then said, "They told me to give you a message when I seen you again. They said tell you to lay off, or they're really gonna kill you."

"Who are 'they'?"

"I can't tell you."

"You said the Japanese, before."

"That's them."

"*Which* Japanese?"

"Can't say."

"Do *they* pay you to tell me these things?"

He looked guilty, and his eyes lost contact with my own.

"Look," I said. "Why don't you tell whoever is giving you these messages to come and talk to me. We can straighten things out without anyone getting hurt."

He looked hangdog and terrified, all at the same time. "I can't."

"Why not?"

"Because I don't see them.

"Then how do they talk to you?"

His eyes became shifty again. He glanced from side to side, then leaned in close. "They make me blind, then put their messages in my eyes."

I felt my heart sink. "Kenny, are you doing Ice *and* booze? What's happening to you?"

"Nothing. I'm okay. It's just these people. They used to send me a check every month, but now they come and steal my thoughts and put their own in, through my eyes."

"What people?"

He looked furtively around again, then said in a whisper, "The Union."

"Ah, man, Kenny—what have you been doing to yourself? Look at you. Those garbage drugs you've been putting into your body are destroying what's left of your brain. Why won't you let me help you? If you'll wait right here, I'll get my car and drive you up to Habilitat, this very minute. Think about it. Clean food, clean sheets, medical help. And I promise, you won't have to go to the state hospital—"

"Shut up or he'll hear you."

"Who?"

"Snake. He works for them, he tells them everything."

I ignored the absurd comment. "What do you say? I'll go get my car."

"You owe me a hundred." He was turning surly. I remembered the last time I'd tried to help him, how he'd stomped down the street upending trash cans.

"I'll bring some money," I said quickly. "Just wait here while I go back and get my car."

His eyes were dark with hostility now, but he solemnly nodded his head.

I thought the promise of money would make him wait for me. I jogged back into my building, took the elevator up to the parking lot and retrieved my car. I also grabbed my wallet and withdrew a twenty, just to use as bait.

But when I pulled out of my driveway and turned toward the bus stop, Kenny was nowhere to be seen. Nor was Snake. I cruised the streets for the better part of an hour, looking for either or both of them.

They were both long gone.

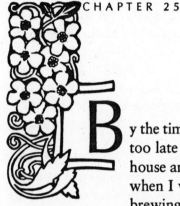

CHAPTER 25

By the time I'd finished looking for Kenny, it was too late to jog up to the Diamond Head lighthouse and back. Troubles had come home, and when I walked into the kitchen, where he was brewing tea, he said, "Derrick phoned. He wants you to call him."

"Later," I said, heading for the fridge.

"You should return his calls."

"I usually do." I had the door open and was looking at some browned apple slices and dried up cheese. "What are we going to eat?"

"I'm going out with Tess. Want to come?"

"No, thanks." I opened a jar of pickles and lifted one out. "I'm too agitated to sit through a meal."

"Why don't you go out with Derrick?"

The question surprised me. "Why do you ask?"

"I—well, I just worry about you, being here—" His words trailed off and he gestured around the room.

"Don't worry about it, I'm okay."

"When are you going to bring Derrick home so I can meet him?"

"It's not that kind of relationship."

"Why not?"

The inquisition was beginning to annoy me, so I said, "Because Derrick is a womanizer. I could never trust him. Believe me, I'd never get involved with someone like that, no matter how good-looking he is."

Troubles held up his hand, offering truce. "Okay, okay. I just thought maybe you had something going there. I stand corrected."

Troubles left half an hour later. I nibbled on some chips and an avocado, which satisfied my appetite for the moment.

But I was still restless. So after I ate, I walked over to sit on a bench beside the Ala Wai Canal to scatter millet seed for the birds while I savored the last daylight and thought some more about my peculiar situation.

Many Waikiki residents think the birds are pests and want to get rid of them. But I figure it's like Joni Mitchell said a long time ago; someone paved Paradise and put up a parking lot. Now that we've covered over their feeding habitat, the least we can do is share a scrap with them now and again. Fifty pounds of birdseed costs just over ten bucks at one of the big discount houses. That feeds a lot of birds. So now, when I walk over to the canal for the fresh air and a change of scenery, I take along some birdseed or dried bread. I've made quite a few feathered friends that way.

Which is good. Some days, you need all the friends you can get. Because there are a lot of people in this world who are going to be your enemies, no matter what you do. And just moments after I sat down I saw one of those people bearing down on me, from the Diamond Head end of the canal.

It was Snake. He had apparently crawled out of his lair for the second time that day. I saw him coming from a long way off, a tall, thin man with a limp. Today, he was using a cane. I scattered millet seed and watched the clouds above me transform from dusky schooners into fairy-tale castles against the darkening sky, but I was tense, watching him from the corner of my eye.

As he came closer, the birds panicked and swirled into the sky, abandoning me. They found harbor in the palm trees. I had to stay and face him.

He finally reached my bench. He stopped, glaring down at me. His eyes were dark and dead as stone, like the eyes of a serial killer.

In all the years I'd seen him around, I'd never spoken with him, I'd never been close to him. Now, I suddenly realized why David had so vehemently warned me to stay away from him. His broad, bony shoulders were permanantly hunched. His face was out of alignment from either an accident or repeated beatings that had broken a few bones and left one side of his jaw lower than the other. His skin was rich, weathered mahogany, too deep to be the sole result of our Hawaiian sun, though his ethnicity was unclear. His black, coarse hair was matted against his neck, greasy and dirty. He wore a soiled red shirt today, dirty twill slacks. He'd probably been living on the beach or under an abandoned building or bridge. But the most immediate and pungent impression he gave was the scent of death, the same scent carried by a lot of gutter junkies who become addicted to their own and others' destruction. He looked me up and down—probably imagining what I'd look like dead.

He works for them. He tells them everything, Kenny had said earlier. I forced a tight smile to my face. "Hello, Snake. I was looking for you and Kenny just an hour or so ago."

Something kindled in his serpentine eyes, then vanished.

"I know we've never met, but my late husband—"

I stopped short as he loomed in closer and snarled, "Shuddup."

His breath was stale and unpleasant, as if he had eaten something rotten. It crossed my mind that either his teeth were very bad or he had ruined his stomach with drugs and alcohol and other various poisons. Just then, the sound of an ambulance siren whined past on a nearby street. He glanced in that direction so I caught a glimpse of the jut of his profile in high relief. And in that chilling instant, I recognized his stale smell. The outline of a fleeing figure came back, racing down a hallway, pushing through a fire door, and I saw that same profile, in motion.

I was staring at the person I'd caught breaking into my condo.

I immediately tried to talk myself out of it. After all, I had misread almost everything about this situation so far. What if I was wrong again? I sat there, skewered by his evil stare, as I searched my memory. No doubt about it. Snake was the man who'd been in my condo.

I felt a rush of anger and started to ask him, right then and there, what he'd been doing. But my common sense outweighed my silent and growing fury, and I bit my lip and said nothing.

But in that moment of confusion, an even more terrible realization eclipsed my memory. I saw him again, in full relief. This time, I was standing on my balcony, looking through my telescope into a crowd of tourists. I pulled the telescope back, as an unusual motion caught my eye, and in that moment I could again see Miro Ochinko, placing something on the ground beneath the shrubs, standing back up and straightening his clothing; then in my peripheral vision, just as a brown UPS truck turned the corner, I glimpsed another furtive motion, something so common as to be invisible: a street person, one of the people I have learned to see straight through. But this one was ducking into an alleyway between Ochinko and the UPS truck, just a split second of motion, and then he was gone.

Was I forcing the memory? I had tried and failed to recollect a suspicious presence at the scene of Ochinko's death, over and over again. Why the sudden memory now?

It was simple. Seeing Snake up close brought the memory back, it was that simple. And in that instant I knew it had been no accident that Snake was searching the trash cans that day. I went back through the event, trying to dredge up a more salient memory, wishing I'd actually seen Snake following Ochinko or in a position to push him. But my mind played back a swirl of people, a carnival of sirens and police lights and colors and brilliant tattoos, but nothing more precise.

Still, Snake had been there, long before I'd seen him rummaging through the trash can and the bushes. I was even more certain of it now. He had pushed Miro Ochinko in front of Sonny Malinta's van, and later he had been looking for the briefcase.

He seemed to see this new certainty flood into my eyes, for he froze and his own eyes slitted up. He looked more reptilian than ever. I did a quick take of the surrounding area, looking for possible help. But since it was dinner time, no one was walking along the canal. The traffic whizzed past on the street behind me, far too swiftly for me to flag anyone down.

I turned back to face Snake. His eyes were lizard-flat, dead as tombstones. What I saw in them made me deeply, desperately afraid.

Snake sensed my fear. Perhaps he saw my eyes widen or saw my pupils dilate, but the change excited him. His eyes slitted deeper and his hand slipped into a pocket—and I knew in that instant that he was going to hurt me.

Something hellish flickered in his eyes; they came alive with a gnawing evil. I was looking into his pupils, and at the same time into a fury of hatred that was beyond him, consuming him.

I believe in hell, a real hell, where evil will be entombed for all eternity, once the conflict on this planet has been played out. And I believe in an evil that sometimes manifests itself through human beings—perhaps even in human form. Certain drugs deaden the human senses. They facilitate demonic infiltration, they consume people, they form a catalyst for death.

I was staring into death's black vortex, the inevitable end of us all. Even if there is a heaven beyond, all of us, at one time or another, have to step into that grim, black void we call death. Snake's eyes told me that this, my own death, was going to be painful.

I managed to distance myself for an instant. I actually managed to intellectualize the terror. And as I did, I felt the fear recede into a mental pattern of fizzing, sparkling, subatomic particles, knit together by some physical force, unifying into that object I knew as my body. It was as if I was spirit in that instant, looking at myself from a distance, and I knew that death would be nothing more than an escape, at last, from an earthly prison, followed by a grand, glorious entrance into the splendors of a Christ-ruled eternity.

But immediately I was staring again at the other, dark face of death. Snake's hand moved deeper in that pocket—it was as if I was stopped in time—and my stark terror surged back. I saw the evil glee licking at his eyes, I knew that at any instant life would regain its momentum and an explosion of pain was going to rip life from me. That knowledge caused fear to tear at my guts, to constrict my heart. My throat closed up and my skin literally went clammy from terror.

Death. I saw it coiling in his eyes, I saw it swallowing his own life even as it devoured mine. How many people had he been responsible for destroying, in how many different ways? At what point in his own life had he decided to embrace death's inevitability? I could see it in his face. Death, to him, was an addiction to the putrid sweetness of decay; it was power and prescience and rotted coffins with grinning skulls, and to him it was beautifully exciting.

These thoughts flooded through my mind with that rapidity that occurs only when you stare death in the face and your entire life flits before your eyes. This was the culmination of all I had ever dreaded; this vile, creeping harbinger was about to touch me with that stark reality of death, and however he did it, he would be very good at the administration.

I was poised, still numb yet wanting to defend myself, when his hand came out of his pocket, holding a fillet knife. It gleamed, razor-sharp. I brought my hands up, hoping to use karate blocks to deflect his stabs so my forearms would take the first blows. He stepped toward me, the evil excitement shining in his eyes—

"Alex! Run!"

It was Derrick's voice, and even before I could react to his order, he was flying at Snake, catching him sideways, both of them reeling backward, then down the embankment and into the darkening water. The water thrashed, then they came up once, Derrick sputtering, and I could see that he had a hand woven into Snake's hair. The knife had vanished, and then they were under the water again. Suddenly Derrick bobbed up, spitting water, looking round him, and began to swim toward shore. I leaned out and over the stone embankment to help pull him out.

He stood on the pavement, dripping and angry, as he scanned the darkening waters, trying to see Snake. I watched, too, and within an instant I pointed at what looked like a slimy water creature crawling up the far bank and vanishing into the foliage at the edge of the golf course.

Derrick cursed, then turned to look full at me, and, as if he was just now really seeing me, he said, "Sorry, Alex. I'm a little tense. Are you okay? Did he hurt you?"

"He only scared me to death," I said. I was surprised at how normal my voice sounded.

"What happened?"

"I don't have a clue. I was sitting here feeding the birds, and he came up and pulled a knife on me."

Derrick snorted in disgust. "This street scum. Somebody ought to put them all in front of a firing squad. Look, I'm off duty so I don't have my squawk box. I'll have to go find a phone and report this. But—are you sure you're okay?"

"I'm fine," I said. "I just spilled my birdseed." I looked down at the heap of grain on the grass beside the bench.

"I've been watching Snake for a while, expecting him to crack up for good. He's dealing Ice and using it, on top of the heroin and all the other junk in his system." We were walking, already, toward my condo, and he added, "I'll walk you home then come back and handle this."

I hesitated. I hate the role of damsel in distress, hate the idea of a knight in shining armor having to rescue me. Yet the truth of the matter was, if Derrick hadn't shown up at the precise moment he did, I would at the very least have some badly sliced arms. Or perhaps I'd be a corpse, like Ochinko, lying on the pavement while sirens screamed and garish lights flashed and people in uniforms ran to and fro, arriving far too late to keep me from careening into that dark finality of death that comes too soon to us all.

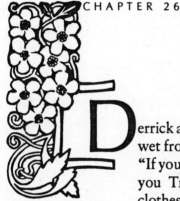

errick and I reached my front door. He was still wet from his swim in the Ala Wai canal. I said, "If you'd like to come in and shower, I can lend you Troubles' bathrobe while I wash your clothes and dry them."

"No thanks. I want to call HPD so they can start looking for Snake."

"Use my phone while I get you a towel."

"No, I can handle a little water. I'll run over to the substation and get some uniformed cops to help me look for Snake."

I was still fumbling in my bag for my key, I was still shaking. Suddenly, he reached out with both hands and held me at arm's length, one protective hand on each shoulder, and gazed deep into my eyes. "Alex, I tried to warn you."

I frowned, puzzled. "About Snake?"

"Not about him specifically, just that someone wants you dead. I mentioned it the last time we talked, remember? One of my informants said you were into something you needed to get out of, badly."

"You think Snake was *paid* to attack me?" The thought astonished me.

"That's exactly what I think," he said. "And I'm going to find him right now, I'm going to find out who paid him and why."

"I'll go with you."

"No. What I do when I find him may not be pretty."

"Don't do anything foolish, Derrick. That man is a killer. Catch him at a time when he isn't ready for you."

I knew it was good advice, but I felt foolish saying it, as if I had no right to speak. Furthermore, I was grateful to Derrick but embarrassed again, too. After all, I was supposed to be able to take care of myself. And I felt uncomfortable with his hands on my shoulders in such a familiar way.

Sensitive to my discomfort, he quickly removed his hands and stepped back. "I still want to help you, Alex. Anytime you feel like talking, I'll be there for you."

"I can't talk about what's happening, Derrick. I don't even understand it myself."

He frowned. "It's time you took this seriously. Snake could have gutted you in under a minute, thrown you in the canal to feed the fish."

I shuddered. "I know, Derrick. I really do appreciate you."

"Well, look, why don't I come back later and help calm you down. Maybe we can have a glass of wine—oh, I forgot." He gave me that charming grin of his. "You don't drink. Look, I'll pick up some espresso at the shop on the corner."

Quickly, I said, "I'd rather go out. Someplace where we're not likely to be interrupted." I really didn't want to talk at all, but I felt like I owed him something, at least some appreciation. And I certainly wasn't going to invite him to sit and have a chat inside my bug-infested living room.

"Whatever you want, Alex. I'll phone before I come back."

After he left, I took a long hot bath. I was still wired tight from Snake's attack on me, trembling inside and out. This situation was getting more and more bizarre—a fact that wasn't lost on my nerves.

As I sat in my hot, vanilla-scented bathwater and soaked, I thought about Yoshida. He had wanted to use me to smoke out Ochinko's killer, and it looked like that was exactly what had happened. But why? Had he primed Snake to come looking for me? And why had Snake broken into my condo?

I'd been trying to get Kenny to go to Habilitat earlier that day. Had Kenny told Snake? Had Snake felt threatened? If he was dealing Ice, then he should have felt threatened. It wasn't at all unusual for a newly admitted addict to rat out the person who'd been supplying him. Yes, that was one possibility. But Derrick had suggested Snake was in the pay of Shinda and Takio. He'd also said they wanted me dead.

But *why* would they want me dead? That was another thing that still didn't make sense. Did they suspect I'd actually seen Snake push Ochinko in front of the van? Or did the whole thing link back into something else, something that had happened before David's death?

My thoughts were tangled and circular, and no matter how I tried to puzzle things out, the picture just wouldn't fall into place. Finally, after soaking for almost half an hour, I felt a little better. I climbed out and dressed in a gray warmup suit.

I wandered back into the living room. It was uncomfortably quiet. Troubles was still out with Tess. He'd been spending more and more time away from the condo. I turned on the TV, more for the noise than for entertainment. Though I wasn't quite so tense as before, my mind was still fixed on Snake. I considered going out on my own to look for him, then decided against it. What could I do, track him down and shoot him? No, for the moment this one was better left in police hands.

Still, as I continued to rehash Snake's attack on me, I started looking at the incident from a slightly different perspective. It was wonderful that Derrick had shown up at the exact moment necessary to save me. But maybe it was a little too convenient. Of all the places he could have been, why there? Was he watching me, playing big brother? Or was he just flat-out spying on me? I moved on past those suspicious thoughts and tried to shake loose more memories of Snake at the scene of Ochinko's death. But I was getting a blank picture again; perhaps that fleeting glimpse of him darting into an alley was all that was stored in my memory.

There was a kids' show on the first channel I tuned into. Automatically, I started hitting the keys of the remote, channel-surfing, filling up the empty spaces with the visual equivalent of white noise as I tried to think about all that was happening to me.

There are several Japanese channels aired in Honolulu, some of which play only at certain times of day, and I had never before been interested enough to figure it all out. But today, as I scanned past, I caught a glimpse of the exterior of a huge stone castle; then there was a quick cut to the inside where a man—obviously a bad guy—was chugalugging cup after cup of hot sake. Delicate, pure of heart geisha dancers swayed to music while he leered at them. At the same time, he was busy with his gang, putting together some sort of scam against a rich man they called the *shogun*.

Even though my adrenaline was still singing through my veins, the scenario snagged my interest. But not because of its story line. No indeed. I was captured because in that moment I remembered that the *yakuza* almost totally controls the motion picture industry in Japan. The stereotypical portrayal of the bad guy caught my fancy, for I realized it was a sort of self-portrait designed by one of the same type of people who had just tried to kill me, if Derrick's assessment was correct. What kind of people were they? What made them tick?

The Mafia in the United States devoured books about organized crime, fact or fiction, and they often financed movies about themselves. Even those they didn't finance, they devoured, especially if they were romanticized. People in federal law enforcement were always surprised to find that the mobsters modeled themselves after their screen images—just as other people do. After the movie *The Godfather* came out, all the New York mobsters were dressing exactly like the characters, all the would-be capos were mumbling out of the sides of their mouths, the way Marlon Brando did. Did the *yakuza* do that—idealize themselves, then try to live up (or down) to the idealized image? As I watched, I began to see that the plot similarity to the old Hollywood extravaganzas was unmistakable. Since the movie came complete with subtitles, I could at least follow the action.

The gist of it was that a *shogun* had a vault in his castle that was full of fabulous wealth—and naturally all the bad guys wanted to get the loot. The bad guys were for the most part caricatures: jovial misfits, nasty-spirited buffoons, and handsome young men who would risk all for love and honor. Was this the way Takio and his merry men saw themselves? Perhaps. Many American mobsters had just such idealized self-images, and the American public was often all too eager to buy into the lie. Why should the Japanese be different?

The subplot centered around a middle-aged thief who loved the daughter of a fellow thief who refused to let them marry. The smitten thief naturally got his hands on enough of the *shogun*'s loot to offer up a dowry that changed the father's mind. When the middle-aged, lower-class couple were married, the group of lovable misfits lionized them yet teased them mercilessly, mostly about their advanced age.

The movie ended with the revelation that the *shogun* himself—a tall, handsome fellow—had infiltrated the group of thieves and at the critical moment there was a fierce sword fight, which the *sho-*

gun—surprise—won, although there was much backslapping between the men, for the *shogun* apparently understood why the men were so desperate to rob him and bore them no ill will.

There were fascinating eighteenth-century sets, lots of atmosphere, good shots of the looming, stone castle, magnificent swords, fragile-faced women in kimonos who proved, in a pinch, to be anything but fragile. But most of all, there was a lesson here for me. Watching the movie brought home the fact that there were many differences between me and the Japanese criminals who had somehow invaded my life. But we were also much the same. I thought about that. Someone had said there were certain basic needs common to all human beings: food, shelter, clothing, and a need to be respected. Fair enough, though I would have added the need for spiritual salvation to the list. Besides, respect wasn't something you just gave out, wholesale. Some people earned respect, some didn't . . .

I used the remote to click off the TV, then crossed my legs like chopsticks, thought for a moment, then said to the bug in the VCR:

"Someone tried to kill me today. I don't know why. If possible, could you, who live in my walls, shed some light on this situation?"

I was silent for a minute, praying. Then suddenly I remembered the Bible verse, Matthew 10:16: *Behold, I send you out as sheep in the midst of wolves. Therefore be wise as serpents and harmless as doves.*

Still silently, I prayed, *God, show me what to say, show me what to do. I'm way out of my depth here, I can't handle this situation without You.*

Aloud, I said, "You all seem to want to know what I'm up to. Believe it or not, I plan to tell you. All of you. Without bias, without pulling any more punches than are absolutely necessary in order to avoid making this situation worse instead of better. I am, at this moment, in the process of trying to extricate myself from this situation, and I'm in the process of trying to understand why someone would want me dead.

"Toward that end, let me just take a minute of your time to let you know that what we apparently have here are at least two opposing factions with various opposing goals, and if we take things from that point of view, what we're all going to have sooner or later is an explosion—because believe me, all the gunpowder and plastique is well in place, all the detonating devices have been laid. In other words, someone is going to get killed here sooner or later if all this doesn't stop. And I don't plan to let that someone be me. Or anybody else, if I can help it. Nor do I plan to turn myself over to the feds for protection. I wouldn't like to live anywhere else besides Hawaii, even for a short time. So here I am, and here you all are, and it looks like we're all in this together.

"So—what are we going to do? Plenty. Someone is going to jail. That much is certain. Someone else is going to have to give up some money, probably a lot of money, money they'd counted on to consolidate certain power positions both here and in Japan. Yes, Japan. As in Japanese *yakuza*. I know who you are, more or less. I also know what you want. Well, I'm sorry to tell you, but you can't have it.

"Anyway, I think you'd all agree that this situation has been building to some sort of serious crisis point. On that, we surely must all agree. Which just goes to show, we *can* all agree, at least sometimes and on some things. There is hope.

"The question is, how are we going to resolve all this without someone getting killed? The answer is, we won't. But God will, if we let Him. Because whether you like it or not, there is a God, and He is ultimately in charge here, and what happens is going to be up to Him, in the final analysis.

"And so—I just wanted to let you know, all of you, that I'm hedging my bets by placing my trust in Him. As far as the rest of you are concerned, you'd be wise to do the same because none of you, not a one of you, is on your way to any place you want to be with this situation. I am absolutely certain of that."

At that moment, the phone rang.

No problem. It was a good place to sign off.

I said, "That's it for now. *Sayonara, sochi.* And may God give you—all of you—wisdom."

I let the phone ring four times, then it stopped ringing. And then after a moment, it rang twice more.

Jess. He needed to talk to me, he was at home.

I phoned him back from the lobby. He was breathless, excited. "Alex, are you someplace where you can talk?"

"At a pay phone. Why, what's up?"

"You were right on target. I've found a link between Alton, Ed Grappner, and Ko Shinda. You're never going to believe it. Can you meet me right away?"

I thought about Derrick. He was supposed to be phoning soon. I didn't want to see him. But I was going to. Not only did I owe him that much courtesy, but I wanted to learn why he'd been so conveniently nearby when Snake attacked me.

I said to Jess, "Can't you tell me now? I have something cooking."

He hesitated. "Are you absolutely sure your phone is clean?"

"Yes. I actually swept it yesterday." Which was true. I'd brought my bug-sniffer downstairs, then checked out this phone when no one was looking, wondering all the while if I really was getting paranoid. But there was a possibility that someone was watching me, knew I was using the pay phone a lot these days. And the feds had been known to bug pay phones.

Jess said, "Okay, here's how it works." He proceeded to explain.

Andrew Alton, political aspirant and Jess's most powerful nemesis, had been "twisting" Japanese real estate deals before his appointment to Commissioner of the HSP. He'd been working in tandem with none other than Ed Grappner, President of the Commercial Loan Division of the Bank of Oahu.

Twisting worked like this: A real estate broker would find a financier who was willing to shave corners. Then, together, they'd find a sucker—usually a foreign client who didn't know the true value of Hawaiian properties. The broker—Alton, in this instance—would quote a price way above the assessed value. The commercial banker—in this case Grappner—would verify that price, assuring the client he was getting a good deal. Most foreigners still trust bankers.

Take, for example, a property assessed at $500,000. If that was a fair price, the seller would be happy to get it. But the broker would charge the foreign client maybe $750,000, or even a million. The mortgage banker would help the broker get that inflated price, then would actually finance the mortgage at the inflated price. Then they'd split and pocket the difference between what the seller received and what they'd charged the client. Some really big bucks had been made that way during the heyday of Japanese investment. Some of the foreign investors who were going bankrupt had fallen victim to this chicanery.

Twisting was not always illegal. It depended on how it was done. But it always fell into the category of highly unethical business practices. It was, in short, a high-powered scam, and if you got caught, nobody ever trusted you in business again.

When Jess had finished explaining, I said, "That's enough to ruin Alton and Grappner. But where does Shinda come in?"

"You're going to love this. Ko Shinda was investing some loose *yakuza* change in several single-family homes here on Oahu. Alton and Grappner didn't know who he was, and they tried to reel him in. Instead, Shinda caught them working him over and made a deal with them. His silence in return for their souls."

I bit my lip. "So *that's* how he coerced Grappner into abandoning Victor in midstream."

"That was part of it. There was also some pressure applied to the parent bank, back in Japan. Plus, Alton seems to be in even deeper, maybe even supplying Shinda and friends with HSP intelligence."

"And this also explains your suspension?"

"That still has me puzzled. Ko Shinda is unhappy with me because I still won't sign Victor's papers so he can get the variance permits for the Golden Palms. He may have applied a little pressure to Alton, convinced him I'd be more pliable if I had less job security. But that doesn't explain it all."

I said, "Maybe this would be a good time for you to bail out of the Golden Palms altogether."

"If it was just me, I'd walk away in a heartbeat. But that could leave Anne and the boys high and dry. Victor had more money wrapped up in the project than I'd initially realized; Anne's inheritance depends entirely on what happens there."

"What about the theory that you were suspended because you refused to accept Ochinko's death as an accident? How would Alton's relationship with Shinda fit into that?"

"I've been wondering about that ever since I got back from Hilo. That's where I learned about Grappner and Alton. The manager of the Golden Sands is ticked at the whole deal. He was supposed to get some bonuses for setting up clients for them to twist, and they pocketed his money, too."

I looked around the lobby to make certain nobody was watching me. Mrs. Shipley from Number 408 was going out the door to walk her poodle. A security guard I didn't know was lounging outside the front door, smoking a cigarette. No obvious spies, but still I leaned in close to the mouthpiece, cupped my hand around it so no one could even lip-read what I was about to say, and then I told Jess about Snake attacking me.

"I'll be right there. Why didn't you say anything?"

"Don't worry about it. I'm safe here, and the HPD is already out looking for him."

"Why would he attack you?"

"There are several possibilities. But that doesn't matter right now. What does matter is—I believe Snake pushed Ochinko in front of Sonny Malinta's van."

There was a silence on the other end of the line, then Jess said, "I guess Snake just proved he's capable of murder."

"Indeed." I thought about the look in his eyes again and shuddered.

We talked for a moment about the possibilities. Jess quizzed me about Ochinko's death again, and I told him what I'd recently remembered about seeing Snake slip into the alley near the death scene. Then, Jess said, "Alex. I kept something important from you. I believe you should know this now."

"That Ochinko was an informant?"

There was silence on the other end of the line, then Jess chuckled. "You never cease to amaze me."

"Someday I'm going to be a real private eye," I said. Then I got serious again. "So it isn't just that Shinda is trying to threaten your financial security so he can manipulate you like he did Victor. No, he also wants any interest in Ochinko's death to die down. Maybe you can figure out a way to crack Snake, once they bring him in. You might find out exactly who hired him and who paid him. That should be sufficient grounds for a RICO charge that would bring down the whole organization."

"I can't interrogate Snake. I'm still persona non grata at the HSP."

"Maybe Derrick Green will help."

There was an unusually long silence, then Jess said, "No, bad idea. Anyway, things are finally beginning to sort themselves out. I may not be able to get Alton indicted for what he's done, but if I can gather a bit more evidence, I may at least get him out of the picture so I can get reinstated and back to work."

I said, "God's blessing, Jess."

"Thanks. I'm going to need it."

t was almost ten P.M. when Derrick finally phoned and said he was on his way. I suggested we meet at the beach and go for a walk, he agreed, and half an hour later we were strolling along the darkened sands, pant legs rolled up, shoes in hand, beside the inky sea and beneath the star-strewn sky. As we walked, we discussed our respective days and the unpleasant way in which they had overlapped.

"Snake is long gone. Probably on the other side of the island by now," Derrick said. "We had six squad cars combing Waikiki and the far side of the golf course. He vanished. But HPD and HSP are both still looking for him. We'll get him."

"I'll feel better when he's off the streets. He scares me."

"He's violent," Derrick said.

"It's a wonder he hasn't seriously injured someone before now." I was fishing.

But Derrick merely said, "He's getting worse. I'm glad we have an excuse to put him away."

We had reached the crescent where the hotels tower up beside the beach, their lighted windows glittering. We walked along silently for a while. The trade winds rippled the black water, which answered by spooning frothy breakers onto the sand. The neon and streetlights bathed the area in distorted shadow-shapes and garish, muted rainbow light; I felt uneasy, as if there might be demons lurking in the shadows.

We came to an outrigger canoe, turned upside down on the sand. Derrick sat down on the hull, I sat beside him. He looked down at me. "You're not saying much."

"Sorry. I was thinking about life, about the drug traffic and all the other corruption. About how this world is fraught through with trip wires and traps that seem to sabotage everything good I try to accomplish."

Derrick shrugged. "It's not all that bad. In fact, life is actually pretty good. Almost anything can happen. You might win the twenty-million-dollar lottery tomorrow, or you could be mugged and murdered in the street. You just never know till it happens, so you have to learn to live for the moment." His arm snaked out, found its way around my shoulders.

I gently removed it and instead loosely held his hand. "It seems to me that the violence is growing worse. There are too many people like Snake, too many drugs. I should be furious about what he did to me today, but in a way I feel sorry for him. He's so swallowed up by the drugs and the misery, he probably hasn't had a lucid thought for decades."

I felt Derrick tighten up. "Snake is a zero. An insignificant cipher. We'll catch him and put him away, and sooner or later he'll die behind bars where he belongs."

"I know you're right. But sometimes I look at the walking dead out there and I think, they were babies once. Innocent, pure. With promise and humanity. Why can't they see what's happening to them? Why can't we get them out of it?"

"You'll drive yourself nuts that way, Alex. You can't fix people, most of them are doing what they want to do. Anyway, it's all in how you look at it. You're like me—we both see too much of the dark side of life."

"That's certainly true."

"You need a break. A vacation. Say, I have some time coming up. Want to fly over to Kauai and kick back on the beach for a few days?"

"I can't. I have some things to straighten out."

I felt him tighten up again. "You'd be wise to leave for a while, Alex. From what I hear, you're treading on dangerous ground."

I felt a slight shiver, and suddenly I was traveling through a parched, black land. What he said was true. But did he really know something, or was he just guessing?

"Give it up," he said. "You're fighting forces that are so much bigger than you that you'll pound yourself to death just battering up against them."

There was something in the tight, almost threatening way he said the words that made me look up sharply at him. What I saw in his face startled me. There was a feral gleam in his eyes, a wolfish tightness in his mouth. But immediately, it melted into a charming grin. "*Now* look what you've done," he said. "I'm getting as uptight as you are."

I was still in the same position physically, his hand was still in mine. But mentally I'd taken a step back from him. I quickly monitored my feelings, and I realized I'd been playing a little fast and loose with them. *Watch it, Alex,* my little voice said. *There are strong undercurrents here, swift treacherous streams of emotion that will knock your footing right out from under you if you try to cross these raging waters.*

I gently withdrew my hand and said, "But a person has to fight back. I, especially, have to try. I'm a Christian, you know. I'm morally obligated to try to make things better, but lately it seems that everywhere I go, I make things worse."

"Because you're stubborn," he said. "You need to smarten up. Stop looking at the situation in a negative way, and start seeing the potential."

"What situation is that?" I tried to sound nonchalant, but I was suddenly on edge. He indeed knew more than he was supposed to.

But he grinned and said, "Us. I'm here for you, Alex. You need to know when to take advantage of a good thing."

I managed to hide my relief and work up a faint smile, but there was nothing I could say that wouldn't seem rude, so I kept quiet.

He was silent, too. The breakers crashed against the sand in a soothing rhythm and the triangle lights of cruise ships twinkled from far out on the black water. I began to forget about the day's tangled events as I thought about the vastness of the earth around us; as I inhaled the eternal, musty scent of the sea.

I was actually beginning to relax and get into the natural serenity of the night when Derrick snapped me back to reality. In a bitter tone of voice, he said, "You're on some kind of self-destructive trip, Alex. Wearing a hair shirt. Sometimes I think you believe it was your fault that David was killed."

I turned my head to stare at him.

"Seriously," he said, the edge coming off his voice a bit. "I know I'm out of line here, but I'm worried about you. You need to start dating again, get past it. Even if you and David had been getting along at the time of his death, David still would have done what he did. You know David. He was determined to bring down those scumballs."

I was still staring at him. "David told you we weren't getting along?"

Derrick shrugged, looked uncomfortable, then said, "I wouldn't worry about it. Partners talk about everything, you know how it goes. He knew you were catching on. But it's no big deal. A man spends so much time in the streets, he starts to look around a little. Believe me, it doesn't mean a thing."

I was staring harder. "He knew I was catching on to *what*?"

Derrick looked at me then as if he was really seeing me. "You didn't know?"

"Know what?"

"That . . . I mean—"

"Are you saying David was fooling around on me?"

Derrick looked sick. "Not really fooling around . . ."

I felt like someone had sucker punched me in the gut. "What are you trying to tell me?"

He dodged the question. "Look, Alex. There's no point in kidding you. Things happen. But just because things don't work out with one man doesn't mean you can't trust any of us. You need to learn to give people a chance."

My head was spinning. I felt anger welling up in me, but right behind it came the hurt, like a splintering ball of ground glass. Could what he was saying possibly be true? Had I misread my entire relationship with David? A lot of cops in Vice and Narcotics ended up having affairs with the people they met in their street world. The work was brutal, the assault of the immoral lifestyle was relentless. But it didn't matter what other cops did. What mattered was what David had done. And he had not cheated on me! Had he? Suddenly I thought about Anne Seitaki and her long avoidance of the truth with regard to Victor's infidelity. Nobody ever wanted to believe that the person they loved was being unfaithful. But things did happen in the brutal, ever-grinding world of the streets. Still, I had trusted David so much that the possibility of his infidelity had never even entered my mind. But what if I'd been wrong? The possibility was terrifying. If I hadn't known David, I had never known anything. If my perception of his honesty and integrity was inaccurate, then my whole life was an illusion, an exercise in self-deception, the bottom fell out of my very world.

Derrick scowled as he watched me, but then he brightened and said, "Sorry, Alex. It's just that—well, David said you knew, that you didn't mind all that much . . ."

"Derrick, this conversation is making me sick. Literally. I'm going home." I rose to my feet.

He stood too. "Alex—I'm sorry. I didn't mean to upset you."

But the black mist, the shrouding fog, had swept into my mind again. I was confused, hurt, the world around me had once again turned ever so slightly alien. I felt the threatening, suffocating sensation again that some dark, evil, unknown force was swirling into my life to smother me beneath decades—even centuries—of deceit, hatred, and vile, defiling lies.

But—*were they lies?*

Maybe, maybe not. In fact, I would never know. Because I couldn't even go home and confront David, ask him if it was true, and if so, why. David was gone from me and from my concerns about his fidelity. He had pitched face first into that deep and evil labyrinth called death, taking his life and all his secrets with him.

I was almost shivering as I walked home, moving quickly, silently, Derrick keeping pace beside me, trying to talk, but every word he said was whipped away by the increasingly violent wind.

He finally said good night as I entered my lobby. I barely managed to acknowledge him. Then he said, "I'll let you know as soon as we pick up Snake, so you can come down and sign a complaint."

"Yes," I said, "please do."

I turned toward the elevator. He stood there for a minute, and I knew he was watching me. Suddenly, he sprinted forward, catching up with me, and said, "Alex, I really am sorry about David. I—I just thought you knew."

"It's okay, Derrick. Don't worry about it. Look—I have to go. I'll talk to you tomorrow."

I turned my head quickly and entered the elevator. I didn't want him to see that I was blinking back tears.

CHAPTER 28

During the night, the trade winds died. By morning, a torpid, windless pall had settled over the Islands, to remind me that I wasn't in Paradise after all.

I lived in the relentless subtropics; we were on the same boiling latitude as Mexico City. Without the cooling winds the sun-warmed island landmass baked the air, creating towering white clouds that stacked up motionless above the Koolaus. The greens of land and the blues of the sea were enhanced by the purity of the air. The suffocating heat gave me a headache.

Troubles' motorcycle was acting up, so he took the Honda to class, then to the windward side of the island to a friend's cookout. I stayed in my condo, air conditioner on full blast, ignoring phone calls—especially the three from Derrick. I was deeply damaged by his insinuation that David had been unfaithful. I couldn't quit thinking about it. The heat further depressed me, stifled me, made me feel listless and stupid and old.

But shortly after noon, gentle Kona winds began to blow in from the south. I opened my balcony door to welcome them only to see that a thin, blue-gray smoke was beginning to touch Oahu like a glaze on an especially fine oil painting. It enhanced the richness of the shadows, the clouds, the rubbery green foliage on the mountains and the fearsome blues of sea and sky. A languid gecko sat dazed on the milky brown stem of my tangerine bougainvillea. A fat, black hornet buzzed listlessly past my face, then spun downward and away.

Kilauea was erupting again, over on the Big Island. A new vent had opened up and the molten lava was bleeding off a thick, choking haze of ash and smog—called vog—that would blow to us on the Kona winds, blighting the air, causing children to stay inside, tempers to flare, people to snarl at one another over the slightest things.

I went back inside, shutting the sliding glass doors behind me, sealing myself, again, inside my chilled cocoon. The suggestion that David might have been unfaithful to me reopened the possibility that he had been corrupted in other areas. I suspended my disbelief and tried to analyze the situation in light of that possibility.

If David had been involved in something dirty, it would have implicated Miro Ochinko, because Ochinko had obviously either known David or known of him. The chain of criminal activity would have included Ochinko's *sochi*, Kuzio Takio. The next link would be the Shinda Corporation—Ko Shinda, and therefore Victor, and probably even Jess. How else would David have gotten involved in such a mess? But the other participants were a subject for another time. Next to David, no one else mattered.

What *if* David had sold out? Was it possible that he had facilitated the traffic in Ice, that his hatred of drugs was only pretense, fabricated for the sake of deceiving me? If so, he had literally sold his soul, and I had lived for two years with a stranger.

But why would he have done it? For money? We hadn't been rich, but I'd drawn a good salary at the university and his police salary was adequate. We'd had enough. No, money wouldn't have swayed him. That part didn't add up. And—no motive, no crime. *That* was a solid deductive equation in criminal analysis. On the other hand, perhaps he'd had a motive, something I couldn't yet fathom. After all, how well had I really known him? What *if* David had been corrupted? What if he *had* been involved, before his death, with Ochinko, who had therefore known where to find me, who had grasped at the straw of my proximity when he was being followed and threatened?

I tried and tried to make sense of things from that angle, but it just wouldn't fall together. So I decided to look at things from a different perspective.

The streets. They'd been known to snag more than one good person. When I'd worked as an Intelligence Analyst, that was one of the things I had to watch out for, the possibility that certain under-cover agents might become co-opted through acclimation to the subculture in which they worked. Adaptation. When you were exposed on a daily basis to moral corruption, unless you had a strong personal center of morality that you could draw upon, the lines between right and wrong tended to fade. As the ethics of your parent world became indistinct, it became easier to borrow the ethics of the world you inhabited: drug addiction, destructive sex, even murder could become the normal way to live.

So what did I really know about David's life as an undercover narc? Not much, really. We'd discussed some things, but for the most part he'd seemed to turn off that side of his life when he came home.

Snake had been David's snitch. I knew that. Snake was a drug addict and a small-time dealer, and he'd proved to me that he was capable of violence. But why was Snake still working the streets, if everyone—even I—knew what he did? Was his information really that valuable? And if so, why hadn't I learned of larger dealers he'd brought down? That sort of thing hit the papers, after all.

And what was David's true relationship to Snake? Had David merely looked the other way in return for Snake's information? Had he indeed wanted to protect me from Snake's potential for violence? Or was something worse going on?

I sat back and sighed. No matter how much I tried to fit David into the framework others were indirectly painting for him, the pieces just wouldn't fit. I continued to tick off the possibilities, but the David I knew and the one I was trying to imagine became so unlike one another that I began to feel disoriented by the juxtaposition. Still, I had to look at every possible angle if I was going to sort this out. And wherever the trouble originated, whether in a *yakuza* boardroom or a police headquarters, the deepest reality of the drugs always filtered down to the streets. Snake was a key to what was happening. I knew that now. So was Kenny. He knew something—his wild ravings cut just a bit too close to the truth I already knew to be pure fabrication.

I had walked into the kitchen and was cutting limes in half, preparing to make some fresh limeade while I brainstormed, when the wall phone rang. Something told me to answer it this time, so I lifted up the cherry red receiver—the one with the bug in it. "Albright Investigations."

There was a long silence. Then an accented, muffled voice said, "Look beneath your balcony." Before I could reply, the caller hung up.

Bewildered, I walked into my bedroom and stepped out onto the balcony, looking down. Parked at the curb was Ko Shinda's long, expensive limousine. Standing beside it, in livery today, was the beefy-necked chauffeur. He was holding a portable phone and gazing upward, and when he saw me, he furtively beckoned for me to come down.

I thought for a moment about the wisdom of complying. I hadn't heard from Agent Frank Yoshida yet regarding the possibility of the *yakuza*—Shinda's buddies—having signed my death warrant. Still, this wasn't exactly the way most contract hits were done.

But just in case, I quickly opened my desk drawer, withdrew my .38, checked to make sure it was loaded, then slipped it inside an ankle holster, strapped the holster onto my lower calf, and pulled my baggy acid-washed denims down over it. Perfect, not so much as a bulge.

The elevator was slow, and the chauffeur was pacing back and forth in front of the limo, holding his hat down against the growing wind, by the time I stepped out of the side door and walked up to him. "What's up?"

He stared at me, his pit bull face expressionless; then he stepped back and opened the rear door. I felt a rush of cold air as I stepped forward and bent to look inside. Ko Shinda himself sat there, his face as impassive as a kabuki mask. He wore a black suit and white-on-white shirt, a business tie, a diamond tie tack. *He* certainly had not been corrupted by the casual life and dress in the streets of Honolulu.

I did the bobbing thing, and he responded with one swift, abrupt nod, and then he made a quick, angry motion that told me to get into the car.

I did.

The chauffeur threw the car into gear, and we rolled away.

The interior was even chillier than my condo. The television set had been tuned to a Japanese channel, to the Tokyo stock market report. Shinda reached over and turned it off, so it stared at me with a cold, dead eye. The fold-down bar was firmly closed, the sliding window to the chauffeur's compartment was sealed tight.

I looked through the smoky windows and saw that we were driving toward Diamond Head, taking the same seaside route we'd followed the night I visited Shinda's roof garden. Out on the ocean the waves were increasingly choppy; the palm trees were bending with the increasing wind.

I said, "Mr. Shinda, please tell your chauffeur to drive around Waikiki while we talk, or let me out right here."

He raised his straight black eyebrows imperiously, as if he had been insulted. But at the same time, he lifted the speaker phone and said something in Japanese to the chauffeur. Then he said to me, "We will drive down to near the zoo."

"Good enough."

I settled back into the seat, pretending to watch the scenery pass, wondering what he wanted, waiting for him to talk first. But he just ignored me, his eyes hooded like a lizard's.

Finally I lost my patience and blurted, "Okay. What am I doing here?" The cultural niceties suddenly seemed like childish status games, especially considering what Shinda might be planning for me.

Predictably, Shinda arched his eyebrows again, like a parent gravely insulted by the behavior of an especially unruly child. The limo pulled into the tree-shrouded parking lot beside the zoo and stopped. Shinda turned to give me a Buddha's stare and said, "You wish for enlightenment?"

I frowned, puzzled.

He said, "Someone tried to kill you."

I remembered then. The bugs. He had actually heard at least one transmission.

I hid my astonishment, and said, "Yes. Thank you. I would deeply appreciate some enlightenment."

He shot me a swift, sideways glance, full of muted curiosity. "You are a most unusual woman."

"Not really. Not for America."

His eyes narrowed, as if he thought I was criticizing his culture. Which, of course, I was. Then his eyes hooded over, and his face went hard. "At any rate, this situation has escalated and it must be resolved. And so—I enlighten you. You have no place in this. Say no more to anyone, and go away until this conflict is concluded."

An unexpected burst of courage welled up. I asked, "Mr. Shinda, were you responsible for someone trying to kill me?"

He leveled an icy gaze at me that told me why the Japanese police called them "the violent ones." Then he said, "We do not wish you dead. Yet. But if this interference continues, we may not be so kind.

Now—please forgive our intrusion into your life. This will be the end of the matter."

I was speechless. Anything I said at this point would give something away, and I wanted to gain information, not give it.

But Shinda was through anyway. He lifted the speaker phone, and said, in English, "That is all."

Almost immediately, the limo began to move.

I sat back, silently. I wanted to ask a million questions, but all of them were dangerous. Again, I stared through the smoky windows— in order to keep from staring at Shinda. The sensation of an overwhelming black incense had rolled in, almost smothering me. There was an immense power here, a sulfuric toughness and a carefully controlled hunger for violence.

We had reached my building, the limo pulled to a stop. I had already turned toward the door, preparing to climb out, when Shinda surprised me by tilting his darkly elfish head to look at me again. He said, "This God you speak of. Do not trust Him to help you. He has no power over me. I do not believe as you do."

And suddenly there it was: one of those rare moments that God handpicks for you, then hands to you like a priceless gem, all weighed and polished and perfectly set. For once, I knew exactly what to say and do.

I gazed respectfully downward and said, "You believe the world was created by the Shinto sun goddess, Ameratsu Omikami."

He looked surprised. He of course had no way of knowing the extent of my tutelage at the wise hand of Mrs. Osaka, who had taught me a great deal about the theocratic underpinnings of the traditional Japanese culture. Shinto (in company with a certain sect of Buddhism) remained the basis of the value position that allowed the *yakuza* and other ultranationalists to believe they were an exalted people. This was the basis of their racism and protectionism, for they were not to taint their race by mingling with or being ruled by inferiors.

Shinda, obviously surprised by my question about Shinto beliefs, said, "I do believe in the Shinto way, yes."

Eyes still lowered, I said, "Then I respectfully advise you. The God I worship created your sun. Therefore, if there *is* an Ameratsu Omikami, my God also created her. In other words, my God created the star in the sky upon which your religion is based. And so I *will*

trust Him to help me because He has absolute power over everything—even you."

At that moment, the chauffeur opened the car door and peered in
at us, indicating that I was excused.

I nodded respectfully again as Shinda studied me, eyes unreadable,
face impassive again.

I managed to get in the final word. "*Sayonara, Shinda-san.* And
may the God who created the Rising Sun give you much wisdom."

Only moments after I returned to my condo, the phone rang again.
And again, I answered it, to hear Jess Seitaki's voice.

"Alex?" The word was an axe stroke of tension.

"Jess. What's wrong?"

"It's Troubles. Come right away."

"What?"

"There was an accident."

My heart hit the floor, my throat wouldn't open, I couldn't
breathe. But I swiftly forced my physical body back under control,
and heard my voice come out surprisingly calm. "How bad is it?"

"We're not sure yet. My good friend Nathan Wong is working
traffic detail now and he recognized your car. He couldn't reach you
so he phoned me. I'm on my car phone, I just arrived at the scene.
They're rappeling down now to get him—"

"*Rappeling?*"

"The Honda went off the road, on the mountain above Kailua,
just above the old monastery. It stuck about a hundred feet down—
almost straight down, but the car caught on a ledge and seems secure.
Troubles is still in the car; he's been down there a while. Someone
saw him go off the road and phoned it in fast; it's taken emergency
services a while to put a rescue team together. They have to rappel
in, but a chopper is standing by to medi-vac him to Queens Hospital
as soon as they can get to him. . . ."

I was already moving out the door. "I have my car phone with
me. Call me as soon as you know anything at all," I said. "I'll be
there as quick as I can."

I was praying, of course, even while I was talking. Sometimes all
you can do is pray without ceasing. But in spite of the prayers, my
throat was closing up like drying catgut. I glanced at myself in the

hallway mirror as I rushed past. My face was so white I almost didn't recognize myself.

By the time the elevator had taken me to the parking garage where I stored the van, I felt the confusion and terror begin to firm up into fury. This so-called accident was too much for coincidence. This was bad *nichibei*, very bad *nichibei*. When someone didn't like me, that was one thing. But when it came to my family—the only family I had left—that was something else again.

Now I was driving the van, cutting through traffic, down the H-1 freeway and to the Pali turnoff, speeding past the grand old mansions that now held various foreign consulates, the Japanese among them, past lush tropical greenery and up the mountain, causing more than one car to curse or honk at me as I darted around them at well over the speed limit.

Finally, I crested the mountaintop, passing through two tunnels. And just past the turnout that offers a glorious vista of the serrated green cliffsides and the aqua blue waters of the windward side of the island, I saw the emergency equipment, the yellow safety lights blinking, the red-lighted ambulance, the police cars with their flashing electric blue lights, cordoning off all but the inner lane of traffic.

There was a chopper in the sky, but as I watched, it whirled up and away. Was Troubles inside? Was I too late to see him?

I spun gravel as I skidded to a stop beside the police cars, earning a scowl from most of the officers in attendance. Jess was standing apart from the others, his hand shielding his eyes against the morning sunlight as he watched me arrive.

I ran up to him. "What's up?"

"You got here fast," he said.

I nodded.

"They just got him out," he said.

I shielded my eyes with my hand too, and looked up at the chopper, which was receding into the distance. "Are they transporting him to Queens?"

"No, he's—"

And at that moment, Troubles stepped out from behind the ambulance. "Hey, Alex! Over here, they're checking me out."

I gave Jess a look full of conflicting emotions, and he grinned. And then I strode over to the back of the ambulance, where Troubles was standing, two white-coated paramedics taking his blood pressure and bandaging his left wrist, and for some reason, I wanted to scream at him and pound him.

Proudly, he said, "Look! No internal injuries, not even any broken bones, just a sprained wrist so far."

"Which means that God answers prayer," I said, sounding annoyed. I was so grateful that he was okay that I wanted to sag to my knees and bawl, but I was also furious that he had put me through all this for what appeared to be nothing.

Jess motioned for me to join him. I looked questioningly at Troubles, who said, "Go on. I'll be stuck here for a while."

He smiled at one of the paramedics, an especially pretty young woman, who shyly smiled back.

I stepped over and looked down the mountainside, toward where Jess was pointing. My crumpled car was dangling at an impossible angle from the side of the cliff. It had been pinned there, about a third of the way down, by a small outgrowth of trees and rock. Nothing indeed! If Troubles had missed that single obstacle, the plunge would have been almost straight down, impossible to survive.

Jess steered me toward his black Jeep Cherokee, which was parked a short distance from Troubles' ambulance. He opened the passenger door for me, and I climbed in; then he went around to the driver's side and climbed in himself. Except for the portable red dome light and the radio tucked well under the dash, you'd never have known the car belonged to a cop, even one on suspension.

As soon as he was in, he turned and leveled a long look at me. "Someone tampered with the brakes," he said.

I felt myself go weak.

"Troubles told me how it happened. He was going down the grade when the brakes went out. He tried to work the emergency brake and it was out too. It's too much for coincidence. In fact, it sounds to me like someone cut the cable to the emergency, then drilled a pinpoint hole in the brake line, so the fluid would pump out when you started using the brakes a lot. Which means, when you needed them the most, they wouldn't work. How often does Troubles use the car?"

"Almost never. His motorcycle was acting up today."

"Then they wanted you."

"I agree," I said bitterly.

His eyes slitted up for a minute, then he relaxed and shook his head as if he was looking at a hopeless fool. "I asked you not to get involved. I jeopardized our friendship to keep you out of it. But you are so stubborn—you're the only person I've ever known more stubborn than a Japanese."

I thought about that. Two stereotypes in one, the Japanese stubbornness and the Scottish-German stubbornness. I wondered idly how I was ever going to break free from stereotypes when they permeated every part of my reality, especially when the victims of stereotypes were also the perpetrators of them. I said, "Too late now."

"Almost too late for Troubles," he said, grimly.

But Troubles checked out perfect, except for a nasty sprain of his left wrist, a fact which caused more than a few of the cops and paramedics to talk about miracles. Nevertheless, they took him to Queens in the ambulance, for overnight observation. I followed along and stayed with him until almost midnight. When I finally went home, I sat down on my plum-colored sofa and crossed my legs like chopsticks, then leaned over and played back the single message that had come in on my answering machine. It was another muffled voice, but this time I recognized it as Agent Frank Yoshida's. He said, "Regarding that matter we discussed. The answer is a negative. That is, a definite negative. That is all."

I smiled cynically. He was telling me, of course, that he'd checked into the tapes from Shinda's end of the game, that there was no indication that the *yakuza* wanted me dead. But I was betting, at that moment, that Shinda had lied through his sharp little teeth to me that afternoon. And that Yoshida was flat, dead wrong.

CHAPTER 29

It was the Season of the Dead.

O-Bon.

Time for the Festival of Souls.

During these torpid, languid days of high summer, the spirits of the Buddhist dead returned to their families. Colorful paper *chochin* lanterns were hung on porches and in trees throughout the Islands, to welcome them back. *Yagura*—short, square towers which held drummers and singers—were built in parks and in the courtyards of temples, in preparation for the Bon dances, which were performed out of doors, in the evenings, after the *segaki*, the services to honor the dead. Special sutras were chanted by priests. And then the summer nights filled with the slow, deep, hollow beating of the *o-daiko* drums and the poignant, dissonant music of the wooden flutes, lutes, and gongs. Wailing voices chanted *hayashi*—nonsense syllables interspersed between the haunting verses of the dance songs. Huge bonfires were sometimes built on beaches and open areas to guide the spirits back. Offerings to the dead were set adrift in the ocean to lure back those who came reluctantly.

The Bon dance was as much a cultural event as a spiritual one now, and I had come to enjoy the annual festivals—though of course my beliefs about death were exceedingly different from those offered by the Buddhists. But the occasion itself was cross-cultural. There was no attempt to proselytize, and persons of every persuasion could be found at the festivals, picking and choosing what they would believe and what they would enjoy.

My favorite Bon dance was on the North Shore, at the Haliewa Jodo Mission, where the festival always took place under the full moon. There, the lighted *yagura* was set up beside the glistening black waters of Kaiaka Bay. The Bon dance started just after dark and lasted for hours. Jodo chanters explained, between dances, where the dead had been (often doing spiritual battle in the demon world), and the *choba*, or food booths, were amply supplied with delicious shaved ice, saimin, almond cookies, and other local and Japanese treats. Island children darted between the legs of tourists, enjoying the summer's night. Teenage lovers strolled hand in hand. All were welcome to dance, so long as they were respectfully dressed. Tourists occasionally stepped into the dances to try their hand at the slow, circular promenade with its emphasis on squarish hand gestures and delicate postures and pauses. The dance involved a shuffling gait, the result of the kimono and the wooden slippers and *tabi*, or white socks, worn by the traditional dancers. But though the guests often wore Reeboks and sandals, slacks and muumuus, they would shuffle along, and sometimes even chant with the singers.

And then came the climactic part of the ritual, when the souls said good-bye and were released, once again, to the vast, dark spirit world. These partings were symbolized by farewell lights—hundreds upon hundreds of tiny floating lanterns known as *toro-nagashi*—which were strung together then floated out upon the dark, moon-glinted sea to catch the currents and sail off into oblivion.

I hadn't been to the North Shore Bon dance since the year David died. He and I had attended it together for the two years we'd been married, and now the memory of moonlight, crashing waves, and flickering lanterns delivering souls back into the suffocating blackness of death made me think too much of him. It was easier to miss the festival than to risk awakening the sorrow, so I'd stayed away.

But Troubles—fresh out of the hospital and feeling better—had commandeered me, Tess, and Mrs. Osaka to accompany him to the Ala Wai tonight. Here another smaller Bon festival took place.

Now the four of us were sitting on the Waikiki side of the Ala Wai canal, on the swath of grass that separates the water from the boulevard. It was just after sundown, the Kona winds were still rising. The black coco palms swayed, and the water was wind-rippled into shining black isinglass.

Mrs. Osaka—remarkably limber—had preferred a thick blanket to my folding aluminum lawn chairs, so we had tumbled down beside her, close to the fragrant, grassy earth. She had pulled her white wool shawl around her shoulders and was watching everything with the keen interest that allowed her to miss little and remember everything. Troubles and Tess were acting a little bored as they waited to see what would happen. So far it hadn't been very exciting.

Clusters of people were everywhere, and muted conversations floated on the night breeze. Cars and other vehicles rolled past on the boulevard, but we scarcely noticed. We were facing the canal and the black expanse of golf course that rolled out beyond it, but our attention was drawn to where the canal dead-ended near the darkened Kapahulu Library. There, a dozen long boats and outrigger canoes were berthed up against the shore, in the shadows of the trees and ferns at the end of the canal. The boats were decorated with bulbous paper lanterns shining pink, green, and gold. Some were tiny, some were larger than a man. The lantern light showed the gracefully draped banners and other decorations that identified various Buddhist temples, the lettering drawn in *kanji*. Dark people in kimonos were flitting about like newly returned ghosts, busily putting last minute touches on the water floats.

At the base of these larger boats, bobbing on the black water, were the hundreds of *toro-nagashi*: toy-sized wood-and-paper boats with small colored lanterns securely attached. As we watched, a dark figure in a tiny dinghy rowed out and with a long taper began to touch fire to each of the *toro-nagashi* candles, setting hundreds of tiny fires atop the water. The sound of a drumbeat rolled out across the island. Then another. The procession would soon begin.

Each tiny movement had a deep symbolic meaning, of course. This was, after all, a sacred Buddhist event. And at that moment, Mrs. Osaka—a walking encyclopedia of cultural lore—was beginning a careful explanation of the origin of this festival to Troubles and Tess, who had admitted ignorance of the history behind the ceremony.

"It began with the Sanskrit," Mrs. Osaka said. "In India. That is where all Buddhism originated of course, not in Japan."

I loved the way she talked. Solemn, each word chosen as carefully as a gemstone, to fit in just the place she wanted it in the sentences and memories she was stringing out for us.

"Shinto was the original religion of Japan," Tess added. She was taking Religion 101 at the university, trying to get her spiritual land legs and still laboring under the delusion that she was going to learn something that mattered there. She knew that I was deeply interested in spiritual growth, so she sometimes asked me questions or instigated discussions about various things her prof said. Unfortunately, said prof was a withered little man who was prone to intellectualizing the divine, and he said quite a lot that, when passed along by Tess, made me angry. He leaned toward exotic religions and constantly made the common quasi-intellectual's mistake that if it wasn't Judeo-Christian, it must be good.

Mrs. Osaka, on the other hand, had a deep fascination with people and their peccadillos, which made her information enchanting and beyond cultural prejudice. That was the most wonderful thing about my elderly friend—her ability to remain constant in her faith and her declaration of it while still accepting others without judging them. She truly knew that Jesus loved them just as much as He did her and that force and castigation would not win them into the fold; they'd come only in their own time, attracted by understanding and love. She also appreciated even the smallest courtesies and efforts toward multicultural friendship, even when the rough edges of ignorance showed through, as I knew they often did with me.

As she acknowledged Tess's contribution and continued her explanation, I let my thoughts drift afield. I had been agitated all day, explaining to Troubles how the car brakes had been tampered with—they'd towed the car up the mountainside, and Jess's theory had proved to be true. I was afraid someone might truly hurt him. I wanted him to drop the last months of summer school and go home for a while, till I got this situation under control. But he flatly refused to leave me.

"If you're in trouble, so am I," he'd said. "But let's take a break from it, okay? They've got you hurting yourself, you're going to have a heart attack from all the worry. Let's go to the Bon ceremony tonight, we'll figure out what to do later."

And so here we were, and I was finding it had been a good idea indeed. As I was relaxing, I thought about how events were beginning to fall into perspective. Though someone had tried to kill me, they had failed. Troubles had been only slightly injured, just enough to send us both a good wake-up call. Our angels were with us; we were, after all, under the divine providence of a loving and almighty God. I plucked out a blade of grass and chewed on it as I began to appreciate the beauty that was spread out around me. I could hear the wind's song as it brushed lightly through the palms. The faint, musty scent of the sea wafted from the Ala Wai, where the salt water mixed with fresh.

The blemishes on the canal had vanished with the scrutinous light of day, and now the near-black waters gently effervesced where the reflections of streetlights touched them as symmetrical sparkles of light. I enjoyed the lights playing golden on the water for a while, making various changing patterns. Then I gazed up and toward the dark mountains.

Sometimes at night the far side of the Ala Wai reminds me of a negative of a rural New England ice-skating scene: a frozen river in the foreground, shoveled free of snow to expose the sheen of polished ice, overhung by trees sagging down from new, wet snow. Except that the Ala Wai is golden and black and the sagging trees are really palms with languid fronds. Still, there is something warm and cold about it, all at the same time. When it rains or mists, the impression of a negative of a Currier & Ives winter scene is even more keen, especially when the mist fuzzes over the reflections. Just a squint of your eyes will transform it into a snowy, black night.

Perhaps that impression occurs because the city directly behind the golf course—from my perspective—breaks the blackness like tiny pinpoint jewels climbing symmetrically up the steep foothills of the Koolau mountains in the general shape of an immense Christmas tree. I studied the scene and decided that was indeed the case. I was a child again, looking upward at a huge, glittering Christmas tree. I felt a wonderful sense of well-being.

Then I swiveled my head to look again at the lighted floats. They were still in preparation. Diamond Head loomed like a sentinel against the sky to the far right behind them. I followed the skyline back toward the city, back to the Christmas Trees St. Louis Heights, then to the darkness which marked the Manoa Valley. From there my gaze moved to the wide inverted triangle of blackness where the Nuuanu Valley—Mrs. Osaka's home—cut between the mountains. A distant scattering of blue-white and amber street lights spread out over the next volcanic hillside; and to my left, the city was an outline of light against jagged cuts of polished ebony.

I eased back so I was leaning on my elbows and looked up at the sky, Mrs. Osaka's voice making a pleasant hum in the background of my mind. The full moon etched out a swarm of wide, wispy clouds. They rode like sheer smoke, escaping from some giant cauldron brewing just beyond the hills. Behind the wispy, gold-etched scraps of cloud were the stars, and beyond them I could see the endless black vastness of outer space, rolling all the way to eternity.

I suddenly felt frightened by the immensity of the sky. I sat up and shivered. I had become conscious of the isolation here, had suddenly realized that this city is just a puddle of huddled humanity in the middle of a vast, voracious ocean, separated from the rest of the world by the endless, eternal sea. The night seemed overpowering, almost alive.

A sudden roll of drumbeats brought me out of my self-instilled terror and back to the conversation. Mrs. Osaka was explaining that the Bon dance originated when one of the disciples of Buddha had been granted the power to see beyond the surface of his world, only to learn that his own mother had been condemned to eternal suffering and hunger because of ill deeds she had performed during her lifetime.

"The disciple sent his mother a bowl of rice," Mrs. Osaka said. "But it burst into flames. He tried other things. And finally, under the guidance of his priest, he discovered that he was to feed the priestly spirits on the fifteenth day of the seventh month, and his mother's soul would be set free from the curse. This news made him so joyous that he danced, and that was the beginning of the Bon festivals."

Tess and Troubles were listening like children hearing fairy tales.

"Look!" I said. The lanterns and floats had begun to move.

The drumbeats became even, the wailing, eerie music of the Bon season began to waft out across the water, and the floats with the large, colored lanterns and the *kanji* flags began to move toward us, down the black canal. The foliage feathered out as a backdrop, and the tiny soul boats with their miniature lanterns dragged along behind the floats on latticed ropes so they spread wide across the canal.

The floats, however, were moving slowly, pushed back by a growing wind. The tiny lantern lights were being whipped here and there, sometimes going out, and a dark-shrouded motorboat—visible only in the occasional shine of a flashlight—plied the waters, relighting them.

Troubles said to Tess, "It's going to be a while before they reach us. Let's go down to the end and walk back with them." They stood up and strode, hand in hand, down toward the library.

When they were gone, Mrs. Osaka turned to me and said, "He's a good boy. You're very lucky."

I nodded. I wished David and I could have had a child of our own, but I knew I was lucky to have Troubles with me at the moment, as a surrogate child. And then, suddenly remembering, I said, "By the way. I haven't heard anything lately about Anne. Have you spoken with her?"

"I phoned her a few days ago, to express my regards. She's still in mourning, of course. But I'm afraid for her."

"Why?"

"She's waiting, you know. For Victor to come for her."

That got my full attention. "For *Victor*?"

She looked at me smugly, pleased to have caught me out. "Of course."

"Okay," I said. "Explain this one to me."

"There was no doll in Victor's coffin, and he was cremated on a *tomobiki* day," she said, nodding her head with satisfaction like Sherlock after an especially brilliant deduction.

"I guess I missed the lesson on *tomobiki*."

"Of course. It has become a very obscure tradition. But Anne is a very serious traditionalist, and she would understand exactly what she has done. I will tell you, Alex, because you like to know."

And tell me she did. *Tomo* translated to "best friend." *Biki* meant "to pull." Which meant that the person who had died would pull, or call, his most beloved friend or spouse within three years after his death, when and if the dead person's cremation or funeral services were held on a so-called *tomobiki* day.

"Now the Japanese calendar is the lunar calendar, and every year is named after a creature," Mrs. Osaka said. "They are: *ne* (short for *nezumi*) which is the mouse; *ushi*, the cow; *tatsu*, the dragon; *ni*, which now pertains to snakes; *uma*, the horse; *hitsuji*, the sheep; *saru*, the monkey; *tori*, the cock; *inu*, the dog; and *e*, the boar. Do you understand?"

"I'm following you so far." As I listened, I was also watching the floats. The wind was pushing more heavily against them, and the outboard motors were cutting out now and again from traveling so slow, though they continued to press toward us. The ropes that towed the tiny lantern boats were tangling up, the *toro-nogoshi* were still blowing out.

"This matters because the days of the month have different names, too," Mrs. Osaka said. "They go in cycles of ten, and they are repeated every ten years. I do not remember all the names for the different days—"

Quickly, I said, "That's okay."

"—but there are many." She smiled. "However, the one I am most knowledgable about—it was pounded into me as a child—is *tomobiki.*"

She explained that the traditional Japanese mourners looked in the lunar calendar to check the day they chose for the cremation or funeral services of the dead one. "It absolutely must not be a *tomobiki* day," she said. "If they ignore this prohibition, the dead person will always call the one that's nearest to him within three years."

I was beginning to understand. "So Anne deliberately buried Victor on a *tomobiki* day, so he would come for her?"

"Yes. You see, if one absolutely has to bury their dead on a *tomobiki* day, the only way to appease the dead person's spirit is to put a little doll in the coffin with them, to take the loved one's place. Anne would have known that. She didn't put the doll in the coffin. She wants him to come for her, she wants to die, and so she sits alone in that huge house, waiting for him. She as much as told me so."

"What about the boys?"

"She has sent them with her family, back to Japan."

"Then we have to spend time with her," I said. "To pull her out of her despair."

"Yes," said Mrs. Osaka. "She is deeply grieved. Even though she was disdainful of Victor when they were first married, she needed to believe he was her husband in every sense of the word. And though, like most traditional Japanese women, she accepted his infidelity, she still wanted to believe that she was the only one who truly mattered to him and that he would otherwise honor her." Her voice turned scathing. "But Victor was a *poi* dog," she said. "He had no morals. And Anne can't resolve this now because Victor is dead."

Her words scalded me, brought back a flood of feelings as I thought again about David and the possibility of his own infidelity. But before I could really go under and get busy licking my wounds, a harrowing scream brought me to my feet.

There was shouting then—I tried to see over the heads of the many people who stood or sat beside the canal, but I had no luck. And then a bedlam broke out at the point on the banks where the lead float was laboriously motoring past.

I thought at first that something must have happened with the floats—perhaps the growing wind had blown one over—but no, they seemed fine, they were still proceeding toward us. But even as I watched, a surge of people began to hurry toward the spot.

Troubles! Had something else happened to him?

Mrs. Osaka was on her feet now, too. I wanted to run, but it was impossible, the crowd was too thick. We began to thread our way through the clusters of people.

I heard the alarm spreading through the crowd even before we reached the spot. "Someone saw it . . . hidden in the brush . . . pushed up under the wall . . ."

When we reached the scene of the confusion, I saw Troubles and Tess standing beside the water and felt a vast relief. They were gaping downward like all the others who stood staring. I followed their gaze to see a black hulking shape washed up against the bank, floating partly in the water. It appeared to be a body. The form was wedged up against the wall, probably something—maybe a sleeve—had caught on a jagged stone, and the tail of its shirt was rippling in the small waves.

I heard a siren; apparently someone had already phoned the police. And then a man pulled out a flashlight and shined it over the floating horror, sending a shock reverberating through me that made my knees sag. I grabbed onto Troubles' arm to stay upright and suppressed a sob.

It was Snake.

His dirty black hair floated out around his bloating face, his soggy, soiled clothing weighing him down so a thin sheen of water covered him. The flashlight played on his opened eyes, staring blankly into the death that had always tracked him. And the light showed a single blossom of red in the center of his forehead, the kind of wound made by one solid, lethal gunshot.

Death always saddened me; Snake's death was no exception. But at the same time, I felt a fleeting sense of relief, though I was instantly shamed by my reaction. And then slowly, resolutely, a new awareness began to build in me. What if this death had something to do with Snake's attack on me? What if whoever was pulling the strings from behind the black curtain had pulled the curtain down on Snake's life, as punishment for his failure?

Death. It seemed to surround me, these days. First Miro Ochinko, then Sonny Malinta, now Snake. Why *would* someone kill Snake? Was there a connection between the three murders? Was that connection, somehow, *me*?

The possibility seemed almost arrogant. And yet too many people were dying. It was time to understand why. And a man whose life had been increasingly intertwined with my own now lay here in these suddenly frightening waters, dead.

As the police arrived and pushed back the crowd, cordoning off the area, my brain started a rapid-fire of possibilities about Snake. It darted in and out, sorted data, added speculation and vestiges of personal prejudice, then summed it all up with the conclusion that there were a lot of reasons why Snake might be dead, and most of them had nothing whatsoever to do with Miro Ochinko or Sonny Malinta—or me.

But the most compelling possibility indeed had to do with me. This was the possibility I'd first considered: that someone had indeed hired Snake to attack me, then had killed him when he'd botched the job so he could never snitch on them. The thought was chilling. Because if it was true, the person who was behind Snake's death *was* also behind Miro Ochinko's and Sonny Malinta's deaths, and this person was totally ruthless, with no regard whatsoever for the sacredness of human life.

I knew this person. I was certain of it. I mulled over the possibilities in my mind. Ko Shinda seemed far removed. He was the type who would have others do his evil. Kuzio Takio, however, seemed far more likely to do his work hands-on, though the bulky-necked chauffeur with his cold, dead eyes and arrogant attitude would probably have performed the actual task.

And then there was the local talent. The street dealers and others who had deadened themselves to the value of the most exquisite treasure to ever grace God's universe—human life. And to be fair, I even had to consider those I thought of as friends, Jess and Derrick, both named to me as possible culprits by Frank Yoshida of the FBI.

I wracked my brain, analyzing the possibilities of each of them in turn, but came up empty-handed. Still, though I couldn't force the face of the killer to materialize out of the black smoky mist of my confusion, it was there, in my mind. I knew it.

I turned to glance back at the water floats with their hundreds upon hundreds of flickering soul lights, floating past and down the Ala Wai, toward the sea, the souls on their way back to the mythical void of the spirit world. And in that instant I also knew that death was drawing in all around me. I was only one false step away from being next.

he winds were growing stronger, growling through alleyways, scattering branches and loose debris through the darkened streets. Troubles, Tess, and I drove Mrs. Osaka home, and by the time we reached the upper Nuuanu Valley, branches were being stripped from an occasional tree and a neighbor's trash can had been ripped loose from its mooring to rattle menacingly down the street.

Mrs. Osaka assured us she could batten down the hatches and ride out any storm, so we returned to Waikiki. I had invited Tess to spend the night. She phoned her parents, then bedded down on our living room sofa, exhausted and distressed from seeing Snake's dead body. She fell asleep swiftly.

Troubles and I went out to the balcony, the glass door sealed shut behind us so that our words didn't float back to our ever-present listeners inside the condo. We pulled the rattan shades tight around the balcony, tying them off on the railings created for just that purpose. The growing wind whipped angrily at the ties, trying to rip them loose so it could again invade our night and batter directly at our shelter.

We sat at the table and talked for a few minutes about Snake, about the accident that Troubles had so blessedly survived, about what we needed to do. Finally, at around midnight, the wind had risen to a serious gale, making further conversation impossible. Troubles helped me drag the plants and balcony furniture into the kitchen and we took down the rattan blinds, so they wouldn't be blown away during the night if the wind intensified. We put crosses of black tape on the balcony doors, to strengthen the glass against the wind and to protect the interior in case the wind won. Then Troubles went to bed.

I went into my bedroom and turned on my radio to the all-weather station. A massive tropical storm was moving past the Big Island; winds there had been clocked at eighty miles an hour, just above hurricane force. The winds were expected to move past the Big Island and out to sea, and we would get just this dangerous edge of the storm. But these storms had been known to stop on a dime and change direction. Though this wasn't a hurricane, there was a high wind advisory out for the northernmost islands and a high wind warning out for Oahu. Large sections of the Big Island were already without electricity, and the surf had reached dangerous heights on most south shores. The Coast Guard was already looking for one fishing boat that had disappeared, and all the residents of the Islands were advised to stock up on hurricane supplies, just in case the storm did decide to change its path and gather strength.

I listened to the short announcement twice, then turned it off, showered, and turned in. But I couldn't sleep. I kept seeing Snake's face, empty of life and floating in the water, and the vision sickened and saddened me. Everything was coming to the surface—all the pain, all the confusion and tension and misery and lies, and I was agitated to the point that I turned from one side to the other, over and over again, until at last I gave up on sleep.

I got up, made some carob tea, and checked the balcony doors. Though the wind was rattling them, they were sturdily built and holding fine. I didn't want to disturb Tess, so I went back into my bedroom and stood just inside my bedroom window, looking out over the choppy, moon-glinted sea. I was still troubled by something, some emerging pattern, some fleeting scrap of memory.

Then suddenly, starkly, I saw it. I had been trying to understand this puzzle by looking for one salient clue that would, like a kaleidoscopic miracle, cause the whole picture to shift and fall clearly into place. But in my quest for the perfect clue, I had missed the bigger picture. The pattern itself. It had been emerging slowly, surely. Snake's death had once again shifted the paradigm. I didn't have all the answers, at that moment. But I finally knew exactly where to look to find them.

I flew to my closet and pulled out my albums, throwing things right and left until I found the one that held the newspaper clippings I'd saved from the swirl of chaos surrounding David's death. I swiftly found what I wanted, then I tore out the page, plastic covering and all, folded it in half, and stuck it in my black purse.

I checked my watch. Only 1:30 A.M. I still had half an hour till the bars closed. I dragged my denim pants and faded T-shirt back on, strapped on my ankle holster with my still-loaded .38, and knocked on Troubles' door to tell him I was going out for a while, then I headed for Rosie Malinta's work place, the Black Cat.

Many hostess bars had moved closer to Waikiki—on Keeamoku or Kapiolani. But the Black Cat was in the old Chinatown red light district, just off Hotel Street, in a section of Honolulu that visiting sailors still called "The Gut." The stage-style lights around the doorway were partly out, giving the place the look of a sleazy carnival arcade. Trash had blown in off the streets to swirl and catch at the bases of streetlights, and a brisk, cold wind blew in from the nearby piers.

Hotel Street had once been flanked with thriving skin emporiums of every kind, but the city fathers had shut down the largest section of it through urban renewal. The remaining action was contained in a two-block, sad and sleazy caricature of glamor, excitement, and fun. On the corner opposite the Black Cat, a newly opened *pachinko* parlor—Japanese pinball, illegal till a few months ago—had sprouted the typical crop of rough, young multiethnic thugs who loitered just inside the door, taking side bets and obviously looking for trouble.

I'd been lucky enough to find a parking place on the same block as the bar, so I didn't have to walk Chinatown's dark streets. As I shifted into reverse and backed into it, I was suddenly aware of predatory eyes on my back.

I turned.

Kicked back against the wall in a small alcove that sheltered them from the lashing wind, ready to spring, were two hard-time hookers. Their faces were garish Halloween masks in the pink and green neon lights. Their eyes were cold, unblinking. They were probably junkies, as were most of the downtown prostitutes. From the spindly, desperate look of them, they might have also been dying of AIDS.

I forced my sympathy to the back of my mind and pulled my purse in close to my side as I climbed from the car. The .38 rested smoothly in my ankle holster. Kindness is all too often mistaken for weakness in the streets, and addicts are invariably desperate for money. Fortunately, boldness is often mistaken for strength, and when they saw my lack of fear, they apparently changed their minds about plundering me, for they withdrew into the shadows, perhaps to wait for weaker prey.

The hostess bar is an Asian invention, the poor man's geisha house, where the male patrons can purchase expensive illusions forged in a harsh reality. This particular hostess bar was at the end of the block. Beside the front door were two glass display cases. Inside them, on a background of faded red crepe paper, were photographs of women in various stages of undress. Some women were old, some young, some Asian, some Caucasian, some Black. The photographs themselves were so old the faded edges curled.

I pulled open the door and stepped into a small, dark foyer, rank with the stench of stale smoke, booze, and disinfectant. A faded, wine-colored curtain hung across the entryway. From within, headbanger rock played on a tinny jukebox. It was deafeningly loud.

I pulled back the curtain, expecting a meaty hand to stop me, a booming voice to snarl, "No single women allowed." But the usually inevitable doorman had apparently stepped away, so I waltzed right in.

The room had all the ambience of the hold in a fifteenth-century African slave ship. It was dark and thick with smoke, twisting and writhing with people, almost all of them men in various stages of intoxication and of all types, ages, and sizes. Several colored lights illuminated two small stages at the center of the room. On one of them, a painfully thin local girl in a bikini costume moved listlessly in a semblance of dancing. I'd seen enough druggies to know she was heavily sedated. Most of the girls had to be in order to work these joints. Heroin, Quaaludes, marijuana, Ice—and booze. When they worked the hustle bars, they almost always drank, in addition to their illegal addictions. All in all, I was looking at a walking, breathing chemical formula for perfect anesthesia against even the worst human degradation—but also a walking formula for a short and miserable life.

I scanned the room, looking for Rosie. I couldn't see her anywhere. I moved into the crowd, ignoring the leers from several drunk patrons. There was only one word for the general pall in this room: *pain.*

The facial expressions of the people, their postures and attitudes, all were expressions of pain. Their catcalls at the drugged automaton reeling on the stage, their insults and whistles, even their brittle laughter. This was a deep, blue-black bruise on the collective inter-activity of the human race, a wound on the dignity of all humanity. And, in fact, it caused me pain to realize that the integrity and nobility inherent in the human race could be reduced to this banal degrada-tion.

And yet—I could also understand the economics of the situation. Most of the women who worked these places did so out of stark hand-to-mouth necessity. When I researched my doctoral disserta-tion, I had occasion to interview a number of women who worked in various aspects of the skin trade, from bartenders to bar hostesses to dancers to outright prostitutes. I'd been surprised at the number of them who were supporting families with their hard-won earnings, even the ones who were hard drug addicts. This fact made the inherent degradation all the more depressing.

The doorman suddenly appeared, a huge Polynesian in a black sweatshirt and slacks. "You lookin' for somethin', seestah?"

My voice came out small. "Rosie Malinta?"

"She's busy."

"I'll wait till she has a free minute."

"No free time here."

"Then I'll pay to talk to her. But only if you'll get her right away." I fished in my pocket, pulled out a twenty, and handed it to the doorman. He blinked once. Then he stuffed the money in his pocket, turned, and started walking. I followed him to a booth set off by itself at the back of the room, where he gestured for me to sit down, then swaggered away. After a moment, a waitress came over, looking annoyed. I ordered a pineapple juice, overtipped her, and waited.

Halfway through the jukebox song, Rosie came through a side door. Her face was still set in a sullen scowl, but tonight she had her hair combed and swept up off her face, and her makeup was less smeared, showing her worn yet pretty face off to better advantage. She was wearing a green sequined dress that looked okay until you got up close; then you could see that many sequins were missing and the shoulder straps were frayed. Her eyelids were smeared thick with matching oily green eye shadow, and I could smell the cheap perfume and booze long before she reached me. I had moved out of the light, to the far side of the booth, and she was right up next to me before she recognized me. She stopped short, just like the last time, and glowered at me. Then she turned to the doorman, and snarled, "She cop, you *lolo*. Why you call me for cop?"

The doorman shot me an evil look.

I tried to salvage the moment by rummaging in my purse again, and pulling out two twenties. She cocked one painted eyebrow when she saw the money and studied me with renewed interest. I said, "Rosie, I just need to ask you a few quick questions, then you can get back to work. Please. I understand you're working, so I'm willing to pay for your time."

She looked greedily at the money.

"Think that would buy me ten minutes?" I was probably offering way too much, but this wasn't a time to worry about getting a bargain.

"Ah. Okay." She slid into the booth opposite me, snatching the money from my hand as she moved. Then she added, "But you buy champagne, too. Ten dollars, one bottle, make boss happy."

"I'd rather just give you the money," I said. "Then if you insist on using it to destroy yourself, it's your business and not mine." Even as I said it, I was biting my tongue. *Come on, Alex, this isn't the time for a temperance speech. You've got bigger fish to fry.*

But she either didn't understand what I'd said or chose to ignore it, so I reached in my bag and pulled out one more ten, reluctantly handing it to her, whereupon she passed it along to the doorman. He nodded and vanished back to the front of the bar.

When he was gone, I said, "I need to know more about the man who paid to bail out your husband."

She shrugged. "He nothing. Just come and knock on door, say he friend of Sonny's, give money for bail. He tell me where to go, I take cab and pay money."

"You'd never seen him before?"

She didn't have to think about it. "No."

I fished in my bag one more time and pulled out the page I'd ripped from my album. I unfolded it and placed it on the table in front of her, careful to catch the wedge of light that provided the only illumination available in the dark booth. "Is this the man who gave you the bail money?"

She cocked her head and looked at the newspaper photograph. "No. I see man just a little bit, he stay in dark, wear hat. But this not him."

I'd been so sure she was going to identify him that my heart sank. I said, "Take another look at it. A good one. It's very important that I know for sure."

She whined then. "Why you bother me? You come here, make me look bad for boss. I no make money, they fire me, I got no money to pay rent, feed kids. Why you cops no leave me alone?"

"I'm not a cop, Rosie. I'm a private investigator. And I really need to know who paid to get your husband out of jail because that same person probably killed him and hasn't stopped killing yet."

She was looking at me craftily now. "You no cop?"

"No, I'm not. And anything you tell me stays with me."

I hoped she had been holding back and was now ready to talk, but she shook her head and repeated her original line. "No matter. I no see man good. But he younger, not this man."

The doorman came back then with the champagne, and I realized I needn't have worried about my ten-spot being used to get her drunk. The four-ounce bottle was wrapped in green foil and had a snap-off top. He popped it, poured the contents into two thimble-sized glasses, shoved one in front of me, one in front of her, and left. I pushed my glass to one side and leaned forward. "You're absolutely certain it wasn't the man in this photograph?"

"Yes. Not him."

I felt my shoulders slump and didn't even try to revive them. I said, "Okay, Rosie. You don't need to drink that junk, you can go back to work now."

But she took one small sip of the rotgut, smiled slyly, and nodded toward the picture just as I was sliding out of the booth, starting to pick it up. "Man no bring me bail money, but I see him anyway," she said.

I stopped short and held my breath. "Where?"

"He come here sometimes, he cop, too." She said it flatly, with a deep and abiding hatred.

I felt myself deflate. The fact that he came in here didn't mean a thing. I said, "Okay, Rosie, sorry I bothered you. Thanks a lot."

But again, as I was standing and reaching for the photograph, she said, "And I see him when man come with bail money, too."

I skidded to a stop.

"He stay outside in car," she said. "He bring man with money to see me. He park in dark place, but I look out window, see him in car headlights when other car come around corner. He no know I see him, but this is man." She tapped the newspaper photograph of Derrick with a long, red fingernail. "Same one, for sure."

I had what I was looking for. She pronounced it with such finality that I knew it beyond doubt. I thanked her profusely, then walked back out into the gathering storm.

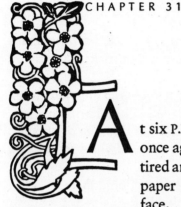

CHAPTER 31

At six P.M. the following evening, Derrick and I once again sat in the Mirin. His blue eyes were tired and frozen, but the light from the colorful paper lanterns softened the hard lines of his face.

The tiny fairy lights that had once seemed so charming now made the whole room seem cheap and garish. I was exhausted. Torrential rain and high winds had plagued the island all day, and I'd also carried a fierce storm around inside myself. But even at the practical level, I'd had a busy day: talking with Jess, with Agent Frank Yoshida, encouraging Troubles to spend the rest of the day and evening with Tess after he'd driven her home.

I really didn't want to be here with Derrick. But there was no direction to go but forward, I had to follow this all the way through. So when Derrick had phoned me—as I'd known he would—I had sweetly accepted his invitation to dinner.

The hostess had seated us at the same small, square table where we'd sat the first night. The piped in music was reedy and haunting, the wood carvings, the prints, the glass and rattan sushi bar were all the same. But I wasn't the same person, this wasn't the same place. My world had irrevocably changed into something savage and alien and threatening.

The waitress, a different one tonight, brought us our hot tea while we talked. By the time she served our meal, we were discussing Snake's death and his attack on me while I worked hard at keeping the hatred out of my voice and my face and my eyes.

"I found out today that his Ice connection learned he was snitching to me," Derrick said. "Snake was losing his ability to keep things straight. Plus, he was cutting his dope too heavily, chiseling everybody. No, I wouldn't worry about it, Alex. I'm sure his death had nothing at all to do with the attack on you. It's just the nature of the drug trade."

"I have something to tell you, Derrick."

"Of course. You can tell me anything." He was having *kitsune soba*. He skillfully twirled noodles onto his chopsticks, then raised them to his mouth. "You know I want to help."

"Snake broke into my condo a while back. I found him there when I went home, but he got away before I could talk to him."

Derrick's head was still down, ready for another bite of noodles. But he looked up at me from under hooded eyelids, and there was a sudden alarmed caution in his eyes.

I said, "I'd really like to know what he was doing there."

Derrick made a swift recovery. "Probably trying to rob you for drug money. He snitched for David, you know. David had him pretty much under control, like I did. But he'd spot *you* as a soft touch, just because you're a woman who lives alone."

I twirled my own noodles onto my chopsticks and gave him a gently amused look. "I think he was there because he was trying to get a handle on the bugs," I said, trying to sound innocently amused. "He wanted to know what type they'd put in and what frequency, so Shinda and friends could more easily penetrate the signal. Furthermore, I think you sent him, at Shinda's request."

Derrick's head shot up and he stared hotly at me. "Huh?"

"Really. You know my condo is bugged, now don't you?" I made the words sweet, almost playful.

He frowned. "Alex, you're losing it. You'd better take that vacation we were talking about." He'd been ready for me this time, and he gave me a charming smile.

"You've been working for Shinda and Takio for years, haven't you? And you and Commissioner Alton have been giving top secret information on the joint FBI/HSP investigation into Shinda's little drug-dealing sideline to them. So all of you could stay ahead of the feds." I kept my voice friendly.

I waited for a second to see how he would react, but he sat stiff and motionless, like he was torn between fight and flight. So I forged ahead. "That stuff about you and Alton being on the outs—that was all *shibai*, wasn't it? And then Ochinko stole some cricital papers from Takio's office in Tokyo and came to Honolulu to help the FBI put the final nails in Shinda and Takio's coffins. Shinda or Takio found out, contacted you, told you to watch for Ochinko and kill him."

He had stopped in mid-motion. His mouth was hanging ever so slighty open, as if he couldn't believe what he was hearing.

"You missed Ochinko at the airport because he came via Los Angeles and you were watching the direct flights from Tokyo. But you found out where he was staying—using your police sources, I'm sure—then sent Snake to follow him and kill him at the first opportunity. But as it turned out, Ochinko realized he was being followed and tried to detour the papers to me, where they'd be temporarily safe, at least until the FBI could come for them—and him. And so that's why Ochinko ended up getting killed in front of my building. But Ochinko managed to slip away from Snake for just a moment, just long enough to stash the papers in an unlikely spot. And when Snake went looking for the papers, he couldn't find them. There were too many people around for him to do a full search, and I got them instead."

"Alex, I don't know where you're getting all this garbage, but you're fishing in dangerous waters. I'm seriously worried about you. This situation has made you snap." There was a growing rage in his face, and he was using his hands to talk again, the chopsticks becoming an extension of his right hand, as he stabbed them in my direction, to punctuate his words.

I looked sweetly up at him. "What situation is that, Derrick?"

"The—uh—"

"That's right. You're not supposed to know about my situation. I've never told you what's going on with me. So how do you know so much?"

He stared at me, motionless.

"You overplayed your hand. You kept trying to convince me to open up to you so you could pick my brain and see what was happening from my end; and you used Snake and Kenny—your snitches—to make me think Shinda and Takio had a contract out on me so I'd have to come crying to you. But as you tried to convince me to talk to you, *you* ended up talking too much. Oh, you never said any one thing, you were too slick for that. But a pattern began to emerge. And then that bit about setting Snake up to attack me, so you could ride up like Sir Galahad and rescue me? That got to be a little much, Derrick. I mean, of all the places in Honolulu you could have been at that particular moment, why would you be right on the scene, to rescue me?"

"Is that what this is all about?" He was under control again, and he gave me a look of fond indulgence. "I was keeping my promise to David. Watching you, Alex. Trying to make sure no one hurt you, that's all."

"Why? So you could have first shot? And when Snake was killed too, right after you'd *rescued* me from him, that iced the cake. I suppose he threatened to tell the truth unless you did something in return, and you figured what's another body among so many? A really stupid move, Derrick. You were David's partner. You should have learned a few things about professionalism from him."

His eyes went flinty. He pointed his chopsticks at me and said, "You're crazy."

"Don't point at me with your chopsticks," I said. "It's bad luck and bad manners. And while we're on the subject of David, why don't you tell me the truth? Tell me about every time he betrayed me and who with and when. I'd like to hear a little proof."

Derrick lifted his eyebrows, in feigned innocence. "Hey, I'm not the one who slept around, Alex, don't kill the messenger."

"You're not a messenger, you're a liar."

He blinked, hard, still trying to pretend. "Alex, what on earth is wrong with you?"

"You're also an emotional cannibal," I said.

"A *what*?" He actually laughed.

"You did to your wife what you said David did to me. I know. I finally made it a point to find out something about you today. You betray people, everyone close to you."

"Alex, you're not yourself tonight. Why don't you try a cup of hot sake and settle down. Here, let me get the waitress—"

But I brushed his words away. "You exist at the expense of others. Emotionally, sexually, and economically. You're a necrophile. A death lover. You diminish and destroy everyone you interact with in one way or another."

"You're nuts." He was paralyzed, eyes wide, trying to figure out what to do with me.

"Actually, I've finally regained my sanity. I can see what's happening. *Finally.* And what I see is that you and the others like you are insatiable because what you're trying to gain by hurting others can't be had that way. You're ghouls, sexually and emotionally and economically. You need a constant supply of fresh objects, fresh conquests, you have to constantly try to enlist others in your perverted morality in order to justify your own disintegration. So, instead of trying to heal yourself and find something meaningful in your own life, you try to pull others in after you, into the black hole that funnels straight to hell itself."

"What is the *matter* with you, Alex?" He gestured around us with a tight little smile. "Keep your voice down a little. You're causing a scene."

"For sure. Let's be charming. That's what you do best, isn't it, Derrick? Your charm is an act. You turn it on and off at will. It's a disguise you wear so you can enlist others in your nasty little dealings, in your invariably exploitative schemes."

His teeth were clenched now, and his fists were balled up. I could tell he wanted badly to hit me, but we were, after all, in a very public place. "This is all none of your business," he said tightly.

I ignored him. "You're a truncated human being. You lack the most important human attribute—empathy. You commit the most atrocious evil, that of reducing others to objects. That's what the drugs are really about. It's not the money, it's the power you gain. Maybe you get some power from the money, but most of all you can enslave others. That's the true reward. And you're insatiable, you'll spend the rest of your miserable life enslaving others so you can manipulate them into your ugly, pain-predicated lifestyle, then control them."

He'd slapped his napkin down on the table. "You've lost it, Alex. I'm getting out of here."

"Good. Run. But you're taking yourself with you. You can't get away from it. You're empty, Derrick. You're emotionally frozen, empty at the core of your own being. And you can't kill or desecrate enough other human souls to thaw yourself out or fill yourself up. You're the loneliest person I've ever known, and every person you seduce, every junkie you string out, is going to leave you lonelier than before. And you're addicted to the behavior that causes this, too. You're lost, Derrick. And there's no way out except Jesus."

"There you go with that nutty religious talk again." He stood up.

"It's a lifeline, Derrick. I'm trying to throw you the last hope you're going to get. Because you're eternally damned the way you are now. You're not just bringing death to others, *you're* also banished from love and life. But most of all, you're dangerous. You've turned from a corrupted, drug-dealing cop to a cold, calculating hit man who kills for expediency to a serial killer who's out of control. It's a natural procession of disintegration. Think where you'll be tomorrow."

He paused for an instant, the wild, trapped look on his face a horrible sight.

I smiled sweetly. "You underestimated me, Derrick."

He shook his head in disgust. "No, I never underestimated you. I knew from the minute you stuck your big nose into the middle of this thing that you were going to turn into my biggest problem unless I could stop you."

I frowned. "*How* did you know that?"

"David. Jess. People talk." Then, as if catching himself saying too much, he spun on his heels and stomped out of the restaurant.

I heaved a sigh of relief. At several points in my tirade, I'd thought he was actually going to tip over the table and punch me. But all in all, I'd said my piece. It had all been true, and I had achieved the desired response. Still, it wasn't over, not by a long shot.

I put the bill on my credit card, then pulled on my windbreaker, and strode out of the shopping mall. I leaned into the cold wind.

The streets were emptied, for a change, of the throngs of tourists and locals. A bone-chilling rain was falling, and the gale was shaving palm fronds from the trees, then blowing them end over end, down the rain gutters.

I pulled up my hood, then headed for the beach. Toward the same spot where Derrick and I had sat on the outrigger and talked the other night. The beach would be empty tonight. The tide was high, and I could see from the street that the waves were enormous and choppy, strong enough to rip your feet right out from under you.

I was walking beside the seawall, head down against the falling rain, and had almost reached the overturned outrigger when Derrick made his try. He came out from behind the foliage, gun ready, and I'll have to give him credit—he didn't mess around.

He looked swiftly from right to left, then back again, then rushed me, his head slamming straight into my stomach, sending me reeling backward and into the cold, powerful waves.

I fought the chop as I sucked for air, swallowing some of the salty water as a huge wave crashed over my head and I went under again. But then I found the sand, I regained my feet, and I was half walking, half swimming, toward where Derrick stood, beside the water, ready for me.

I tried to dodge him as I came out but he hit me again, this time with his fist, a blow that should have knocked me out but instead glanced off my face as I managed to jerk away. He'd put his gun in his waist holster—I saw a quick glint of metal there. Which was a good sign. He wanted to either drown me or get me out of here before he finished me. Otherwise, instead of his head I'd have felt slugs go into my gut. The instant I deflected the blow, he was on me in another way and I managed to dodge the first blow, but the second one folded me up, and I fell to my knees, gagging up the salt water I'd just swallowed.

"You should have left it alone," Derrick said behind me. "I was really starting to like you, Alex. I didn't want to hurt you, we could have—"

But the last gag had been feigned, and I was suddenly rolling, catching my breath and regaining my momentum. I used my karate training to leap to my feet like a cat so that I caught him off guard. He came at me again, his hand up and ready for a mortal chop to my neck. But he was off, just a fraction of an inch off, and I managed to catch him with a precise side snap-kick, just behind the knee. It was his turn to fold forward, and then I had my .38 out of the ankle holster—I'd known this would get rough—and I was standing over him, aiming the gun dead at him, my breathing ragged, every nerve and fiber in my body tight as I waited for him to try something.

But suddenly, he changed. The fury melted out of his face, so fast it startled me. He said, "Okay, Alex, you've made your point. Now let me up."

I saw it then—his gun. It had come loose from the holster and was lying on the sand, near where he'd fallen. His hand was inching toward it. Still aiming dead-steady at the center of his forehead, I stepped forward and kicked his gun. It went skidding across the dark sand and beneath the canoe.

His hands came out, now, in the classic posture of truce—*look Alex, no weapon, no threat here.* What a liar. I felt a flood of fury, felt my trigger finger squeeze ever so slightly.

"Alex!" He'd rolled to his knees, and now he was backing away from me, his eyes ticking from side to side as he searched for a route of escape. "Don't do this. It's crazy. I don't know what's happening with you, I was just trying to help . . ."

"Derrick," I said, "shut up." I felt my trigger finger tighten again.

He saw it. His lip furled back, and he looked suddenly frightened. "I thought you were supposed to be a Christian. Thou shalt not kill, and all that—"

I lost it. I stepped forward, loomed over him, the gun braced between both hands now, my trigger finger ready to spring the surprise. But something soft washed through me at that moment, and I caught myself, just in time, heard myself say in a steely robot's voice, "You'd better get on your knees right now and thank our God in heaven that I *am* a Christian, Derrick. Because the fact that killing you would probably cost me my immortal soul is the single, solitary thing that is keeping me from blowing your sorry hide straight into eternity."

"Alex." His voice turned whiny. "Can't you see it? That I never wanted it to be like this?" He was playing for time, trying to figure out how to take me. "I really care about you. I tried to talk them out of killing you. Look, we can work something out . . ."

I said, "Derrick, just tell me now. About David. What happened? I just want to hear the truth. Did you shoot him?"

"You don't want to know."

"Yes, I really do. It—it might make a difference."

His head tilted oddly, then he shot me a hideously defiant look. "He found out. He couldn't leave it alone, just like you. He was going to take me down. He figured it out that night, when we were about to make our bust. I had to do it. I shot the dealer—he was one of mine, I caught him off guard. Then I fragged David."

It took me a minute to realize what he was talking about; I mean, that isn't a word you hear every day unless you're a military man in the heat of combat. What he was telling me was that my husband, rather than dying in the line of duty, had been killed by so-called "friendly fire."

"Ah, Derrick," I said, "good-bye to you."

His eyes slitted up and fixed on the gun in my hand.

"No," I said. "I don't have to do the dirty work. That's your department. And by the way, are you the one who tampered with the brakes on my car and almost killed another person I love?"

"I didn't want to kill you or your nephew. I just wanted to scare you so you'd get your nose out of my business." He started looking around again for a way to take me down and escape.

But I had squinted, looking past him. At last, belatedly, I could see Yoshida and Jess and one more FBI man, my back-up, running up the beach.

I had spent the afternoon with them, brainstorming about the easiest way to bring Derrick down once and for all. We'd finally decided that I'd make him angry enough to follow me out here, where they were supposed to hide nearby and monitor his confession while guarding me. Ha. Here was yet another lesson in why I shouldn't trust people.

But the wire-pack taped to my stomach hadn't gotten too wet when I'd landed in the water, and hopefully it had beamed them every word Derrick and I had said since we'd first arrived at the Mirin. If so, maybe I'd still managed to gather enough evidence for an indict-ment. And Rosie would testify, if we handled her right. Derrick didn't even know yet that she'd seen him and could therefore link him to Sonny Malinta's death. And the person who had actually handed her the bail money would certainly be convinced to come forward and further implicate Derrick, once he was found. My guess was it was yet another of Derrick's street snitches, or other snitches. Commis-sioner Alton would also give up Derrick, in a heartbeat. In fact, the FBI had planned it so that Alton would be arrested at this same time, and with luck Alton was probably already ratting out Shinda, Takio, and everyone else, in an effort to save his own *okole*.

Derrick had his back to the three men and was unaware they were approaching. He looked up at me, pleading. "Look, David didn't understand. Some things you have to do, Alex. You know that . . ."

But I was still looking past him. I said, "You're late."

Derrick started to reply, but Yoshida had reached us, and he spoke instead. "A tree blew down, hit a car out on Kalakaua. We had to help get the driver out and into an ambulance."

Derrick's head spun so that he was gazing up at the three men who had joined us. Until that moment, he had thought it was just me, that he would still bring me down, shut me up and run. But now he saw the truth, and the full extent of his vile, hideous hatred came to the surface and burst through in a grimace of such absolute loathing for me, for these men, that the sight of it almost stopped my heart.

Yoshida held his gun on Derrick while Jess cuffed him. I put my own gun back into the ankle holster, then scratched at the mike taped to my chest. "Did you guys get all of it?"

"We lost some of the signal in the wind. Then it went dead for a few minutes, shortly after you got here—"

"That would have been while I was underwater, struggling for my life and expecting my partners to swoop in and save me," I said sarcastically.

"Sorry. We got tied up saving someone else. Anyway, when the mike came back on, the transmission was clear as a bell."

"Then we've got him."

"Yes, thank God."

"I'm going home, then. To thaw out," I said. "I'll strip off this wire myself. And by the way—"

"Yes?" Yoshida said. He had pulled Derrick to his feet and was frisking him.

"In the middle of all our furious planning this afternoon, I didn't get a chance to ask you: why didn't you just tell me that Derrick was your prime suspect when you first talked to me? I know now that you must have suspected he was Shinda and Takio's point man for the drugs and guns and other street action, even back then. So why not come right out and warn me?"

"Because we didn't know *you*, Alex. You were close to Derrick and seemed to be getting closer."

I interrupted him. "Ha."

"Well, we didn't know. We thought you might actually let Derrick put you together and you'd tell him what was up. We couldn't risk that."

I was getting a headache from Derrick's punch, and my stomach was upset from drinking salt water. But I said, "What about the missing papers? Do you still need to find them, now that you have all this evidence?"

"They're probably still in Takio's safe in Tokyo," he said, "but fortunately, we don't need them. You've given us the missing pieces. We can put them all away now."

I felt good about that for a moment. Deflated yet strangely satisfied. I said, "Then things seem to have worked out. See you tomorrow."

I nodded a farewell, then I turned toward home, suddenly realizing that the rain had stopped. I desperately needed some rest. But before I did anything else, I was going to take a screwdriver and rip the bugs out of my home and out of my life, then throw them off my balcony—just as far as I could throw.

t was the following night. The storm had passed, leaving the Islands cleansed and pleasantly cool.

Jess had groomed and manicured his backyard into perfection. The side of the yard where the plum trees reigned was dark tonight, the yard light turned out. But Jess and Yoko had strung Japanese lanterns on the branches of the sprawling banyan, cherry, and willow trees that surrounded the rest of the yard, and now their reds, golds, and greens cut soft, circular glows against the canopy of foliage and the liquescent blue of night. The stream rushed melodiously into the *koi* pond, and soft underwater lights showed the large carp swimming languidly about—black, orange, and golden streaks of sequined beauty.

On the lawn, a picnic table was laden with food, and two *hibachi* were smoking with freshly lit coals, waiting for the fresh fish that Jess planned to grill. Sitting in lawn chairs, chatting in groups, were a dozen of my favorite people, including Troubles, Tess, Mrs. Osaka and her gentleman friend Yoshi Tanaka, and several others from our church.

The party had been Yoko's idea, planned on the spur of the moment. She'd phoned me just this morning and said excitedly, "Alex, let's have a cookout tonight. I have a wonderful surprise for you."

"Splendid," I'd said. "By the way, how goes Jess's reinstatement to the HSP?"

"Oh, the Chief has handled all of that, with profuse apologies. I'm married to a full-fledged cop again, thanks to you."

I felt good about that. In fact, even though my head and stomach were still sore from Derrick's blows, I was feeling altogether good today. I'd learned earlier that Jess had been working diligently behind the scenes to resolve the problem of Anne's inheritance, with regard to the tangled affairs of the corrupted Shinda Corporation. And even though Shinda and Takio had flown out to Tokyo this morning, the Japanese National Police already had indictments drawn up for both of them as well as a number of others involved in their corruption. The scandal was already rocking Japan, for the corruption went all the way up to the Minister of Finance and several other high-ranking members of the Diet.

But that was their problem now. Here, things were getting straightened out. The largest part of the Golden Palms project was going to be saved, although a lot of it would go to new investors, who were bailing it out. But there was still a large inheritance for Anne and the boys and a smaller one for Jess. That news had also apparently put Anne in a much better mood, though she was still in official mourning and therefore was not here at Yoko's party. Mrs. Osaka had talked at length to her and assured me she bore us no ill will for our part in exposing her corrupted uncle as a *yakuza* front. To the contrary, she had never liked him and was pleased he was out of the way. Besides, Victor's involvement with the *yakuza* had been layered and discreet and would be minimized during the trials. So, though the Shinda family name would be disgraced, the Seitaki family name would not. For once, Anne was one up on her family. A good deal, from her point of view.

I'd had another piece of good news that day. The director of Habilitat had phoned and asked me if I knew a man named Kenny Dexter, who wanted to sign himself in for drug rehabilitation but had no permanant address. I vouched for Kenny and promised I'd be up to see him right away. Apparently, Snake's death had hit him hard. He'd been busted yet again, and this time he had spent enough time in jail to dry out a bit and partially come to his senses. So after getting out, he'd hitched a ride to the rehab center.

Yoko was in a bubbling good mood tonight, wearing a gold cotton shirt and matching slacks, her hair pulled back into an elegant chignon, her enthusiasm touching all her guests as she flitted from one person to another, welcoming them and cheering them up.

She chatted with Tess and Troubles for a moment, then came over to me. I said, "Nice party, Yoko. But what's the surprise?"

Her eyes sparkled. "Just wait. Right after we eat. Oh, Alex, it's so wonderful. You'll see."

But though the party was beginning to roll into full steam, as Jess brought out the large swordfish he'd bought for the occasion and began to cut it into steaks, my happiness began to fade.

This was the first time I'd attended a party in this yard since David's death, and predictably, I started thinking about him. We'd helped paint the white gravel for the carefully swept paths through the Japanese garden; we'd helped build the dam for the *koi* pond. There were so many memories here, and now, seeing the comfortable camaraderie of the couples in attendance, I wanted David back again, wanted him here beside me, laughing and enjoying the night. It wasn't fair that he was missing. I felt the old anger rise up again.

I walked over to a stone bench a distance away from the others, beside the pond, and sat down, to gaze out over the Japanese garden with its elegant perfection. But after a moment, my gaze shifted to the dark tangle of forest beyond. There had been so much death around me lately. I had waded into deep waters thick with evil things and hatred. Now, the sorrow and turmoil and anger of the past few weeks suddenly boiled up to the surface, and I felt my face set into a tight-jawed defiance at the way this universe had been set up.

If I ruled the world, things would be different. There would be no death, no greed, no suffering . . .

Mrs. Osaka came up just as I was heading full-steam into my silent tirade and sat down beside me. "Alex, you've left us."

"I think I'm just burnt out," I said, forcing myself to be polite. "I need some space, nothing serious."

"Ah, but it is serious. It's about David, isn't it? You have captured the man who really killed him. It must have been very hard to do."

I opened my hands in a gesture of dismissal. "I didn't set out to do it, it just happened."

"I see." She sat back then and also gazed out over the delicately lighted Japanese garden. "I understand better than you might think," she said. "I still miss Curtis."

I tried to lighten the mood. "You mean this misery *never* goes away?"

"I mean," she said, "that I remember well how I felt for the first few years after Curtis's death. But that was before I finally understood."

"Understood?"

"Yes. Before I finally understood death."

I always had a hard time talking about it. I said, "Yes . . . well . . ."

She nodded to herself, then was silent for a moment. Then she pointed at a lava boulder with an unusual shape, set like a stark gray gem in the green rolling carpet of grass. "See that?"

I nodded. "A rock."

"Do you know why it is there?"

I thought. "For symmetry?"

"That is a small part of it. But mostly, it is there because of tradition. *Shinto* tradition. You see, the Japanese gardens were originally built only at temples. The traditionalists believe that the countless thousands of Shinto gods called *kami* inhabit everything natural yet unusual, and the gardens were built as shelters for them. And so my ancestors would say that rock is not just a rock—it is a home for *kami,* and it is hallowed."

I wondered where she was going with this. What did it have to do with death? With David?

She was watching me closely, her chocolate-black eyes glittering with intelligence. She said, "So that is the origin of the tradition of the garden you and I sit beside today. But do Jess and Yoko believe in *kami?* And do they believe, like traditionalists, that if one stone is asymmetrical, it opens the doors to demons, who will come to lurk in their garden?"

In spite of myself, I laughed. "Hardly."

"So you see, traditions die, but the good that comes from them may live on."

I thought about that, then nodded my agreement.

She said, "We have kept the true beauty of the garden, but now we have stepped beyond the traditions that blind us, and we attribute that beauty to the right source—the one true God."

I suddenly remembered a Bible verse from the first chapter of 1 Peter. I said it aloud. "Conduct yourselves throughout the time of your stay here in fear; knowing that you were not redeemed with corruptible things, like silver or gold, from your aimless conduct received by tradition from your fathers, but with the precious blood of Christ."

She smiled. "Exactly. A good part of our perception is shaped by our parents, and theirs by *their* parents, and so on, and much of it is indeed aimless conduct. And so, we find ourselves doing many things that harm us, because we have learned that is the way things are supposed to be. And so it is with the way we view death, Alex."

I tilted my head. She had me listening now.

"In fact, death is a word we Christians need to do away with," she said, "except when it pertains to those who have not given their lives to God. Because once we accept God's salvation, there is no true death for us; we are already eternal beings. There is merely a changing, at some point. A shedding of the physical body. That is what I learned about death. And I began to heal when I learned to stop thinking of Curtis as dead. Just as you must stop thinking of David as dead. He has merely changed into something more than he was, into the being he will be in eternity. And you will change, too."

"You mean I'll *die*," I said flatly. "Why kid yourself. Even if we go to heaven afterward, we still leave behind everything we love. Death is cruel."

"Yes, it is. But God had to do it. There was no other way to teach us what we had to know in order to find eternal life."

I thought about that for a moment.

Mrs. Osaka said, "God has given us physical death only because He loves us."

That one threw me. The sorrow, the bereavement, even the physical suffering of death—how could they come from a loving God?

"Because eternity is the thing," she said. "That's why God tells us not to get too attached to this world. He warns us over and over again that we are just mists and vapors who will quickly fade. Our treasures must be laid up in heaven. Because the things that really matter are happening in that dimension, not this one. This world hangs like a bubble suspended in the water of the true reality, Alex. This is not the real world."

I accepted that on the theological and intellectual level, of course. But now I tried to really see it. And as I did, a vast mysterious *something* darted into my consciousness, and I had a heart-thumping glimpse of the scope of all I did not yet understand. I shook my head slowly, in wonder.

Mrs. Osaka fixed her gaze on me, and said, "Physical death is hard, whether it comes to us or to those we love. But all lessons worth learning come hard. You see, as difficult as physical death may be, spiritual death is far worse. Yet how would we know what spiritual death was without some way of understanding death? That is the lesson. Because God understands us. He created us. He realizes that we will never see what He means by spiritual death unless he provided a metaphor for that death in this world. And so, we die, physically. And though the spirits of the departed live—at least, those who live in Christ—God shuts us off from that world of spirits, so we can no longer communicate with our loved ones who have died in Christ. But they still exist. David still exists, Alex. He's probably more real than you and I are. But God *wants* you to experience the finality of total separation. It may seem cruel, yes, but how much more cruel to have to assign spiritual death to those who refuse His salvation without letting them realize what death really is? Physical death is only a small sampling of spiritual death, a small taste of the real thing. It is a lesson, like touching a match to a child to keep them from leaping into a flame."

Suddenly, I saw it. Amazing!

She continued: "We're trapped in our traditions about death. We see all the dark illusions: the physical decay, the terror, the suffering. And every culture has these traditions, some worse than others. But we Christians must break loose from this legacy of fear and grief and horror about death, just as we must break free from all harmful traditions. We must learn that the only death we have to fear is spiritual death, and we must do everything we can to see that that horror doesn't come to *anyone*."

Suddenly I saw that too. But just as I was coming to terms with the full, mind-boggling impact of the realization, Yoko came over and dragged us back from our metaphysical journey. The steaks were grilled, and it was time to eat.

I made small, distracted conversation throughout the meal. I couldn't quit thinking about what Mrs. Osaka had said. I felt my anger dissolving in a flood of renewed hope. She had answered a question that had hindered my spiritual growth ever since David's death, by showing me how a God who truly loved me could build the fact of physical death into His universe. Still, my sorrow and fear and anger ran deep; it was going to take a good long while to resolve it all.

We had just finished the meal when Jess stood, and said, "Now for the surprise we promised all of you."

Yoko stood too, clapping her hands together like an excited child. Jess strode to the side of the yard and threw a switch, and a carefully filtered light fell on the plum trees like a silvery moonbeam.

There was a collective silence, an awe at the beauty we saw before us. And then, the crowd began to make sounds of appreciation, and then the buzz of conversation turned into excited glee.

"They blossomed last night," Jess said. "All of them at once. Just look."

The plum trees were in full, pink-white bloom, the canopy of foliage a spilled lacework of fragile beauty against the dark of night and the feathery black forest.

Yoko came up beside me and put her arm around me. "Do you remember when we talked? You said the trees needed a Hawaiian *haru ichiban*?"

I had forgotten, but I smiled at the memory.

"We've had one, Alex. You've been at the center of it, and Jess and I appreciate all you have done for our family. But the long winter is over. We've all struggled through the despair and hardship to emerge strong and beautiful like the plum blossoms. And now you are a plum blossom, too."

I blinked back tears. I didn't know what to say. But then Yoko hugged me once more and left to talk to other guests.

And I stood back and looked at the plum blossoms, thinking about the people whose hospitality I enjoyed and the feudalistic oppression they had finally escaped and all the rest of the pattern of life, for all God's people.

It was going to take a while to work all this out, to come to terms with this new flood of feelings. And yet I felt proud, too, at what Yoko had said. And I knew that slowly, certainly, I would work through the remaining tangle of grief to truly deserve her respect.

I looked up at the dark, star-strewn sky. And I spoke in my heart. "Good-bye, David. I miss you, but I know I have to get on with what's left of my life. So, I guess I'll see you in eternity."

The gentle wind rustled through the trees, sending a cascade of the fragile pink blossoms to earth. I watched them for a long moment, then I felt a sense of peace descend on me. It didn't matter whether or not I could trust people. I could always trust the God who held us all firmly in His loving hand, and that was all that really mattered.

ABOUT THE AUTHOR

Janice Miller (aka J.M.T. Miller) is an accomplished writer and author of several books. She has published both non-fiction and fiction titles for the Christian market and has published a detective series for the general market. *The Plum Blossoms* is her second novel with Thomas Nelson.